Ceoran Rising

THE CEORAN CHRONICLES VOL. TWO

CEORAN RISING

VIOLETA M. BAGIA

VULPINE
PRESS

Published by Vulpine Press in the United Kingdom in 2024

Cover by Claire Wood

ISBN: 978-1-83919-657-7

www.vulpine-press.com

To Talia, when you're old enough to read these books, you'll be as strong as Alex, as wise as Eric and as caring as Kieran.

PROLOGUE
WHEN I WAS YOURS

Alex

I couldn't believe after all this time he was still chasing me around with that damn camera. We were all hanging out on the strip of terraced garden that ran alongside my parents' driveway. My legs were tiring from running up and down so much.

Emelia had made him swear he'd take a billion and one photos to commemorate my birthday. When I'd complained, she'd whined that it was a special one.

"You only turn seventeen once," she'd said as I rolled my eyes. Eric, on the other hand, had sided with his sister. Surprise, surprise.

As annoyed as I was, I couldn't help the smile that crept across my face when I saw Eric's expression. He was happy. Truly and unequivocally at peace. How could I take that away from him? Like my own consciousness confirmed that I was in fact being an idiot, I caught a glimpse of that perfect smile again. "You're not taking this seriously," he said, and my mind snapped back to the camera in his hand.

"It's just a picture." I shrugged, running my finger along his arm. Instinctively he tightened his hold on me.

"It's not just a picture," he answered. "It's important to me."

1

"Oh alright," I gave in, looking over at Emelia. "Make this quick though. I hate taking photos."

She pouted, but the half smile she gave made me laugh.

"Hold this," she said to Lana, who of course did everything Emelia said. They were so in love it was disgusting. "I want to make sure I catch everything."

She chuckled when Eric tried to kiss my cheek and I pulled away.

"Hurry up," Eric muttered. "Alex is about to go full *Exorcist* on us—head spin and all."

"Hey!" I slapped him playfully across the shoulder. "Don't listen to him. I'd only go *Exorcist* on him, never you two."

Lana laughed, unhooking Emelia's tripod and setting it up. "You're all set."

"Thanks." Emelia pressed a kiss on Lana's lips before turning all her attention back toward me and Eric. "Smile!"

Eric pulled me against him, and in a quick motion he'd swept me up into his arms and twirled me around.

"Too cute!" Emelia shouted with a laugh.

Before I could register what she was doing, she threw a book at me, which made a loud thud as it hit my arm.

I'd let her borrow it.

"Hey!"

Eric laughed, throwing his sister a thumbs-up. He'd clearly told her to do it.

A grin snuck up on me before I could stop it. I was sure the surprise attack had made for a great picture. Eric picked the book up and grinned as he charged at me.

A sudden shriek left my lips as I jumped down onto the next step at the bottom of the garden, trying to get away from him. I lived with my parents at this house and Eric, being responsible for my safety at all times, was allowed to live with us. Mom knew there was more to the relationship than that, but she never said anything about it and so, Eric and I stayed as neutral as we could in their presence and everyone else's. But out here, when it was just the two of us, it was different.

Taking another step down, I leaped over the potted plants lining the driveway, eliciting a series of not-so-pleasant words from our neighbor Mrs. Grier. She was ancient: she'd lived on my street since I was five, and even then she was a fossil living among the ancient ruins of her seventies Art Deco house. In hindsight it wasn't too bad. With the right color scheme it could have looked nice.

She was one of the few Ceoran who were dead set on keeping everything the way it was originally intended to be. This included the ancient laws about Ceoran Council members and soldiers not being involved with one another. That fact alone made me want to call on a little burst of my power and knock her stupid plants over.

Eric had always reminded me that I was of pure blood, high on the chain of command, and that my patience and perseverance as the people's leader came above all else. Including him. It killed me to act like that, to pretend like I was better than everyone else. But Eric, ever the gentleman, reminded me that he could take care of whatever they threw at him—but he couldn't deal with me being alienated because of it.

"Your parents will hear about this!" Grier shouted.

Great. I rolled my eyes. As much as I wanted to tell her to cram it, I absolutely wouldn't be doing that. She was a big deal. She was one of the founding members of the Ceoran compound we were living on, which meant that she had enough sway to make my life miserable if she chose to. Luckily for me, though, she and my mom had a good relationship, and she would simply look the other way, unless I destroyed more of her flowers.

"Sorry Mrs. Grier. It won't happen again," I called over my shoulder as I ran, evading Eric.

The less she saw of him the better. Maybe she'd blab to my dad and I'd get another lecture, or maybe we were getting away quickly enough that she wouldn't recognize him anyway.

As the last flower bed came into view and I leaped over, Eric moved around the side and caught me, his fingers wrapping tightly around my wrist and pulling me back. We both fell into the soft ground cover, disappearing from the old woman's view, and erupted into laughter.

His hold on me tightened when I tried to break free from his arms. He was ruthless: his hands snaked around my body, dragging me back down into an attack of tickles. I shrieked again when he caught me in the ribs.

"I will punch you, Eric Raine. You know I hate being tickled!"

He laughed, and a giggle broke free from me before I could stop it. I couldn't be mad at him even if I tried. He obviously hadn't taken my threat seriously, because he was far from giving up. So I did the only thing a girl could do: I forced my elbow down, wedging it between us, buying a single second to make my move. When I managed to catch a breath I focused on him, and slowly, carefully called on the power running through me. Then I released it.

Eric stilled, immediately snapping his eyes back to mine. I burst into wordless laughter watching his eyes widen with confusion. Then it clicked. He was slowly floating into the air like he weighed no more than a feather.

"No, Alex, this is not cool!"

"Told you to leave tickling out of it," I teased.

"I hate heights, you know that."

"I hate being tickled," I countered.

"Alex, please."

"Promise."

"Alex!"

"Promise to stop tickling me and I'll let you down."

"I promise I will never tickle you again." His hands shot up in surrender.

"Good." I smiled, releasing the power.

Eric floated down carefully. When his feet were safely on the ground he shook his head, eyes downcast.

"You're cruel," he muttered.

"You're worse."

"That was some serious power, Alex," he murmured, stopping a foot away.

"Does it scare you?"

"No. Of course not," he said, closing the distance, "but you have to be careful. You never know who's watching."

"No one will find out," I said quietly, looking around. Emelia and Lana had disappeared for a private rendezvous leaving me and Eric alone. "It's just us."

"It won't always be."

I glanced over at him. He wasn't just worried, he was scared. His eyes flicked away from me as the creases above his brow took shape.

"Just promise me you'll be careful. We don't know who we can trust."

"I promise, Eric. I'll be careful."

CHAPTER ONE
THE COLD HARD TRUTH

Now

Panic was at the forefront of my mind. Eric was safe and he was healed thanks to me, but I was going to be in a whole world of not-okay if I didn't get out of here.

My head was splitting and all I could think about was the pain, and the cold, and the damp earth beneath my knees soaking through the torn jeans I'd worn to death.

"You're the Halfling."

My ears perked up, making out what Silus was saying, but barely able to piece it together.

"What...what are you talking about—"

My focus was abruptly realigned when a rough hand around my throat dragged me up to my feet.

"You thought you could stay hidden forever," Silus mused. "Interesting. Perhaps even formidable."

My lungs seized up as his grip tightened. He wasn't making any sense.

"But I must say, I am disappointed in how quickly you crumble when one of your own is in danger."

My eyes watered. *Eric. Think of Eric,* I kept repeating to myself. I had bargained for Silus to heal him in exchange for information on the Map. But this, this was not part of the deal. I couldn't do this.

"You are a warrior, the strongest of all your kind, yet you break like a common Ceoran." He paused for a moment; maybe he was trying to work out what to do next. "Such a simple death it would have been for you, but now? No. No such mercy for the Halfling. Now you're going to be of use to me and my men."

Fear tightened its hold on me, mirroring the fingers around my throat.

"Now you're mine."

A series of hollow laughs echoed around us while all I could focus on was the fate worse than death staring me in the face. I should have tried to fight or move. But whatever I *wanted* to do was moot. My body was frozen. My legs were useless beneath me, and my arms were limp by my side. Silus was doing this. He was somehow managing to keep me sedated, and that in itself was a level of terror I'd never felt before. To have that kind of power was insane to me. I might have been newly reintroduced to this world after regaining some of my memories, but even I knew how unnatural this kind of gift was.

Before my mind could drag me down into the vast array of things that were about to go wrong, a shot echoed in the distance. Silus jerked to one side and his hand tightened firmly around my throat.

Another shot, much closer this time, rang through my ears and caused Silus to drop me. I crashed to the ground, grunting loudly as my knees crunched against the wet earth. As soon as his physical hold on me was broken, so was the telepathic. I regained control of my body.

I dragged myself to my feet and recalled how to work my legs. The actions were jarring. Every muscle ached but I managed to get a few feet away from Silus. With limited mobility and even less energy, I pulled myself upright and started running.

I made it a little less than twenty feet before another explosion, louder and even closer, sent the tree to my left into the air.

The only thing I could do was scramble out of the way as it came crashing back to the ground. As I dodged falling debris, I ignored the stinging of wet grass against the torn skin of my palms and focused on the distance I had still to run.

"Alex!" My name drew my attention away from Silus' raging, pale and grotesque form and gave me incentive to move. "This way!"

When my brain and limbs finally got on the same page I scrambled through the debris field, moving into the darkness of the tree-covered woods and away from the fight erupting behind me. The Reapers were engaged in a battle I could no longer see.

Explosions sent tremors through the earth and caused me to trip over an upturned root.

Stifling my scream, I quickly picked myself up again. Scanning the vicinity, I choked back a sob of pain and kept moving.

That's all I could think; that's all I knew. *Keep moving.*

Shot after shot echoed through the dark, and my breath slowly became rougher and sparser.

I couldn't work out where Kieran's voice had come from, and I couldn't for the life of me work out which way I needed to go. The darkness grew dense, and with it the heavy feeling coursing through me.

Silus was gaining, the Reapers were closing in, and I couldn't get my brain clear. The haze he had me under was still making my head fuzzy and my legs weak.

Once I'd reached a tree large enough to shelter behind, I threw my weight against it and dropped. Tears burned in my wind-blasted eyes, and with each shaky inhale another sob shuddered through me. I shook my head, hoping that it would clear some of the fog. It didn't.

"Come on Alex," I muttered to myself, pinching the bridge of my nose, "get yourself together."

The moment that thought caught on, I laughed, then quickly composed myself. I was losing it. Then again, I don't think anyone would give me losing it a second thought. It was literally only days ago that I was bedridden with Reaper venom paralysis; only weeks before that I learned that I was some kind of intergalactic hero; and not to mention the fact that the entire planet went to hell in a matter of weeks taking everything I'd ever known, including my family, with it. I'd say I was well within my rights to have a mini meltdown.

Still, this wasn't the time. I tried again to calm myself by taking a few deep breaths and some well-placed fingertips on the pressure points in my temple.

When that did nothing, I leaned harder against the trunk and exhaled through my nose, bringing my trembling knees up to my chest, and buried my face against them. If Silus found me, it'd be over. I knew I had to keep going. I knew I was too important to be captured, but I was done. God, I was *so* tired. I didn't know if there was any fight left in me, and I didn't know if that was Silus' doing or if I was burning out. Both possibilities dawned on me as I sank further into my stupor. I couldn't even react when a series of hurried footsteps closed in on me.

"Alex?"

My heart sped up and something came to life in me as I peered around the tree. "Kieran?"

"I didn't know how far you'd make it. You look like hell."

Normally I would have scoffed. Normally I would have come back with a quip so good it would burn him, but right now all I could manage was silence and a half-grimace meant to resemble a smirk.

"We have to go, come on." He kneeled, gently pulling me up-right, linking an arm through mine, and helping me to my feet. "Can you walk?"

"Yeah."

"Okay." He looked around. "Do you remember where we are?"

"Yes."

The Reaper base was a few days' hike from the Ceoran com-pound we'd escaped from, and luckily for us the Reapers were lousy at hiding their presence. The decaying trees surrounding us and the rotten grass beneath our feet was like a neon sign pointing us in the direction of how many Reapers were gathered and where—more decay meant a higher concentration of Reapers. That, and I could also feel them. I could sense their presence, like when you can feel someone watching you from a hiding place, though I still wasn't sure exactly why, or how.

"Good. There's another outpost a mile from here. If we keep moving, we should reach it before they catch our scent."

"We can't just leave," I balked. "Did you see how many there were?"

"That's exactly why we have to leave."

"They're going to hit the compound if we don't stop them."

"I know," he bit back. "But right now you're in no condition to fight, and you'd be no good to me in the field."

When I could barely form a reply, he tightened his hold around my waist and dragged me forward.

"Keep moving, Alex. I've got you. Just focus on the steps, okay?"

He turned his face to me; his skin was sickly pale. There was a gash under his eye and an even deeper cut across his arm.

"We're going to make it," he said. I didn't know if he was convincing me, or himself.

With each painful step, my mind began to quieten. Kieran's words seemed less frequent, and a comforting hum filled the space in my head around my wildly beating pulse which had also started to even out now...

That didn't seem right.

Soon all I could hear was a low thrumming inside my skull. The dark green shrubs surrounding us got darker, and the path underneath my feet less clear.

I was slowing down. Or was he speeding up?

Kieran was saying something; I felt the vibration of his chest close to mine, but the words weren't there...nothing was.

I knew he was gripping my arm tightly, but even that seemed gentle now, almost comforting. I let my body relax. Wow, that felt good. Why hadn't I done that before?

Sleep. Yes, sleep was good. That's what I needed.

Warm, cozy bed. Sleep. Soft pillows. It was all calling to me.

"Alex, I need you to keep moving," Kieran said through the haze.

"I'm so...tired."

"I know, but you have to keep moving. I mean it. I can't get us through this alone."

11

The words barely registered before my eyes drifted shut. Softness enveloped me, and I felt my body go limp.

Chapter Two
News Travels Fast, So Does War

Eric

There was little warning. First came the sirens and then the lock-down protocols.

All the doors slammed shut. The mechanical locks engaged in seconds, sealing us in and them out. I fought my father's hold on my shoulder and struggled to break free from him. Panic shot through my body, instantly urging me into action.

His hold was ironclad and despite the burst of energy I'd suddenly inherited, I couldn't push him away.

"You need to rest," he said.

"There's a legion of Reapers out there!"

"And you're in no shape to help anyone. Sit." He shoved me back down and pressed the side of the earpiece. "What's your six, Rogers?"

I ground my jaw, waiting for the inevitable response that would tell my father how absolutely screwed we were, and that the safety of our compound was now at risk, probably forever.

His face changed. His jaw squared and he looked away for a moment before tapping the side of the earpiece again and meeting my gaze.

"What is it?" I asked.

"Worse than I thought."

"Are you planning on being cryptic indefinitely?"

His brows furrowed. Again I tried to push past him and again he shoved me back down onto the bed, the sheer force of his large hands momentarily stunning me. In an instant I felt like a kid being reprimanded for getting up when I should have been sleeping.

Commotion just outside the room drew his attention from me. There was screaming, followed by unintelligible shouting. The few words I managed to make out were *Reapers* and *outside*.

Damn it.

Dad's eyes landed back on me. "We have no choice, son. We're locked down now and we have to stay put."

"We have to get out of here. We have to find Alex. If the Officials come—"

"If the Officials come, we're all screwed. But it won't get to that if we fix this now."

The Officials didn't usually concern themselves with what happened outside of Ceora. They only stepped in when things got really messy and we were going to be on the losing side of the battle. They were high-ranking Ceoran, given powers by the Karatoi and they simply existed to keep order and nothing more.

"And if we fail?" I challenged.

"Then let's hope the Collective doesn't come for her and do it their way."

My chest fell with a sharp exhale. The Collective was very rarely, if ever, spoken of aloud. If they came, he was right, we were all screwed on a scale I couldn't even fathom. It would mean that we'd failed and someone even more powerful than the Officials would have to come and clean the mess up, someone who didn't answer to Ceoran powers—they answered to the United Universe Assembly, and only them.

"This is the safest spot for us right now," he reiterated.

"She's out there!"

"Kelly is with her, and soon Carter and Clark will be too. They'll lead her to the next outpost."

"And then what?"

"Council protocols dictate that they make for the next available, non-compromised compound."

"And we can't direct them anywhere else?"

He shook his head, looking down at me. "External comms are down as of an hour ago."

"Damn it."

"It's not ideal, but they're trained for situations like this."

"That's not what worries me."

"Elaborate."

There was a significant chance that Alex wouldn't be safe out there regardless of how good the men we sent to protect her were. She was a fighter, a soldier in her own right, and that made me anxious. She would fight. She would disobey direct orders because she didn't believe her life was worth more than everyone else's.

The other thing that increased my worry was Ashfield. He wasn't to be trusted. He was determined to make my life a living hell, not just now but even before Alex went through with the Clean Slate. He was jealous and conniving, and I didn't think for a second there weren't underlying motives. I didn't care who he was or that his parents were on the Council. He was bad news.

"You better start talking, son. We don't have the luxury of time here."

"We need to keep an eye on Ashfield," I said.

15

"You've already made your feelings about him known."

"He's bad news. You know I'm right."

"I don't like the kid any more than you do, his pompous attitude and pedigree upbringing makes him about as liked as any of the other royals here, but we don't have anything concrete to go on."

"He's set me up numerous times. And not all the royals are like him."

"You're right, they're not all bad. And I agree they were immature pranks but that's all they were—"

"He's insubordinate."

"And your feelings for Wynter have nothing to do with this?" He raised his brows, challenging me to lie to him.

"What?" I snapped. "No. I just don't trust him."

"Because of his history with her?"

"There is no history," I bit.

He pursed his lips and before I had a chance to question him, a loud crash sounded just outside the door, making us both jerk around in response. The door flew open and Emelia rushed in. Two red sight dots appeared on her chest as she tried to push past two guards with a glare.

The soldiers rushed in with her, coming to form a protective barricade between my dad and her.

"Let her pass," Corteza said. "And get your weapons off my soldier."

"Sir. It's getting hairy out there," one of the soldiers said, lowing his weapon. I didn't know either of them; they were assigned to the Council post when I was assigned to go off-site and guard Alex.

"Understood. Give us a minute."

16

Once the three of us were alone and secure inside the room, Emilia rushed over to the bed and threw her arms around me.

"Eric!" she shrieked, then stood back with her wide eyes darting between me and Dad.

"Keep your voice down," he ordered but with a gentle undertone he always reserved for my sister. She promptly shut her mouth and leaned down toward me.

"How did this happen? Why didn't anyone tell me earlier?" she demanded.

Dad looked over at me, and then apologetically at Emelia.

"Because I told him not to," I said.

"Why would you do that?"

"Because of this," I snapped, gesturing at her reaction. "I was in a shitty place as it was, I didn't need you on my back as well."

"And you thought I wouldn't have liked to know my brother was hurt?"

Her voice rose another octave before a stern look from Dad told her to tone it back down.

She sat beside me and threw her arms around my neck. "Do you have any idea what it was like finding out that my brother nearly died?"

I looked down feeling her scrutinizing gaze on me.

"After all we've been through together, Eric, after all the near misses, the adventures, the law breaking..." She said the last bit quietly. "You didn't think I'd want to know something this important?"

"I'm sorry, Em. But I'm okay now, it's fine."

"Only because some crazy-ass miracle brought you back to world of the walking."

"Not a crazy miracle," I corrected her. "It was Alex."

17

She jerked back. "What are you talking about?"

When I didn't reply, she looked to Dad. "What is he talking about?"

"It appears we have to reassess our protocols here."

His eyes closed momentarily and when they found mine again, he bowed his head.

"Alex has revealed who she is. The Reapers know she is the Map."

"What? How?"

"She went to barter for Eric's life," Dad explained.

"Oh no." She pressed one delicate hand over her mouth.

I forced back a pang of hurt at the gesture. Mom used to do that too. It was funny the traits of Mom's that Emilia had considering she was our stepmom. Our biological Mom had left us when we were babies.

I took her other hand in mine and gently squeezed it.

"I'm okay, Em. I promise. But we have to find Alex. She needs us now and we need to make sure she doesn't get caught."

Easing one leg over the edge of the infirmary bed which I noticed wasn't nearly as comfortable as those reserved for Alex and the other royals, I pushed away the nagging reminder that we really did come from different worlds. It wasn't just about where we ate, where we slept, it came down to what they were willing to give to us versus what we were willing to give up for them.

Dad leaned in and stopped me. "You need to rest, son. Alex will be alright."

"No, I can't just sit here and wait to see what happens."

"Dad, no offense, but you don't have the best track record for trusting her, or even liking her," Emelia interjected. "You know she loves Eric; you know she would do whatever she has to for him. Just like he would do the same for her," she added.

For a moment Dad stayed quiet. It was unnerving. He was always full of quips and ready to bark an order. This time, he bowed his head and looked over at me.

"This isn't just about her, Eric. It's about the bigger picture. Preserving her is in everyone's interest."

"She's not a condiment," I muttered.

He gave me a steely look. Even though he was my father, he took order and law seriously. I was about two comments away from being called out for insubordination.

"What I meant is that her life is important." He pinched the bridge of his nose in frustration.

"Yeah, it is," I bit back. "Help me." I turned to Emelia. "Please."

"You cannot go out there in this condition. You're pushing it," Dad muttered.

"I'm fine."

He applied pressure to my lower back making me yank away and hiss.

"What use will you be out there if you collapse before you even get outside the walls?"

"He won't. I'll help him," Emelia shot.

"I can't stop you then." He frowned, cupping Emelia's cheek and looking over at me. "I won't order you to stand down, Eric, but I'm begging you to reconsider."

"I can't, Dad."

He expelled a long breath. "Your mother made me swear that I would keep you two safe. I cannot lose you. Do you understand?"

"I know, Daddy, you won't. I'll keep Eric in line. You know we're alright out there."

19

Emelia hugged him before the door behind us opened and two soldiers came in, standing to attention. I recognized them from before we'd left the compound.

"Sir, we've got word from Carter. They've crossed the outer border and located Kelly and Wynter. They're making good time reaching them."

"Good. Keep me posted," Dad said.

"Yes, sir."

Once they were dismissed, I turned back to my sister and watched her for a moment. She was so willing to do whatever it took to keep us together as a family, and it broke my heart knowing how much guilt she still carried for our stepmom's death. It wasn't her fault, I told her daily, so did Dad, but no matter what we said she still believed we were wrong. Her death was an accident, and nothing Emelia could have done that day would have saved her. The love that woman had for us was enormous.

"You don't have to come with me," I said.

"You're not getting rid of me. Either I come or you stay."

"Your sister drives a hard bargain."

A smile pulled at my lips.

"Come on, we should go now if you're serious about doing this." She helped me up and toward the door.

"Be careful," Dad said, his features hard and strained.

For a moment I didn't know what to do or say but when he approached, I threw my arms around him.

He stiffened, but as I pulled away, he gently squeezed my shoulder.

"Find her. Keep her safe. For all of us."

"I will."

Emelia and I began to move toward the door. We barely made it two feet before a loud, glass-shattering explosion rocked through the foundations. Everything went up in flames as the south side of the compound was razed to the ground.

The last sound I heard as the beams around us caved in and the solid concrete surrounding us came down was Emelia's frightened shriek and my father's cry cut off mid scream.

Chapter Three
Hiding Is Harder Than Running

Alex

Striding toward me were four figures dressed in matching combat gear made up of obsidian black suits and helmets that reflected everything around them. My stricken face reflected in the suit as one came closer, hand outstretched. I didn't know who they were or why they were here, I just knew that it had everything to do with the end.

My eyes flew open as the memory of the four strangers dissipated into the chaos of my fragmented mind. A strong metallic taste filled my mouth and the pounding in my head intensified.

I looked around. We were no longer in the woods, and I was obviously no longer walking.

There was also a weird feeling. Something I couldn't put my finger on. It came in and out of focus, pulsating through me like a faded memory. I groaned when it slipped through my fingers once more. Whatever it was, it wasn't good. My body broke out in a slick sheen of sweat accompanied by fine tremors.

Something was wrong.

I looked up, hyper aware of Kieran's concerned gaze. He gave nothing away.

He sat cross-legged on the floor on the opposite side of the room to me, watching my every move with an intent curiosity.

"Where are we?" I asked.

Kieran tossed over a bottle of water. I downed half of it in one gulp noticing how dry my throat was.

"Outpost. We're safe here for a while."

He went silent again. I couldn't tell what he was thinking. It seemed he'd perfected his poker face.

Another stronger pull of that weird feeling caused me to wince and jerk back. Kieran didn't respond. Instead, he kept watching me passively. I released a slow breath and looked down at my hands. They were shaking too, muscles involuntarily convulsing with every pump of blood through my veins.

What was going on?

Why was I feeling like this?

Eric was okay, I knew that much. Thanks to my long-range connection to him and the teleportation healing courtesy of Silus, I had enough to go on to know it couldn't have been anything to do with him. But the sense of pure dread forcing my heart into my throat wasn't easing up.

Still, I couldn't help but wonder if something had gone wrong. I'd seen him get up, but what if something else had happened? What if Silus had tricked me? Another tremor rolled through my hands and I closed them into fists. My hands, these hands had coursed with alien power. I'd seen it, I'd felt it, but I couldn't make sense of it. I released another low breath and this time when I shook my head, Kieran got up and sat beside me. After a few seconds, he squeezed my knee.

"Do you remember everything?" he asked finally.

"No," I croaked. "Some of my memories are still locked. I remember some of my life."

"You remember the work we did?"

I nodded slowly.

"Then you remember how important keeping you hidden was."

The jab cut deep. I looked away.

"What happened back there?" Kieran asked.

"I asked Silus to help Eric."

"I figured that part out for myself. What happened when you asked him?"

"Well, let's see." I paused. "He did some…weird connection thing, where he linked us with Eric, and then he healed him through me."

"Seriously?"

"Yeah. I saw him, it was like he'd opened some kind of portal or door. I have no idea."

"You were there?"

"I saw Eric as clearly as I'm seeing you right now."

"And Eric, he's…Is he?"

"He's okay. I saw him before Silus pulled me back out. Whatever he did, he didn't bluff. Eric was moving. It worked."

"But you're still worried about something?"

"I don't know how to explain it. There's this feeling of dread. Like something is really wrong."

"You've had one hell of a ride, Alex. Maybe you're still coming down from it all?"

"Maybe," I said without conviction.

Kieran glanced over my shoulder for a moment, seemingly composing himself. When he looked back at me he sighed.

"I'm going to take a wild stab here and say Silus now knows who you are."

"Yeah."

"Crap." He scrubbed the back of his neck. "This puts us in a bad situation."

"I know. I made a mistake. But I would do it again if I had to. Every time."

"That's what makes you dangerous, Alex."

"It's what makes me strong."

He gave me a long look and then ground his jaw when I didn't reply.

"What now?" I asked, slowing.

"Now we do whatever we can to stop this mess from getting any worse, save as many lives as we can. If we don't, I'm afraid we'll be dealing with a lot more than conniving Elders and Ashfields."

"What do you mean?"

"Taking it you don't remember this?"

"No."

He blew out a long breath and nodded, "Alex, there is a bigger, more powerful presence out there that fixes things when the balance gets knocked out of whack."

"That doesn't sound good."

"It isn't, the Officials who watch over the way Ceoran conduct their business won't take lightly to what's happening here on Earth. If we can't sort it out, they'll step in."

"And then what?"

Kieran exhaled. "Then we deal with the fallout of whatever their decision is. They might decide we've failed and that the people of Earth are to be left to their own devices."

"No, that can't happen, they'll die!"

"They will. But at the end of the day, the Officials only care about Ceora, and those who belong there. They won't allow anything that threatens that to exist."

"Including me."

"Including you."

My breath got stuck somewhere between the giant boulder in my stomach and the razors in my throat. It would have been really handy if my brain decided to give me back this kind of information.

"And what if they fail to contain the threat?"

A dark look crossed Kieran's face. "Then the Collective steps in and overrides everything. If that happens, this planet might as well get ready to meet the stone age again."

"The Collective? I don't remember that either."

"Trust me, Alex. You don't want to remember about them."

"Tell me."

"They're a bunch of super-powered freaks from all different races who only care about one thing. Eradicating threats that shift the balance of the universe. They don't care who they destroy or how they do it."

My tongue grew heavy in my throat.

"Come on, we need to think about what's happening now. We're meeting two soldiers in the clearing at sunrise. There are protocols we must follow now."

"What, no that's—"

"It's not up for discussion. I've made contact, and our orders are to meet them."

"And go where?"

"Nearest outpost, meet reinforcements, then head to the next safe compound."

"I thought you said we were safe here."

"Only until you're rested enough to move. We need to get somewhere safer."

"And what? Hide while our home is under attack!"

"It's because it's under attack that we have to follow protocols. We have orders to go elsewhere and get you to safety."

"That's not good enough, Kieran. I can't walk away from this."

"You can't fight it either. You saw how strong they are."

"I outrank you."

He smirked. "Now you're acting like a leader. But unfortunately, no. Not in this case. When the compound falls under attack, you fall under military rule which means we call the shots."

I closed my mouth and ran my hands over my hair. "I have to do something."

"Staying alive and staying out of their hands is doing something. You know the threat that looms over us."

"What about the soldiers?"

"What about them?"

"Let's say we meet them as planned, get them to help us. They'll understand, right?"

"Alex." He sighed. "There are hundreds, maybe thousands of Reapers. We are hilariously outnumbered, not to mention up against some serious firepower if the Officials decide to pay us a visit."

I brought my knees to my chest and slumped forward. "They won't, we can fix this. I can fight. I'm strong, right? You said so, you saw what I did."

"You are, and I did. But you're also too valuable to be in the field. You need to be kept safe at all costs."

"I remember this part, from before the Clean Slate," I said, a warning rising in my voice. "This is exactly what I lobbied to change, Kieran. You were by my side. You fought with me."

"Yes, for the right for you to learn how to fight and get your hands dirty in a safe environment. Not when something this serious threatens all of us. This isn't the time, there's too much riding on us keeping you alive and making sure things don't get worse."

"So, you're just benching me?"

He shook his head, a small frown creasing his brow.

"I can help," I tried again.

"I'm sorry, Alex. This is the way it has to be. I signed up to protect you should Eric be otherwise unable."

I frowned. Eric and Em were at the compound, and as much as worry tightened inside me, I had to keep reminding myself that they were both skilled soldiers, surrounded by hundreds of other skilled soldiers. Way more skilled than me. And they had a whole army there. So why did I feel like this?

Had I been too quick to act? No. I convinced myself of that straight away. Had I not sought out Silus, Eric would be stuck back there, hurt and unable to protect himself. When the Reapers attacked he'd be worse off, possibly dead. There was no way that I would risk his life ending to keep mine going.

"What are you thinking about?" Kieran asked.

"Eric."

With a deep breath, he bowed his head.

"I'm sorry, I know there are bigger things to worry about right now—"

"Don't apologize for caring about someone."

"It's—"

"What is it?"

"We're not alone," I whispered, stopping to focus. "Something's moving out beyond the trees."

His shoulders squared as he moved over to the window and carefully pulled back the rickety blinds. "I don't see anything."

"I can feel them."

Kieran's radio crackled to life and both our eyes shot down to it. The soldiers were close, at least within range of the radios. He quickly put in his earpiece and flicked it on. "Yeah, I've got her, and we're about to have some serious company—"

I shot to my feet as his face changed from confused to downright terrified. He jerked his head toward the window, and I followed.

Outside, several dozen Reapers were circling, now directly in our line of sight. Evidently they didn't care about staying hidden anymore. They ranged from the new, slimy kind which were still humanoid but completely alien looking, to the more refined, older ones. They were the ones that managed to blend into a crowd, disappear among humans and wait until they could strike.

A shallow breath came loose as my heart raced against my rib cage. Kieran nodded, then looked back at me.

"Okay. Plan C. Got it." He disconnected the call and dragged me into the hallway outside the bedroom we'd been hunkered down in. "We have a problem."

"What kind of a problem?" I followed him toward the storage room at the rear of the building. "And what is plan C?"

"The compound is completely overrun, so this has now officially become a salvation mission."

No. No, no way. That couldn't be right. I stopped halfway down the hallway.

"Alex?"

"I felt something. This is it. It has to be."

"What are you talking about?" he gripped my bicep trying to pull me forward, but I snatched my arm free.

"That sense of dread I was talking about, this is it. I felt it as it happened, I felt the compound being overrun. How is that possible?"

"I don't know, Alex. I really don't. But we need to move. Now."

"Damn." I followed him down the hallway while my mind raced back to the hideous feeling that coasted through me and invaded every cell inside my body. Was it really possible? Could I somehow have felt what Eric was feeling?

"Help me," Kieran called, dragging my mind back to the disaster unfolding around us.

He gestured to the storage room door and wasted no time pulling it open. When it was wide enough, he shoved me inside. I reached for the light switch but he swatted my hand away and urged me deeper, down a steep slope into the dark underground. This didn't feel like just a storage room.

Thousands of Ceoran, young and old were now out in the open, danger calling at every angle. Nowhere was safe. Not even here, by the sound of the clamor filtering through the soil above us. They were trying to get into the cabin we'd just been in.

"What is a salvation mission?" I asked, my voice small.

We reached another door and Kieran pulled it open. He stopped and looked over at me.

"Kieran?"

"It means get the asset to safety, drop everything else."

"The asset being me?"

"Yes. Move."

"No. This is outrageous. Do you know how many people are going to die?"

"Yes. A lot," he ground out and then rushed over to the end of the small room, and started searching.

All I could do was stare as he rummaged around, searching for something, anything, we could use. I knew I needed to help. I knew I needed to be able to survive this, fight our way out. Maybe I'd even have to use my powers, whatever they were. I tried to summon that familiar feeling, but nothing happened.

My heart slammed against my ribs, pounding and pounding until all I could hear was the rushing of blood in my ears. Would I really be responsible for the Officials coming? I couldn't let all the humans here die because of me. Oh God. What had I done?

I staggered backwards, feeling the cool walls against my sweat drenched back.

"Alex!" Kieran grabbed both my shoulders and shook me. "Hold it together, I need you!"

"This is my fault."

"Yeah, it is, not gonna lie, but you have to pull yourself together if either of us are going to walk away from this." His blunt comment made my eyes snap to his. He stopped what he was doing, holding out a shovel to me. "Feeling sorry for yourself isn't going to salvage the compound or bring back those who've died. But you can help those who are left. Now come on, help me."

"Okay, yeah, okay," I mumbled, chastened, and took the shovel.

He pointed to a hatch in the floor I hadn't noticed until now. I jammed the tip of the shovel into the small opening and applied pressure until the splintering wood gave way and the hatch popped open.

We peered into the darkness of the small, underground tunnel and after a few seconds of deliberation I dropped into the hole.

Kieran followed, taking the shovel with him and closing the hatch behind him.

"What is this?" I asked, fumbling through the crumbling tunnel.

"Used to be a tunnel for bootlegging. It's ancient."

"Oh."

As we made our way through the dark, winding passage, I heard the Reapers breach up above and start smashing up the place. Familiar sounds of guttural grunting along with splintering wood and smashing glass filtered down through the foundation. Not long after, I heard the roar of flames setting everything alight. They were trying to smoke us out.

A dim, orange glow broke through the blackness giving us an edge in the dark. We still had a bit of time before being overrun with smoke.

"I'm sorry about what I said," Kieran said through the dark.

"You were right."

"Still a dick move."

"I deserved it."

"No, you didn't."

I shook my head, loosening the knot in my shoulders. "Let's keep moving, I don't like the sound of those voices. They're getting closer."

Smoke had started to filter through the hatch and straight down the tunnel. I pulled the collar of my shirt over my nose and avoided taking any more breaths than absolutely necessary.

Kieran continued behind me in complete silence. When I finally reached a caved-in dead end, I stopped and turned to Kieran, wide-eyed with worry. He held up the shovel triumphantly and got to work clearing the path. While he worked, I moved aside whatever

I could. After dragging back three large beams and a few exposed bricks, I exhaled loudly and examined my handiwork.

"Good work, city girl."

I shot him a look, to which he replied with a grin.

The banter was familiar, it was nice. I realized now how vacant the darkest parts of me were. It wasn't just like a blanked-out memory; it was a blanked-out existence. I didn't know who I was, not completely, or who I had been. I was just trying to blend in wherever I could without ever really succeeding. Even before the Reapers' descent, in that short period of time I wasn't a Ceoran, I wasn't popular, but I wasn't on the fringes either. I was just a nobody. Nobody bothered to bully me, nobody bothered to befriend me. I was just gliding through the last year of senior school without knowing why. Knowing that Eric performed the Clean Slate to wipe my memories under my orders should have given me some comfort now. It didn't. All it did was cement how lost I felt. The life I had before my false memories of school were planted was lost and I didn't get a chance to grieve it.

I told Kieran that I didn't remember everything and that was scary. Would I ever know what I'd missed out on? Would I ever remember it all?

"Grab that end." He nodded to one end of a large beam.

I gripped the end of it and after a few determined attempts, we got it to budge.

After he checked the stability of the newly excavated tunnel, he went in first.

"You know we have no home now," I said with a long breath. "And I don't know how to make that better."

"We'll work it out, Alex. We always have. You remember that, right?"

"Yeah."

"So, no more of this pity party, got it?"

"Got it."

"Now move. We have to get into the open and make a run for it."

"How much fire power can we expect from our reinforcements?"

"Enough. Carter and Clark pack some serious punch."

I continued half-crawling through the dark; the tunnel was rougher now and I was having to yank my clothes free from protruding roots. I wondered what kind of power the soldiers possessed. Would they have explosive power like Eric? I'd never seen it, but I remembered hearing the loud crashes in the woods before he found me, and then again when Em and I were running from the Reapers. Or were they more psychic like mine? I didn't exactly understand how it all worked but I did know that it was powerful. There were countless times I made people obey me just by thinking it. Like when my 'fake parents' and I were hiding out in the building right after the Reapers came down on New Year's Eve. We'd heard them scouring the floors, searching for what I now knew was me, and I'd made them leave just by thinking it. I had no idea then, bit it made sense now.

Every yard we put between us and the Reapers made me more anxious. I knew what was back there, but I didn't know what was ahead. As Kieran continued crawling, I slowed. I could help. I could buy us some more time. I still wasn't certain how my power worked exactly, but I was confident that I could make it show when I needed to.

Kieran kept going, oblivious, and I hoped it would buy me enough time between now and when he realized I wasn't following.

I focused a little on the familiar coil of heat inside me and this time, unlike before, I felt a tiny spark. I had to focus every ounce of my energy on it and hope that it would come to life. After a few moments of homing in on the energy coursing deep within, I took a deep breath, and when I was certain that I was ready, I turned and made sure Kieran was safely ahead.

A fine tremor rolled through the earth and vibrated beneath my fingertips. I looked down and carefully lifted my hand, realizing it was originating from me. Holy hell.

The Reapers' voices got louder and the orange light brighter, drawing my attention down the tunnel.

I only had a few minutes left until the Reapers reached us, and I hoped that it would be enough for Kieran to get out of danger. I wiggled my fingers, feeling the heat roar to life just as the first Reaper's face appeared. My breath stalled as we came face to face. The hollowed-out eyes and sullen cheeks took on a ghostly hue of greyish white, the fine sheen of slime that covered the entire being and seeped through the ill-fitting clothes it had chosen made me shake.

"Alex! What are you doing?" Kieran shouted.

"Keep moving and get plan C ready!"

Before I could hear his response, I thrust my fingers into the earth on either side of me and released the blast of power into it.

The rumbling began low and quiet, quickly building into a deafening roar far too loud to hear over. Yet somehow the shouting from both ends of the tunnel pierced through the noise. When I concentrated and dug my fingers even deeper into the soil, I focused on the calm sensation that the cool earth gave me. The tight coil of energy twisted around my hand, almost like a whip, and then fired outward. I screamed as the power erupted and drowned everything else out. The opening to the tunnel fell away and landed on top of the Reaper. Its alien face twisted in agony until the falling earth covered it completely. The vibrations continued, erupting out from me and away down the tunnel until our pursuers were all gone, snuffed out and silenced.

It wasn't over yet, though. The tunnel was now unstable, the earth above me threatening to fall and give way. I turned as quickly as I could in the small space and started crawling for my life. Behind me, a wave of falling soil was catching up. My breath raged in my lungs as I pushed myself through the narrow opening that Kieran had disappeared into.

His hand appeared ahead. "Hurry!"

"I'm hurrying!"

As the tunnel widened into a space big enough to stand in, I grabbed Kieran's arm and hauled myself up. With no time to draw breath, we ran. I sprinted harder than I ever had as the roar of my impending, earth-crushing death sounded behind me. We were heading back up toward the surface. We threw ourselves through a bigger opening that marked the end of the tunnel, followed by an explosive crash as the tunnel and cabin caved in.

"You're insane," Kieran muttered, helping me to my feet.

"You're welcome."

I dusted myself off and gave the smokey rubble behind us a quick look and started running again. I made out at least four Reapers emerging from the chaos and start gaining on us. Kieran muttered something under his breath as he sped up; I didn't waste any time and followed. A clearing came into view ahead and Kieran gripped my arm urging me on. Before the footsteps came right on top of us I rejoiced as I saw two Ceoran soldiers standing tall with wide open stances, arms out and ready to fight.

As Kieran and I ran beyond them, a roaring sound erupted behind us. I didn't dare look back. There were only a handful of Reapers left now but it didn't mean they weren't able to do some serious damage.

"How did they even find us?" Kieran hissed when we slowed and took cover behind a tree.

"I'm guessing they can smell us?"

"Yeah probably." He grabbed his gun from where he'd stashed it around his waist and reloaded it. I checked mine too.

Once I was done I made a move but Kieran's hand wrapped around my wrist and he stopped me, pulling me back.

The woods were filled with the guttural, alien sound of Reapers screaming as they burned to death. I clamped my hands over my ears and sunk to the ground. Every cry seemed to pierce through my eardrums, and I could have sworn my ears were bleeding.

Then it was over.

I uncovered my ears and checked my hands, exhaling in relief when there was no blood.

"We're good, come on," Kieran said, helping me to my feet.

The two soldiers I'd seen earlier who saved our asses gave Kieran a curt nod before casting their gazes over me.

"Wait here," Kieran said.

I stood beside the tree watching him walk over. If I wasn't mistaken, I could have sworn he looked tense; his shoulders were squared and body rigid with each tentative step. Were they not on good terms? The two figures which had been shielded by shadows cast from the overhead moon stepped out into the clearing and when Kieran greeted them, I relaxed.

The soldiers holstered their weapons and waved me over.

"Kelly, good to see you alive."

"You too, Clark, Carter." Kieran nodded at the two soldiers dressed like Eric had been the first time I saw him.

"Chancellor." Carter nodded. He looked at me with a nod before looking back at Kieran. "You two hurt?"

"No, we're good. How bad is it?" I asked, making sure I sounded as confident as possible and not as shaken as I really felt.

"Overrun," Clark explained. "The Council took the younglings underground, Corteza engaged the older ones."

"They've been deployed?" I balked.

"No choice, Wynter. The shitshow you two caused set a lot of wheels into motion."

"They're not ready."

"No, they're not," Carter muttered. "Most will probably die."

His blunt response made angry tears burn my eyes. My throat tightened and the heat inside me roared to life. I quickly shut it down. That was weird. I'd never felt my power, or whatever this was, course without me willing it to. Was it related to my emotions?

"What about everyone else?" I demanded.

It didn't take a genius to figure out I was referring to Eric. And the way they both looked at me suggested they knew a whole lot more than the others at the compound.

Carter turned his face from me.

"Did they get out?" I demanded.

"I don't know, Wynter."

My heart constricted, but before I could ask anything else, Kieran squeezed my shoulder. "He's fine, Alex. They both are."

"How can you know that? I felt something shift inside me, Kieran, I felt dread."

"You could have felt dread because of the attack on the compound, like you said."

My mouth dried up.

"Trust me, they'll be fine. I know it. Eric wouldn't go down without a fight."

It did very little to appease me.

"As it stands now, we're on our own, and plan C is in effect," Clark announced and then looked at me. "You good to move? We need to get this show on the road."

"No," I muttered.

"We're ready." Kieran shot me a warning look. "Relax."

I let out a long breath and focused on inhaling and exhaling slowly. Kieran said it before and I agreed, tears weren't going to do anyone any good and they certainly wouldn't change what happened. I just had to focus on what I could do now.

Carter looked over me, his hazel eyes narrowing. "We need to get moving. Here, take these." He held out two earbuds. Kieran and I took one each and put them in.

"Surprised you're letting me have one of these," I muttered.

Kieran shot me a look. I was being petty, but I didn't care.

A quiet beep told me they were active and then we were moving.

Kieran hung back beside me while Carter and Clark kept their weapons trained ahead. I kept my eyes scanning the tree line and occasionally checking up on Kieran. He was tired, his footsteps slowed and faltered every few yards or so. When I reached over and looped my arm around his waist to help him, I abruptly stopped.

"You're hurt."

"I'm fine." He pulled his arm free.

When I looked down at my hand, he did too. My entire arm was covered in blood. Kieran's eyes rolled to the back of his head and he went down. My body reacted before my mind did. I

dropped to my knees as he hit the ground and threw my hand under his head before it made contact.

Clark and Carter moved quickly but I held out my bloodied
hand. "Stand back, I can help him."

Clark opened his mouth to object, but I forced the inner heat
to the surface of my hand. I watched his eyes widen as his gaze
landed on the deep, burning glow coming from under my skin.

"I can help him. Stand back," I repeated.

Carter pulled him back, and they did as I said.

Kieran's eyes fluttered open as I turned his face toward me.

"Stay calm, I'm going to heal you."

"Alex, no…"

"It's okay, you're going to be fine."

"Don't."

"Stay still."

He began to argue but as soon as I pressed my palm over the
gushing bullet wound in his abdomen, he snapped his mouth shut.

The heat surged through me and poured into Kieran. This I
could do, this was within my realm of ability, I hoped. His abdomen seized under me, tensing with each passing second. I felt him
struggle for breath, and then I felt him relax. A shudder rolled
through me and then it was all over.

I pulled away and fell backwards. Carter caught me against his
chest before my body could crumple the ground.

"I've got you, Alex. Come on." He pulled me to my feet and
Clark rushed over to help Kieran.

"Is he…is he okay?" I asked.

"He's fine, you did good," Carter said, leading me into the cover
of some heavy pines and toward a large root. "Sit, easy."

I leaned back against the bark and closed my eyes. Two sets of footsteps told me that Kieran was okay. I breathed out in relief and blinked through the pounding headache. It was like being drunk and hungover all at once. There was a deep sickness that made me want to throw up but at the same time, euphoria, like it was the best feeling in the world. I could tell why it was addictive to some and why the Council banned it. I also now understood a little more about how these powers worked—emotion, that was the key. Powerful emotion, good or bad, it didn't seem to matter.

Kieran kneeled in front of me, his face blurry through the strain of reactive tears in my eyes.

"You shouldn't have done that."

"Don't lecture me," I managed.

He scrubbed his jaw and got up.

"Speaking of which, *how* were you able to do that?"

"I've been able to heal small things, figured a bullet wound would be easy enough."

"But not Eric's injury."

"No." I shook my head slowly. "He was paralyzed. It was bad, I don't think I could have done it without Silus' help."

He ground his jaw turning from me.

I took the small moment of solidarity to close my eyes and focus on my breathing.

"She needs to rest," I heard Kieran say.

"I understand that, but we have to keep moving," said Carter. "It's too dangerous out here."

"It's too dangerous to move her," Kieran shot back.

"I'm fine, guys, seriously."

Kieran's gaze found mine. We had no choice. He must have seen it in my eyes, and in the desperation of the situation. The compound and any promise of safety was as good as gone. And it was on me. There was no way I would let these two soldiers and Kieran risk any more for me.

"I'm good, let's keep moving."

"Alex, no." He shook his head, scrubbing the back of his neck.

"Please just help me up."

Kieran frowned but he walked over and reluctantly held his hand out. Together, the four of us continued under the cover of darkness.

Every step was difficult. Every breath rattled my lungs. Every single meter was a challenge. Kieran watched me as I walked, and I did whatever I could to make sure I wasn't displaying any outward signs of the pain I was feeling. The euphoria was gone. Now I just felt like crap.

"How are you holding up?" Carter asked, slowing up ahead.

I couldn't hide the trembling in my voice when I spoke next. "Fine."

"She's not fine. We're stopping now," Kieran said.

Using so much power was obviously not good. After I took out the tunnel it took hours to feel somewhat reenergized again, healing him now, same sort of deal on a lesser scale. That much I knew, even if I didn't fully understand everything else.

"We're just up ahead," Carter announced. "Can you make it?"

"Yes. I'm fine."

Kieran sighed and left me alone.

I looked over to where he nodded and spotted the distinct shape of a vehicle. Cars hadn't worked for months, aside from the one the siblings somehow had. The secret stash of gas like they'd said really came in handy, and so too did their obvious ability to keep that kind of thing under wraps until I came along and ruined it all.

This must have been supplied by the compound. It made sense they would stockpile gas for emergencies.

Carter and Kieran cleared the area while Clark and I stayed low behind a tree, then they nodded to us when it was safe to cross to the car. Once we were all belted in, Carter took the small sedan out onto the main road.

"How do we contact them?" I asked.

"We'll have to get in range; by my estimate we're about two miles out from being able to make contact" Carter explained.

"In range of what, exactly?"

"The next secure compound's comms towers," Kieran added.

"And the compound itself?"

"A day's drive at least, assuming nothing goes wrong," Carter muttered.

I looked between them. "What if it's too late? What if they've been attacked too?"

"Too many what ifs, Alex, I can't function like that," Kieran muttered. "We work with what we know, which right now is getting you to safety. Then we worry about everyone else."

"Even if everyone else is dead," I muttered.

"Even if everyone else is dead," Carter confirmed.

Chapter Four
Under Attack

Eric

The sounds of soft whimpers and agonizing cries surrounded me. I couldn't tell where the voices were coming from. I couldn't even tell where I was.

A dull ache spread through the back of my head, and when I reached back and felt the wetness come away from my hair I held in a groan.

Ceoran Almighty. My head ached something fierce, and my body wasn't faring much better. My muscles protested as I craned my neck, trying to assess my situation.

With each small movement my heart pounded erratically, struggling to regulate. As I finally brought myself up into a seated position among the crumbled cement, I remembered what happened.

"Em!" I screamed without even thinking. "Dad!"

I scrambled to my knees and shoved whatever debris I could out of the way. I stopped abruptly when my hand grazed something soft and warm. A hand. Holy Ceoran hell, it was a hand. A hand attached to a body that had been crushed beneath a pillar of concrete. I yanked my own hand back and looked down in horror.

It wasn't a female hand. It wasn't her. And it wasn't Dad either. He wore a large signet ring with our stepmom's initials on it and this hand was bare. I tore my gaze away as nausea rose up inside.

"Em!" I screamed again, and then waited. "Dad!"

The whimpering voices continued, but none sounded like my family. Everyone who was able was calling out for someone they loved, someone they had been here with. And some of these people would never hear their loved ones respond. I only prayed that I wouldn't be one of them.

Tears pricked my eyes and I told myself it was just the settling dust. I wouldn't break before I found them, one way or another. I carefully moved past the crushed body and kept my eyes scanning the wreckage. Wherever I looked I realized how dire the situation was. A large pile of smoking rubble separated me from everyone else, trapping me. Live wires danced dangerously, sparking to life every few moments causing me to shield my eyes. Eventually I spied a small gap in the rubble, just large enough to crawl through on my stomach. I got down on the ground and slowly pulled myself through, stopping only when I saw the mangled mess of the gurney I'd been on. I shuddered.

How long had I been out? Maybe only a few minutes had passed since the building came down, or maybe it had been hours. Panic started to set in.

"Em!" I screamed again once I'd pulled myself up.

This time, there was a response.

"Eric, is that you?"

"Em?" Her voice was coming from behind another crumbled wall at the end of the hallway.

"Yeah, I'm okay, Dad's here too."

I exhaled with relief and followed the sound of her gentle tapping.

Once I reached the end of the caved-in hallway I saw her hand waving frantically through a gap in the rubble.

I grabbed it and she squeezed my fingers. I couldn't see my family, but at least I knew they were alive.

"Are you okay?" she asked.

"I'm fine. You?"

"We're both alright, son," Dad replied. "Can you get out?"

I looked around. I was blocked in. "No, see if you guys can shift any of this."

On the other side of the pile of debris, I heard them get to work. Once I'd assessed where it would be safest to start, I joined in.

The sounds became clearer as we pulled more and more cement away. After what felt like a solid half hour of work, we'd cleared enough rubble for me to crawl through to them.

Dad grabbed my arms and helped pull me through the gap.

Emelia threw her arms around me, and then Dad. For a quiet moment, the three of us stood embracing, counting every blessing we'd been given to survive this when so many others hadn't. I wasn't blind to the blood pooling beneath piles of crushed cement that had once formed a respectable room filled with our people.

When at last we separated, I steeled myself and looked around. It was a war zone. Bodies lay strewn all around us. People were bent over their loved ones, their colleagues and friends, crying and sobbing. It took every fiber of my being not to crumble and weep alongside them. I pulled Emelia close and held her against me.

The young Ceoran Alex had bravely helped when the compound was first attacked was dead. Her eyes wide and unseeing, blood smeared across her unearthly pale skin. Her friends were screaming unintelligible words while others tried to pull them away from the danger of unstable ground.

"We have to keep moving," Dad said gently.

I pulled my gaze away and followed him through the wreckage. Every caved-in corner we rounded we found more bodies. I stopped counting after twenty-eight. Twenty-eight people I'd known and worked with, shared drinks with, shared laughs with.

Once we reached the common rooms, we split up and started helping whoever we could. The compound's first responders were already working, healing those in need and delicately covering those who were beyond help.

My eyes surveyed the open space and stopped when they landed on Ashfield. He was nursing what looked like a broken nose and some minor scrapes.

"No, it hurts!" he yelled, then swatted away the nurse's hand. I rolled my eyes.

My wary gaze left Ashfield for a brief moment and stopped on a nurse who was trying to help an uncooperative kid.

"Hey kid." I smiled and kneeled in front of him. He was covered from head to toe in dust and ash. His wide blue eyes brimmed with tears. "How are you doing?"

"I lost my mommy and everything hurts."

I glanced over his body. He seemed fine aside from a few cuts and scrapes on his elbows and knees. The nurse gave me a curt smile and tossed over some of her supplies before leaving to tend to another patient.

"Tell you what. You let me take care of these cuts and then I'll help you look for her. Deal?"

He nodded quickly.

"What's your name, little man?"

"Tommy."

"Nice to meet you, Tommy. I'm Eric."

A tiny smile formed on his lips.

"You know, I heard from my super-secret source that you're a really brave boy."

He grinned. *Okay, good. This was good.* I applied antiseptic lotion from one of the nurse's bottles to a gauze and brought it to his knee. Poor kid.

His leg stiffened in my grasp. Before he could start crying, I applied more pressure and looked up at him with a smile.

"And my sources tell me that you're going to be a soldier someday. Is that right?"

"Y-yes. Like you."

"I knew it."

"You did?"

"Of course." I nodded seriously. "We recruit only the best. And I'm impressed by how brave you've been."

Tommy's eyes lit up and he immediately put on a brave face as I applied another gauze pad to his elbow. I knew better than most that the sting of antiseptic was a bitch, but this kid was staying strong. As he began to tell me how he looked up to the soldiers at the compound my attention returned to the corner where Ashfield had been. He was now limping over to another nurse. She wasted no time rushing to his aid when he planted his ass on a bench.

Anger gripped my insides. Son of a bitch.

I turned my attention back to Tommy. "Alright Petty Officer, where to?"

He bounced to his feet; the ache of his grazed knees long forgotten.

"She was in the hallway when I saw her last."

"Okay, let's go and find her." I kept my eyes on Ashfield as Tommy took my hand and started leading me away.

Our eyes briefly locked before he looked away. I didn't trust him. I didn't want to take my eyes off him.

"Hey."

My eyes snapped forward in response to the voice.

Emelia stood in front of me, cradling a small baby wrapped in a green army blanket.

"Want me to take the kid?" she asked.

Tommy looked insulted.

"This is Petty Officer Tommy," I corrected. "He's looking for his mom."

"Oh, Petty Officer. I'm so sorry." She saluted him and he was immediately appeased.

Emelia looked over my shoulder and then back at me with a long, understanding look.

"Tommy, this is my sister, Lieutenant Emelia Raine."

Tommy loved every second of the official introductions.

"Nice to meet you." He beamed.

Emelia smiled and took his hand with a professional air.

She gave me another quick look, which I'd learned early on meant 'don't mess this up.' I nodded and returned my attention to helping other Ceoran survivors while mentally keeping note of where Ashfield was.

Meanwhile, Dad went from nurse to medic, checking in on whoever needed help. When Ashfield got up and started making his way toward the exit, I shot to my feet.

Dad must have known what I was doing because as I moved to follow Ashfield, he appeared in front of me.

"You need to stay back, Eric."

"Dad, I don't trust him."

"I know that," he said sternly. "But if you rock the boat anymore than you already have you're going to be held in contempt, and there won't be a damn thing I can do to protect you. Not my word, not your ranking here, do I make myself clear?"

"I can take care of myself."

"To what end?" he challenged. "Get yourself locked up and you won't be able to help Alex and then you've really sealed your fate, and hers."

I shut my mouth and kept my eyes ahead.

"Leave Ashfield to me, son. Keeping order is my job. Yours is to help the others."

I ground my teeth. Damn it.

"Go, now, Major."

"Fine." I gave him a firm salute.

He left and I watched him disappear behind the makeshift doorway, hopefully after Ashfield. I bit back the anger and simmered down. I reminded myself that he was my general first, father second and a part of me wondered whether I resented him for it. We were raised to put rank and royal first meaning everything else we felt was null and void including familial relationships. Still, didn't mean it was easy.

"Major Raine, could we get a hand here please?"

Turning to meet the voice, I recognized the nurse as Kristian Hall. We'd studied together, fought together and after a few patrol missions he opted to go into helping people rather than killing. In the end it was all semantics. We were all a means to the same end.

He was trying to help an elderly man to his feet, but thanks to the injury and the awkward position of the patient, the task was proving futile.

I slung the man's left arm over my shoulder while Kristian did the same on the other side. He counted down and together we lifted the older man's weight.

"Where are you taking them?" I asked.

"Away from this room, it's not stable."

I looked around and noticed for the first time that the structure was in fact crumbling. What fallen beams could be moved had been used to prop up the cracked ceiling.

"Have you been checked over?" Kristian asked.

"Yeah."

He frowned. "Still a shitty liar."

"Still a shitty medic."

Kristian looked down at the bleeding gash in the man's abdomen. He smirked.

"We'll patch him up once he's safely out of here."

I shielded a grin.

We got the man settled in the newly set-up med bay, outside on the lawn within the confines of the now secured inner wall system. Still, there were plenty of soldiers guarding the area just in case, some mildly injured themselves. Tents would have been erected within the first fifteen minutes of the explosion and the patients would have started rolling in shortly after. It was our protocol. Kristian and I walked back into the unsafe hall and repeated the process with at least seventeen other patients.

Sweat broke out across my body as the ache of the hours spent shifting heavy rubble took their toll. While I worked tirelessly and without rest, my mind kept returning to Alex. Where was she? Was she okay?

Over and over my mind kept repeating that all I needed to do was find her. Despite the worthiness of my work with the medics, my mind kept telling me I was in the wrong place. I needed to be out there, searching for Alex, seeking to destroy everyone who had ever tried to hurt her.

Chapter Five
Where Are You Running To?

In the few hours I'd been working with Kristian, I'd lost track of time. Crap. While I'd been stabilizing patients and delegating tasks, Dad and Ashfield had been gone for a long time—and I needed to know what the deal was. I dropped the bag of bandages in my hand and pushed my way through several soldiers who up until this morning had still been in training, and made my way into what was left of the hall.

"Em!" I spotted my sister talking with a young woman who was holding the baby Em had been cradling.

As I approached, both women flashed wide smiles at me. The gesture kind of threw me off. Everything here had been so grim; we'd been surrounded by so much death. A smile felt out of place, yet oddly comforting.

"Tommy helped me find the little one's mom, and she fortunately also knew where Tommy's mom was." She beamed.

"That's great." I smiled. They would be a family; they wouldn't have to deal with the loss Em and I had. "Em, can I have a word?"

"Ah, sure." She gave the lady an apologetic smile before standing up and following me. "What's up?"

Once the woman and her kid were out of earshot, I pulled her aside into a doorway. "Ashfield's up to something and I need to know what. Dad went after him and ordered me to sit this one out."

"And you don't want to."

"Of course not." I frowned. "When have I ever agreed with him?"

Emelia sighed, pinching the bridge of her delicate nose. "Since he's your superior."

I raised my brows at her.

"What can I do?" she offered.

"See if you can find anything out. He's going somewhere, he knows something, and I get the feeling Dad does too."

"Records room."

"What?"

"There'll be something in there."

"Last time I checked that place was a fortress," I said.

"Last time I checked, I was pretty good at breaking into places others can't," she countered.

"I don't want you getting in trouble, Em. These people don't take us messing with their shit lightly."

"I know. But it's worth it. All of it is if we get answers." She began to turn, but when I caught her hand she gave me a quick look. "Trust me, Eric. I've got this. And besides, I've got an ally."

"Who?"

"Lana."

I grinned. "Now that's a team even I wouldn't mess with."

"Exactly. We'll be fine. You stay on the front line. Everyone expects you to be doing the dumb stuff. So if you're accounted for, no one will think to suspect me."

"Dumb stuff, really?"

"Yes, really. Go. Show your face." She smirked at me then disappeared down the hall.

I shook my head with a smile. Lana had been out on missions for the last two years, watching over some rich Ceoran couple who'd adopted a human kid. The Council wanted them protected by the best of the best, so Lana and her highly specialized team were assigned as personal detail. No one external to the small group of guards knew why they were so high on the list, but I did. They were basically a bank to the Ceoran High Council. They did whatever they pleased, including playing make-believe families with a human kid and the Council turned their gaze as long as the cash kept flowing. She hated the babysitting of pompous royals as much as any of us did but Alex was different, of course. Not just because I'd fallen in love with her, but because she was a force of change. She made people rethink. She challenged the status quo after two centuries of the same mundane, demeaning crap. Not just here but back home on Ceora. So if my sister told Lana this was for Alex, she wouldn't think twice about helping.

When I lost sight of Emelia, I made my way back through the corridor and found Kristian. For another two hours we continued working. Most of the flames were now out, the wounded safely tucked away and the crumbling building secured.

When I finally dropped into a chair, fatigue etched all over my body, I closed my eyes letting the pain settle deep into my muscles and bones.

"Alright man, your turn."

I looked up and sighed when Kristian appeared in front of me with a med kit.

"I'm fine, there are others who need help."

"Everyone is taken care of. You, on the other hand, are a mess."

"Did I miss the memo where everyone's just roasting me today?"

"Isn't that every day?"

I stuck my middle finger up at him.

He laughed and proceeded to shine a light into my eyes.

"Follow the light."

"Sure thing, doc."

He rolled his eyes.

"No concussion. You're good."

"Told you."

"I know, but it's my duty. You know how it is."

"I do."

Kristian packed away his equipment and looked around. The eerie silence of the usually bustling common room was unsettling. It drove home how quickly we could become undone in our own sanctuary. Nowhere was safe, no one could protect us but ourselves and it was my duty now and always as a soldier to do whatever I could to protect them.

"We've known each other for a long time, right?" I said, getting up and stretching out the ache in my muscles.

"Yeah man, years. What's going on?"

"I need your help."

"Name it."

I jerked my head toward a private corner of the common room, tucked away from everyone else. When we were alone, I turned my back to the door. I hated relying on other people, but I knew when I was backed into a corner that being arrogant was only going to put others in danger. More than that, I was growing paranoid. The attack on the compound had come from within. Someone here was responsible, and I didn't need concrete evidence to know that it had something to do with Ashfield—but it also made me realize I didn't know who I could really trust here.

"What's going on, Eric?"

With everything that had happened, I found myself at a loss. What was I really about to ask him? And could I live with it? I shifted in my spot and scrubbed the back of my neck.

"Emelia's breaking into the Elders' vault to get into the records room," I said.

"Okay, I was not expecting that."

"Someone here is responsible for this attack and the last, and that someone has been protected and hidden from the rest of the Council. I need to know who."

"What are you going to do when you know?"

"I'm going to stop them."

"You're going to stop them," he repeated flatly, and then looked away from me. My reputation here reached far and wide. That might have been advantageous when I needed people to stay away from me, but definitely not when I needed to stay off the radar. "What do you need from me?" he asked after a moment.

"Chancellor Wynter is in danger out there, and I am her primary guardian. But Kelly's her detail and if I'm right about whoever is orchestrating this, they're going to know all of the protocols and Kelly will be walking into a trap. Somehow they are always one step ahead of us."

"Alright? So, how can I help?"

"I need you to gather whoever you can, whoever is on our side. We need numbers."

He twisted around and looked over the debris in the common room. The sight was horrific to say the least. The bodies were gone but their blood, their clothing, the trays of food they'd been enjoying earlier were strewn around as a reminder of the mortality we all faced.

"I know what I'm asking of you. I get that it's a lot, but I can't protect her alone. I don't trust anyone else."

Kristian paused for a moment.

"I need to stop this. What happened here is just the beginning."

"I'm in."

To say that I was relieved would have been a gross understatement. Exhaustion and emotion rolled into one big, overwhelming mess. The sting of grateful tears burned the back of my eyes.

"Tell me what to do and it's done, Eric. I know how important she is." He forced a tight smile.

He knew how important she was to *me. He'd known since we were training together.* And I knew he'd never said a word to anyone about it, even when he was questioned. He'd risked his position to cover for me.

"I can never thank you enough, Kristian."

"You don't need to. What do you need me to do?"

"Gather whoever you can, whoever you trust, and meet me on the north side. We're leaving the compound tonight."

"Where are we going?"

"Plan C is in effect. This is now a salvation mission. They're going to be regrouping with nearby soldiers and heading to Compound 2."

"Who knows about the protocols?"

"Only me and the soldiers who'll be escorting Alex, along with the High Council."

"But you think someone else here knows?"

"Yes, someone definitely knows," I bit.

"And I bet I know who you suspect."

"I can't prove anything yet."

"Alright, so we intercept whoever it is and stall plan C?"

"That's the idea. North side, two hours," I said.

"Got it."

I waited for Kristian to leave before I backtracked through the common room and down the hall to where I'd seen my dad and Ashfield leave. I stayed quiet and close to the walls, oddly grateful for the downed tech that let me move around unmonitored.

People were busily tending to their loved ones and paid me no attention as I rushed by. With my own disheveled appearance, I blended into the environment of post-disaster chaos, which I was trained to use to my advantage.

The central part of the compound was still standing, even though the power was out, and the rooms and halls were bathed in the eerie green light of backup generators. Through every crack in the windows and holes in walls, I made out the strong perimeter defenses around the compound. Most of the soldiers on guard were a lot older than me and had opted to stay on as ground crew rather than be deployed on missions like I was.

That was another advantage for me. I knew how to evade them, and I knew how the outside world worked better than they did. Aside from outranking them, I also out skilled them.

I slowed when I heard hushed voices. There were several people inside a closed room, secured only by a door that didn't sit properly on its hinges, and thanks to the small square pane of blacked out glass that was broken I could make out who they were, well, at least one of them. I moved closer to the wall and stopped just short of it, focusing on the conversation.

Inside, Ashfield was talking to someone who sounded old and frail. Most likely a senior Council leader. My face immediately heated with anger and I caught my own scowl in the reflection of the glass shard still stuck in the doorframe. These people were asinine. They were out of touch, had no idea what kind of hell was raining down upon us out there while they still maintained their own cushy protection in here. And worse still they dictated every single aspect of what my life was.

"I can find her," Ashfield said, his voice muffled.

"And what then, James? You've already proven to us that you're not as efficient as you'd like to think you are."

"I was dealt a hand of unplayable cards, sir. I can do this. I assure you; I have a card to play."

"How will you do this? Please, enlighten us," another voice said.

"I know what their protocol dictates. I know where they'll be. I can intercept them. She'll need my help, and she will accept it."

"What makes you think she'll accept anything from you?"

"I'm sure her memories will not have completely betrayed the past we shared. She will listen to me. I know it," Ashfield said.

My ears pricked up. The delusional son of a bitch was even crazier than I thought.

"If I remember correctly, your relationship was shrouded in secrecy and ended in a way that shall we say…wasn't amicable?"

"The relationship ended because she fell in love with the soldier, is that not the case?" the first voice said.

My heart fell through the floor.

Ashfield cleared his throat. "Yes. She left me for the soldier. Her guardian."

"And do tell, why will she listen now?" the second voice asked. "If I'm not mistaken, the guardian is still in her life now?"

"Because I can offer her something she wants."

"What's that?"

"Answers Raine can't give."

I jerked forward furrowing my brow. What the hell was he talking about?

"What then?" the first voice asked.

"Then I make sure she's safe, keep her away from Raine," Ashfield answered.

"You have serious competition there, Ashfield. You know Raine won't willingly leave her alone in your care."

"He will when she orders it."

"You play a risky game."

"A game I know I can win. Let me."

"Fine. But if you fail this time you will be hard-pressed to find anyone here who will endorse your next term. Understand?"

"Yes. I understand."

"Good. Now leave us."

I pushed away from the door and hid behind a downed shaft. Next term? What was happening here? I crouched into the shadows, waiting until I heard footsteps approach the door, open it and then exit.

Anger raged through me. *What the hell was he playing at?*

It didn't take long for my mind to conjure up all sorts of things I didn't want to entertain, each one worse than the last. I was about two seconds from rushing down the hall after Ashfield and throwing the bastard down when I heard another familiar voice stop him instead.

"Oh, I'm so glad I caught you!"

I risked poking my head around the corner and frowned, *How did she know he'd be here?* Emelia flashed him a brilliant smile, the kind that was reserved for hardcore infiltration, namely flirting with boys to get them to do whatever she wanted. Who was I to judge?

"Emelia, the nicer half of the Raine duo."

She giggled, and I could only imagine how much acid hate was running through her veins right now.

"James, the nicer of the Ashfield trio."

"What can I do for you?"

"I'm running a clean-up down in the mess hall for the kids. I was hoping you could help me. You know, give them some hope as a royal, make them smile for a bit."

He looked her up and down.

Dear God. If she didn't knock him the hell out, I certainly would. But Emelia was playing a role. This was what she excelled at. She wouldn't go in for the kill until the opportune moment presented itself. He shifted onto his other foot and looked around. He was getting irritated; she was losing him.

"I really don't have the time."

"We'd really appreciate your help," she tried, flashing her best smile again.

"I have a lot to tend to."

"The kids have been through a lot, and I said I'd try and bring their favorite councilor down to see them. But I understand, you're extremely busy. I could maybe ask someone else—"

"No, no it's fine, I'm more than happy to come and visit the children."

He flashed a pearly white smile of his own and shimmied closer to her. I was going to vomit.

Emelia, though, was definitely the more mature of the two of us. She held back her bile and played right into his ego and insecurities. Ashfield was a people pleaser. He wanted to be the guy everyone went to for help, like the two-faced bastard he was. Every forced smile was perfected by hours spent in front of the mirror learning how to conform to what the politicians expected, and the people ate it up.

"Really?" Emelia bounced on her heels. "That would mean so much to them."

"Who am I to deny the children?"

She chuckled and led him away before shooting me a look down the hall. This woman was good. How did she even know I'd be here? Then it dawned on me. Kristian probably found her and made sure she knew all about what was going to go down in two hours. That meant I had to get my ass moving.

Chapter Six
The Plan Has Changed

Alex

Static filled the silent car, causing me to straighten in my seat. Beside me, Kieran did the same.

"What is that?" I whispered.

Carter held his hand up beside his head the way soldiers in movies do to tell comrades to stay quiet. I caught Clark's concerned gaze in the mirror and kept my mouth shut. I might have been gung-ho before, but I was smart enough to know when I needed to stay put, stay quiet, and let the experts do their job.

The car slowed and came to a jarring stop just on the cusp of a fork in the road. I wasn't used to such silence. Even though there hadn't been much life in the way of animals since this all started, it was still unnerving. There was nothing, not even the horrific sounds of gunshots in the distance or screams from camps fallen victim to Reapers or Scavengers. It was blacker than black and more silent than anything I'd ever heard. I shivered.

"I think we should move," I heard myself say.

"Car's dead," Carter whispered. That made sense of the sudden halt.

"Where are we? Shouldn't we be in range by now?" I whispered.

"We should be, I'm not picking anything up though," Carter said quietly.

"You're joking?" Kieran unholstered his weapons and looked around in the darkness.

"Sadly, no. No comms, no anything. It's a tomb out here," Clark whispered.

I followed his gaze, squinting. It was pointless. You couldn't see anything even if you had a flashlight. Considering how our Ceoran eyesight far outranked human vision, I was surprised.

"Stay low, and stay quiet," Kieran instructed before reaching for the door. "Something's off here."

"What are you doing?"

"We have to check the engine."

"You're kidding, right?" I hissed.

"Enough," Carter hissed back. "Stay quiet and lock the doors behind us."

"You're not seriously going to leave me behind," I muttered.

"I'm staying," Clark said. "They will check the car. Nothing will happen to you."

"I'm not worried about me." My eyes snapped back to Kieran and then coasted across the unnaturally still darkness outside.

Kieran gave me a reassuring nod. "We'll be fine, trust me."

A sound off to the left of the car alerted us to a new presence. I wasn't overly confident.

"Move out, make it quick," Clark ordered.

Carter and Kieran disappeared outside, closing the doors with a quiet thud. I quickly locked the door. It was impossible not to worry. I couldn't see more than a few feet beyond the car and the coiled tension inside was doubling with each second.

The car jolted slightly as the hood was lifted. Clark shifted in his seat and his eyes darted from left to right as the noises continued outside. A cranking sound, and then a low whir.

Clark flinched again. So much for watching out for me. He was just as scared as I was. That was the moment I realized how *human* we all really were. No one was ready for this. In the *old* world we would have been going to gigs, watching movies and hooking up. Not preparing for war.

"What's taking so long?" I whispered.

"I have no idea."

"Should we help?"

"Not a chance."

"What if something attacks them?"

"Even more reason for you to stay inside." He turned his whole body around in the seat to face me. He didn't like it, treating me like I was worthy of extra protection. I didn't either.

I reached for the door handle and his eyes narrowed. Before he could tell me not to go outside, Kieran's face appeared at the window making me jerk back in shock.

"Oh my God!" I hissed, unlocking the door. "You scared the crap out of me."

Carter gave me a bemused smile.

When both of them were seated I shook my head, playing it off.

"What was wrong with it?" Clark asked.

"Loose wiring," came Kieran's response.

"Seriously?" That was so ordinary it was almost laughable.

Kieran didn't share the sentiment. His brows knotted and he turned to stare dead ahead. Carter wasted no time pulling back out onto the road.

After what began as a dangerous night, the journey soon became uneventful. As I leaned back in my seat, a twang of pain shot through my midsection. Right on cue, Kieran shot me a concerned glance.

"Before you start, I hurt myself running. Not healing you."

Carter's eyes met mine in the mirror. He'd seen me heal earlier, but I think even he hadn't really believed it was possible for me. I'd never developed the skill.

"Why are you looking at me like that?" I sighed, looking at Kieran.

He wordlessly pressed his hand to my forehead making me flinch at the coolness.

"You're burning up," he said.

"It'll pass."

"Do you need us to stop?" Clark asked before Carter cut him off.

"We can't stop. Help her while we're on the road."

"I'm right here, guys," I snapped. "And I'm fine, I don't need help. I told you, it'll pass."

"And when will that happen, when you drop because you're drained?" Kieran demanded.

"I won't drop. Just let it go, okay?"

"Not okay."

"Oh my God."

Before he could further chastise me, I shot him a look and he closed his mouth. In the front, I caught Carter's smirk. I couldn't help but shield a smile as I turned away.

***

Eric

I gathered a few items I thought might come in handy, including a flashlight and a few trail bars, and shoved it all into a backpack.

A quick glance at my watch told me I had a little less than thirty minutes to meet Kristian, and I could only hope that Emelia had found what she was looking for. It was too dangerous to look for her, and the anticipation was making me edgy. I paced the small room four or five times before I finally slung my bag over my shoulder, grabbed a med kit and made my way to the makeshift medical center out in the erected tents.

Given the attention being paid to the victims of this evening's blast, no one looked twice as I dumped the med kit and snuck out the back door. As I approached our designated meeting spot, I saw Kristian navigating his way through the small crowd gathering around another fallen soldier. Friends and comrades paying their last respects. My heart broke for the loss, and had I not been working behind the scenes to keep Alex safe from the same threat, I would have cracked. With each step I reminded myself that my resolve couldn't falter now.

"Em?" he asked, looking over my shoulder.

"She's not here yet?"

"No, man. Thought she was with you."

"Damn it." I shoved the backpack into his arms and began to turn. Just then I saw her approach from the shadows cast by the rear of the compound on the north side of the facility.

"Where were you?" I hissed.

"We need to go. Right now." She grabbed my arm roughly and pulled me into the shadows.

68

"What's going on?" Kristian began to ask as she shoved him forward too.

I could take a hint. The three of us weaved through the downed rubble and sidestepped a group of medics running toward another casualty. Once we reached the far north perimeter, which was about a hundred yards from the compound, Kristian pointed to a small group huddled by the remains of the gate.

Just as he was about to start the introductions, a roaring explosion erupted behind us, sending what was left of the compound burning to the ground.

"Dad!" Emelia and I screamed in unison.

Before we could even think of running back, Kristian grabbed my shoulders and threw me backwards. Someone else did the same to Emelia, but all I could think about was the sheer terror of watching the last of our home go up in flames with our father inside.

"Get everyone you can and move now!" Kristian yelled.

Whether I wanted to or not, I couldn't run back. Hands were around my arms, pulling me forward and away from the burning compound.

We ran. Out of the perimeter gates and into the world outside.

We followed Kristian and the team he'd gathered deep into the dark cover of the barren tree line. I lost track of how much I'd cursed every Ceoran and Karatoi being. My sister, on the other hand, was deathly still when we stopped.

I pressed my hand to her shoulder, and she jumped.

"Em..."

"He's okay. I know he is, Eric. I know it."

Kristian squeezed my forearm. "Come on, we need to get out of the open."

Silently and without question, the eight of us—maybe the last eight survivors of the compound—disappeared into the night. Up ahead on the horizon, a new day was starting to bleed into the darkness, a new day filled with the unknown.

It didn't take long for nerves to get the better of me. Emelia clutched her satchel tightly and gestured for me to follow her, breaking from the group. I gave Kristian a nod and let them get a few yards ahead of us.

"I found something," she started, keeping us walking at a steady pace.

The change of topic was jarring, but it was needed. I had to get my head in the game. Dad was probably okay, just like she said, but Alex might not be.

"Tell me."

"Alex lied to you, she lied to all of us."

"About?"

"About Ashfield."

Heat reddened my cheeks recalling the cryptic as hell message I'd heard him convey earlier. "Explain."

"I will, but we need to find somewhere safe to stop. There's a lot, and I think it will impact what we do next."

"Okay. Let me tell Kristian, and we'll sort something out."

Emelia sped up and I followed closely behind. As I released a long, labored breath I found my mind racing. My father. Alex. Kelly. Ashfield. The thoughts tumbled over each other, hellish and rampant. My mind wouldn't slow, it wouldn't quieten. And through all the noise in my skull, different meanings behind what little information Em had given me wove insidiously through my brain. Alex had lied to me. How? And why? Unable to bear it, I walked past my sister and tapped Kristian on the shoulder.

70

"We need a place to rest," I said.

"There's an old outpost up ahead."

"Enough for all of us?"

"Should be. It was a training post we used while you were out in the field."

"Alright, tell the others."

He did as I asked, and within a minute we were on a new path, tracking through the woods and toward an unmarked path. Not long after, Emelia pulled back a thin covering of branches to reveal a small, nondescript entrance to an underground tunnel.

Emelia jumped into the manhole first, and a few seconds later signaled for the rest of us to follow.

Once we were all in the bunker, and covered by the woodland's disguise, I found Emelia and pulled her to one side.

Kristian and the others spread out, finding their own places to rest in relative privacy. The bunker was somewhat underwhelming. I half expected high-end tech, or at the very least some indication that our kind had utilized this space. When I sat down at a desk with a basic computer, I realized that the reason it was so plain was that this was merely a training hub. No one actually spent more than a few hours at a time here. One central room where I sat at the desk, and two smaller rooms off either side was all that was here.

Emelia opened her satchel and placed two thin in front of me. My eyes traveled down to her neatly folded hands, strategically placed over the files.

"You and I were certain that all of Ashfield's intentions with Alex were merely to get ahead in the line, right?" she began, and I immediately felt myself getting ready to argue.

"Yeah."

"So, I found something that says otherwise."

"What?"

"You were worried about him being involved with the attacks on the compound." She opened up the first file and slid out a sheet of paper. "You were right."

"I knew it, damn it." I snatched it up and read over the first few lines. Once I got down to the middle of the page, I stopped abruptly.

"This has to be wrong."

"It isn't." She frowned. "I looked over three other reports, all of them indicating the very same thing."

"No, there's no way she and Ashfield were involved in any way, especially not like this." The conversation I'd overheard said otherwise. I shut that thought down.

"Not only were they involved, Eric, they were attempting to make changes within the Council. And what I've read indicates that Ashfield wasn't always the jerk we knew him to be. At least not to the same extent…at least not to her anyway."

"How so?"

"He genuinely cared for her, Eric. There were documented accounts of their conversations, private talks within his household. Eric, I think he loved her."

My throat closed, drying up. I wet my lips and looked across at my sister. "So everything he's doing now is jealousy?"

"Wouldn't put it past him."

"No." I shook my head. "He was pressuring her, blackmailing her. Making her say things, I don't know. Maybe he was forcing her, Em…"

"I doubt that." Em shrugged, making my stomach recoil. "But this is serious, Eric. If she and Ashfield were in a relationship and now they're not, he could have multiple reasons to want to get back at her."

I sank into the seat and leaned back. "Why would she lie to me about this?"

"Maybe she was ashamed."

"Maybe she was scared," I added.

"Maybe."

"This is going to complicate things." I scrubbed my jaw and opened the next file.

While Emelia stayed silent and let me read, I found out more and more information about the girl I thought I knew better than myself. I read about her secret life, a life I had no idea about. She and Ashfield had a partnership; I couldn't imagine it was anything romantic, but a pang of jealousy coursed through me just the same. There were talks in the Council about making them an official delegatory pair which meant that if they wed, they'd be privy to all the Council protocols, books, every piece of information someone would need to bring the whole thing crashing down from within. And the more I read the more I started to piece together the possibility of what she had been hiding and why—she was planning on taking them down.

"They were together," I finally admitted out loud. "In one way or another, they were working together."

"Does it change how you feel about her?"

"No, of course not."

She nodded and turned her eyes down to the folders between us.

"He plays the game well. Too well. It's scary the way he can manipulate people," Emelia said.

"So does she."

Emelia's eyes met mine. "You read the same file I did, what's your take on it?"

"Infiltration."

"Exactly. So what changed?"

"Maybe she changed her mind, couldn't go through with it."

"Why?" Emelia asked.

"I don't know." I shrugged, scrubbing my jaw.

"I think it has to do with you."

My eyes snapped up to her. "What do you mean?"

"Come on, Eric. She is obviously so in love with you that doing this, even for the greater good, would have destroyed her."

"You think that's why she canned the infiltration?"

"Is it so hard to believe?"

"Guess it isn't," I mused. "Why wouldn't she tell me then?"

"It would have eaten her alive, could you come clean about something like that?"

I hung my head. There were a lot of unknowns and until I could ask her myself, I wouldn't pass judgement; my dad would call me stupid and naïve for it, the hell did he know though?

"Look, I know he's a jerk and he's done a lot of shady stuff, Eric, but do you really think he could work with the Reapers, with Silus?" Emelia muttered.

"You think it could be someone else talking in his ear?"

"It's possible; he's just one of three very motivated brothers, and their family has been on the decline for years. I'd say there's a lot of motive."

"And that—that is what worries me. Ashfield is nothing compared to the real threat," I realized.

Acknowledgement burned a hole in my chest. I was agreeing to Alex, *my* Alex, having been involved with Ashfield, the one and only asshole in the compound who could make my life a living hell and probably lived for it too. I oscillated between anger and sadness. My hands shook under the table, safe from Emelia's gaze. What had she seen in him? What had he done for her? What had they meant to each other? Was she seeing him when we were together? Was there more to their relationship than the infiltration? Was she seeing him at all? I thrust my fingers through my hair. No, Alex wasn't that person. I knew she wasn't.

She must have had a reason to have kept this from me. She must have had a reason to stay with James Ashfield for as long as she did. She and I were a secret, kept away from most prying eyes under my request, not hers. With him, she was free to be in the open, yet still no one knew about it until now. What if she'd been in trouble? What if he had something over her that would put her in danger if she left?

"Eric?"

"What?"

"You didn't hear a word I said."

"No. Sorry." I frowned, meeting my sister's bright eyes.

"I don't think he hurt her."

"What?"

"I know that look," she tried, "and I know how your brain works. You go to all the worst-case scenarios. But I honestly don't think he hurt her. At least, not in that way."

The thought alone brought a rage I hadn't known in a long time to the surface. I looked away and composed myself with two long breaths.

"Ashfield is an asshole," Em continued, "but he's not that kind of asshole. He's more of a blackmail kind of guy. His brother David, though—I wouldn't put that kind of crap past him."

"That's it." I looked back at the files. Once I found what I was looking for, I handed it to her. "David Ashfield was the golden boy and on the fast track to sitting on the Council until he had that assault charge brought against him."

Emelia's eyes widened as she kept reading. "Keep going."

"He always presented himself as the champion for the elite, who if elected would make sure that their people would never have to raise a finger to do anything for themselves ever again. They would get even more protection at the cost of even more of our lives. You remember all his rallies, right?"

She nodded slowly.

"What if he set the whole thing up, ensured James would make it to the Council in his place via his relationship with Alex, and then when he was in power, he would have an in to all that information those relics are hiding in their ivory tower. But when she dumped his ass all those plans went out the window."

"To what end though?" Emelia set the file down. "After he was so easily booted out, I don't think he'd be wanting to do anything that could benefit the Council now."

"You're right, but he might want exactly what Alex wants, but for revenge."

"That's seriously reaching, Eric."

"Is it though? Is it hard to imagine what lengths someone like David would go to in order to exact vengeance on those who destroyed his entire livelihood and image?"

She considered what I'd just presented and looked back at the files.

"Think about it, Em. He served and did everything they asked of him, and they tossed him out like trash."

"I get it, he would be pissed."

76

"People like the Ashfields live for the name, for the pedigree and what their sway can buy. Now, he's a pariah, no one, elite or otherwise looks at him twice. I know I'd have some feelings if that were me."

"I don't know."

"It doesn't matter now. Outcome is the same. She's in danger, and if we go off this we're no longer just dealing with Reapers. We have multiple variables to factor in."

"So what now?"

"Now we fill in the others and work out what to do next."

"You know you have to tell them the truth, about you and Alex?"

I bit down hard.

"You know what that means," she said gently.

As simple as the statement was, the truth of it was anything but. The truth meant outing myself and what Alex and I had shared. It meant being open, putting her in the spotlight, risking my position and probably exile, and it most likely meant losing her. But if I could save her, and stop all of this from getting worse, then it didn't matter. Then it was worth it.

"I know," I relented.

"Are you sure you're ready to do that?" she asked tenderly.

I looked down at the evidence, spelled out in black and white. Ashfield and his brothers, and the potential plot to change the landscape of our world. Who knows what it would mean for non-elite soldiers like me and my family. I couldn't let that happen. I thought about the other soldiers here, resting, getting ready for a fight they knew nothing about, and then I looked back at my sister.

Whatever came next, my priority would be to protect her, and Alex, and everyone else who wasn't out to get us.

"Yes, I'm sure."

CHAPTER SEVEN
WHAT ARE WE WILLING TO RISK?

Alex

Kieran tapped Carter on the shoulder to wake him up. He jerked, then mumbled, then quickly turned red when he realized we'd all heard him mutter how much he missed his mom. It was cute, despite the crap Clark gave him afterwards.

"We should stop for the night," Kieran suggested. "The compound is still eight hours away."

The impromptu stopover we made to fix the wiring in the engine cost us a bit of time, that and the two times we had to stop for Carter to puke meant we were delayed by a few hours.

"I don't like it, Kelly. We should stay on the road," Clark muttered.

"I agree," I added.

"Everyone is exhausted. Taking turns to sleep in the car isn't ideal," Kieran said.

"Being dead on the side of the road isn't ideal either," I said. "We can take turns driving, but we should stay on the road."

"I think she's on the ball here, man. Sorry," Clark sided with me.

"Fine, let me take over for a while then," Kieran offered.

Once they'd swapped and settled back in, I closed my eyes and decided to try and get some sleep. Once my eyes drifted shut, I focused on the soft sounds of the CD playing in the car and the rain on the windows outside. It was a song I knew well. I had planned to have it at my wedding. Of course, I didn't know who the groom would be but I always dreamt about deep pools of green and a smile that took my breath away. I felt my cheeks flush as I smiled to myself. Before long, sleep had taken over and I found myself pulled into a dream, out of body, standing in front of Eric and myself.

It wasn't *me*, me. It was a dream version of me, and I was watching from the outside, kind of like an old movie being replayed. Eric and I moved toward a corner and his hand landed on my forearm. Our voices were hushed and arguing about something I couldn't quite make out. He stopped talking when Carter walked past, giving him a look. He straightened and took a small step back, removing his hands from me.

When Carter was clear of the corridor, Eric stepped a little closer and I watched the me in front of him step back. It was painful, even if I wasn't experiencing it again for real. The class division was prevalent in all our lives. We lived and breathed the rules. The soldiers were seen as lesser than; the Ceoran like Ashfield wanted to be the elite, and then there was my family who was considered *royal* in human terms. It was sickening. We weren't allowed to form relationships beyond the scope of guardian and subject let alone fall in love. The repercussions for me and Eric would have been catastrophic.

"I need you to let me go, Eric. This ends now," I heard myself say to Eric in my vision.

As small fragments of my past found their way into my memories while I stood here, I remembered what Ashfield had said to me one night, though the context wasn't quite there....*do this or I tell them all about you two. Can you live with yourself if Eric is kicked out because of you?*

Pain seized my heart.

Surely there was more to this conversation. Surely there was a reason I was sucked back into this memory.

I moved toward the Eric and me in my memory and tried to listen.

"I don't understand why you're pushing me away," I heard Eric say.

"I'm not trying to push you away, but you know what the risks are. I don't want to do that."

"And you're making that decision for me, then?" he bit.

"No..."

Eric stepped away from me when I paused, and ran his hands through his hair. I noticed that he didn't have any of the burns or the scars I'd become accustomed to. This was before the attack on the old compound. Why didn't I remember this conversation?

"I'm not making the decision for you, Eric, but I'm hoping you can understand where I'm coming from, what I'm trying to do here."

"Is someone threatening you?" he asked.

"No. I just finally realized how childish I'm being, how much I'm risking. I won't do it anymore."

"Your career."

"My chance to make real change here."

"You're serious?" he asked.

"I am and I need you to understand. I cannot do that with you. I'm sorry."

"Does this have anything to do with him?"

"Don't be ridiculous."

The me in front of Eric was cold. Emotions were there, I knew they were I just wasn't showing any and Eric looked at me with wide, pleading eyes probably trying to work out what in the hell was happening. I was too.

"What do I do, then? Pretend were just friends, ignore you? Pretend I don't love you?"

"Yes, it's for the best. I need to do my job; I need to make things right. And James will help with that."

"Make what right, Alex, I don't understand. And you cannot be serious, he's an asshole!"

"He can help me with this, all of it!" My voice rose an octave, I was losing my composure.

"No. I can't do that."

"You have to."

I watched in disbelief as the me in front of Eric started crying. The same hopelessness I'm sure I felt then coursed through me now, but I stood there frozen, cold and emotionless. I was breaking, I saw my own pain through his eyes but I knew now what I was doing. Ashfield had whispered his threats, but I heard them loud and clear.

"Please, Alex, please rethink this."

"This is how it has to be. I'm sorry, Eric."

I was jolted back to the present with the heaviness of the dream conversation pushing me into the seat.

When I noticed that the car wasn't moving. I jerked. "Why did we stop?"

"Change of driver, thought I'd stay in the car with you in case you woke up," Kieran said.

"Oh." I looked up and caught Clark sneaking a cigarette outside.

While Carter gave Clark a piece of his mind about taking a smoke break, Kieran leaned over to me.

"You okay?"

"Fine. Just a dream."

"Sure?"

I seriously considered telling him to butt out, but I was straight up exhausted carrying all of this on my own.

Kieran was, as far as I was concerned, one of the most trustworthy people I knew, even if I hadn't remembered it all immediately. Some people just gave off good vibes and Kieran was one of those people.

"Remember when I told you I was breaking up with Eric?" I asked.

His brow knotted but he nodded.

"Did you see something in your dream?"

"A few weeks ago, when Eric first brought me back to the compound, Ashfield was being really weird. He was saying stuff about us, insinuating that we had some sort of history. Obviously I thought he was out of his mind because why would I ever have a relationship with a person like that?"

"What are you saying?"

"I did have a relationship with him, Kieran."

"What?" he balked. "You never told me this, I never knew."

"All I know, is Ashfield was threatening to out me and Eric. I think I gave into his blackmail. I don't know why else I would have…and then I ended things with Eric."

"Oh Alex."

Shame burned my eyes. "I don't know what I did and I don't know why—I honestly can't remember all of it, but what if it was all for nothing anyway?"

"You were under a lot of pressure to be a perfect leader your whole life. You kept a lot of what you did from us, and there was a lot you had to do to be a part of that world. But I know for a fact that whatever you did, whatever you agreed to was for a reason."

"God, I hope so."

"Is that what you dreamt about?"

"I think my dream wasn't a dream. It was like I was there, Kieran. Watching myself from the outside, like I was really there as a presence when the me there with Eric was talking. Is that even possible?"

"It could be for you."

"What do you mean?"

"It's not a Ceoran trait," he said simply.

It took a moment to realize what he was saying, and why he looked away from me as if I could kill him with one look. I folded my arms across my chest. Well, he wasn't really wrong, was he? I'd taken him down with a touch not long ago. I shuddered. That was terrifying. I looked at the other two outside. They didn't know what I was, nor would I be telling them.

"What does that mean for me?" I whispered.

"I have no idea, but it could be serious."

"This has to mean something, Kieran."

"And whatever it is, I know you would have done it for a reason, a damn good one at that."

I thought for a moment, deciding that yes, whatever I chose to do then was for a reason and a damn good one, I just had to trust myself the way Kieran trusted me.

I wound down my window and Carter turned his head slightly. "What's up?"

"I need to stretch my legs."

"Right now?"

"Yes."

"Stay close and don't stray too far."

I shot Kieran a look and he followed me outside.

When we were out of earshot, I dragged him a little further into the privacy of the darkness.

"I think I'm the reason all of this is happening."

"You know how pretentious that sounds, right?"

"Yeah, but unfortunately it's probably legit."

"When you say everything, you mean the attack on the compound?"

"Yes."

"Why?"

"I don't have the exact answers, but I think it had to do with our *relationship* ending."

"Because he misses you?" he scoffed.

"No, absolutely not. At least not entirely. There has to be something more, something I don't remember yet."

"What would you need to find out?"

I expelled a breath and met his eyes. "No idea. That's the problem."

"That's a big problem."

"I know," I groaned, pressing the heels of my palms to my face.

"But you're sure you're on the right track?"

"Positive. I can feel it. This is the closest to an answer that I've ever had, and I need to find out why."

"What can I do?" he asked.

I glanced over at Clark and watched him pace beside the car. When I looked back at Kieran, I stepped closer making sure that no one could hear us.

"Keep it between us for now, and when we reach the second compound I'm going to try and get into the digital records."

"You sure that's a good idea?"

"Probably not, but I have to try. Got any contacts?"

He grinned. "Definitely. I know a girl, I trust her. She can dig up any info you need."

"Thank you."

"Don't thank me until we're free of being charged for treason." He gestured back to the car. "Until then we just have to remain open and honest with each other. I don't want you doing this alone when you don't have to."

"Scout's honor."

"You're not a scout." He grinned.

"Neither are you."

Once we were moving again, I gave Kieran a knowing look and settled back into the seat. Whatever answers I was after would be at the new compound. Everything I needed to know would be there. Until then, I had to wait. I had to hope that Eric and Emelia knew how to find us, I had to trust that they knew where to go and how to protect themselves. It wasn't just about me, it was about everyone now. Everyone who counted on me to keep them safe. Not only as their leader but their trusted guide who could lead the

Ceoran back to the Bridge when the time came for our kind to go home…if that ever happened.

CHAPTER EIGHT
THE PLAN

Eric

Emelia got the attention of the rest of the group in the cramped quarters, and I felt their eyes slide over to me. Holy hell, I was really about to do this.

She gave me a small nod, then stepped back. The chatter quieted, and I found my nerves spiking. Strange. Usually I was good at this sort of thing. Though, granted, I'd never really spoken about my personal life to a bunch of people, let alone something that was such a bombshell, as I'm sure they'd put it.

Kristian looked to me and, like Emelia, gave me an encouraging nod. I was going to be sick.

Eventually, I took a deep breath and held up the two reports my sister had brought. As much as giving them the full, unaltered spiel would have been easier, I couldn't do it.

This had to be approached with tactical finesse.

"We're all here because we know there's more to the Council's rule than we've been led to believe. We're here because we know that whatever took place weeks ago, and again last night, wasn't just an opportunistic attack."

A few nods came in response. So far so good.

"Over the last few weeks after Chancellor Wynter's return to the compound, Emelia and I have been running recon and gathering as much intel as possible related to keeping the Chancellor's position safe. One recurring theme was the involvement of James Ashfield and potentially his brother, David."

"And the other?" Leah asked.

"No word on Jonathan being involved, that's not to say that he isn't," Emelia added.

"To what end?" Kristian asked.

"At this stage it's all speculation," I responded, careful not to put myself in a position where I might have made things worse for myself should anything happen.

"Speculate away. No one here cares much for them," Kristian said. "And you're definitely not going to offend any of us by saying what you have to."

Emelia gave me a look. This was it. I couldn't back out now. Everyone was waiting for something tangible, something we could work with. Up until this point, speculation was all we had—and as much as I hated to admit it, this was a little more than an educated guess.

"We suspect that there may have been plans prior to the Clean Slate procedure which wiped Chancellor Wynter's memories for her to sit on the High Council with James Ashfield. Together, they would have possessed the required pedigree to make decisions. They would have had the innate leadership that the Ceoran have been lacking."

"And before anyone starts, we have proof," Emelia said.

She took the files from me and handed them to Kristian. For a while we stood quietly in the dark of the shelter, our faces illuminated only by a dim light until finally, he looked up at me.

"These are huge allegations. You're telling us that Ashfield got butthurt that Wynter wouldn't date him anymore so he went to the Reapers to get payback?"

"It's not that simple," I muttered, exhaling loudly.

"We all heard the Wynters's declaration that they would never share the *throne* with the Ashfields, there's just no way what you're saying is true. There's no way Alex would be dating him despite the rumors." Kristian handed over the files to Zayne who had both Lisa and Leah reading over his shoulder.

"I know." I ground my teeth. "We all heard the same thing years ago when the rumors started swirling."

"But he is right, we did see them cozy up at a few events," Katya reminded me. "Looked real to me."

"Because she was playing a role," I emphasized.

I loved Katya, considered her one of my oldest friends but dear Karatoi she could get on my nerves in a split second.

Katya's brows rose like she was insulted by my reaction. "No need to get snappy, just calling it how I see it."

"I know that, but I'm telling you, there's no way there was a real relationship, regardless of the rumors and what we saw." I hoped.

"So what's changed now?" Leah asked, putting a stop to the shouting match.

"What's changed now is that his plan to get his family to the throne has been overthrown because Alex is starting to remember her life before the Clean Slate. His goal was to get her back, win her over with the notion that she wouldn't remember me or anything she did before the Clean Slate, including shutting him out, and considering everyone on the Council saw their union as an obvious pairing, no one would have said a word against it," I said.

90

Zayne gave me a pointed look, thinking for a moment. "And Alex ruined his plans again."

"Exactly, we're dealing with the Ashfields, we know their power over the Ceoran is immeasurable," I added.

"That's a dangerous comment," Kristian muttered.

"I know it's a risk to make these kinds of accusations, but what do we know about the Ashfields? We know they're conniving, willing to do whatever it takes to get to the top and if that's what we've seen so far, what says they wouldn't orchestrate something as big as an attack on the compound?" I tried.

Silence greeted me.

"Our working theory is that those rumors were true at one point; perhaps Chancellor Wynter's family did agree to a peaceful arrangement to bring their own change requests to the table, perhaps Chancellor Wynter had her own reasons to partake," Emelia said, looking at me briefly. "But she might have changed her mind and perhaps because of this the Ashfield family was locked out of the winning seat and sought retribution."

"But, they rested their hopes on her being brought back into our world without her memories," I reminded them.

"And what reasons could she possibly have to get all cozy with that scumbag?" one of the girls asked.

"You're looking at him," Katya said nodding across at me. She was one of the few who knew about us.

A few people genuinely looked shocked, which was good, it meant our relationship wasn't tabloid news, the others looked like they weren't surprised.

"You're going to have to explain that one," Zayne said.

"Alex and I were dating, we were in love, obviously that's forbidden and here we are," I muttered, feeling every eye on me.

"When Alex ended things with me, the attack on the Hampton Compound happened not even a week later, a few days after that she asked me to initiate the Clean Slate."

That's when talks of Alex's identity really started swirling. It became too dangerous to for her to remain in our Compound and so, I did as she asked. Now, speaking these words aloud to this group I started to wonder if there was any correlation. The timing was too close to be coincidental.

The attack, as we all knew, was designed to take her, kill her family and everyone protecting her. They didn't account for me being away from the building on account of our breakup, so I was able to get there and get her out.

The skin on my arm tingled as a timely reminder for what took place.

"I'm so sorry," Leah whispered.

"So am I. But right now, we need to focus on what this means for us," I began. "I think the two older Ashfield boys needed a way into the Council chambers and when David's sexual assault charge threw him out of contention, his middle brother, too, leaving James the only one eligible to stand in their place, and with Alex pulling out, it ruined their plans."

"What exactly would they want in the Council chambers?"

"Not a clue. All I know is that whatever is in there, is enough to make them kill mercilessly and sacrifice countless Ceoran and human lives to get it."

"What about Chancellor Wynter?" Zayne asked.

"She, along with Kelly and a small group are out there right now heading toward the next compound, as is our protocol. I have reason to believe it's been compromised and they're walking into a trap."

It would have been irrelevant to say how much the admission hurt. The whole thing tore a hole right through my chest and my sister knew it. With a sympathetic look, she took the lead.

"Regardless of the potential outcome of these allegations, we need to take them seriously. We're here because we're the best, however you look at it. We have more combat hours in this one room than the entire compound combined."

"Pretty sure our compound is gone, man, we might be the only ones left," Kristian muttered.

"Which means all of this falls on us." I searched each of their eyes.

Skepticism and fear looked back.

"So, what is the play here?" Zayne asked off to Kristian's left. "I can't imagine this being a tactical execution, someone like James Ashfield would no doubt be packing some serious heat with the protection detail on him at all times, which I assume means we're going in guns blazing."

Zayne was a big, burly guy who looked like a bouncer in a high-end club—rough on the outside but a huge softie who loved a chat on the inside—so the fact that he was already thinking about the hostility waiting for us set me on edge.

"I want to set out at first light and start heading toward Compound Two," I said.

"You just said it was compromised, why one Earth would we go there?" Zayne asked.

"Because protocol dictates that's where they're headed so we need to intercept them and stop them from walking into the trap," Emelia explained, sighing like she couldn't believe she had to explain this. I felt the same.

"What then?" Leah asked.

"Then…then we work out what the Ashfields are up to and stop them," I said with fierce determination.

"Stop them. Just like that," Kristian deadpanned.

"Well we have to start somewhere," I shot back.

Each of them gave me a quick, curt nod. They'd followed me to the end of the earth before this. They'd trusted me endlessly, counted on me to lead them and provide sound intel. Could they still trust me after this? Had my run ended?

Katya gave me an encouraging nod.

"You lead, we follow. It is our way," Lisa said.

A smile tugged at my lips before I could stop it.

"It's definitely our way." Emelia smiled, squeezing my forearm. "We should all rest up, including you." She furrowed her brows and nudged me toward the back of the low-ceiling cavern.

Before I could argue, she'd shoved me toward a milk crate. I turned it upside down and sat, waiting for my sister to do the same.

She didn't seem to be in the talking mood as she snuggled into her oversized coat and met my eyes.

Guess there wasn't much to say, was there?

We were all about to embark on something which had never been done before. Not only were we a small army, we were also a bunch of non-elite soldiers about to go up against a fury of counselors and their big hitters.

"I know you're worried, Eric. I am too. But this is the right thing to do. I know it is."

I sighed but nodded. Emelia had a smidgen of Ceoran seer ability, which came in handy whenever we went up against the unknown. It's also how she was always one step ahead of most of us when it came to strategic planning; come to think of it that's also how she probably knew where I was when I was eavesdropping on

Ashfield and the Elders. It's how I knew Dad was okay when she said so. It also meant we were always a little ahead of whatever came next. The problem was, when it came to Alex no power she or I possessed could come close—and I could never tell her why. Keeping secrets from Emelia was special kind of torture, but revealing that Alex was part Reaper was a secret that could never leave my mouth. I'd told Kieran because I had to, right now, was different.

As if she'd sensed that something was on my mind, I evaded her questioning with an exaggerated yawn, and leaned back into the rough surface of the wall behind me.

The fact that I had to lie to my sister twisted my stomach into knots. Ugly, tense knots. But something deep inside whispered like an insidious storm on the horizon I had to, and by whatever was guiding me, I did as I was told.

***

Alex

No sooner had I fallen asleep than I was jolted awake by the car screeching to a halt followed by a loud, unmistakable thud. We'd hit someone. Or something.

"We're under attack!" Carter shouted first. My blood ran cold.

Before I could gather my thoughts, the thud was followed by a very forceful jab to the side of the car closest to me. I held in a surprised shriek and looked out of the tinted window. There were four Reapers outside, about a dozen Scavengers, and some Ceoran in the background. I gasped.

The shocked silence inside the car confirmed that none of us could comprehend what we were seeing. Why were Ceoran working with the Reapers? We knew, or at the very least we assumed, that Ashfield and his brothers had a stake in Reaper operations for their own personal gain. I knew what I'd cost them by recanting on my parents' promise to stay with James, but this seemed to be a free for all. There was no reason behind it. No logic.

"Get into formation, now!" Kieran said hoarsely once the shock wore off.

I didn't even have a moment to stumble out of the car before Kieran dragged me to the ground beside him. My thin leggings immediately soaked through in the damp earth.

"Stay beside me and stay down. Got it?" he said sternly.

"Got it."

"Good, follow me." He started moving toward the back of the car, and I stayed low just as he said.

Beyond my line of sight, I heard Carter and Clark barking out orders, which I now realized must have been to the Ceoran at Compound 2; we were finally in range. As Kieran dragged me further away from the firing my earpiece sparked to life and through static and erratic chatter I could hear the conversation. Backup was on the way but they wouldn't make it on time.

"Get her out of here!" Clark shouted.

I held my breath as Kieran and I moved as one away from the fighting.

As we neared cover in the form of a large group of trees nestled amongst a formation of large rocks, I heard one of the soldiers scream. I couldn't tell if it was Clark or Carter. It was short and sharp, and then there was nothing aside from the constant yelling and gunfire.

"We should be helping them!" I shouted to Kieran.

"We need to keep you out of sight."

"And let them die out there alone?"

"That's their job, Alex. Mine is to keep you alive."

"This is bullshit, and you know it."

"No, Alex!" he snapped, standing so close to me I could feel the heat of his breath on my forehead. "What's bullshit is that you put yourself and all of us in this situation."

The second the words left his lips, he clamped his mouth shut and took a step back. Not a huge step, a tiny one. The kind you take when you're absolutely flabbergasted that you could have possibly said something so mean. True, certainly, but mean, nonetheless.

"Alex—"

"You're right," I snapped and gave the direction of the fighting one quick look before continuing past Kieran.

He followed in tow, silently, until we were both far enough away from the commotion that the shouts were barely a whisper.

His eyes landed on mine. I couldn't let him see how hurt I was, and I could never let him know that the hurt went deeper than the small tremble in my knees or the grinding in my gut. It was soul deep. This was a burden I knew I would carry for the rest of my life. Every drop of Ceoran blood spilled now was because of me. I'd already established that, but hearing Carter and Clark fighting out there and possibly dying for me was a lot to deal with.

He paused for a moment, his jaw grinding.

"Stay here," Kieran said urgently.

"Where are you going?"

"I'm going to help them. Do not move from this tree."

My heart kicked up. "Yes, I promise. Go! Hurry!"

He turned on his heel and dashed into the fading light of the forest. In little less than a minute, I heard more shouting and gunfire as another set of weapons joined the fight. He'd made it, and I only hoped it was in time.

As the fighting got louder and the echoes in the surrounding tree line more prominent, I kneeled beside the large trunk of the tree Kieran had left me at. I needed to do something. I couldn't just stay here and wait. I buried the fingertips of my right hand into the soil and closed my eyes. The moment my skin connected with the earth I felt a sudden pull that winded me. Low, shuddering breaths escaped my lips as a warmth that started in the core of my heart started to spread out through my veins and into my hands.

A low grumble started in the earth closest to my hand before it picked up momentum. Within seconds it blasted outward—a smattering of debris from the trees overhead and the branches all around exploded in a brilliant flash of power causing me to shriek.

My scream was cut off as my breath hid another cry. With little more than a gasp, my knees collapsed from under me and I folded over like a broken marionette, my strings cut loose, my body no longer controlled. What the hell just happened? This was not like the tunnel…this wasn't like anything I'd felt before…

Darkness swamped my vision, and I was out.

***

"Is she okay?"

"I don't know, give her some space."

"Damn, we need to keep moving, Kelly."

"I can't move her right now."

Voices swam in and out of focus. My fingers tingled. They weren't covered in dirt anymore, and I was no longer soaked in the damp earth. There was a gentle hand on my cheek and then another at my wrist.

"We don't know how long she's bought us."

I groaned. "What did I buy?"

"She's coming to," the first voice said.

Fragments of what happened before I passed out came back to me. Oh. I'd done some freaky Ceoran/Reaper stuff.

"Get her up, Kelly, we have to move. It's too quiet out here. I don't like it."

That was definitely Carter's voice. A little huskier than usual, but definitely his.

The gentle hand fell to my cheek again and this time when I groaned, I also tried to open my eyes.

"Easy, kid. You've been unconscious for a bit."

"*Kid*," I muttered, when my mouth decided to work.

As my eyes opened, I was greeted by all three pairs as wide as the moon above.

"Backup?" I stammered.

"They didn't make it on time, we had to cut our losses and get out. You did buy us some time to haul ass though," Carter explained. "They told us to keep our heading and keep moving toward Compound 2."

"Glad to hear it," I bit through the building pain in my head.

I dragged myself to my knees and Kieran leaned in closer helping me.

"You scared the shit out of me," Kieran said.

A quick, sharp jolt of pain sliced through my head making me wince, and as soon as I did that, my body shuddered, and a surge of energy coursed through me electrifying whatever was in contact with my skin.

Kieran jumped backwards; his eyes locked onto the spot his hand had just been.

"What is going on?" Carter snapped, backing away like I was a coiled snake about to attack.

Clark didn't need an invitation to get the hell away from me either. Both of them kept their eyes on me but they were so far from trusting me it wasn't funny.

I wondered whether they ever questioned their directives, or why they were tasked to certain jobs? Maybe they did, just never overtly because that's what made a good soldier, right? Obedient, *loyal*.

My heart lurched when I thought about Eric and the way they treated him. He was nothing more than a soldier tasked to do whatever they said whenever they said it. There was no regard for his safety, his own personal dreams or aspirations. He was born into that world, and he would die in it.

My teeth reactively ground down in an angry kneejerk reaction. As soon as I did, the same rush of energy coursed through me. I looked down at my hands and arms to see a river of highly illuminated blood coursing just beneath my skin. My eyes snapped up to Kieran's.

"What is happening to me?" I whispered.

His mouth gaped.

It might have been funny if I wasn't so scared.

I looked back down at the glowing rivers snaking their way under my skin and took a long, deep breath hoping that I would calm myself and whatever *it* was.

Kieran moved closer to me and I jerked back.

Maybe I wasn't in control of myself…that, that reaction wasn't me.

God my head hurt.

I doubled over and felt the power surge through me again. Kieran moved closer but I held out my hand stopping him.

"Don't touch me, okay?" I whispered. "I don't know what's going on, I don't want to hurt you."

"Whatever it is, it's defending you," he said quietly, out of earshot from the other two.

My eyes lifted meeting his.

This was getting harder to contain and hide. We both looked down at my arms and the lit-up blood had disappeared. I was normal again. Normal skin and normal veins.

A broken breath escaped my lips as I helped myself up and stood by the tree using it to prop myself up while the other two brought a car over.

It wasn't the one we came in, instead it was one of the Ceoran military Hummers. Carter popped the hood, searched for a moment and ripped out a small device which I now saw was flashing.

"Stole it from the a-holes who attacked us," Carter explained, catching me eying the vehicle.

"Right," I muttered.

"They won't have eyes on us now," he added, gesturing for us to get in, avoiding eye contact with me.

"The Council?" I asked.

"Also, radios are dead." Carter sighed.

"What do you mean?"

"Can't reach anyone, anywhere. It's all dead."

I looked up at Kieran.

He nodded, brushing his hair back. "We're alone now."

My stomach soured. That was not good.

Carter got back in the car and I followed.

Wisely, no one got too close, and no one accidentally brushed up against me. Had I just become like Cleopatra, except instead of paint to ward people off, I had some fiery as hell blood that blasted people ten feet into the air?

Chapter Nine
Rules of Engagement

Eric

Emelia's voice droned on and on as she and Kristian debated which road to take. She insisted that staying on the highway was safer as we'd have more of a vantage should anything happen, and he was adamant that we needed to know we were hidden by trees and the cover of night.

I pinched the bridge of my nose and exhaled loudly.

They both stopped bickering and looked at me.

"Are you okay?" she asked gently.

"My head is pounding."

"More than usual?" Kristian joked.

I shot him a look; the usual lighthearted banter wasn't coming out right now. I was in pain and the pain wasn't new to me. I'd felt this before and that's what stressed me out. He got the point.

"Eric?" Emelia said, a lot sterner this time. "What's going on?"

"I think something is going on with Alex."

"What?"

"She's exerting a lot of power and I'm worried she can't control it."

"Is it more than you've felt before?"

"I've never felt this before, Em. This is new. And it's big. I think she's hurting too."

Kristian looked at me through the rearview mirror making sure the other two vehicles were still along for the ride. "The rumors are true then, I take it."

"Which rumors are you talking about exactly?" I asked, wincing as the pounding in my head intensified.

"The ones where you can somehow feel her."

I bit down. "Yeah, they're true."

"How?"

"I'm not really sure, it just started happening when I was assigned to her," I explained.

"It's how we were able to keep tabs on her when she was out in the world without us," Emelia added.

"And the part where Alex is something none of us have ever seen before?" Kristian narrowed his gaze.

"That part is true also." I leaned back in the seat and let out another long breath, leaving out the Reaper hybrid part.

Each time I caught their concerned gazes I felt more and more pulled toward Alex. Whatever she was going through right now felt a lot worse than what she'd endured in the warehouse with Silus. That made me sick. My stomach tightened into coils and the pressure in my head intensified. Damn it, we needed to hurry.

"How far out are we?"

"Still too far for comms."

"Shit." I tapped my foot on the floor of the car and thought. There had to be another way to check in.

Emelia gave me a small smile which immediately made me realize I was doing the thing—mindlessly tapping and fidgeting and on the verge of meltdown. I took a deep breath, closed my fists, composed myself and then looked back at her.

"We need to change direction," I said.

"Where to?"

"Instead of heading directly to Compound 2, we need to cut Alex's convoy off; which direction would they be taking?"

"Hard to say," Kristian mused. "Depends in what direction they were heading to begin with."

"Where were they at last comms?"

"Southeast of our location, about seven miles."

"Okay good, that's where beta team noted they were last, right?" I asked.

"Right."

Beta team was assigned to stay in the shadows, keep tabs and send reinforcements if needed. They were the team who'd told my dad that they were heading toward the next protocol dictated location before the compound was dropped on us.

"What are you thinking?" he asked.

"It's safe to assume that they would have continued along the same road. Kelly knows how we work, so he would be following the same rules of engagement," I said.

"Okay, so head southeast, hit the river and find them."

"That's the plan."

"You got it, man. If you think that's the best course," Kristian agreed.

"I do," I said, hoping to Karatoi I was right.

He reached for the walkie and it clicked to life. "We're changing course, follow close."

"Where to?" Katya's reply came first.

"Southeast, riverside."

"Cutting them off before the compound?" Zayne's response crackled through.

"That's the plan," Kristian said.

"Okay," Katya replied. "Copy that."

Kristian veered off and I looked behind me watching the two cars follow suit.

The sense of irrefutable dread was starting to weigh down on me more and more. With each passing second speeding through the clear, eerie night, my mind raced with thoughts about Alex and how far we'd come only to be thrust here again.

Every few hundred yards or so there'd be telltale signs of camps set up by survivors. Tents that had been left behind, discarded cook wear, sometimes embers of campfires. I sighed, pinching the bridge of my nose. So much had been lost.

I hadn't seen anyone in weeks out here, but I knew the humans moved silently and expertly these days. Those who were left, were left because they knew how to evade us and the Reapers. The rest, I assumed were deep in the cities, hiding out in skyscrapers where there were more hiding places.

But a realization dawned on me not long after I'd grieved the world as we knew it. Nothing we could have done would have spared all those lives lost. I was certain of it. I'd done my duty. I'd kept her safe. She was always the priority above all else, that's what they'd always told me and that's what I'd always believed in my heart.

I just hoped that someday soon, she'd get to live that life out in peace, the way she deserved, and a selfish part of me hoped that she'd allow me a place beside her.

Emelia looked over at me, that small smile was replaced with a grimace I'd seen all too many times. Her eyes traveled along my scarred cheek and then away. No one could make me feel the pain as much as my own sister. She hated what happened; she hated how we were treated which made this even harder.

I stretched out my neck and focused on Alex again. She was calmer now. Her mind slowly resting, her pain easing up.

"Eric, what do we do when we intercept them?" Emelia asked, her voice low and quiet like she knew she wouldn't like the answer I was going to give.

When I looked away and out at the trees we were speeding past, she shook her head.

"Please don't tell me what I think you're going to tell me," she said.

"You know it's the only way."

"It isn't."

"What are we talking about, guys?" Kristian asked.

"Eric, no," Emelia pleaded.

"I have to go off the grid with Alex."

"You mean alone?" Kristian asked.

"Yes. Just the two of us."

"That's madness," Kristian muttered.

"That's what I was going to say, and yes, it's absolutely insane." Emelia turned briskly to face me. "Why do you think that's a good idea?"

"Because they're looking for a group large enough to protect her, they'll be looking for a flashing sign made up of a lot of Ceoran energy. We're basically a beacon to them."

"And you two alone is safe?"

"It is. With me being able to cover her, she'll be safe. Her light will be out and no one will bother chasing down a single Ceoran."

Neither of them said a word until Kristian cleared his throat. "I hate to say it, but your crazy ass brother is right about this."

"You can't be serious!" Emelia snapped.

"You know how they track us, Emelia, you know they can see our true form, sense it. Eric can cover her, and for all intents and purposes he'll just be a single Ceoran, like he said. They won't bother with him considering they're hunting for a group," Kristian added.

I gave him a curt nod silently thanking him for voicing his opinion against my sister. She was a fiery one and not many dared to speak up against her. Especially those who ranked under her, not that she ever looked at people like that, but it didn't mean they didn't see things that way.

"This is stupidity at its finest, even for you," Emelia shot back, looking at me with that last jab.

"One Ceoran is a lone wolf, maybe even a rogue, no one will bother looking for Eric, but even a small group is enough to raise suspicion. They'll come for us and they'll find her. How much more carnage will come of that?" Kristian challenged.

"That's what we've signed up for," she deadpanned. "Every person in this car and the two behind us knows what we're in for."

"Agreed. But that's not what Alex wants. You know that," I said softly.

Emelia conceded and slumped her shoulders retuning her attention to the front.

"I'm sorry, Em."

"Don't be," she whispered, keeping her eyes dead ahead. "You're right. You always are. That's why you're our leader."

"Believe me that's not why," I bit.

Kristian looked across at me in the rearview and then averted his gaze. He knew just as much as I did that I was their leader because I was willing to do the things no one else was. My unwavering dedication to the role was spotted early on, not just by my father but by the Council. They saw that I was willing to make the tough calls, get my hands dirty and get the job done no matter what it took. A sour taste coated my mouth when I realized that Alex fell into that camp too. I'd done the unthinkable to her. She compelled me, I knew that, but I could have fought her. I felt the pull, I felt a gap in her shield, I could have broken through, but I didn't because I knew that it was the right thing to do. It was an order and I obeyed. But I was a damned hypocrite, wasn't I? I spoke a big game about doing things by the book, obeying every order that filtered down, yet I almost ruined her life and mine, putting us all at risk by falling in love with her.

The revelation burned through me. I'd never admitted that to myself.

If I got to her and got her out, things would be different. I was done with this world. And if she wanted out too, we'd make it happen.

"I know you've thought about this for a long time and that it's weighed on you, but are you sure this is really the right course of action, Eric?" Kristian asked quietly, drawing my eyes to his in the rearview.

"I have thought about it for a long time and yes, it's the right course of action."

Emelia rolled her eyes at my response. "Don't have to be an ass about it."

"I'm not. I just know how much easier it'll be when I don't have to worry about anyone else."

"Sometimes, and it might shock you to hear this, people are willing to help if you ask."

With that, she turned her gaze away and I let out a long breath. Kristian didn't push the matter anymore either.

She was right, but asking for help and getting it were two different things and sometimes I wondered whether anyone could really help with a job this big.

"Take a left," I said spotting the familiar turnoff.

Kristian clicked the button on his walkie-talkie and waited for it to connect to the other two cars. "We have a change of plan."

The convoy sped off the highway onto a merge lane and into the city streets. Discarded cars were stopped every few yards or so, some ransacked, wheels and body parts missing, others were burned out. Some looked like whoever had occupied them left in a hurry—clothes, bags and other personal items hung haphazardly across the seats and doors, reminding me of how quickly everything had descended into chaos.

"When will we know if we've really made a mess of things?" Kristian asked.

"Well, we need to make sure we intercept Ashfield before he finds Alex, and considering they were on the road long before us we're already at a disadvantage. And then we still need to avoid being ambushed ourselves, so, not long," Emelia said flatly.

"We're two hours from the intercept location," I said simply, ignoring Emelia's rant.

"Yep. Give or take two hours and we'll know whether we've made a mistake," Emelia said, syncing her watch.

Yep. Two hours until we found out if Ashfield got to her before we did.

Chapter Ten
The Unlikely Ally

Alex

Kieran took over driving when Clark started to look a bit pale.

"Do you need us to pull over?" I asked, craning my neck to check out his injuries.

He'd probably sustained a broken jaw, maybe a few ribs too, the rest was superficial: cuts and scrapes.

"No, keep moving."

"Fine, got a first aid kit in here?" I asked.

"I'm fine, Wynter."

"You're not fine. Besides, your face is making me queasy. You're bleeding all over the place."

Carter chortled but kept his eyes ahead. "There's a kit under one of the seats. Standard issue."

I reached under my seat and when my fingers brushed a cool, plastic box, I grabbed it and put it between us.

"Show me."

Clark reluctantly turned.

"I'm not going to hurt you," I muttered, noticing the way he was so tense in his seat; he looked like he was about to be sick and then I realized he was actually scared.

I didn't know what to say or do, for that matter. I dropped everything back into the kit and lowered my gaze, turning back to my seat.

"I'm sorry," he said softly, "it's just, back there…"

"I get it."

"Alex—" Kieran started.

"Forget it. I've got this weird ass crap going on, no one wants to be around me but I'm a chancellor, so you have to be, right? So can we leave it?"

They did. Not one of them said another word and I turned my face away so no one could see how hurt I was.

Clark took it upon himself to sort out his face and Carter even patched himself up. Kieran drove silently, his eyes dead ahead never once turning to meet mine.

As the drive reached the two-hour mark, I started to see the cresting of the sun on the horizon. This used to be my favorite part of the day. If I had been scared throughout the night, I always felt better when I knew the sunshine was just a few minutes away. Today, though, the glistening of the morning rays cutting through the sparse canopy above did little to appease me. We were getting closer to our location.

Everything was shrouded in a sense of dread, a heaviness I couldn't quite place, nor understand. It didn't take much digging to figure out that it had something to do with the road ahead. We were heading to the second compound, but it didn't feel right. Something about this journey was tinged in a cloud of confusion I couldn't work out. Something was off. Deep in the pit of my gut I felt a knot form.

Just as I was about to tell Kieran to slow down, a single Hummer cut into the road ahead of us and slammed on its brakes making me jolt forward and curse every living thing under the stars. Once I regained my senses and my vision after the bright red taillights blinded me momentarily, I released my seatbelt and craned my neck.

"What the actual..." Kieran muttered before we all saw the sole occupant exit the vehicle.

"You've got to be kidding me," I hissed. Before anyone could stop me, I'd thrown open my door and started for the asshole who'd been the bane of my existence since before I even remembered who he was.

"What the hell are you doing here, Ashfield?" I spat.

"Just hear me out, Alex. Please." He held out his hands defensively.

Kieran, Clark, and Carter were behind me in a second flat.

"The compound has been compromised, we need to get you to safety and comms are now down."

Carter shot him a look and then glanced over at Kieran who had stepped between me and Ashfield. That's what they'd just told me. How did Ashfield know?

"I'm telling you, it's not safe, Kelly, we need to get Chancellor Wynter to the next safe location."

"That's why we're heading to Compound 2," Carter explained.

"No, not Compound 2." Ashfield shook his head. "I just told you, it's compromised, it's at risk of an imminent attack."

"How could you possibly know that?" Carter challenged.

"Because logic dictates that if they know what our protocols are, they would hit the next one on the list. Wouldn't you?"

"He has a point," Clark pointed out.

"In any case it's not secure there anymore, we have to go to the next safe place on the list," Ashfield added matter-of-factly.

"And that's where?"

"Base of operations. The military towers."

"And you expect us to believe you, why?" Kieran demanded, his tall presence absolutely towering over Ashfield.

"I want her alive, why would I put her at risk?" Ashfield shot back like it was the most obvious thing in the world.

I recoiled at the notion.

"Doesn't make me not want to knock you out," Kieran muttered.

"Be my guest," Ashfield said with a grin, though it wasn't the usual dose of smarminess. "But you know as well as I do, that it's your job to make sure she's safe. So, are you willing to risk that I'm lying and take her to a compound you know might be overrun or, will you do your job?"

Kieran ground his jaw and took a step forward. I pressed my hand to his shoulder and eased him back.

Ashfield looked at each of us, paying careful attention to me, immediately setting me on edge making me take one full step back.

"I know you've no reason to trust me, but I am here, of my own free will, alone. I've risked a lot to get the message to you. Raine and his army are heading that way as well but they're out of range to let you know," he said to me.

My eyes snapped to Kieran's.

"So, what's it going to be, Kelly?" Ashfield offered. "Risk her or listen to me?"

"Can I have a word. Now." I grabbed Kieran's arm and dragged him to the side of the road and behind our car leaving the other two guarding Ashfield.

When we were out of earshot, I looked up at him "I don't like this, I don't trust him."

"I don't trust him either, but he has a point."

"You think the compound is at risk?"

"If I was orchestrating attacks and I knew the inner workings and protocols—"

"You'd attack the next one on the list."

He nodded, looking over my shoulder at Ashfield before looking down at me again.

"What do we do?" I asked quietly.

For a moment he didn't say anything, he just stood looking completely at a loss, completely broken by the two choices laid out before him. On the one hand he could call Ashfield's bullshit and risk all of us walking into a potential ambush; on the other, he could take him at his word and follow him to the military towers and again, risk walking into a potential ambush.

"Kieran…"

"We go with Ashfield."

"How far are we out from being able to contact anyone else?" I asked.

"Based on my mapping, too far, hours. And that's if anyone's radios are still operational."

"We don't have hours." I glanced up at the sky. The previously tiny crescent of the sun had become a full-blown orb ready to glide across the sky.

"Can we really trust him on this?" I ground out.

"Trust? No. Absolutely not. But we have to go with the possibility that he's right and if he is, we would be walking into a trap. It does make sense tactically."

"And if we do, we could be falling into another trap," I muttered.

"I know, I've thought of that."

"Well shit."

"That about covers it," he ground out. "You with me?"

"Yeah, let's do this."

We walked back to the others and my guard went back up. Ashfield, as much as he presented as someone I wasn't used to seeing, was still untrustworthy. He never did things out of the goodness of his heart, there was always an agenda and it would only be a matter of time before I found out what it was. I remembered enough about our time together to know that.

"We have to move now, Chancellor," he said. "There'll be Reapers on our tail. Your move back there caused a bit of a stir."

I shot him a look.

"I could see it all the way out where I was." He gestured behind him. "It's how I was able to locate you."

Damn. If my power had flashed like a beacon enough for him to find me, he was right about Reapers being able to potentially track us. It didn't leave us much option, but it did beg the question, would Eric have been close enough to see it too and if he did, why wasn't he here?

"What about Major Raine and his team?" I demanded.

"They'll know where to head, that's what they're trained for," he said simply.

"Did you leave the compound together?"

"No, we were separated, he was with his sister when I saw them last, helping fallen soldiers."

I narrowed my eyes at him. "General Corteza?"

116

"Last I saw, he was hurt but alive. Now come on, Chancellor. We need to go," he repeated.

"If he's hurt and so many others are dead, we should be going there to help!"

"Even more reason to avoid going back, Alex," Kieran nudged us forward, away from Ashfield. "I mean it, you need to let me take the lead on this."

Before I could open my mouth to argue, Ashfield gave me what I could only describe as a pity smile.

"Raine and co will be at the towers. You have my word."

I remained rooted to the spot.

I didn't want to take him on his word, but I didn't want any more carnage either.

"We really must move now, Chancellor," Ashfield said again.

Kieran looked at me and then Carter and Clark. Eventually he gave Ashfield a curt nod.

Despite us deciding to trust Ashfield right now, it wasn't without suspicion. But he was right about one thing: he had risked a lot to come out here, and if he was right about us heading into yet another compromised compound, we could have walked into a trap.

"We'll take our car," Clark insisted, and to my surprise Ashfield didn't argue.

"Let me get my bag. I packed in a hurry, didn't know what we'd need," Ashfield said.

"Fine. Make it quick," Carter replied.

Within a few minutes, Ashfield had collected his bag from the Hummer and after a thorough check by Kieran to make sure he wasn't carrying anything suspicious, we were all loaded in the car, with one new occupant making our journey just that bit more unnerving.

***

Eric

We were nearing the location where we should have intercepted Alex. Emelia confirmed it by holding out her watch and signaling to Kristian to take a sharp right onto a small, less used path.

I was half expecting to see a small convoy of cars but instead, there was nothing aside from an abandoned vehicle in the middle of the road.

"Stop the car," I said as soon as I caught sight of the license plate.

"What is it?" Emelia asked.

"Stay in the car."

"Not a chance."

I rolled my eyes and got out.

The other two cars came to a rolling stop. Katya rolled her window down and Zayne did the same in the car behind her.

Emelia and Kristian followed me.

"What's going on?" Katya asked.

"Checking something out."

"An abandoned car?" she chuckled.

"Wouldn't be worried had it actually been an abandoned car," I muttered and walked over to the trunk. As I suspected, the trunk had a code and the number I keyed in worked.

Emelia sucked in a sharp breath.

"It's one of ours," she said.

"Seriously?" Zayne asked poking his head out of his window.

"Yep," I called out, taking a look through the contents. There was nothing identifiable, nothing that told me whose car this had been or why it had been left here.

"Doesn't look like there was a struggle. Everything was taken and locked up neatly," Kristian explained.

"Everything except the way it's parked," Emelia added. "Reckon ambush?"

"With a single carload?"

"Maybe, depends who was packing what in this car."

"True," I mused and looked around, stopping when I noticed the tire marks ahead. "Someone was here, stopped in the middle of the road."

Kristian kneeled, touching the depth of the indentations the car had left behind. "It's deep, I'd say it was an SUV."

"SUVs are Ceoran standard issue. Help me check the computer," I muttered.

Kristian got inside, popped open the hood and Emelia got to work rummaging through the engine bay until she retrieved what we were looking for. A small, nondescript *black box* of sorts. This was installed on all our military vehicles and would tell us via the trip computer, where it had been and how long it was driving.

Emelia took the box to our car, found her laptop and plugged the device in. After a few moments, she called me over.

"You were right about this being one of ours."

"How right?"

"Compound one, military faction, taken approximately six hours ago."

"And who did we lose sight of approximately six hours ago?" I muttered.

"You don't think he's out there hunting for her?"

"I think he found her."

"Eric, you don't think—"

"I don't think anything yet. I can't let my mind go there. There're no signs of struggle, no bodies, the car was left in an orderly fashion. I have to think that whatever went down here went down with some semblance of a plan."

"You're a lot more calculated than I would be, brother," Kristian muttered, closing the hood and shutting the doors.

"I have no other choice," I said dryly. "Let's keep moving."

"Compound two?" Kristian asked.

"Yeah. They'd be getting closer now."

"You heard him, move out!" Kristian called to the drivers.

Chapter Eleven
Thinking Like a Soldier

Alex

Kieran slowed as we neared a grouping of trees which looked suspiciously like an organized shelter.

"Why are we slowing down?" I asked.

"There's movement out there," Kieran answered.

"We shouldn't be stopping at all," Ashfield said. "I don't like this."

"Well we have no choice," Kieran answered, pointing ahead through the window. "See that over there, trip wires. We hit those, who knows what comes at us."

Both Ashfield and I looked in the direction he had been pointing. Now that he'd shown us, it was easy to see. He and the others had been trained to spot these things, Ashfield and I had not.

"Maybe it's an old installation?" I suggested.

"Maybe. Maybe not," he replied. "I'm not risking it."

"So what do we do?"

"We go around."

"I know this is your forte, but what if that's exactly what they want us to do? What if it's like a secondary trap?" I supplied.

Kieran grinned.

"What?" I asked, confused.

"Nothing."

"You grinned at me. That's not nothing."

"You're just starting to sound like Eric, that's all," he said gently.

"Oh."

"It's not a bad thing," Carter added. "He's where he is on the ranking board because he's that good."

"The ranking board?" I asked.

"Ah, the fresh one has never heard of the ranking board." Clark grinned.

I ignored the fact that he called me *fresh* and looked at Kieran for answers.

"It's where all the soldiers are ranked, unofficially of course," Kieran said. "Your man has been riding the top spot for almost six years."

"Who ranks you?" I asked.

"We do, among ourselves. Heaps of things are considered, training, combat, saves, losses," Clark explained.

"Where do you guys sit?"

"Kelly the powerhouse is second, only followed by yours truly at fourth," Clark said. "Carter over there is fifth."

"And Emelia?"

"She and Kelly have been battling second and third as long as Eric's been number one," Clark explained.

Ashfield watched the entire exchange with curiosity.

"Has it always been the same top five?" I asked.

"Nah, there was Colonel Addams, he was seriously competitive, he and Raine were always assigned for training combat missions together because they were pretty close in skill. Some said he was possibly better than Eric," Carter said.

"*Was...* is he dead?"

"Not dead, just moved up the ranks to protect the super wealthy over at another compound, doesn't participate in our stuff anymore, naturally," Kieran said, looking over at Ashfield who was now looking out the window seemingly losing interest in this conversation.

"Well I'm glad I've got the best then," I said lightly.

"Definitely the best." Clark nodded while Kieran assessed the road ahead.

"What do you suggest?" Kieran asked me finally.

"About the route?"

He nodded.

"Ah, I don't know." I looked at the now obvious wires laid out across the road.

"I know you don't want to go around, that's a reasonable aversion to have. What do you think we should do instead?"

Ashfield looked at me, like he too was expecting some sort of magical answer that would cement Kieran's observation of my tendency to sound and think like Eric.

My cheeks flushed and I found myself wondering whether he would have been proud of that...or annoyed.

"I think we should stop off to the side, scope out the surrounding area on foot, meet back here and then proceed once we have more information."

"I like it." Carter nodded and reached into the glovebox for his weapon. Clark did the same, finally looking a bit spritelier.

"Spread out. Ashfield, stay close to Carter; Alex, you're with me." Kieran gestured to me.

Before long, our, *my*, plan was in action.

The car was parked safely behind the cover of some trees, which was surprising considering how much light the sun was casting now.

"Stay in the tree line wherever possible, we need to remain hidden," Kieran explained as the two of us separated from the others.

"The sun is going to make that hard work."

"Agreed, but at least we can count on the fact that if these trip wires were set by Reapers, they wouldn't be out here in the daylight since I don't think they want to be spotted. And if it's Scavengers, well let's just say I'm not that worried about some humans."

"Even the ones that work for the Reapers."

"They're still just human, Alex," he said, carefully stepping around the base of what I now saw was a hinge holding the trip wires in place. It was a simple contraption, a small hinge, some wire and a coil. I shuddered.

It was all too eerily similar to the Scavengers I'd run in to what felt like a lifetime ago. I recalled the feeling of their rough hands on my body as they held me down, threatening to enact their sick and twisted plan. I thought about what could have been had Kieran not been there, I thought about it often to be honest, and my mind wandered to Pa's last living relative who was spared by Kieran that night. Did he make it out? Was he part of this new clan?

"You okay?"

"Fine," I bit, hating how close I'd come to becoming a notch on their belts.

"Some people don't deserve any less than a bullet to the head," Kieran said simply, carefully pulling apart some leaves and branches that had been fashioned together to make a sort of camouflage.

"I know."

"I had to shoot them. They would have done God only knows what to you."

"They weren't too shy about their plans," I bit.

"You know I would do it again in a heartbeat if I had to. Does that bother you?"

He stopped and looked at me.

"No."

"Good. Help me with this."

We dropped all conversation about my near miss and the disgusting people that turned to crap out here. Instead, I focused my attention on looking for any clues, however small, as to who had left these trip wires and whether they were still lingering around.

Once I was certain my section of woods was clear, Kieran confirmed it.

"Must have been an old installation. Whoever was here, they're long gone now," he said gesturing to the rusted-looking screws holding everything in place.

We carefully disarmed the tripwire trap and collected the hardware in case we could use it for something else.

"All clear on your end?" Carter called.

"Yeah, all clear. Yours?" Kieran responded.

"Whoever was here hasn't been around for months. Everything's overgrown," Carter said.

"Same on this end," Clark confirmed.

"Straight through it is." Kieran nodded, gesturing back to the car.

The second we had allowed ourselves a moment to breathe comfortably in the sunny woods, a loud creaking sounded through the surrounding tree line, followed by an enormous bang. It took two seconds for me to work out that someone had literally broken a tree and it was about to crash down onto us.

Before the falling branch reached us, a hard body slammed into me forcing us both to the ground. A shriek escaped my lips as the thud of the impact winded me.

"You're okay!" Ashfield shouted, pulling me up. "We need to move!"

"My ankle, damn it, I think my ankle is sprained."

"Hold onto me." He hauled me up against his body and despite how gross I felt being so close to him, I couldn't find it in me to care.

"You got her?" Kieran shouted.

"Yes! Get your asses out of there."

I noticed now that the *there* he was talking about was inside the tree line, precisely where the traps had been, and Ashfield and I were in relative safety but the others were not. Clark and Carter had been knocked down by the huge tree that had almost wiped us out.

"Can you move?" Ashfield asked, dragging my attention back to him.

"Yeah, slowly."

"Okay good, we have to keep going."

"We can't leave them!"

"We're not leaving them, but you can't help right now, you need to get to the car."

"What are you going to do?"

"I'm going to go back and help."

"You're not trained to fight."

"I know," he ground out, "But what choice do we have."

As we reached the car and he shoved me inside, I gaped when he made me lock the doors and ran back to join the fight.

I peered through the window and watched in shock as Ashfield the asshole ran headfirst into a group of Scavengers who'd appeared seemingly out of nowhere and braved the onslaught.

He took a beating at every turn. His perfectly styled blond hair was instantly stained with blood and dirt as he tried to execute clumsy punches. He managed to reach Kieran and together they ran back freeing Clark and Carter.

As more Scavengers joined, Ashfield went down but managed to get back up, ready for more. I was in shock. Who was this person? Was he someone I'd grossly underestimated? Parts of me remembered a time where I didn't hate him, surely those memories were real? It was always easier to play a role. The bad boy. The jock, the cheerleader, the pretty one.

The guy fighting with a broken nose and slashed up hands was none of those things I'd pegged him for. He was fighting beside a class he believed was beneath him. No matter how much it ached me to say, he was putting himself in harm's way to get the job done and help people who he'd previously never given a second look.

Sure, I wasn't about to throw him a party and welcome him back to the car with a song and dance, but maybe something more was to be said about James Ashfield and the fragmented memories that painted a very different picture to what I'd been led to believe.

Moments later, several loud gunshots silenced the fighting and I realized Kieran and Clark had retrieved their weapons.

Just like that, in a matter of seconds, the fight was over. The Scavengers went down and those who didn't retreated.

They didn't stick around to see if anyone else was coming, instead they ran back to the car which I promptly unlocked and the four of them jumped in and we were off.

"Holy shit, you're all hurt."

"We're fine, how are you?" Kieran asked, looking over my body for signs of injury. "Are you hurt?"

"Ankle. That's all, I'm fine."

"I'll help."

"No, you need to preserve your energy."

"Lucky you got away with just that," Carter said.

"Lucky indeed. I would have been a pancake," I whispered, as much of a thanks as I could muster.

Ashfield took it gracefully.

"Here." I reached down for the first aid kit and handed them each some gauzes and saline solution, this time not offering up my services.

"What happened back there?" I shook my head. "I thought we'd cleared everything."

"We did," Kieran said. "There was nothing, we all confirmed it."

"Then how did a bunch of brainless humans get the better of us?" Carter nursed his head.

"Your guess is as good as mine."

"Reckon they had Reaper help?" I offered.

It wasn't as much of a stretch as it might have once been. It would explain how they managed to find us when we'd been careful the entire time. I guess if they had been working with the Reapers they could find me by my use of power like Ashfield had. Still, that many Scavengers, almost a dozen, was unheard of. They usually stuck to their smaller, more trusted groups. Something big was brewing and it wasn't just the feeling of dread in my core that said so.

"Maybe. Maybe it was some sort of shielding capability. You ever heard of anything like that?" Carter asked me.

"I know some Ceoran can do it, but you already know that. Question is, do Reapers possess the same ability?"

He shrugged like he was expecting me to say something else, like maybe give up who I was as if I knew all about the Reapers and their dirty secrets. I shuddered and looked away.

"We just have to watch our six, stay safe," Clark said matter-of-factly.

"Damn straight." Kieran nodded. "How far are we from the military towers?"

"Less than half an hour I'd say—stay on this heading and you'll see a set of manned towers approach to your left. When we're close enough, I can contact them," Ashfield explained.

"Good. Until then, keep your eyes open, people. We know we can't trust anything out here."

The car fell into a silent reverie where only the pain in my ankle radiated into my head and caused a sort of thrumming. Other than that, it was relatively calm and peaceful, and damn, I needed it.

I didn't want to fall asleep but at the same time my body was aching, and I felt like I was moments away from passing out.

Kieran and Clark started chatting about their younger days and I closed my eyes, smiling to myself.

Their stories took wild turns, they laughed among themselves, and even Ashfield had something to share.

CHAPTER TWELVE
THE WEAPON AND SECRET ALLY

Kieran slowed the car down and we all craned our necks to get the first look at our new home. Just like Ashfield said, there was a pair of watch towers off to the left. In each one, I saw a flicker of rifle scopes glinting in the afternoon sun. Each tower must have been at least nine stories, give or take, fortified all around by a concrete wall that reached up halfway, enclosing the entire compound in.

"Stop the car here and I'll contact the guards."

Kieran killed the engine and we waited for Ashfield to make the call.

He pulled out the small radio and turned it up so we could all hear the conversation—another point to add to Ashfield's sudden change of nature. He wasn't being secretive but rather totally transparent with his actions, though something still didn't sit right with me. There was a twinge of something I couldn't place in my gut, something that told me not to trust him because he was planning something. But the more I saw him interact with and help our small team, the more I felt that twinge simmer down—there was no evidence to support my theory just yet.

Maybe the prospect of death was enough to change his attitude. It wasn't all fun and games in the safety of the Council's wing; this was real life and it got dark, real quick.

"This is James Ashfield, contacting support tower as advised."

"Copy that, Ashfield. Confirm occupants of vehicle."

"Chancellor Wynter, Council Member Kelly and Officers Clark and Carter."

"Proceed to the gate."

Once the comms were shut off, Kieran drove up to the gate as instructed and, like the guard said, we were checked and then waved through.

It was strange, they didn't ask for physical IDs, they kind of just looked at us, their eyes doing a weird staring thing and then they nodded letting us pass.

"This is different," I said.

"You don't remember this?" Ashfield asked.

"No, I've never been here."

"Interesting."

"Have I been here before?" I asked, keeping my voice low so only Ashfield could hear.

"Not that I'm aware of," he said. "Thought you got your memories back?"

"Not everything, no."

His brows lifted briefly before he turned away from me.

I didn't believe him. Clearly I had been here at some stage, but why was he lying about it? And, more importantly, why was this still missing from my memories?

He kept his eyes ahead and Kieran shot me a look in the mirror. We weren't there because we trusted him. We were there because we needed answers. I kept reminding myself of that every time we drove through another secure gate and down yet another small winding road.

It was much less hospitable than the compound we came from, not that that was saying much. These small streets were grey and concrete, not much greenery at all and very little lighting. It was like a small concrete town. It probably looked creepy as hell at night. There were spotlights set up at every corner that I could see, which flooded the area below in a sterile white light. I had to squint to avoid the blaring light they emitted. The concrete walls before us were blackened in some areas like flames had licked their surface, and all around stood stern faced Ceoran who barely blinked. If they didn't shift from post to post every few moments, I could have mistaken them for statues.

The street which Kieran drove us through was narrow, barely wide enough to fit a marginally larger SUV than the midsize one we were in without scraping the mirrors. At each turn there was another Ceoran standing guard, and above us more security cameras than I'd ever seen in one place. Each one pointed in a different direction which told me that every inch of this fortress was covered. It immediately set me on edge.

"This is us," Ashfield said, pointing to a gated entry to an underground car park.

Kieran pulled up to it and waited. A few minutes later the gates opened, and we were waved through by a guard.

"Anywhere is fine," Ashfield said.

It didn't take long for Kieran to find a spot beside an obnoxiously large, blacked-out Hummer. Bet they didn't come down the street we just did.

Kieran caught me eyeing the vehicle as I got out of ours, and chuckled beside me. "It's what all the military guys drive out here."

"I've never seen one like this," I said, noticing that the shiny wheels were as big as me.

"Yeah, the Ceoran posted here tend to stay out here in their own neck of the woods. They don't really have much to do with us."

"Aside from letting us stay here."

"Not so much us, but you," he said grimly.

My eyes snapped up to his, torn away from the glossy tires.

"What do you mean?" I asked.

"We're allowed to be here because we're with you."

"Surely they'd let people stay here for refuge?"

"Not likely, Alex. These people aren't like us. They're not even like the other guys we work with."

A shiver rolled over me. "What are they like?"

"Cold. Systematic."

"Systematic?"

"Everything here is a job. Everything. They have no empathy, no sympathy, no remorse."

"That sounds horrific." It was almost like they were a different species altogether. Nothing like the Ceoran I know at the main compound, *domesticated* for lack of a better term, able to blend in with the species of this planet and be pretty much human. *How did I not remember this?*

"Like I said, they're not like us. We're here now and that's fine with me. At least we know they have enough firepower to take on a small country should we need it. Other than that, I've no interest in getting in their way. On or off the field."

"Why are they like this?" I asked, feeling like a small child the second the words left my lips.

"Because they don't believe in mixing with the human world. On Ceora it's like this. You're either royalty or you're not. There's no kindness, no saving face, there's no pretending to make friends. It's just the way it is."

"So they're jerks."

"Careful, you never know who's listening."

A shiver rolled up my spine. It's what Eric had said to me once. "I don't like it, I think coming here was a mistake."

"So do I." Kieran ground his jaw.

"Chancellor Wynter?"

My back straightened at the overly formal and indignant address.

Kieran's eyes traveled over my head and a tiny muscle in the corner of his jaw twitched. I slowly turned.

My attention landed on a tall woman dressed head to toe in black. Well-fitted pants, a tailored jacket and an immaculately fitted black shirt. Dark hair was tied back neatly into a low bun and the Ceoran insignia on her uniform with two gold stars above it told me she was higher on the ladder.

I didn't know whether I was meant to salute her or bow. Luckily for me, she approached looking uninterested in my inner turmoil.

"May we have a moment of your time."

It wasn't a question, despite the way it was framed.

"Ah, yeah, of course." I looked at Kieran and hoped he'd say something to save me. He did not. Carter and Clark, too, kept their heads down and mouths shut.

Something told me that this woman was running things here and no one, not me, not Kieran, could do anything that went against her. As she addressed me, another similarly dressed woman approached the others.

"Council member Kelly, kindly come with us for your debriefing."

Clark and Carter shot Kieran a quick look before he spoke up.

"I'll be needing my detail if that works with you?" he said to the woman.

She nodded and Clark and Carter went with them but I didn't miss the look Kieran shot me. I couldn't make sense of it but it didn't seem like it was at all positive.

"Follow me please," the woman who'd addressed me said.

I did as she asked and we left the car park, heading inside through a nearby door.

I swallowed hard and ignored the building bundle of nerves in the pit of my stomach.

"My name is Commander Morales," she said.

"Alex Wynter."

She nodded. That was it. The only response. I shuddered and continued trailing behind her as she took a left at the end of a brightly lit corridor and then a right into a much dimmer one.

My heart kicked up. It felt wrong being here. That nagging feeling in my stomach said so. It wasn't just not remembering everything, or thinking that Ashfield was lying, but all of it. It was all a weird, macabre farce and I was just a puppet despite what the shiny title I was born with said.

The back of my throat dried up making it hard to swallow.

"Chancellor?"

My eyes snapped up to her when I realized I'd slowed.

"Everything alright?"

"Yes. Sorry."

"Please, we have several Elders waiting to meet with you."

I took a deep breath and followed her again.

Once we'd reached a set of large steel doors with a small square window in either side, she stopped.

"Will your ankle allow you to take the stairs?"

135

I pressed my weight on it and winced.

"That would be negative." She turned to the side and gestured to a keypad on the right.

"If you will."

"I don't understand."

"Place your palm on the reader, Chancellor."

"My palm?" I looked between her and the panel.

"Yes, your palm. Please."

I blinked back the confusion but did as she said. Once my hand was on the reader it came to life, and a green laser came out and scanned my hand. When I looked over to her, I noticed she was doing the same thing on an identical panel on the opposite side of the door.

"This facility has been coded to your palm prints, voice and eyes. You can access most of the rooms here should you need to. There are of course, several private areas which are off limits. You understand." Again, a statement rather than a question.

"Ah yeah, of course."

Once we were inside what I now realized was an elevator, we went up two floors and then the doors opened.

A soldier was about to get in when he spotted me then immediately took a big step back and apologized. The doors shut. I turned to Morales but she was as stoic and uninterested as ever.

"Commander, have I been here before?"

Her shoulders stiffened, only just but enough for me to make out the discomfort in my question.

She kept her face ahead. "Not as far as I'm aware."

Another lie. I frowned.

The doors opened once again and she started down the catwalk which separated two areas of work. We stepped out into a very busy hub filled with computers and hundreds of soldiers clothed in the same uniform I'd seen Eric and the soldiers back at our compound wear.

One side seemed to be a lot more chaotic than the other. The staff here were looking at multiple screens at once. The other side was polar opposite—the staff there were seated in single rows of computers and desks. Not much was being said.

"What is all this?"

"This is our head of operations," she answered.

"You monitor all the facilities from here?"

"Yes." Morales gestured toward a room at the far end of the catwalk. "We monitor external threats, the other compounds, our soldiers out in the field and the portal."

"I'm sorry, portal?"

"Yes, Chancellor. The portal through which we, and the Reapers, travel."

"I thought that was the Bridge."

"The Bridge allows them to access the portal. The portal is what allows us to travel between worlds."

"And what stops external threats from accessing planets they want to attack?"

"Ceoran have an aeronautical force. We protect our skies and those surrounding the portal."

"Oh." It was my world, yet there was still so much I didn't remember. I'm sure I understood it once and I hoped that it would eventually come back to me.

"Through here, please."

I followed her through the doors and stopped when I saw two Elders I'd never seen before. I remembered the other relics.

"Chancellor, please, come in and have a seat," the first Elder said. He was much younger than any of the others back at our compound.

My mind raced back to the first, awkward meeting which was unfortunately forever burned into my brain. The Elders were a bunch of old men and women in suits who sat at a ridiculous high table which had probably been dragged straight out of Dracula's castle and dumped in the twenty-first century.

At our first meeting they'd dropped the whole bombshell about me working on uniting galactic forces. It was ridiculous then and even more so now when I saw how cold and sterile this place was. How could I possibly unite Ceoran like this and hope for change?

"Chancellor?" the Elder said.

I straightened and entered.

"Thank you, Commander. You can leave us."

With that, Morales was gone and I was yet again alone with some people I didn't know. Not that my five-minute walk with the Commander had made us best friends or anything, but it was definitely a sense of familiarity I missed right now.

When the door was closed, I returned my attention to the young Elder who looked more like my dad's age than one would expect of an aged Elder.

"We're so thankful that you're alive and well," the other one said. She, too, was quite young, maybe a few years older than my mum had been. "Please, sit."

"Thank you," I obliged.

"We understand that there was an ambush on your compound less than a week ago and that the security of that complex was compromised."

"Yes, that's correct."

"We understand that you've since made contact with the leader of the Reapers, Silus."

"Yes." My voice was small.

"And what came of that contact, Chancellor?"

"Nothing."

"What was the purpose of that meeting?"

Meeting. It wasn't like I'd scheduled a dignitary dinner with some familiar intergalactic leader. It was a little less *inviting* than that.

"I wanted..." I looked at them and changed my approach. "I'd *hoped* that I would be able to come to some sort of arrangement between us and them where we could go about this peacefully."

"And it failed."

"Yes."

"I see."

"It was a mistake," I said.

"A very big mistake," the male Elder clarified. "You put a lot of Ceoran in danger."

"I understand."

"What I need to know, Chancellor Wynter, is what Silus has learned from your interaction."

"Learned?"

"We understand that in the case of your exceptional circumstances, Silus might have learned who you are."

My mouth must have gaped to the point where they could have seen my molars all the way on the other side of the room.

"We are aware of your heritage and what your mother did when you were an infant. The mage and the Reaper blood..."

"Who else is aware?" I found my voice slowly filling with venom.

"No one else, we assure you. Your safety, and by the same token, your value, makes you so much more important than we'd first believed when you were born."

"My value? I'm sorry, what does that mean, Elder?"

The smug grin that met me was enough to make my hands ball into fists without even realizing I'd done it. He didn't miss a beat. He knew he was getting under my skin.

"The power you contain is stronger than anyone we've ever known. That alone makes it incredibly important to keep you safe and available to use should the time arise."

"Available to use?" I frowned. "I'm sorry, I'm not following."

"You are a powerful tool."

"A weapon," I clarified.

"It's not quite that simple," the female Elder said.

"It sounds simple to me," I bit.

The male Elder grinned again. "In any case, Chancellor. You're safe here."

"Noted," I bit.

Funny. I didn't feel safe. In fact, I couldn't wait to get out of this room. Everything about this felt off. I rose and folded my arms across my chest.

"Commander Morales will escort you to a safe area within the complex."

"Thank you," I muttered, remembering that I didn't want to make enemies here. These people scared me. "Thank you for your help, and your shelter."

Commander Morales appeared at the door and gestured for me to follow her. God I was getting sick of following people around like a lost child.

While we walked together silently, my mind did a backpedal when I noticed that we weren't heading back in the direction from which we came, but instead she was leading me down a different set of corridors.

"Where are you taking me?"

"Down to the Elder quarters, better fortification and privacy."

"Where are my friends?"

"They will be relocated down there too."

"I want to see them."

She stopped walking and I sidestepped to avoid crashing into her.

"I understand that you're wary here, Chancellor, but you have to let us take care of you."

"I'm wary because I'm being ushered all over the place and given no clear answers. I want to see my friends now. Thank you."

Morales looked like one of those women who would fire you on the spot for looking at her wrong. I was expecting a cold, calculated answer. What I wasn't expecting was a small nod.

"I will escort you to your friends. You can converse with them for a moment and then you'll all be relocated down in the bunker."

"Thanks," I said, as sternly as I could whilst hiding my shock at her answer.

"This way."

The winding corridors took us to a different set of elevators which we both entered without a word. Soon, we were climbing and the door chimed, stopping at the fourth floor.

"This is tower one. I will wait for you by these doors. Your friends are through there."

"Okay."

I watched her retreat and stop by the elevator, taking post like a guard. She seemed unphased. Had it been me, I would have been annoyed babysitting someone who was clearly not willing to listen.

"Ten minutes, Chancellor."

"Alex. Please," I said, before I turned and went in search of Kieran and the others.

CHAPTER THIRTEEN
DEATH AND DESTRUCTION; THE END OF AN ERA

Eric

Emelia drove straight through the gates of what once used to be a high-tech security system.

"What happened here?" she exhaled, winding down the windows.

"Stop the car," I said.

I got out slowly and looked up at the remains of the once towering, impenetrable Compound 2.

The other trucks stopped beside us. Zayne looked down as he killed the engine.

Trails of smoke rose into the air, embers of a fire that had been burning for hours and hours lit up the expanse of the nearing tree line. My stomach fell through to my feet as I spotted huddled up bodies against the rubble.

"Eric..." Emelia let out a shuddering breath.

"She's not here."

"How do you know?"

"I don't feel her."

The conversation fell away. I walked through the remains littering the street, and a pang of nostalgia shot through me. I'd been here as a child, ran through these streets and buildings, played with my sister and our friends, climbed the smooth concrete walls and hid behind the towering lamp posts. It was similar to our home, same sort of layout, but much more greenery and a huge garden in the middle Mom used to let us read in. Now, there was nothing...embers floated through the sky, the smoke burning my eyes and making them water.

Through the haze I could make out the collapsed main building, evidence of the once luscious and vibrant garden filled with colorful flowers peaked through the ashen landscape. I swatted away the soot landing on my cheeks and continued scanning the horizon for any evidence of what happened. My eyes pricked with the smoke still heavy in the air, as well as the weight of what I was seeing.

There was no way to explain how this much damage took place with no warning, no word. There was nothing. One moment it was here and the next, everything was reduced to ash and rubble.

A few yards ahead, I spotted what I could only describe as a small backpack. As I neared, bile quickly filled my throat. It was the body of a small child, no older than two or three, curled up beside a dead man. My shoulders dropped and I balled my trembling fists at my side. I forced my emotions to simmer down and continued on. If I allowed the anger and the sadness and the pure horror of what I was seeing to consume me, it would have swallowed me whole. I couldn't, I wouldn't let that happen. Not when I had to find Alex, when I had to stop this from happening again. I wouldn't let these people die in vain.

Emelia rushed to my side and I quickly pulled her back and away.

"Oh my God, Eric. Is that?"

"Don't look, okay? Go back to the car."

"No, Eric I need to—"

"You don't need to do anything. You can't help here," I said gently. "Kristian and I will check for survivors. I need you to take a small group and do a perimeter check."

She looked at me for a moment before she nodded and stumbled forward. I took a deep breath and ran my hand over my hair.

Kristian, Leah and Katya joined me and we slowly began our grim search. No one spoke as the weight of the situation settled over us.

The first half of the compound was shattered beyond recognition. I couldn't tell where the bricks came from, nor whether there was anyone alive underneath any of it. Chances were low. The still embers told me that this fire had raged long and hot for too long.

"Take the south side; Kristian and I will veer north," I instructed.

Katya and Leah broke off and silently continued their search. Katya's face was blank, I knew that look all too well. She was holding everything together but it would only take one thing to set her off.

"Help me over here," Kristian said nodding to a large beam which led to an underground system of stairs. "Maybe they had enough time to get people underground."

It was unlikely, but we had to try.

"Got it." I grabbed one end of the large beam and pulled while Kristian used a steel bar he found off to the side as leverage.

After a long haul, we finally got it to budge, but not without half the foundation holding it up crumbling to the side.

"Watch out!" I shouted and ducked out of the way, narrowly missing a brick to the head.

"Christ. You okay?" he muttered.

"Yeah. Fine. Help me with this." We moved a few of the bricks out of the way. "I'll go down first."

"I'll wait for your signal."

Once I was inside the cavity, which resembled a site from an archeological dig more than it did a stairwell into the basement, I kept my eyes ahead and my body close to the walls. The whole structure could give at any time. Any loud noises, sudden movements could send this whole structure crashing down on top of me. No pressure.

With a lot of careful stepping and assessing, I reached the end of what used to be a hallway and found the lower level undamaged.

"Clear down here," I called back.

A few minutes later, Kristian had joined me.

"The door is jammed, need to see if we can get it open in case people are stuck inside," I said.

"I'll grab the top, see if you can get enough grip down there."

I used my fingers to pry open a small gap beside the hinge—it had most likely blown in by the force of heat building down here. It had basically been a steel tube with superheated air flowing freely through it until it blew. The steel was still warm, but cool enough to touch. That instilled some confidence in me. The fire must have burned through this side only.

With a bit of effort, Kristian and I managed to pry the door open far enough for me to get a good look inside. Before I could take in the entire room, the stench hit me forcing me back.

"Dear Karatoi," I ground out.

"What?"

"There are people in there."

"Can we get them out?"

"No." I shook my head, holding back the vomit. "They're dead. Cooked." This time I couldn't stop the tears that came.

Through the charred remains I saw dozens of people with their faces etched in permanent agony.

"The fire burned right through there, everyone is dead. They didn't have a god damn chance. There must be at least thirty students."

"Fuck me," he choked out, stumbling forward. "Were they all the soldiers in training?"

I nodded, wiping my face with my sleeve. On the floor I spotted a piece of the uniform student soldiers wore to distinguish them from the rest of us. "Back up. There's nothing we can do here."

Kristian retreated up the way we came as I gave the bodies one last look. Some of them were burned so badly you couldn't tell whether they were wearing their uniforms or casual dress. Others were huddled like they'd died hours later, waiting and hoping that someone would come to rescue them. No one did.

How in the hell did this happen?

Anger quickly replaced the shock.

We did a quick search of the rest of the compound and when we were certain there were no survivors we met back with the others.

Emelia's eyes were red, as were Zayne's.

"They're all dead, aren't they?" Lisa asked quietly behind her. She'd stayed back to watch the cars and didn't witness any of the horror we just did.

I couldn't make my mouth work. Instead, I just nodded.

"Perimeter?" I asked, keeping my voice even.

"Clear. There's no sign of anyone sticking around," Lisa whispered.

With nothing more to say, we all piled back into the trucks and pulled out onto the road. A heavy silence blanketed us all. There weren't enough words to describe what a toll this had taken, how much of a hit this was and how deeply it would be felt.

They'd attacked us at our core. We'd lost hundreds of Ceoran in a matter of weeks, countless young, countless innocent. Not only was the future of our kind at risk, the future of all the humans we were here to protect, those who were left, was all but lost.

I bowed my head as Emelia's eyes filled with fresh tears and spilled over her cheeks.

"This shouldn't have happened," she whispered, almost to herself.

"I know." I tried to remain as composed as possible in the current situation.

It hurt me to see people I cared about in pain, and it made it even harder knowing that there was nothing I could do about this to help her either.

"We need to keep moving, I know this is hard on everyone." I cleared my throat and spoke into the walkies we'd kept between the vehicles. "Our next target is the military towers."

My voice didn't falter but everything inside me shook. I had to be strong for everyone here.

Emelia knew me better than that though. She looked away, probably seeing the pain in my eyes. This was what it took to be a leader. Nothing came easily with this role, nothing worth doing or fighting for ever was.

"Copy that," Katya replied before Zayne chimed in two cars behind us.

With that, we drove through the embers and crumbled remains of Compound 2. More than four hundred lives and countless generations had been lost in a matter of seconds. But now we had to leave, put it behind us and move forward with our mission to ensure that not a single Ceoran soul was lost in vain.

CHAPTER FOURTEEN
DO WHATEVER THEY ASK!

Alex

Kieran seemed less concerned about the state of things here than I was. Maybe I was being uber paranoid or maybe I was just across it more because of my *valuable* position. Either way, it didn't bode well.

"You're really worried about this, aren't you?" Kieran asked when my eyes kept darting between Morales and the door to my escape. She was standing with her shoulders squared, face up and eyes on the window ahead.

"Yeah." I turned back to Kieran.

"Why?"

I glared at him. "Seriously? We're being held here."

"We're not being held."

"And we can just leave then, whenever we want?"

He shifted on his spot.

"Can we?"

"Well, no. But it's safer here," he said.

"Because they said so."

His lips pursed.

"And don't tell me I'm doing the Eric thing. You said so yourself, he's where he is because he's always thinking. I don't like it here; I don't think we can trust them," I pleaded.

"You need to tell me why, Alex."

"I just have a feeling, okay? Can we go with that?"

"I'm going to need a lot more than a gut feeling to take you away from a place that is dedicated to protecting you."

I sucked in a breath when he didn't relent and rethought my approach.

"I know you don't understand, and I don't expect you to. But I have a *feeling* about this, I can't stay here. I need you to trust me."

His eyes softened. "What is it that has you on edge?"

I glanced around the room, there were a dozen others sitting around having lunch, obviously doing their own thing but everyone was a suspect in my eyes.

"Let's step outside," Kieran said, gesturing to the small door which led to a balcony.

My eyes darted back to Morales who was still standing by the door. She didn't seem to mind that we were heading out onto the balcony.

"Come on."

Despite the unease, I followed him out. No one looked up as we walked past, obviously because they were just normal people using their lunchroom.

God, I was losing my mind.

Kieran shut the balcony door behind us once we were outside, safe in the warmth of the evening sun.

"The balcony wraps around; we can walk around there."

"Fine."

The moment we were far enough away from the door and the windows, I looked out over the horizon and let my eyes take in the treetops and the oddly colored clouds speckled with purple rays from the weirdly colored sun. Everything was tinged in a strange orange hue like the way California looked during the bad fires. No matter how much it rained, it never washed away the haze.

The trees didn't move and there was no rustling in the branches showing signs of scurrying wildlife. It was silent, frozen and devoid of life. No matter how much you strained your ears, you wouldn't hear the sounds of faraway traffic or voices carrying on the wind.

It was a stark contrast to the sound of chatter and normality behind the closed doors.

"The Elders here know," I said without looking up at him.

"Know what?"

"About me, Kieran."

He gripped my shoulder and turned me. "What exactly?"

"Everything." I ground my teeth, my eyes flicking up to his. "About what my parents did, about who I am, the Map, the Reaper blood, all of it."

"How?"

"I don't know. The commander took me to meet with them before she would let me see you. They said only the two of them and other important parties know."

"Alex, this is serious."

"I know. That's why I'm worried. I don't like it here. Kieran, I'm scared. They were talking about me being valuable, *useful.* They called me a *tool...*"

His eyes shot out to the horizon. Before I could say a word, he ground his jaw and slammed his palm on the beam.

"We have to stay," he said.

"I just told you they know about me."

"I know. That's exactly why we can't go anywhere right now."

"I'm not following."

"If they have a vested interest in you, they will hunt us down and eliminate us to get to you. Understand?"

A cold chill settled on my skin.

"Alex, you must do everything they say. This is more serious than we thought."

"What if they want me to do some crazy stuff?"

"Do whatever they ask you. I don't have any doubts that they will do whatever it takes to keep you here."

"I don't want to do anything; let alone what I can only imagine they would cook up."

"They won't hurt you. But they will test you. I will find a safe way for us to get out."

"How?"

"Leave that to me. I swear to you, we'll get out of this. All of us. First, I need to find information that we need."

"What can I do?"

"Stay out of their way, make yourself invisible. Go where Commander Morales is taking you. Don't draw any more attention to yourself."

"Okay." I nodded, though I was far from okay with what he was suggesting. But a quick look at the serious fortification of these towers, and the surrounding walls through which we drove, I didn't really see any way out. I sighed and looked out over the horizon.

I wanted to see Eric and I didn't care how needy that made me sound.

"We need to get you back," Kieran said after a quiet moment.

I looked over his shoulder and noticed that Morales was looking impatient, now standing by the balcony door.

"You owe me. If they turn me into some sort of pin cushion, I'll stab you."

His lips quirked into a smile. "I won't let you become anyone's pin cushion."

We parted ways at the door and I followed Commander Morales down to the Elder Quarters like I said I would after I spoke to my friends.

Having achieved what I'd needed to, I went down the elevator with a sense of a plan, or at the very least hope that one would be made. With Kieran handling things on his end, I knew I could focus on my own.

I had to do what he said, lay low and avoid any unwanted attention, and if that meant playing the role of their Chancellor, then that's what I would do.

"Here is your room, Chancellor."

I rolled my eyes. Guess she wasn't going to start calling me by my name any time soon.

"Thank you, Commander."

The room was large, opulent. Bigger than anything I'd lived in before. My *old room* back in the real world was nice, the one at the compound was pretty too, but this was insane. The walls were painted in a warm white, the lighting fixtures were simple and modern, a slim chain with an Edison bulb hanging from it. The furniture was the same, sleek lines, black and white in tone. A large bed sat by the window which had a digital display of an ocean on it—had you not known you'd travelled six levels underground, you could have believed this was real.

"You will be secure on this level," she said, giving the room a quick glance, her steady façade perfectly in place.

"What exactly do I need to be secure from?"

"From outside threats."

"I don't see how this building could be affected, have you seen the fortress that's built around it?"

"I'm afraid the powers the Reapers possess are far greater than you can imagine. My job is to keep you safe within these walls."

"Like I said, the walls here are a fortress."

"So was the second compound."

"What do you mean *was*?" Had Ashfield been right? Had the compound fallen like he said it would?

"I'm afraid their defenses weren't enough to sustain a stronghold on the facility."

"Are they okay?"

"There were no survivors."

My mouth instantly shut. "None?"

"I'm afraid not. Get some rest, Chancellor. You've been travelling unrested for a long time."

Before I could question her and what the hell she meant by no survivors, even though it was pretty self-explanatory, she was gone. The door shut and if I wasn't mistaken, a lock engaged. I ran over to the door and yanked the handle to no avail.

"Hey! What are you doing?"

No response. Just my own, panicked voice.

Before I even realized how quickly my heart rate was rising, I found myself hyperventilating.

I had to calm down. I had to breathe. This wasn't going to help. My hands didn't stop shaking though, no matter how much I talked myself out of it. When I glanced at my hands, another shallow breath got caught in my throat. The glowy red vein thing was happening again. This was not good.

I clenched my fists into balls and sat straight down, crossed my legs and started counting out loud.

"One, two, three, breathe," I recited over and over until my body stopped shaking and my breath slowed.

When I looked down at my hands this time, the red was slowly fading. This was control...I finally had some control. I took another few deep breaths and released them when I saw the red completely vanish. Relief swept over me and I slumped in my spot.

"Dear god," I whispered into the empty room.

The news of the fallen compound replayed in my head. If it was anything like our compound there must have been around four hundred people there, so many young soldiers, kids who were just there because that's where their family chose to live. Eric and Emelia had relayed how these compounds worked but even still, I couldn't understand how this could happen? Why had the Elders not done more to equip them, or us, with enough firepower to survive?

It was madness. With that many trained, powerful Ceoran we shouldn't have fallen the way we did. Not at Compound 2, not at our compound either. If only we'd been allowed to do more, allowed to learn how to protect ourselves and our families.

The tightness in my chest wouldn't ease up.

Someone else must have played a part in their sabotage, someone I was starting to think had to be Ashfield.

There was no way to tell the others now. They were hanging around him unbeknownst to his deception; he'd lied to us all.

Anger quickly gripped me again. This time, though, I let it fuel me. I closed my eyes in the middle of the floor and I focused. I didn't know whether this would work, or whether I could even do something like what I was about to try. But I had to give it everything I had. Like that feeling that I got in the woods when I was on the run alone sensing the Reapers, I homed in on the sensation and concentrated.

Minutes meditating turned into hours, my mind and body completely independent of each other, my breaths slow and my heart even slower.

There, in the distance, as if I was looking through a foggy winter day, I saw his face kind of like how Silus must have connected us. He was sitting in a car, his angular jaw set in a hard line, green eyes narrowed in focused rage.

"Eric," I whispered to him, "Eric, we need your help now."

*****

Eric

My body jolted at least a foot into the air. A sudden jab of shock pierced right through my heart.

"Holy shit!"

"What?" Emelia screeched beside me.

"Holy crap, that was Alex."

"What was Alex?" she looked around, both her and Kristian's eyes darted around.

"She came to me...in my mind."

"How?" she snapped.

"No idea." I shook my head trying to get the feeling of being invaded out of my core. The more I tried, the harder it seemed to get. The force of whatever she'd done was still inside me.

"Eric." The voice was there again, *her* voice.

"You guys can't hear that?" I looked at my sister, hoping I wasn't losing my mind. Or, if I wasn't, I was hoping Alex was alright and she wasn't somehow reaching out to me from beyond.

No. She wasn't dead. I'd have felt that.

"Hear what?" Kristian asked urgently. "You're scaring me, man. Are you alright?"

"Eric, you're not losing your mind, I'm not dead either. I need your help. Please focus and listen to me."

"It's…it's really her," I said out loud.

"I'm so confused," Emelia whispered, keeping her eyes ahead.

"Let me focus. Just keep driving," I closed my eyes and leaned back in the seat. A few moments later, I felt her, as though she was right here beside me and spoke in my mind. "I'm here."

"Oh, Eric. We're in trouble and I don't know what to do. I don't know whether Kieran can get us out, I don't know if I can help."

"What's going on? Where are you?"

"I don't know. Ashfield brought us to some sort of military installation."

"You're with Ashfield?" My heart spluttered with anger.

"He found us in the woods, Eric, he helped us. He stopped us from going to the second compound, he said you would be heading to the towers too."

"Jesus, Alex. He lied to you, I don't trust him."

"I don't either, but he knew that the compound was going to be attacked, he stopped us from getting involved. He didn't say how bad it was, no one has told me anything."

"It's bad, Alex. Everyone is dead."

"Everyone?"

"We checked. I, I've never seen anything so bad."

"Damn it, Commander Morales told me but I hoped she was lying..." she whispered. "You're coming here, right?"

I drew in a sharp breath, "There are two military bases, I need to know which one you're at."

"Eric, I don't know."

"Can you describe it to me?"

"There are two huge towers. There are two Elders here. Ones I've never met before."

"Did you say two towers?"

"Yeah, why?"

"Do they have underground quarters too?"

"Yeah."

"Damn it."

"That doesn't sound good."

"If it's the military base I think it is, it's fortified unlike anything else around."

"It's secure, for sure." She went quiet for a moment and then she was back. "Eric, they know about me."

"Who?"

"The two Elders I met with."

"What did they say?"

"They said I'm very valuable to them, because of who I am."

"Where are you now?"

"They've locked me in the underground quarters. I can't get out; I've been separated from the others," she said calmly.

"When did you last see Kelly?"

"A few hours ago. One of the guards here let me see him."

"Who?"

"Commander Morales?"

"Okay. Good."

"You know her?"

"Yes. She's good people. We can trust her."

"But she locked me in here," she said.

"She must have a reason."

"I hope so, because I cannot get out. The freaking room is all the way in the basement, like six floors down and I have no idea where everyone else is."

"Don't panic, just keep calm and we will fix this."

"How?"

"I know where the installation is, I know how to get you out. Morales is going to help us. She owes me. Big time."

"For what?"

"Long story, but she was part of the reason we couldn't save your family. I personally held her accountable, and she swore to make things right when the time came."

"What do you mean?"

"I knew there'd be a time when we needed to work against the Ceoran, and she swore she'd be on our side when that happened. I'm guessing that time is now."

"Okay. So, you trust her?" she asked.

"I trust her to uphold her end of the deal."

"Hurry, okay?"

"Hold tight. We're coming. Do whatever she says, she knows that I'll be coming for you."

"And you think that's an advantage to us?"

"Yes, because she put you somewhere safe. When we come in, it won't be a peaceful surrender, I can guarantee it."

"What are you going to do?"

"Whatever I have to."

She went quiet again, only this time I felt the urge to say everything that was on my mind. I sucked in a sharp breath, feeling comfortable knowing that no one else could hear what we were talking about.

"Alex…"

"You don't have to say anything."

Her voice was shaking too.

"I want to, I need to." I focused on the feelings rather than the nerves, and the feelings told me that everything coursing through me was undeniable. "I'm sorry I hurt you and I'm sorry I failed you. But most of all I'm so sorry I lied and that I didn't tell you how I felt." I paused. "How I *feel*."

There was no response. Not even a tiny breath. Nothing. I closed my mouth and seriously considered whether I had some sort of brain injury to tell her everything like this. A normal person would have waited until they were face to face with the woman they were proclaiming their love for, not this, this weird mind connection thing.

"Please say something, Alex," I finally managed. "If I crossed the line, if you don't feel the same, or anything at all…"

"I do."

"You do?"

"I do feel the same."

I exhaled through my nose.

"Even before the memories started coming back, Eric, I saw your face in my dreams when I was out there alone. I knew when I saw you that there was a connection and no matter how much you hid it, you couldn't completely shut it out."

The words I'd so carefully planned out in my head for her rejection disappeared, and instead I was left with this emptiness. I'd hurt her, a lot. Deeper than I'd realized even now.

She'd been alone all this time and when I should have been there to give her the comfort she needed, I'd treated her like a stranger.

I would never forgive myself for that.

"I understand why you did it," she said quietly, her voice barely above a whisper in my head now. "But it still hurts."

"I am so sorry, Alex."

"Me too."

"I will make it up to you, I swear."

"You don't have anything to make up for. You were doing your job and I should have been doing mine."

Thoughts of her time with Ashfield made me squeeze my hands in anger. If she was truly with him before our time and then gave it up for us...did she regret it?

"It's not good enough. I let you down. I get that and I will make things right. Whatever it takes, however long it takes," I said sternly.

"Eric—"

"Please. Let me."

"Because you want to, right?"

"What do you mean?"

"Because you want to, not because you feel obligated or, or bad or whatever."

"Because I want to. It's the only thing I know for sure. This whole thing has been a damned mess since the beginning, and I kept making mistake after mistake. This ends now, Alex. I will make things right by you if you will let me."

"Start by getting us the hell out of here," she said quickly. "Someone is coming."

"Alex!"

"Hurry," she whispered and then she was gone.

Panic raced through me as I shook myself from the haze and gripped the edge of my seat.

Emelia's wide eyes met mine.

"We need to hurry, now!"

Chapter Fifteen
The Commander and the Chancellor

Alex

Snapping back to my reality was like being dropped on one of those horrific rides at Dream World in Australia. My stomach lurched into my throat and did a huge tumble making me gag on the tiny amount of bile that crept into my throat.

It didn't take me long to realize that the reason my mind had snapped me back was to avoid the mess that was about to be unleashed. My mind and body seemed to be working independently to some degree because had I not been snapped back, I surely would have missed the unmistakable sound of someone unlocking my door.

Just outside my room I heard what sounded like loud, bickering voices, followed by a thump and then nothing. I held my breath waiting for them to come through the door.

When the heavy booted footsteps came closer, I jerked back and looked around searching for something I could use as a weapon.

Unfortunately for me, whoever anticipated that they'd be shoving me in here, had de-weaponized the room. There was nothing. Not even a heavy book. I groaned and did the only thing I could, despite it making me cringe—I hid.

As the door was unlocked from the outside and slowly opened, I made myself small behind the oak dresser and covered my mouth with my palm.

They walked around, stalking, taking their time. It was definitely someone of big build, maybe a man, but I couldn't be sure. I pressed myself lower and squeezed my eyes shut, hoping I'd be able to slow my breathing enough to avoid making any unnecessary sounds. It was working. The footsteps went around the dresser and back toward the door.

But my celebration was short lived, because the second I let out a small, quiet breath, rapid footfalls came right at me, and before I could even blink, the curtain was ripped away and a large, rough hand shot out and closed around my throat choking off any stunned sounds I would have made.

"I've got her," his grimy voice said.

I kicked and thrashed with my arms to no avail.

He was huge. Immovable.

"Copy that, we haven't found the others," came another voice just outside in the hall.

I thrashed again, but he was squeezing my throat tighter and tighter, restricting whatever movement I managed.

"Stop struggling, little girl, or I will snap your neck like a twig."

If I could have said something smart in retaliation, I would have. Something along the lines of not needing to try much harder. My eyes started watering while the pressure in the front of my head built.

"Sir, still no sign. All three underground levels are clear."

I was minutes away from passing out.

"Keep looking, he won't be happy if we come without them," the one holding me barked.

"The rich prick can kiss my ass. We're not getting paid enough for this," came the response.

My eyes were rolling into the back of my head as my mind raced through the possibilities of who he was talking about and only one, simple answer made sense. Ashfield had set this up. Another very small, gargled cry came free and I felt everything start to go lax.

The man dropped me to my feet giving me a moment to catch my breath before he grabbed my ponytail instead and dragged me behind him. Hell to the no.

I reached behind with every ounce of strength I could find and scratched at his hand until he hissed and let go. It was only for a brief moment, but it was enough. I scrambled to my feet and found my way to the lift Morales had brought me down earlier. Right beside it was the entrance to the stairwell she alluded to. I shoved it open.

"Get her back!" I heard a voice call after me.

Those same, heavy booted steps came hard and fast.

This time, though, I didn't leave anything to chance. I found my energy and took the steps up two and three at a time. Once I'd reached the next landing, an arm shot out and dragged me through a door. Before I could shove the person back, I was met by Morales. She shook her head and pressed her finger to her lips.

Shrill screams broke through the ventilation systems humming above. Chaos broke out down below and just outside the small section of the corridor we found ourselves in, and my entire body broke out in goosebumps. A battle was raging all around the compound.

"Stay quiet and follow me," Morales instructed before stopping us at another small intersection. "Can you fight?"

"A little."

"Good. We might need whatever you've got."

I nodded and then remembered Eric's promise about Morales being an ally. "I can use *it.*"

Her eyes narrowed while she considered me. She seemed to be taking her sweet ass time considering how much was at stake right now.

"It's dangerous to draw that kind of attention to yourself."

"I'd say right now that's the least of our worries, wouldn't you?"

A small line in her forehead moved, only slightly. That was probably the most emotion this woman ever showed.

"I can fight," I reiterated. "I can fight with *it*. We don't really have a choice right now. Let me help."

"Fine. Stay close and do not exert too much energy. I still need you to be able to get yourself out of here."

"Got it." I nodded.

Together, we pushed through the doors, armed and ready. Morales with her gun held directly in front of her, and me, with the fire slowly pulsing through my veins. The second we got ready to leave, I questioned my sanity. *Could I really do this?* Guess there was only one way to find out.

As we broke through the last remaining distance of peace, I was shocked by the sight before me—there weren't just Reapers, there were men, our men, and Scavengers. They were all on the same side, the side we weren't on. A rich sense of irony forced me to shut my mouth in shock as a gun was pointed in my direction.

As the thought formed and the gun fired, my mind went blank: this was it, this was my end.

Morales lunged forward and took the shooter out. My hands instinctively reached down and patted over my body. I was okay, I wasn't shot.

It wasn't just the horror of what I was seeing, of the bodies strewn across the floor or of the sounds that came from the battle, it was the sheer lunacy of it all. My entire system of belief had been turned upside down. Everything I thought I knew, everything I remembered ceased to exist in a tiny puff of smoke coming out of the tip of the Smith & Wesson that had been aimed at me only a moment ago.

"Move," she barked.

I couldn't see a way that this would ever get better. This war was officially on our doorstep and it had only just begun.

Morales looked over at me as the Reapers up ahead caught sight of us.

She didn't need to ask me if I was ready. The fire roared to life beneath my skin and I dropped my hands out at my side, nodding.

It was game on.

***

Eric

My hands instinctively rolled into fists as soon as we pulled up to what I was sure used to be the gate to the towers. The impenetrable gates that now looked like a pile of scrap metal.

There was a sickening stench in the air, something close to burning flesh and hair. I shut my mouth to avoid breathing it in and squeezed my eyes shut as the embers in the air burned through the night sky. We rolled our windows up, but it was too late. Reactive tears were quick to form, and no matter how much I wanted to pretend that they were just from the smoke, I knew I was lying to myself.

168

Every thought somehow manifested into all the ways they'd hurt Alex and started to cause an uncontrollable panic to surge through me. This wasn't me. I was cool, I was calm and collected. But the deeper we drove into the carnage of the small, narrow streets it reminded me how much was at stake.

I was only cool when I knew things were in my control. Nothing about this situation was in my control. It took one look at the chaos erupting around me to prove that. Alex was out of my grasp; I was spinning out of control and enemies we never knew were creeping out of the shadows at every turn.

"You doing okay?" my sister asked, squeezing my hand.

"I will be when we find them."

"I hear you."

That was the only conversation I had energy for.

As soon as the car stopped rolling, I threw my door open and rushed outside. With no protection of glass and steel, I felt the entirety of what we were faced with. It was as though the chassis and the fabric and the glass had created a cocoon, one we were now forced out of prematurely. I wasn't ready for this. I didn't know whether I ever could have been.

Emelia stumbled beside me, her small frame shook as she took in the sight before us. I'd driven down these streets twice before. First when I was briefed on my responsibility to guard Alex and met her for the first time, and once more when my stepmom died. I was called here for them to make some half-assed apologies that served nothing other than to cement my distrust in the people running the place. The streets looked the same, save for the smoke pouring through the laneways—they were narrow, far too small to outrun anyone and caved in in some areas. We were safe for now, Kristian had found a spot far out of view, but we couldn't stay out in the open for long. The other cars stopped beside us. We had to move quickly.

I gently nudged Emelia forward and gestured to the rest of our small army to take formation.

Katya, Leah, and Lisa stopped beside me and my sister while Kristian and Zayne took a few tentative steps toward the burning building.

"We are surrounded by hostiles. Keep your eyes open and stay alert. I don't know who we can trust here," I said, nodding up to the carefully placed security cameras which showed no red light telling of their operation.

"What's the mission?" Kristian asked.

"Get our friendlies out and get clear."

"What about the others?"

"I can't risk the Chancellor's life. She is my priority. Once we're clear, my mission is to get her to safety. You do what you have to."

"Copy that."

With those simple orders, we split into teams. Emelia and Kristian with me, and the rest forming two more groups. We were tasked to find Alex, we three knew more than the others and we had to keep her alive.

Despite my ego and prior protests, I couldn't in good conscience do this alone.

"Everyone stay sharp," Kristian said, giving me a quick nod.

It was time to let people in and let them help because I knew there was a very high chance that this could end with more of our people dead.

Kristian, Em and I broke off while the other two teams went to their respective locations.

"Where?"

"This way." I trained my weapon ahead and focused on Alex's presence. "She's doing something."

"Your freaky radar is nuts, did anyone ever tell you that?" Kristian asked clearing the road ahead for us.

"Yep," I muttered gesturing for Emelia to take the lead while I cleared behind us.

"Something bad?" my sister asked.

"Can't tell."

"This is seriously weird," Kristian muttered shaking his head.

"It's weird for me too, believe me. I can't work out where she ends and I start. It's like this constant humming in my head." I stopped abruptly and dragged them back. "Someone is coming."

"Where?"

"Up ahead."

She craned her neck and then nodded. "Two bogies, both armed."

"Definitely not Reapers?" Kristian asked.

Emelia shook her head. "Nope. Unless Reapers suddenly started wearing Ceoran uniform and parading around with semis."

"Crap," Kristian cursed, crouching beside us.

"Yep."

"We need to head back around. I have to get up there." I nodded to the tower in front of us.

The towers side by side looked like old, Germanic spires with turrets topping them off which were usually reserved for the Ceoran tasked to watching the nearing areas. They were equipped with enough firepower to take out a small army approaching from any direction.

Given that the twenty-foot cement walls surrounding us were just as efficient keeping us in as keeping enemies out, I didn't think we had many options to work with. I scoped out the surrounding area and looked back to where we came from. That road was probably a no go now, a chance look confirmed that it was crawling with Reapers and screams of falling Ceoran cemented it.

"There's nowhere else to go," I said to Em and Kristian. "The streets are too narrow to try and make it out past them and the damn place is a fortress, only it's keeping us *and* them in."

"And you think getting up there is safer?" he asked me.

I looked up. The bottom few levels of the tower directly ahead were billowing with flames, and the top few were expelling smoke. The turret and the floor below that had access to a balcony were clear.

"She's up there, somewhere in tower two," I said.

"You do realize that tower is on fire, right?" Emelia muttered.

"Only the bottom half."

"How do you want to do this?" Kristian asked, shaking his head at me.

"Go in through tower one. I'll go in from the outside of two. Find a way across where it's safe."

"Through the tower that's on flames?" he scoffed.

"I've got this. Go."

Neither of them looked convinced but nodded.

They split off from me and in a single leap, Emelia threw herself onto a small ledge that was about six feet off the ground on the first tower. Kristian followed suit. Before I could blink, she'd already rushed inside the building and disappeared into the smoke.

I took a quick breath, pulled my shirt over my nose and rushed into the smoke at ground level of tower two. My eyes burned but quickly adjusted to the hazy darkness.

It didn't take long to find myself surrounded by enemies. One of which was a kid I trained with at the compound years ago. He was a little shorter than me, though back then he had light blonde hair and a friendly face. The guy in front of me wasn't that anymore. Deep set scars crossed his features, dark circles made the usual bright blue of his eyes contrast sharply, and he had dark, intricate tattoos lining his arms where the skin was exposed. He was a lot bigger now, too, like the kid had been replaced by a sort of steroided version of himself.

Behind him, there were two more Ceoran-gone-bad soldiers who gave me looks I could only compare to a rabid dog. Anger and adrenaline instantly pushed my momentary shock aside. These people were not my friends anymore, these people stood for everything I fought against. They were the enemy, they sought to destroy the peaceful kind we could have been and instead created a world order within our ranks that only favored those with power and destroyed those with none.

I *hated* what they stood for and I had no time for it.

"You've come far, Peter."

"Wish I could say the same for you," he spat. "You're still just a slave to the institution, I see."

"At least I know what I fight for."

"For what? That little bitch up there?"

My fists balled at my sides as the venom of his words replayed in my head a few more times.

"Isn't that little bitch the reason you're out here looking like Freddy Krueger?" Peter taunted.

"Is that your plan? Keep throwing jabs at me and hope that I'll buckle?"

"No, brother. My plan is to finish you off and then find your little playmate and have a good time with her."

"You touch her, and I will destroy you."

"Or maybe your big sister, she seems like a bit of fun."

I stared at him for a moment, weighing up how I was going to end him. Would he be on the receiving end of the rage that fueled my veins or would it be a swift, merciful death? I didn't have time to toy with him, but I didn't want him to get off so easily.

"Maybe both of them at the same time." He grinned, his unnaturally white teeth baring.

That was it. The last thing this monster would say to me. I didn't wait for any other jabs he was ready to throw out, I went to fire my weapon but in the split second it took for me to do so, Peter had darted out of the way, slamming the gun down and out of my hands.

The two behind him rushed forward. Within a breath of a second, the fight was on.

I couldn't tell which fist was smashing into my jaw and frankly, it didn't matter, the anger had numbed parts of me and at this point it was more than I could have hoped for. These guys were a lot better than I'd remembered. I had to up my game and I had to find some way to get the upper hand. With each minute I was wasting here with these three clowns, the tower continued to burn.

Peter threw down another well-placed hit which, if I wasn't mistaken, fractured my nose. I tasted the blood before I felt it slide down the back of my throat. The reactive tears blinded me for a moment before the reminder of why I was there kicked my ass into gear. One of the others, maybe both, kicked me in the stomach forcing me down and then again in the ribs forcing another angry cry from my lips.

"Come on, Raine, you really going to let me walk away from here and find your girl?"

I spat the blood out and dragged myself to my feet and squared off with the three of them. The few punches I took taught me exactly what moves to anticipate next. So as buzzcut guy to Peter's left ran forward I threw my forearm out in front of my face and stopped his assault. That stunned him for a moment buying me enough time to sidestep Peter's other goon buddy and launch my foot at him. He fell, giving me a split second to turn all my attention to Peter. His expression hardened and his icy blue eyes widened when I dropped my hands at my sides and called on the Ceoran blood coursing through my veins. I knew he suspected that I had more power than the average Ceoran. I knew there were rumors, but I'd always been careful to keep that part of myself hidden, not only for me but for the protection of Alex. If I drew attention to us in any way, it put her at risk.

"What the hell are you?" Peter's voice faltered as his two clown mates stammered backwards.

All their eyes were on my hands. The glow from within paling in comparison to the ferocity Alex could produce. No one knew exactly why some of us were gifted with extra power but there were theories: some of those were that the chosen guardians of the most important Ceoran were given them by the Karatoi in order to fulfil their duties; some speculated it was because there was a reason in our afterlife. All I knew is that it was given to me, and it had saved my ass, and Alex's, numerous times. I didn't want to expose myself to these idiots but deep inside, I knew they wouldn't live to tell anyone about it.

All I could think as Peter watched me approach in fear, was thank the Karatoi that Alex wasn't the one destroying them, but me. The pain of killing someone, especially of your own kind, was never easy to digest. It did something to us inside, something dark and immovable. A part of you began to rot and spread like a disease. How many would I have to kill today? How much would it cost me?

I ground my jaw and stepped closer.

"You're stronger than you let on, Raine," Peter spat.

"And you're dumber than you let on."

"You're not going to kill me. You're not going to kill any of us. You're better than that."

I focused on the burn beneath my fingertips. Despite their words of confidence, they jerked back.

"You're too righteous. Too *good,*" Peter muttered, like he was trying to convince himself.

"You must have missed the memo." I threw my hands up and forced a powerful, soul-destroying burst of energy which permanently silenced the two Ceoran at his side. They dropped without a sound.

Peter gaped.

"I'm not the same person you knew," I hissed taking a step forward.

His eyes darted between the bodies before finally landing back on me. I could have spared them. I could have let them walk out of here. But the venom and the truth in Peter's threats reminded me why I had to do this, why I had no other choice.

If he did leave and he found Alex, he wouldn't have spared her. My mind disappeared into the dark recesses of my imagination. I didn't want to think about Alex or Emelia at the mercy of this animal; I didn't want to think about his large hands touching any part of their bodies.

I stepped closer and he stepped back.

Alex and my sister could look after themselves, Alex could take him out if he got anywhere near her, so maybe this was a selfish need of my own…

"You don't have to do this," he pleaded. Suddenly the tables had turned. The unfearing soldier was now begging for his life. And I wasn't going to give in.

"Too late for that, Peter." I barely recognized my own voice. "I can't let you walk away from here. Not when I know what you're capable of."

"You know I would never hurt your sister, or Alex…"

"I can't believe that, not after sensing the truth in your words. If I let you leave, Alex will be at risk. The Chancellor above everything else."

"Eric, please—"

I called forth the power and threw my hands up at him releasing it all. I killed him before he took his next breath. He dropped to his knees, his eyes wide and unseeing, staring up at the ceiling at a point beyond my head.

I didn't waste any more time on him. Throwing everything into the sprint, I took the stairs up the rounded spire staircase two at a time until I heard commotion a floor up. There were shouts and grunts, unmistakable sounds of bodies hitting the floors and finally the roar of a new, billowing wall of fire raging towards me. I dropped to my knees and shielded my face. The flame roared over my head and rapidly extinguished as it ran out of fuel.

As soon as it was safe, I pushed to my feet and ran up, ignoring the blistering heat still superheating the air around me. My lungs burned with each inhale but the desperation to get to Alex burned harder.

"Now, Alex!" My eyes darted up when I heard Morales' familiar voice.

A large, powerful tremor rolled through the floor beneath my feet and up over the walls and down the stairs. I braced for the impact. A few seconds later, another tremor rocked the foundation and this time, the floor beneath my feet cracked and crumbled. I threw myself forward and grabbed onto the railing, holding my breath as the floor I'd been on seconds earlier disappeared into the darkness below.

My eyes darted up, landing on Morales. She was barely holding onto the doorframe, but she was still here, still breathing. Her eyes briefly met mine before the sound of Alex's small voice drew my attention over Morales's head.

Her feet were firmly planted to the sturdy floor a level above, but the moment she caught my eyes, whatever she'd been focusing on fragmented. A small smile crossed her lips before she dropped to her knees.

"Alex!" I pulled myself up, using the rail as a guide considering I could barely see through any of the dust or smoke that had been thrown up. Once I reached Morales, I helped her to safety and we rushed toward Alex.

Her eyes were closed, body unmoving and a small trickle of blood pooled under her nose. I dragged her up into my arms and brushed the hair from her face.

"Come on, Alex, come on. Open your eyes." I gently spoke to her, aware of the billowing fire taking down the rest of this pyre.

"We have to go, Eric. Get her and follow me."

"The floor is gone."

"Pay attention." She pointed to the door leading to the balcony. "And always know your surroundings."

My eyes followed her hand and landed on Emelia outside the now shattered door. I ground my jaw ignoring the jab.

"There's a way down here come on!" Emelia called.

I carefully drew Alex to my chest and carried her to the doorway. Emelia cradled Alex while Morales and I ripped off the curtains that had adorned the windows in the room and fashioned a harness.

"Has anyone else come out?" I asked, handing her the curtain harness.

"No, haven't heard anything yet. Help me get this around her."

Morales carefully looped the harness under Alex's arms and then ensured it was tight enough to hold her securely.

"You two scale down first, I'll help Alex."

"What the hell happened up here?" I ground out.

"We were outnumbered, there were dozens of them."

"Ceoran?" Emelia asked, climbing over the edge of the turret.

"No, Reapers."

My eyes snapped up. "She took them all out?" I asked, suddenly aware of the energy that would have taken. The eruption, the shaking and the cracking in the floors now made sense.

"Yes. I didn't realize she was so unstable."

I bit down hard. I hated that Morales used her as a weapon.

"Hurry, we don't have long." Emelia motioned to us to get moving.

I watched Morales curiously as she knelt beside a still-unconscious Alex, seated carefully against the wall of the small balcony. Morales pressed a hand to her cheek and moments later, Alex stirred.

"What...?"

"You're alright, Chancellor. But we need to get up and go over that ledge. You think you can do that?" Morales said.

179

Alex's body went rigid as her neck craned up and around, spotting me waiting on the ledge.

"Eric…"

"I'm here, I've got you."

Morales drew Alex's attention back to her and tilted her chin up.

"Are you ready?"

"Yes."

"Good. Come on." She looped her arms under Alex's and then helped her to her feet, though it looked a lot more like she was being dragged.

Alex stumbled, her eyes darting from me to Emelia down below, and Morales right behind her.

"I'm going to help you swing your legs over that ledge; Major Raine will help guide you down and I'll make sure you don't swing too much," she explained. Alex seemed to be keeping up.

"Ready?" I asked gently.

Alex nodded.

"Let's get moving," Morales said.

With that, I scaled a few floors down and stopped, holding onto the pipes running along the edge of the pyre while I waited for Alex to carefully make it down with her harness. No one said a word as the descent took place. The only sounds aside from our own feet scuffing the brick were the shouts coming from inside a battle I couldn't be a part of.

"Hold up," Emelia called from below.

I glanced down and saw her unhook her weapon and scour the surrounding area.

"Are we clear?" I called.

"No. We have company, I heard something, I just can't see where."

"Let me try," Alex said from above. "I think I can use my power to see further now."

"Are you sure?" I asked.

"I can do it, just give me a second."

Everyone else went quiet and Alex turned in the harness, her brilliant eyes searching the area.

Suddenly, she went completely still. Her eyes narrowed and she slowly raised her right hand while holding onto the curtain with her other. She closed her eyes, and I felt another subtle rumble roll through the foundations beginning low and close then spreading out further and with more power.

"Hold on!" I yelled below to my sister.

Morales and I gripped onto the curtain for dear life as Alex worked. The rumble extended beyond the small vicinity surrounding Alex and grew until the force nearly caused me to let go of the pipe. She opened her eyes and screamed out as the force escaped her hand and erupted outward.

Down below, as the energy dispersed, I saw several dozen Reapers appear out of nowhere and immediately fall to their deaths. The cloaking shield they had deployed fizzled out with Alex's power revealing just how many there had been.

"Found them," she whispered, making me laugh.

"Keep moving. We're not safe yet," Morales said, ushering Alex down.

In the short time it took for me to reach the bottom, Alex had caught up. I helped her down to the ground. "Easy."

"Reckon you can walk?" Emelia asked Alex.

"Yeah, I can walk." She pulled herself free from the harness and looked at me.

I couldn't find anything to say. My mouth dried up and my nerves started firing. It felt like it had been so long since I'd seen her properly, through eyes that weren't covered with a lens of fear and apprehension.

"Here," Emelia said, breaking my gaze and handing me my gun. "Saw it down there, thought you might need it."

I tucked it back into my jeans and returned my attention to Alex.

"We should go," she said.

When Morales caught up, she practically shoved all three of us toward the cars we'd left.

"What about the others?" Alex asked, looking back.

"We have to go, Chancellor. Your safety is our priority and we're officially pushing that limit."

"I'm not leaving without Kieran." She stopped walking and looked to me. "Eric, please. We can't leave them."

"I'll go."

"What?" Alex said quickly. "Not alone, you can't face them all."

"And I can't risk you. Go with Morales and Em, you'll be safe."

"Eric, please."

"Go. I'll find Kelly. I promise."

"Be careful," Emelia said.

I gave her a quick look and then chanced another glance at Alex. I immediately regretted it. Her eyes were wide, a coating of dust and ash had settled on her pink cheeks making her look so delicate and innocent and it drove home how close we came to losing each other.

"I'll find them, just go, please," I said to Alex.

"This is a bad idea, Major. You are her primary guardian," Morales said to me.

"You don't get to have an opinion now," I spat.

"Stop acting so childish. This is your duty."

"My *duty* is to make sure she has the best possible chance of coming out of this alive and if that means gathering more of our soldiers then that is what I will do," I snapped back. "Your duty is to be there when it matters."

Morales clamped her mouth shut and looked at Emelia. Thankfully, my sister was on my side. She cocked her brows and shrugged.

"We've lost a lot of soldiers these past few nights. We need whoever we can get," Emelia added.

Morales ground her molars and eventually yielded.

I reined in the emotions and turned back to Alex. There was so much I wanted to say but time wasn't on our side. And before her pleading could break me down and make me see how stupid my decision to leave her was, I broke contact and ran. I knew Morales would have a lot more to say about it than she already had, but I couldn't care less about her or what she thought right now. She'd made sure of that years ago.

Personal differences aside, I trusted her to keep Alex and my sister out of harm's way. Right now, I had to get my head in the game.

Kelly and the others needed me.

So as the car Alex and Emelia were in disappeared into the darkness and the cover of the tree line, I found myself running back into the burning remains of what had once been the most fortified city in all of Ceoran human history.

Chapter Sixteen
Don't Turn Your Back

Alex

Commander Morales ditched the car after a short drive and instructed us to walk. She kept us moving at a swift pace, one that was starting to take a toll on me. I didn't know where the extra reserves of my energy kept coming from but I knew I was finally running low. Those last two bursts of power were too much.

"We have to keep moving," she said sternly when I stumbled over yet another tree root which had rudely grown out of the ground.

What was a root doing on the surface anyway?

"She's hurt, give her some time," Emelia said, rushing over to help me stand straight. "And remind me again why we had to ditch the car."

"We have better chances remaining hidden this way," Morales said.

I groaned and straightened.

"We do not have time, Chancellor, we must keep going."

"I know, I'm okay. I can keep moving."

"She's hurt—"

"It's fine, Em. I can keep going."

She let out a long sigh but dropped it. The silence was thankfully really helpful. It allowed me to focus on keeping my feet going one step at a time, while talking myself into keeping my head together. I didn't need to throw up. It was just a figment of my imagination. I was totally, one hundred per cent fine. Yep.

Just as I tripped over another inconsiderate root, I crashed to my knees and threw up whatever was left in my stomach.

Dear God. I was so not good.

My head started spinning and before I knew it, dark edges quickly closed in on my vision.

I couldn't tell whose arms were around me or which way was up. The only coherent thought I kept having was this sickening feeling of dread. Something bad, seriously bad was coming and I couldn't do a damned thing about it.

As Emelia's voice faded in and out, a clear and sharp image of Eric, Kieran and a gun shot through me making a very slow, shallow breath catch in my lungs.

"What's wrong?" Emelia asked kneeling beside me.

"Something bad is going to happen to Eric and we can't get there in time to help."

***

Eric

It didn't take long to navigate through the haze of smoke of the compound and find Kelly. He and Ashfield were fighting three Reapers. From my vantage point, I could see that both of them were badly hurt—Kelly was still holding his own while Ashfield stammered every few hits. I had to hand it to the guy, as untrained as he was he was still going, albeit a bit bloodied and shaken up.

I unholstered my gun and shot the Reaper closest to me. He dropped causing the other two to turn to me and give Kelly and Ashfield a moment to breathe.

"Was not expecting to see you, man." Kelly doubled over, inhaling sharp breaths.

"You two okay?"

"We are now."

"Ashfield," I said.

"Raine."

"We need to get out of here, the outer pyres are going down." I gestured behind me.

"Alex?" Kelly asked.

"She's safe."

"Where?" Ashfield asked.

A coil of heat tightened around my chest. I knew he'd gotten them here, to *safety* but I didn't trust him. Not in the slightest. Especially knowing what I knew now having read about them in the files Emelia had *sourced*. I had to play this smart, though; going off half-cocked could end in disaster, especially if he was playing the long game. I needed him to think that he was still in control until I knew what we were dealing with.

"Outside of these walls beyond the limits. Let's move, we need to get out before we become a part of the rubble," I said, deliberately leaving out as much information as possible.

"Don't need to tell me twice," Kelly muttered.

Not even two seconds passed before I felt a warning race through me like a sharp, sudden sensation of dread where your mind raced through a million questions and answers within a breath of a second, but by the time I figured out what it was, it was too late.

I spun on the spot, turning to face Ashfield and the simple, nine-millimeter gun he had pointed at me.

Within a painfully quick second, his eyes met mine, a wry grin on his lips. Then the gun went off.

There was no feeling, no sound, no warning. Just a single, white flash that burned through my retina.

Then came Kelly's startled scream followed by a scuffle and pounding feet on the remains of the wooden floor. It must have been seconds; it had all happened in seconds. Bodies hit the floor, mine and someone else's, I couldn't tell.

My lungs spluttered and heaved, desperately trying to suck in futile breaths. The heat from the hole in my chest rapidly filled with hot liquid which warmed the rest of my shirt. I found myself going cold.

It wasn't a cold night. I could remember that vividly. It was balmy, the heat of the fire had kept us all warm and the slight pink on Alex's cheeks proved it.

"Raine!" My shoulders were roughly shaken. "Eyes on me, bother. Come on."

A sort of choked cough left my mouth followed by a warm, sticky and metallic taste. How ironic. I was biding my time to let him think he was still in control and I'd been the fool the whole time.

Hands pressed down on my chest drawing a broken gasp from my lips.

"Eric. Stay with me. Eyes open."

"Ash...Ashfield..."

"He's down. Don't worry, he's down."

Another choked cough rattled through my ribcage. No matter how much I tried to keep my eyes open and pull myself together, I couldn't. The persistent shaking got worse, and I could now feel every single nerve and muscle in my body fire all at once. The ferocity of the pain from the deceptively small bullet made me clamp my jaw shut.

"You're going into shock but you're going to live, I need you to stay awake and keep your eyes on me."

"Go…"

"I'm not going anywhere."

"Alex—"

"Alex is safe, you're going to see her again."

My eyes slipped shut.

"No, Eric. Eyes on me. Now."

"Can't…"

"Yes, you can. You need to see Alex, you need to make things right between you both, she needs you. Keep your eyes open."

No matter what I wanted to do, my body refused. No matter how much Kelly shook my shoulders or pleaded with me, everything was shutting down.

"Eric…I'm so sorry, I'm so sorry for how things are with us, you were my best friend, and I…I need you to come back. Okay? Please."

His hands wrapped around mine and the last thing I could manage was to tell him in the only way I could that I had heard him. I squeezed his hand and then, with a broken breath, I felt everything go lax.

Alex

My chest heaved with a pain I couldn't place. It was everywhere all at once. It was physical, it was emotional, it was all consuming and there was no escape.

Tears poured from my eyes with no sound reason for them to be doing so. I couldn't catch my breath and I couldn't stop the body-shaking sobs that raced through me.

It was so definitive, so complete and intolerably painful. I hadn't even noticed that a whole group of Ceoran had joined us. Some were friends from the previous convoy, others Ceoran I didn't recognize.

Emelia's wide eyes filled with tears; she couldn't have known what I did, she couldn't have felt the connection I had with Eric but she could see the utter devastation breaking me down. It didn't take Reaper blood or supernatural power to see it.

"Please tell me my brother is okay," Emelia said.

"Chancellor, what did you see?" Morales demanded.

Once I was able to stop crying long enough for coherent words to come through, I looked up at Emelia. "I don't know, Em, I don't know. There was pain and then nothing…I don't know, I can't feel him."

She clamped her hands over her mouth and shot to her feet.

"We have to go back," someone shot.

"It's not safe, Katya," Morales said, her face grim, and voice a lot quieter than I had heard previously.

I didn't know who the girl was who'd spoken but she seemed hurt, just like me…had she known Eric?

"I don't care, he needs us," she shot back.

Everything about Morales's body language changed.

All the confidence, all the strength, gone. She hung her head between her shoulders, and I could have sworn that I'd seen her shudder and hold back a single sob.

"Please, we need to get to him. If I can't help…" I said.

"You're weak right now."

"I can manage!" I snapped, unsure of who I was losing it at. The situation, the pain, the constant reminder of my failure to control my power as much as I wanted to.

It was all too much, and I refused to let it continue to control me.

"If you won't help me get there then I will go on my own and I swear to you I will destroy every Reaper and Ceoran who stands in my way."

Emelia shot forward, so too did Katya.

"We're going now," Emelia said.

Morales surprisingly didn't argue. Instead, she gave me a single, curt nod and followed as the two women helped me to my feet.

Every step was a struggle, every pull of every muscle reminded me how low on energy and strength I was, but knowing that Eric was out there, dying in his own pool of blood, made the anger drive me even harder and forget the mortal pain holding me back. I couldn't know for certain but I had no doubt that Ashfield was responsible.

I was a damned Halfling, as they put it. That had to count for something and there was no better time to see what it all meant.

If Ashfield wasn't dead already, I wasn't going to hesitate to kill him myself. The moment the thought formed in my head, I immediately hated myself for it. The realization of what I was thinking sent shivers over me, and Emelia gave me a quick look when I went rigid. Shaking it away, I reminded myself that no, I wasn't that person. I wasn't like Ashfield. I wouldn't do that…

"What is the plan, Alex, what do you want us to do?"

"I don't know yet. All I do know is that we need to find him."

"What if he's seriously hurt, what if you can't…?" Katya trailed off.

"I can," I snapped and kept my pace steady and my eyes dead ahead. *I had to.*

I couldn't look at any of them because the moment I did, they would sense how unsure I truly was. I had to stay positive and keep my mind from swimming. If I let myself wonder about all the *what ifs* I'd never see the sunrise again.

After less than fifteen minutes of stumbling through the dense terrain, we reached the lone car we'd left behind.

The four of us sat in silence as Emelia drove back to where we'd last seen Eric. Not long into the drive, I felt a shift of energy up ahead. My eyes snapped to the front of the car and the surrounding darkness. Morales raised her weapon loading it.

"Stop," I hissed.

"What is it?" Emelia slammed on the brakes.

"Someone's coming, get out of the open."

Emelia slowly took the car through a small clearing off to the side and the four of us got out.

Both Emelia and Katya unholstered their weapons and stepped forward, creating a sort of barricade between me and whoever was coming, while Morales stood watch behind me.

"Lead on, Chancellor."

All four of us went ahead in complete silence, holding our breaths as the heavy smoke haze blocked us from seeing what was ahead. The tension doubled, both Emelia and Morales were as rigid as I was.

Just as I felt like I was about to snap like a twig, two figures broke through the haze.

For a moment I wasn't sure who I was seeing, then I saw Kieran's strained face as he struggled toward us. His shoulder was tucked under Eric's arm. Eric was unconscious, his head lolling from side to side. I stumbled forward and dropped to my knees. Emelia helped Kieran lower Eric down in front of me and Morales cradled his head.

"Oh my God, Eric." Emelia took his hand.

"Give me some space, please," I said.

Morales lowered Eric's head gently to the ground and stood back. Katya pulled Emelia away from us. As I carefully brushed my fingers across Eric's cheek Kieran's eyes locked onto mine, and I saw the fatigue etched onto his features.

He knew just as well as I did that if I didn't do something to help Eric now, he wouldn't be alive long enough to get him to help, and no one else here could do it.

My hands trembled as I carefully pulled his shirt up. He stirred beneath my touch and his eyes found mine. When I reached down for the wound, his hand shot up and closed around my wrist.

"Alex…no."

"Shh."

"Please."

"You're badly hurt, you won't survive if I don't."

His eyes were barely staying open, but he did his best to keep his gaze on me and I could only imagine a fragment of how hard it must have been.

"I've got you; you'll be okay. I promise," I whispered, again getting my hand into position.

"Is he going to be okay?" Katya whispered beside me.

"Yes," I ground out. I wasn't about to fail him.

The familiar heat started to build beneath my palm and the power of Esper began to course through me. The powerful body of water under the Bridge that all Ceoran were sworn to protect would now be protecting me. Without Esper, we were powerless. It's where we drew our power from. Without it, we were as defenseless as humans. It took every single ounce of concentration not to break apart when I was already so drained.

"Damn it, we have company!" Kieran yelled.

"Where?" I heard Emelia reply.

"Coming from the east and the west," Morales responded.

"Alex, we don't have much time," Kieran called over.

He didn't need to tell me. I could feel the Reapers' power surging all around just as much as I could feel the energy of Esper rushing through me. It was too much. Too many things coming all at once. I ground my teeth and focused on Eric.

'Time to work your magic, Chancellor," Katya said gently, though I felt the edginess in her words.

"We're outnumbered, any great ideas, Kelly?" Morales yelled as firing erupted.

"Let me think for a beat. Keep them off Alex and Eric, we need to cover them."

While they formed a solid barricade between the oncoming attack and me and Eric, I focused on the task at hand.

The strain made my brain feel like it was going to explode. I held my breath and very clearly noticed that it did nothing to help me. Blood, or at least it's the only thing I thought it could be unless my brain was leaking, started pouring out of my nose.

Firing all around us kicked up while the power inside me raged to life. Just as it did, I felt another sensation roll through me. We weren't alone at the mercy of Reapers anymore. There were dozens and dozens of Ceoran, good Ceoran who had made it down here to fight on our side. They'd found us.

I ground out a strained cry as Eric drained more and more power from within me. His hold on my wrist tightened with each passing second and the build-up of energy forced a scream to erupt. As Eric's hold on my hand tightened, I felt myself go lax and collapse over him. I didn't fall, and I didn't feel the impact, instead I felt his arms around me, holding tightly and pulling me up against him.

"I've got you. I've got you," I kept hearing his voice repeat over and over as the aftershocks continued to make my body tremble.

I finally caught my breath and managed to slow my heart rate enough to look up at him. His face was white, the blood loss evident and his eyes unnaturally vivid and green, yet he still looked so perfect.

His hand cupped over my cheek, gently wiping the tears from my face with his thumb.

"You are seriously crazy, you know that right?" he asked, making me laugh.

"Just the way you remembered, right?"

"Exactly." He chuckled.

"Ah guys, reunion time can wait. We need to kick ass and then promptly leave," Katya called over.

That's right. There were a bunch of Reapers waiting to kill us while we were caught up in each other's arms.

Eric chuckled again and pulled me to my feet.

"Are you good to run?" he asked.

"I'll have to be." I bit back and hoped that the adrenaline of the fight would be enough. "Are you?"

"I'll have to be."

I grinned and together, with some newly found strength, we ran. Soon, Kristian, and the team he'd brought along appeared beyond the tree line.

"Thought you'd bailed on us!" Kieran yelled, a ghost of a smile on his lips.

"You know me, I like to keep everyone on their toes," Kristian replied, gesturing to the truck Carter had gotten out of. "We were occupied by the second tower, had a rough time getting out!"

Dropping the small talk, we all ran, rushing toward the waiting cars.

"You guys go, we need to hold the fort. Reinforcements are coming and we're going to need somewhere safe to stay," Morales explained.

"What?" Emelia shook her head. "We need you; you can't leave us now."

Both Emelia and Eric stood before this hardened woman, someone who seemed to be almost incapable of showing emotion, or at the very least, unwilling. Yet, as the siblings who I now saw had an uncanny resemblance to her long, wavy dark hair and bright eyes stood before her, pleading for her not to leave us. It all made sense.

"I wasn't there for you both when it mattered most, when you were growing up and becoming the wonderful people you are today. But I will be here for you now. I give you both my word."

"No." Eric shook his head, looking away.

"Look at me, Eric."

He turned and met her gaze and after a painful moment, she placed a hand on his shoulder. "I will not let you down."

A line in Eric's jaw pulsed but he nodded.

"You have your duty, and you must fulfil it," she said looking over at me and smiling, which was the craziest thing I'd seen all day. "And you have done wonderfully, both of you have. I'm proud of you."

Before either of them could say any more, Morales shoved Eric into the back seat beside me and closed the door, tapping the top of the car.

"Go now. I'll send word when this location is secure."

With that, Eric, Emelia, Kieran and I were leaving the smoke and the flames behind us letting Morales, Kristian and the rest of the Ceoran on our side do what they'd promised. They would rally people to fight with us and we would get to safety and find our new home.

CHAPTER SEVENTEEN
WE FOUND EACH OTHER

Alex

We'd been driving for hours before I'd lost count of the number of intersections and highway turnoffs we'd driven through. All I could say with certainty was that it was almost dawn now. There was a pinkish hue creeping across the sky as the blackness of the night bled into the coming day.

Eric was silent beside me as he clutched the spot on his chest where the bullet had very nearly cost him his life. He was as stiff as a log, not even the rise and fall of his chest made his body move. My body was strung tightly too. I felt the pull of Esper coursing through me whenever my mind recalled the faint beating of his heart beneath my fingertips. It's as though it knew what he meant to me on a deeper level. The whole thing was so strange.

Emelia on the other hand was overly animated. Maybe that's just how she dealt with tough things. She turned the radio on, heard the same, usual static then changed it to the CD that had been left behind when the Takeover happened. A few minutes into the song, she turned that off too and sighed loudly.

Kieran gave her a look and then let out a long breath.

"How do you feel?" I asked Eric.

He kind of stiffened, and then turned his head slowly.

"Weird."

"Weird how?"

"Like there's electricity running through me." He frowned.

"Are you in pain?"

"No." He shook his head and looked away for a moment. "It's like I can still feel your power. Like it's still inside me."

"Has that ever happened to you when you heal?"

He shook his head, leaning back into the car's mammoth headrest and turned his face to the window. I folded my hands in my lap and turned my attention outside my own window. My breath made a small cloud on the cold, frosty glass.

"Can't believe I was actually beginning to trust that asshole," Kieran said breaking the silence.

"Didn't really have a choice," I muttered.

"If he's not dead, I'm going to kill him myself if I see him again," Kieran ground out.

"He shot *me*, why are you pissed?" Eric said lightly.

Kieran's eyes snapped up to the mirror and then when glaring Eric down through a reflection wasn't enough, he turned back and gave him a look.

"If anyone's going to shoot your sorry ass, it's going to be me."

I shielded a smirk, glad that both of them were starting to relax. In all seriousness, it was horrific that Ashfield did what he did, but we all got out, *alive*. I couldn't let myself or any of the soldiers who'd come with us carry that. It was too much, too heavy a burden, one that would ruin us with distraction when we needed to be focused unlike ever before.

"We're going to have to stop for gas," Kieran announced a few minutes later.

"You do know we're in an apocalypse, right? There aren't functioning gas stations around," I said.

"Luckily for us, this car doesn't need much. We can get by on a minimal amount."

"Even minimal is going to be hard to find." Emelia sighed.

"If you're all going to be so damn miserable, I might just leave your asses on the side of the road," Kieran muttered.

Eric's lips quirked into a smile.

"There," Emelia said, pointing to a car parked off the road and down a shallow ditch. "Might find your minimal fuel there."

Kieran rolled his eyes and pulled over to the side.

"Watch my six," he said to Emelia.

"Watching your six," she confirmed.

Kieran and Emelia got out leaving me and Eric alone. While one checked the abandoned car the other watched ours. While they took their positions outside, I kept my radar up watching out for any signs of company.

Eric kept his gun at the ready. I would ask for a new one of those one day. Mine had been long since lost and it hurt knowing I'd lost something my father had given me, something which had saved my life more times than I could count.

I cracked my window, "Any luck?"

"We've hit gold on this one," Kieran replied.

"Won't always be that way," Eric muttered beside me like Kieran's celebration was for nothing.

"I know." Kelly sighed.

"Come on, guys, hurry it up," I called over to them. "I don't like being this exposed."

"Finishing up now," Emelia called back.

She opened up our car's tank and poured in the fuel they'd siphoned. Within a few minutes we were all back inside and back on the road. The tension lessened.

As much as we joked when we were out here, it was hard to look past the stress etched onto all our faces.

Danger was at every turn, hidden behind every tree. We didn't know who was on our side or who we could trust. That in itself became the daily challenge.

I looked over at Eric and felt a deep sense of sadness rush through me. For the first time in a long time, I felt emotionally vulnerable and I couldn't think around the sense of panic that coiled through me. I should have felt some semblance of comfort being with these three but instead all I could think about was the unknown. What if this was it? What if this is the way the rest of my life, however long that was, would be? What if we could never stop running?

Eric, as though he sensed the tumultuous emotions racing through me, scooted over and put his arm around my shoulder. For a moment I didn't know how to react, but that moment passed quickly. What replaced it was comfort, familiarity. I closed my eyes and rested my cheek on his chest.

"Rest, Alex," he whispered into my ear. "You're safe with me."

***

Eric

Alex fell asleep the second she closed her eyes and the shallow rise and fall of her chest deepened, evening out. She was exhausted and it didn't take the obvious notion of her sleeping to know it. I felt

200

the aftershocks of what she'd done course through me for hours, as though we were somehow linked. I couldn't even imagine how damaging that much use was to her.

The thought scared the hell out of me. I'd seen that kind of power only once before and that woman met a very early, very tragic end. She was a Seer, the kind of Ceoran we kept hidden away and used entirely too much for our own advantage whenever we needed them. She was only twenty-nine when her soul gave out. She couldn't harness the power anymore and the Council used and used until she just ceased to exist. I shuddered and tightened my hold around her.

"We need to talk about what we're going to do next," Kelly said, meeting my eyes in the mirror.

"I know."

"One option right now is to keep heading south toward our safehouse and stay off the main roads and keep her away from all Ceoran," he explained.

"Another option is to take shelter, and ask Dad for help," my sister said, turning to look at me.

"Both options suck." I sighed and looked out at the rising sun on the horizon, continuing to run my fingers through Alex's hair. Having her right here with me was surreal and I wouldn't take it for granted.

"Which option sucks less then?" Emelia asked.

"Honestly, I have no idea right now."

Kelly slowed and pulled over when we reached the next highway exit. "We need to choose, Raine."

I pinched the bridge of my nose and nodded. "Get off the main road, keep heading south and when we're sure we're safe for the time being, I'll find a way to reach Dad," I said, looking directly at my sister. A compromise if ever there was one.

"Find a way?" she deadpanned. "How do you plan on doing that?"

"Somehow," I snapped. "Let's keep moving, we need to get to shelter before we're caught out here."

Emelia gave me a pointed look.

"I promise I will call Dad. I'm not looking to be a hero out here. Not after everything."

"Fine."

Kelly took that as his cue to go.

He turned off the highway and started heading for the smaller, less traveled roads ahead.

"We need to talk about Morales," Emelia said.

"Later."

Kelly kept his eyes ahead and his foot on the gas. We were making good time and I hoped it would be enough rest for Alex.

Given the amount of time we still had to pass, I settled into the seat and tipped my head back.

Emelia had the same idea. She turned the heater up and closed her eyes.

Kelly met my gaze in the mirror again. "Get some sleep, brother, you need it."

"You sure?"

"Definitely."

He smiled and returned his attention to the road.

It didn't take long for Alex's gentle breaths and steady heartbeat to help me drift off to sleep.

Alex

The warmth all around me woke me first, then the gentle strokes through my hair and quiet chatter.

I cracked my eyes open and noticed Eric's hand on my arm.

"Did you sleep well?"

"Yeah, really well." I smiled, looking up at him and straightening in my seat.

"We're here."

I followed his eyes to the front. "What exactly is here?"

A small building appeared before us. I peered through the window and frowned when all I saw was a quaint cottage with weatherboard panels and a cute bay window at the front. For all I knew, it could have been a little old lady's forgotten retirement project. But as we approached and a laser grid blocked our entry, I realized that no little old lady owned this, unless she was a doomsday prepper or general badass. Worst thing was, you couldn't really see the faint lines of the lasers unless you looked at just the right angle. It gave off major *Resident Evil* vibes. That scene where the laser spread out into a thousand small squares and chopped the guy up made me rethink wanting to stay here.

"This is a safehouse Kelly and I set up years ago, it's not owned by the Ceoran, it's owned by us," Eric explained.

"Em, you're up," Kieran said drawing my attention to the front.

"Magic time," she muttered, jumping out of the car clearly not seeing the horror in the situation like I was.

She approached the long metal pole that housed the very ominous laser grid and pressed her hand to it, touching the surface in a few different spots. After a few seconds where nothing apparent happened, I saw a small hatch open outward revealing a control panel. Emelia grinned at us and reached into her pocket and pulled out what I could only describe as a Frankensteined screwdriver— one end was a small blade concealed beneath a bit of fabric and the other was a flat, spatula looking thing. She turned back to the hatch and jammed the blade end under the control panel where it seemed to be installed into the hatch and then when a screeching, wailing sound started, she got to work typing something into the keypad all while humming something overly cheery I didn't recognize.

I didn't see what she was doing but a few seconds later, the screeching stopped, and the laser grid vanished.

"We're good to go," she said waving Kieran through.

"If this is owned by the two of you, why are we breaking in?" I quirked my brows.

Eric chuckled. "We're not breaking in. It's a false code reader made to look like Ceoran security. That *screwdriver* Emelia used is actually a key, it was Kelly's idea."

"How is she going to get in if she has to hold the key in place?" I watched as Kieran drove through and Emelia hung back.

"It gives us thirty seconds to make it past before it all comes back online."

"Thirty seconds?" I balked. "That doesn't seem like a long time."

"Long enough if you run, but not long enough to let uninvited guests in either," Eric explained.

Kieran parked the car in front of the garage and I looked behind us and watched with fascination as Emelia pulled the screwdriver-key thing free, shoved it back in her pocket and skipped across what would have been the laser grid barricade reaching us as the laser grid came back online.

"She's theatrical, loves putting on a show," Eric said gently, his breath tickling the back of my neck making all sorts of feelings rise to the surface.

Hyperaware of the very obvious goosebumps erupting across my skin, I pulled my sweater back up over my neck and hoped that he wouldn't see.

"We're safe here, at least for the next few nights," Kieran explained, getting out first.

We all followed suit and I kept my eyes down and away from Eric knowing how red my face was turning.

Eric walked past me, his arm brushing mine as he did.

I brushed the spot where his skin had left a burning trail and followed Emelia into the house.

"You should definitely get some rest. You're looking a little flushed," she said.

"Yeah, you're probably right, though we have the entire day ahead of us, I don't want to sleep again now and mess up my body clock."

"Trust me, with what you've been through, you'll pass out the second you hit the pillow now and tonight. Go," Emelia said gently.

"She's right, you do need rest. That car nap wasn't sufficient," Eric added.

Emelia grinned and then looped her arm through mine at the elbow. "You and Eric can take the room at the far left; I'm staying up front with Kieran to keep watch."

"What about us? We can help."

"No deal." She shook her head. "You need rest and Eric does too. He's the strongest one of us to guard you and he's looking a little worse for wear right now."

"I don't need a guard."

"Girl, you need a guard now more than you've ever needed anything in your life."

I shot her a look and Eric stayed uncharacteristically silent on the matter.

"Seriously, though, you saw what they did back there and even worse, they saw what *you* did. That power? They're itching for it now. They're going to be coming for you and they can take every single one of us out without even blinking. That laser grid out there will slow them down, but that's it. We get maybe two, three minutes tops for them to work out how it runs and where the weak points are. If we're lucky."

"And if we're not?"

"Then let's pray they don't like toying with their food."

I shivered.

"I'm not trying to scare you, but it is what it is."

"You're right. I know," I said, straightening.

Everything that was happening now was because of the decision I made weeks ago to see Silus and risk exposing myself. I did that, but I would have done it over and over if it meant saving Eric. But I had to live with the consequences now.

"Get some rest. We all need you to be on your a-game," Kieran said before giving us a quick smile then disappearing toward the front of the house, Emelia in tow. I looked away and only lifted my gaze when I felt Eric come to stand beside me.

"Come on, I'll show you to the room."

"Guess sleep isn't the worst idea." I sighed.

When we reached the end of the hall, he opened the door and peered inside. There was one bed with military corners, two pillows placed neatly in front of the wooden headboard. Beside the window blocked by thick black bars, there was an armchair, a small coffee table and not much else. On the muted grey walls there were paintings made up of blacks and blues, white streaks slashing through the canvas in places. Abstract, haunting—it was like everything else in our world. There was an adjoining door which I sincerely hoped was a bathroom.

Eric gestured for me to enter. Once I did, he secured the door behind us and crossed the room and peered outside the window.

"Are we safe here?" I asked.

"For now, yes."

"But you're not happy that we're here."

Eric scrubbed the back of his neck and walked over to the bed and sat. "No, not in the slightest."

"It's your safehouse, do you not trust it?"

"I trust the safehouse and the people here. I just don't trust what's out there. If the Reapers managed to find us before, I don't think hiding out here will stop them now but we had to make a decision."

Great. I sighed and sat on the opposite end of the bed and crossed my legs facing him. Dark circles had formed under his eyes, his shirt was stained with dried blood and his cheeks were still speckled with ash and soot. His chest rose and fell sharply, and every so often there would be a shudder.

"Truth be told, Alex. I wanted us to go off grid together, without my sister or Kelly."

"You said you trust everyone here."

"I trust them."

"Then?"

He sighed, paced around the bed before turning back to face me. "I trust that us alone is safer, that's all."

"So why aren't we going out alone then, why did you agree to come here?"

"Because that plan kind of went out the window when that asshole shot me and you had to exert your energy to save me."

I bowed my head. "But you still think that plan is better than being here?"

"I do. Not just because I can protect us better without worrying about anyone else, but because there's less reason for Reapers to be scoping out a lone Ceoran. It's safer for us and for Em and Kelly."

"You're talking about shielding me."

"Yeah."

I shook my head. "No, that takes way too much energy. You cannot do that, not again."

"I can."

"Not without compromising yourself. When I was out there alone and you and Em were watching me from a distance, you had to do it, I get it. I didn't know who I was or how to fight them off. I do now, so no, there's no way you're using that much power to shield me again."

Eric frowned.

"I know you don't like it, but I'm right."

"Doesn't matter now anyway, we're here for a little while at least."

Silence settled between us but so, too, did the weight of what we were facing down. I didn't like being told I couldn't do something because of my own limits, so I could imagine how Eric felt. All I knew was that I was right about this and I was sticking to my guns. His life was worth more than his pride to me. I could only imagine the kind of pain he must have been in when he was shot. I did a good job healing him but that kind of pain would leave an eternal scar in your memory, and the way his hands trembled every so often confirmed it. He needed to look after himself.

After a moment, he opened his mouth like he was about to say something and then he dropped his gaze. I felt a shift between us. Something was weighing on his mind.

"What's going on?" I asked.

"It can wait."

"Considering things seem to change in our world in a matter of seconds these days, I don't think waiting is wise."

His eyes lifted meeting mine.

"Alex, I know about you and James."

My heart slammed into my ribcage as the words registered in my mind.

"What are you talking about?"

"You and James Ashfield had an arrangement, right?" he said gently. "I know you were together, to some extent. I know you never told anyone, and I get it."

I wet my lips.

"Did it mean anything to you?" he asked.

When I failed to answer, he got up, crossed the distance between us and took my hand kneeling.

"No. It didn't. It was…it was meant to help us. But when you and I started talking…I ended things."

"Okay."

"Okay?"

"I just wanted to know, that's all," he smiled gently.

"Eric, I…"

"I trust you, Alex. I just needed to know. It's okay."

Silence fell between us, and my heart stalled. Eric was tired, he was defeated and for the first time I had no idea what to say or do.

"Do you want to shower first?" I asked, gesturing to the bathroom.

"Yeah, I think that's a good idea."

After a long while, he got up and collected a towel from the dresser by the bed and disappeared behind the closed door. As the water turned on, I focused on trying to control my emotions and much to my relief, I didn't burst into tears. It had been a rough night and a long day. I buried my head in my hands and hung my shoulders. Damn I could really go for a full body massage right about now.

A few minutes later, the water was off and Eric appeared in the doorway, a small cloud of steam following him. My eyes traveled across his body which of course was only clothed in hip hugging trackpants which all the safehouses contained—basic change of Ceoran compound clothing, toiletries and towels. He and Kieran must have stolen these years before they'd even set this place up.

His wound—the huge hole in his chest—was now barely a small pucker of pink on his skin.

He seemed to be in a lighter mood, happier ever. His eyes met mine and a warm smile came in return.

"I'm staring. I'm sorry," I said.

"It's fine, you're allowed."

"Smart ass." I smirked. "I need a shower. A cold one."

He chuckled and sprawled out on the bed while I forced myself to stop gawking and get moving. I slammed the door shut and stripped, got in the shower and scrubbed all the blood away until my skin was raw.

Once I was done and satisfied that all the evidence of last night's battle had disappeared down the drain, I rummaged through the cabinets and found the supplied compound uniform.

The trackpants were decent, the sweatshirt was huge. I rolled the sleeves up and tied a knot in the side hoping that I didn't look like a child who was in over her head.

Eric had nearly died because of me. The rest of our group was nearly killed too. A sick feeling rolled through me, how was I meant to detach myself from feeling things?

Eric raised himself up on his elbows when I opened the door.

"Em brought some snacks over. It's not much but it's the best we could stash here that wouldn't spoil. There are some packs of mixed nuts, a trail bar and water."

"Perfect." I caught the trail bar he tossed over.

"If I'm not mistaken, you're meant to look happier after the shower than *before* you went in."

"I'm fine."

Eric got up and sat right beside me. For a moment I didn't move and neither did he, but when I expelled a long breath and dropped the cheerily packaged trail bar, he cupped my cheek and tipped my face up to meet his.

"I'm sorry about before, I shouldn't have brought it up now," he said.

"It's not that, I'm glad you came to me with it."

"Okay, then I hope you know that you can talk to me too, with whatever's on your mind," he said softly.

"I know I can."

"And will you?"

I pulled back. A small crease had formed above his eyes.

"Alex?"

"You nearly died because of me."

"No, I nearly died because Ashfield shot me. I lived because of you."

"I made you go back."

He shook his head. "You made a valid point and I agreed. Alex, this isn't on you. None of it is."

"I disagree."

"I know you do, and I know that nothing I say will make you think differently. But I'll say it just the same."

"I am dangerous, Eric. Your dad was right. Everything I do puts people at risk, and you shouldn't be out here with me. None of you should. It's not fair to put your lives at risk to save my ass all the time."

"See that's where I disagree."

I swatted the few more tears that fell and pulled my knees to my chest. Eric sat in front of me making the bed dip.

"This is exactly where I'm meant to be. With your crazy ass. Making sure you don't do something stupid alone."

"So stupid is okay if it's with you?"

"Damn straight. If we're doing stupid stuff, we do it together. That's the deal we made long ago, I know you don't remember it all right now, but someday you will."

"Oh no, I do remember that."

He grinned and I smiled to myself.

"I'm afraid that my crazy ass is going to get you killed."

"We're both messed up in different ways, Alex. I know you know that. I don't need to tell you because you've seen it. But the thing we have to hold on to is that we're here, together, whatever it takes. Not just because this is destiny or duty or whatever other cosmic crap you want to assign to it, but because it is my choice. It always has been."

He paused, watching me, waiting to see what I would say or do. Truth be told, I wanted to run, so, so far away that no one, not even Eric or his insane skills, could ever reach me. But I also wanted to fall into his arms and believe that everything would be okay, that somehow we could make it through this. I knew what my choice was going to be. I moved closer to him and I couldn't tell when the nerves started to fire inside me, because the next thing I knew, I was reaching up for his face. Eric moved beside me, his free hand cupping my cheek in response.

I closed my eyes and expelled a shallow breath.

His hand stilled and when I opened my eyes and found his gaze, his lashes lowered momentarily until he looked back at me.

"Don't go, okay?" I whispered.

"I'm not going anywhere."

I kissed him. Every flicker of energy inside me fired at once and when he twisted his hand through my hair, my skin erupted with goosebumps.

He pulled me closer and kissed me deeply until my body was pressed right against his, every muscle wound tightly.

My body remembered everything. I pulled him closer, afraid to let go and he eased us both down into the sheets. My legs moved on their own, tangling between his, my hands raked through his hair and coasted over his skin. He pulled the covers over us and with each breathless kiss, I found myself growing hotter and more impatient. My stomach tumbled into a mess of nerves but each time his hand grazed the skin on my stomach, or his breath tickled my cheek when we parted for air, I found myself spinning.

I pulled back, my hand clutching the fabric of his shirt while I focused on the hammering of my heart against my ribcage.

"Alex?" he whispered breathlessly. "What's wrong?"

"Nothing. Kiss me."

He did. Fiercely. Every time his fingers brushed the bare skin on my arm, I felt a little of the anxiety inside me chip away. And when his free hand reached down and skimmed the edge of the hem of my sweatshirt I inhaled sharply and lifted my eyes to meet his.

"Too fast?" he asked.

"No." I reached for his shirt and pulled it up and over his head.

"Are you sure?"

"Yes. God yes."

My face flushed as my eyes wandered over his chest.

I lifted my hand to his stomach and traced the line of the puckered pink flesh that had been burned, the same marks as mine, the same fate we'd both shared.

A coat of tears filled my eyes and Eric captured my hand in his and brought my knuckles to his lips.

"I'm so sorry that you went through this," I whispered.

"I'm not. You are the reason we are all here, breathing and fighting."

"With no home to go back to."

"It was going to happen no matter what you did. Maybe it would have come later, but it would have come."

I dragged in another deep breath and looked back over the scarred skin. When Eric pulled back slightly, I sat up and took my sweatshirt off.

His eyes widened slightly, like he was seeing me for the first time, and I guess in a way, maybe he was. The girl he'd said good-bye to was not the same girl here with him now. She was haunted and chased by ghosts of a world she didn't belong to, figuratively and literally. But she was also learning how to be a warrior again and that warrior would be damned if she didn't show Eric exactly what he meant to her.

Eric lowered his forehead to mine when I remained still.

"You disappeared for a moment, where did you go?" he asked gently, tipping my chin up.

"Nowhere, I'm right here."

I was done talking.

I brought my hand to his cheek and gently eased his face down to mine, letting the weight of his body settle over me. A small, shallow breath passed between us and the whisper of my name came next.

I closed my eyes and felt his lips close over mine again and then trail over my cheek, down my jaw pressing a few quick kisses to the sensitive spot behind my ear.

My entire body trembled as the warmth of Eric's body sent fresh shivers to the surface. When he pulled back to look at me, I pressed my hands to his chest and watched as he breathed in deeply, his chest rising and falling in time to the rhythm of my own heart.

He moved so fast after that making my head spin. He slipped his hand to the small of my back until our bodies were crushed together. I whispered his name and he whispered mine back between kisses.

When the air around us grew denser, I gently pushed him back and reached for the cord on his trackpants. For a moment we

215

looked at each other, clumsy actions kind of stilled until he lowered his lips over mine and I took it as my invitation to proceed.

My fingers fumbled with the band and trembled when I started pulling them down. But when he took over with a soft chuckle, I laughed and buried my face in his chest. This time he moved slowly, his palms grazed the delicate skin on my stomach and coasted over my ribs, gently taking his time until he reached the hem of my pants. I froze for a second, realizing that I'd forgotten how to breathe.

My head lifted and our eyes met. I closed my hand over his and guided it lower and lower, and when he finally undid my track-pants and pulled them down enough that I could slide out of them I snuggled up against him enjoying the warmth of his skin against mine.

"God, you're so beautiful, Alex."

"Still?"

A muscle in his jaw flexed. "What do you mean?"

My eyes flicked down to the burns on my arm, and a pit of shame coursed through me. The attack when the Reapers first breached our home compound had left more marks I knew would never fade, just like the memories that lay etched on my mind and the horrors of what I'd seen, burned into my retinas. It was a part of me I knew I could never get back, but it was deeper than that. It was the loss of my parents and the loss of who I was the day I lost my real family.

Everything after that day came to me in a tumbling mass of un-intelligible emotion. There were fragments of who I had been before colliding with the person I was now. Throughout all of that, Eric's face came in and out of focus and somewhere deep inside, there was the rest of me and everything I was yet to remember trying to break through.

That day when I lost my family in the blaze that tore apart more lives than I can even comprehend, a part of me was locked away for good. I wasn't the same Chancellor Eric was protecting and a part of me *wanted* the Clean Slate because it meant forgetting the anguish.

But now, as he held me and our bodies reacted to a symphony only we knew, I realized that it didn't matter if I never recalled everything before that point, what mattered were the memories I would commit to my soul now.

"Look at me." He tipped my chin up. "You've always been beautiful, and this doesn't change a damned thing."

"Am I like you remember me?"

"Exactly."

A smile pulled at my lips.

Before he kissed me again, his lashes lowered for a moment before his gaze met mine again. "I love you, Alex."

My heart slammed into my ribs as his eyes searched mine. All the emotion I'd held onto deep inside, the constant reminder that I didn't recognize myself, finally fell away. I wasn't afraid of who I was anymore, or of the notion that I would never remember everything from my past. In this moment I found a peace that I'd never felt before. Like this was how I should have been feeling all along. I didn't need to remember everything from who I was. I needed to focus on now and live in this moment.

The things that mattered, like how I felt around Eric and in his arms, were more important.

"You don't have to say anything—"

"I love you too, Eric," I whispered, twisting my fingers through his hair.

He chuckled and pressed a kiss to each of my cheeks before pressing a gentle one to the tip of my nose.

With that, all the other words and sentences and thoughts were set aside. In this moment all that mattered was us.

Eric kissed me and I kissed him back, getting lost as the minutes stopped counting and all that mattered was his lips on mine. When he slipped his hand under my hip, I held my breath bracing for him. Instead of that, he pulled back, his elbow pressing into the mattress beside my head, and he let out a low groan.

"We don't have any condoms. Obviously. I mean it's not like Kelly and I thought about *that* when we set this place up."

My cheeks flushed but I grinned. "I have the rod."

"No shit."

"I had it put in last year, and it's good for another two. All the girls in my class went together, so…"

He grinned and kissed me again. This time when I braced myself, my breath was stolen as his entire presence invaded me in the most perfect way. I closed my eyes and exhaled. This wasn't my *first* time, we'd been together before, those were the dreams I couldn't stop swooning over which I now knew weren't really dreams but rather memories. But the tumble of emotions buzzing around inside me were relentless, reminding me that it still felt so new, like going to sleep one night and not knowing what the next day would bring. You were still you when you woke, but maybe something in the universe changed you just a little, just enough to see things differently, to feel and experience in a new light.

Eric moved closer and deeper and I tangled my fingers through his hair needing to be closer, to learn who he was, to learn who I was. After the battles we'd fought and the time and distance that kept us apart, I needed to know him more than I'd ever needed anything in my life.

With a firm yet gentle maneuver, he brought our bodies closer and the small, broken breath that came free from his lips was almost enough to undo me.

Like all those dreams I'd had before I found him again, I felt the realness in his touch and in what he and I had shared and no supernatural erasure of memories could ever take that away.

With breathless gasps neither of us came up for air or paused to slow down.

I might've become someone different, and I might not have remembered everything that made me who I was before, but the things that mattered, the feelings that I needed, it was all right here. And above all, I knew that I'd gained something I didn't have before; I learned the most important thing. Eric was, and always would be, the reason I would continue to fight, the reason I would risk everything again and again. He would be there until the end, however close that end might be.

I held on tightly as all the emotions and pent-up fear and sorrow and joy and uncertainty all rolled through me making me cry out and bury my nails into his skin.

He repeated my name over and over until the tremors rolled through us both and exhaustion finally won.

Eric held me tight as I drew the covers over us once we'd both changed back into our clothes. I grinned like an idiot the entire time and then flushed even brighter when he kissed the tip of my nose.

"You're looking a little redder than usual."

"Shut it," I snapped back, a half-smile creeping up on me.

"Are you okay?"

"Why do you ask?"

"That was...kind of quick to rush into, I'm sorry."

"I'm not."

"You're sure?"

"I'm sure." I reached up and kissed his cheek. "I remember that with you."

"You do?"

"It's weird, and I'm about to sound like a total freak right now."

"It's cute when you're a freak."

I chuckled. "Well, then stalkerish maybe."

"Now you have to tell me."

"I dreamt about you."

"Oh?"

Again, my cheeks heated up. "I kept seeing you, small snippets of us together. Before, well before I actually *met* you in the forest that night."

"I've said it before but I'll say it again, it's crazy, Alex. I've never heard of anyone being able to recover memories after a Clean Slate. I don't think anyone has."

"Maybe you didn't do something right?"

"Not possible. I've been employed to perform it countless times, to various degrees because I was so efficient."

"Do you think something is wrong with me?"

"Nothing is wrong with you, Alex."

"Maybe it's the Reaper DNA."

"I don't know. Whatever it is, it's allowed you to make an almost full recovery."

"Does it scare you?"

His eyes found mine again. A deep, concerned expression looked back.

"Yes. It scares me."

"You think they can hurt me." It wasn't a question. It was a deep, fear-fueled realization.

"I know they can, and I know they wouldn't hesitate to. I just don't know what they're willing to do. That terrifies me."

"Given what they've already done, I wouldn't put anything past them." I shuddered.

"It won't get to that. You've got a whole army behind you now."

I nodded.

"Try to rest." He kissed my forehead and I snuggled into the soft covers.

"You know it's blaring daylight out there?" I murmured feeling my eyes start to close.

"I can see how not tired you are." He chuckled.

Within seconds, despite smiling at his comment, I felt my body get heavier and heavier. Eventually my eyes closed of their own accord and the warmth spreading through me carried me off to sleep.

CHAPTER EIGHTEEN
DUTY COMES FIRST

Eric

When Alex finally fell asleep, I rolled onto my back and closed my eyes, hoping sleep would claim me, at least for a few hours.

I must have dozed in and out for a while before restlessness and a racing pulse finally forced me back to lucidity. There would be no more sleeping. I pulled back the covers and swung my legs over the edge of the bed. There I sat for a few minutes listening to her breathing. Once I was sure I wouldn't disturb her, I carefully walked over to the door and slipped outside into the hallway. It was late in the afternoon at this point and the sun was hidden behind a thick cover of clouds, giving the outside world an eerie, dark blue hue. As I made my way through the silent house, I spotted Emelia outside through a window keeping watch on the perimeter. I stopped and watched her for a moment. Her back was to me, but her face was tipped up slightly, eyes closed as the gentle breeze carried her dark hair around her shoulders.

There was nothing I wanted more than to absolve her of her duties, to let her live a normal life. One that wasn't plagued with monsters and perimeter watches. But the truth of our world and birthrights was so much more than something any of us could escape. I sighed and continued down the hall in search of Kieran.

The hall was littered with peeling wallpaper and light fixtures that had long since fallen off. A stark contrast to the very new and very equipped rooms we were used to at the old compound. It was a trademark of the Ceoran and unfortunately for us we weren't able to source anything better when we put the plan into motion. Deadbolts and laser grids protected the assets, the rest wasn't important, so it wasn't touched. Rickety old floorboards continued through to the kitchen, which was thankfully clean and filled with basic necessities; Kelly and I had been incredibly diligent with our stockpile. I stepped onto the cool tiles that separated the hall from the kitchen and cursed, wishing I'd put on some socks.

"This place is as cold as a tomb. We should've probably thought about heating," I muttered, walking into the kitchen.

Kelly was seated at the bench and looked up when I approached and sat opposite him.

"Yeah, well. I don't think we ever expected to really use this place." He sighed.

"You're right about that."

"How are you feeling?" he asked.

"Better."

"Glad to hear it."

I looked over at the plans he had in front of him. It was of the fortified military complex we'd just escaped from, and two other compounds.

"Listen, Kelly, thank you for what you said back there."

His eyes met mine as he took a drink and handed me a mug filled with steaming hot coffee.

"The way things went with us was rough and I don't want to keep holding onto that," Kieran answered.

"Neither do I."

"I also know now that you did it because she made you."

Never had I considered telling him the truth about the way things went down that night. It would have made my life easier having him as a friend and on my side when I was grieving her after the Clean Slate, but it was my burden to carry and I should have been the one to take it to my grave.

"Truce?" he asked, holding his hand out.

"Always was on my end, brother."

"Because you have always been the bigger man."

We both smirked and settled into a comfortable familiarity. I drank my coffee and picked up the files Kelly had been looking over.

"What's the plan from here?" I asked.

"Everything we've ever banked on is now compromised and we don't know what is safe and what isn't. As much as I don't doubt your mom's ability to secure the towers, I don't want to rely on waiting for that alone. We need somewhere safe to stay, somewhere more secure with reinforcements and the possibility to stay longer term. I propose to wait it out here a few days, recoup and properly plan the next move."

"And contact my father?"

"If we can. Otherwise, one of these two compounds is what I'm proposing." He tapped the smaller drawings.

"Why these two?"

Kelly was one of the brightest Ceoran that I knew, and, despite being from a royal family, he actively placed himself into the soldier arena because he genuinely wanted to make a difference. I respected his opinions and the way his mind worked, but I couldn't understand his choice on this matter. Kelly was determined, though, his brows knotted as he nodded down at the bigger sheet with the schematics of the military installation.

"These two compounds are smaller but because of that they have something the bigger compounds don't—secure underground bunkers."

I quirked my brows following his train of thought.

"What about the numbers? Will we have enough cover should the locations become compromised?"

"Not necessarily numbers, but because of the fortification and the proximity to each other, we can utilize both locations, form a comms channel and ensure that only necessary trips beyond the walls are made."

"This is going under the assumption that the Ceoran within those walls are friendlies," I said.

"Yep."

"And you know that's a big assumption. We both know how deep this power struggle runs among our ranks. Those two towers are primarily Alex's people, not ours."

"Which works to our advantage. They won't be skilled enough to put up a fight."

A chill settled over me at the truth of his words. If we needed to, we could take all of them out, or at least enough of them to take the facility. The royal Ceoran refused to muddy their hands which meant that they rarely, if at all, trained in hand-to-hand combat. It was something Alex had been lobbying to change when she was in power, and I knew it meant everything to her to someday see us all as equals. I only prayed we'd get to see that in our lifetimes.

I let out a long breath and massaged the knots out of my shoulders. In some ways, I envied him for seeing things so optimistically; in others, I pitied him. He was a good man, but he was naïve. Chances of the Ceoran in those installations actually being friendlies was low, and I knew we could take the facility if we had to but I didn't think he knew what that really meant for us. It was an offence punishable by death for non-Royals like me to threaten, let alone hurt or kill Royals like Kelly. Kieran, no matter how much he mixed with us, was still one of them. He would never see the world like Emelia and I did. He would never feel the struggles we felt when they looked down on us simply for existing. I guessed that it didn't really matter now, did it? One way or another, I didn't think that we were all walking out of this.

"What do you think?" he asked.

"I think it's a good idea."

"Really?"

"Yeah," I said, "But we have to operate on the assumption that we're going into a den of wolves. We can't let our guard down."

"Got it."

"We need to map the terrain, know what we're working with in the area. Don't know about you but I can't remember it well enough to go out there confidently," I said.

"We do that tonight, get back in a few hours and get some rest before we move in the morning."

"I like it. I want to give Alex as much rest as we can."

There was a pregnant pause and then Kelly looked at me. "I'm happy you two found each other again."

A flush heated up my cheeks remembering just how much Alex and I *found* each.

"Don't worry, I didn't hear anything. I can just tell when you're happy. You're different and you haven't been that in a long time." He chuckled.

"That miserable usually, am I?"

"Yeah," he laughed. "You kind of are."

A hint of a smile broke its way to the surface before the dread fell over me again, "Kelly, give me your word that if anything happens, you'll make sure you get yourself and my sister and Alex out."

"Nothing will happen."

"You know how hostile Ceoran can be; things aren't like what I trained you for at the academy. This is real."

"I know it is. But I also know you aren't going to let anything go wrong. And, you would suck as a coach if you didn't train me well enough to take on some untrained royals."

"Fair point," I said, shielding a smirk.

That was the plan. Whether that eventuated or not was a different story. I finished the rest of my coffee in time for Emelia and Alex to both appear at the kitchen door.

"Hey," Alex said. Her cheeks were flushed with the subtlest hint of pink.

"Did you get enough rest?" I asked.

"I think so. Feel way better."

"Em, perimeter all good?" I nodded to my sister.

"Yeah, uneventful which is what we want."

"That's definitely a bonus."

"Did you sleep at all?" Emelia asked me.

Alex flushed beside her but Kieran kept a straight face being the respectful friend that he was.

"A little," I lied.

"You two should rest tonight, Eric and I will take over for the night watch," Alex suggested.

Kieran gestured at the table. "When we come back, for sure. There's coffee in the pot. Get your fix and then we're hitting the road again."

"We're not staying?" Alex knotted her brows.

"We are, but we need to scope out the area and map our terrain," I explained.

"What's the longer-term plan?" Alex asked, looking at Kelly then back at me. "I thought Commander Morales was going to call us back to the military towers?"

"Compounds three and four out in sector seven are our best bet. I want to create a ring and utilize their underground bunkers," Kelly explained. "I don't think waiting for Commander Morales to call us back is wise. We don't know how long it might take and you need to be somewhere secure."

"And the Ceoran in there?" Emelia asked, when Alex frowned at Kieran's response.

"Valid question and I don't have an answer yet."

"We're going in blind," Alex said.

"So to speak," I added.

Alex pinched the bridge of her nose and then sat at the dining table. Emelia handed out the coffees and sat beside her.

While my sister and Kelly discussed the specifics of what exactly they needed to map out, I kept my eyes on Alex who hadn't broken her gaze from me since she sat down. I didn't know what she was thinking, but I wanted to know everything. I wanted to know more. I was reminded of her and I was hooked. The taste just a few hours ago wasn't enough, I was addicted all over again and I'd missed out on too much time.

I cleared my throat and set my cup down a little harder than intended.

"Can I talk to you, please?" I asked.

She didn't say a word but instead replied by getting to her feet. Neither Kelly nor my sister paid us any attention. I followed Alex down the hall and into the room we'd shared.

As soon as I followed her in, I closed the door, and before she said a word, I cupped her cheek and gently pushed her back against the door and kissed her with everything inside me.

Her body relaxed into mine immediately and as quickly as my mind unraveled, her hands were tangled in my hair.

I gently pulled back and brought my forehead to hers.

"I had to make sure it wasn't a dream," I said.

Her lips formed a beautiful smile.

"I don't think I could have dreamt that up," she replied breathlessly.

"Neither could I."

"Eric, what are our chances out there. Really?"

"Of this plan working out?"

"Of all of this working out. Us surviving. Seeing the light after all of this is done."

"With the skill the four of us have and the Ceoran we do have on our side, I know we'll make it."

"Liar."

I forced a tight smile and wrapped my arms around her. The fact that she carried so much on her shoulders made a new sort of anger I hadn't known before begin to consume me. The Alex I had parted with those years ago had been through a lot, yet she was fierce and immovable. But the woman in front of me today was haunted, weighed down by the power raging through her veins.

The warmth I'd remembered was still there, though. She was still caring and loving, and everything I'd fallen for, but it was distant, like a part of her died that day when I took away her memories, and I would never stop blaming myself.

"You're so tense." Her voice dragged me back to the room. She tipped her face up and frowned. "What's wrong?"

"Nothing, all good."

"Well, I thought we were all good, then you just went quiet."

"It's nothing, asteraki mou."

Her eyes softened and she lowered her face to my chest letting out a long breath.

"Eric, can I ask you something?"

"Always."

I led her to the bed, and we sat side by side.

"Is Commander Morales your biological mother?"

"Yeah. Yeah, she is," I answered without hesitation.

When I didn't say anything else, she looked across at me and then hung her head. "I'm sorry that I don't remember, I mean I assume I would know something this big, right?"

I smiled, nodding. "Yeah, you knew. Only those closest in my circle do."

"Oh, Eric."

"She walked out on Dad when Em was only three; I was barely crawling, so I don't remember, but she did."

"What happened?"

"Duty came first. At least that's how Dad explained it."

"She was always a soldier?"

"Yeah. She and Dad fell in love quickly and intensely. The Ceoran Council suspended her, said she was losing sight of her mission and for a while she was fine with it. Em came along, things were great, and she slipped into the role perfectly. But after I was born things changed. She was reinstated. She jumped at the opportunity to go back to that life, and we were forgotten."

"Jesus, Eric. I'm so sorry. And I'm sorry I'm making you go through this again."

"Don't apologize for that, Alex."

She frowned.

"I just keep wondering if it was me, you know?"

"God, no, it wouldn't have been you."

"I just wonder whether it was too much, two kids and all. Maybe I was a shit child."

"No, Eric, I don't believe that for a second."

I bowed my head, shielding the frown tugging at my lips.

"Did you know who she was?" she asked gently.

"Not in the beginning. Dad wasn't too keen on us knowing about her, but Em is obsessed with knowing everything all the time, as you can see. And she dug it all up."

"How did Morales take that?"

"Well, two teenagers turned up at her door one day in the middle of the night out of nowhere. So, not too good."

"Is that what your father thinks of me? That one day they'll call me to the Council and I'll leave and hurt you?"

"Why do you ask that?"

"Because I made you do the Clean Slate, I'm not naïve. I know how that would have broken you. But it was my duty, right? I had to protect the knowledge in my head and that's how he sees what I did to you. I broke your heart, and I forced your hand."

I looked away from her. How could I have forgotten how perceptive she was?

"No, Alex, he's just…overprotective."

231

"No, I don't think that's it at all. But I appreciate you trying to say it is."

She folded her arms across her chest and looked away, her gaze landing on the small window encased in fortified steel.

When her eyes met mine again, I scooted closer.

"Was I there for you when you first found out who she was?" she asked gently.

"You were."

"I'm glad, because if I wasn't, I was a terrible girlfriend."

I chuckled. "You were there, you helped me a lot. And Em."

For a moment we sat with the information between us before she looked up at me with a steely expression.

"It makes sense, you know? Duty comes first. He's afraid that you will pay the price, again," she said.

"You're not going to have to leave, and if you do, I'm coming with you."

"I don't think there'll be a choice. I've already done it once, what makes you so certain that I won't have to make that kind of decision again?"

"I'll go down fighting for it not to come to that like I should have the first time."

She sighed and pulled back when I tried to wrap my arm around her. "Is this a mistake, Eric?"

"What?"

"You and me. Was it a mistake then? Is it still the same mistake now?"

"Are you asking because of Ashfield?" I frowned.

"I'm asking because everything started to go wrong when I risked your safety and position because I wanted to be with you."

It was the same thing I felt about risking her because of my self-ish need to have her in my life.

"No," I said firmly. "Regardless of why you left him, the fact remains that you did. Whether it was for me or otherwise, he would have had the same reaction."

"How can you be sure? Look at your mother, look at us. We're being ripped apart from every angle, by everyone."

"I am not my father, and you are not Morales. And Ashfield is a jealous jerk, we both know that. Always has been."

"But I am someone who isn't meant to be here, right? I'm meant to be someone who will fight for this planet and this race. Is there room for love, for *us*, in that?"

I was stunned into silence when the corner of her lips pulled down. She got up and paced the room, her hands resting on top of her head. A slow burn of fear blazed through my veins. Was she considering ending this? After we finally found each other again was she about to break us apart?

"Eric, I don't know if I can do all of this."

"You only do what you need to, that's it."

"And what if that isn't enough?"

"No one is expecting everything from you."

"Not yet."

I crossed the space between us and captured her hands to stop her pacing. "Hey, look at me."

She did.

"There is always room for things that matter, and I know I have failed epically on that front, but I won't again. I know where my loyalties, and priorities for that matter, lie."

"You are one mature man, Eric Raine."

"Have to be, Chancellor. I'm your guardian."

She gave me a tight smile and then wrapped her arms around me.

"You're braver and stronger than you know. And I'll be sure to remind you of it all the time," I said when she didn't reply.

"Thank you, Eric. I mean it."

"I know." I kissed the top of her head. "We should get back."

"The mapping begins."

"Yep." I chuckled.

CHAPTER NINETEEN
WE CAN'T WAIT FOR A CALL THAT MAY NEVER COME

Alex

While I freshened up—which basically meant I stared at myself in the mirror for ten minutes, then rushed off to take a cold shower because I blushed when I remembered our rendezvous—Eric and the others put together the basic plan for where and how we would complete our mapping of the area.

We had to make this shack our home for at least the next three days, which meant there was a lot we had to know about the surrounding areas, where our enemies might come from and what our contingencies were. There would be no room for error and absolutely no room for sloppiness. We needed to be sure that there were exit plans, contingencies if those didn't work, contingencies for those contingencies and so on.

I gathered my hair into a low bun and sat beside Emelia at the kitchen table. She was deeply focused on the old paper map of the surrounding area that she didn't even notice when Kieran placed a cup of fresh coffee beside her. She jumped, knocking some of it over before salvaging the rest, startling the rest of us at the same time.

"Jeez. Why so touchy?" Eric asked, forcing Kieran to snort while drinking his coffee.

My heart swelled. I was so glad that they'd made up.

Emelia groaned and wiped the coffee from her hand and the paper on which she'd spilled it.

"So?" Eric asked.

"So what?" her brows lifted.

"You're jumpy. Something on your mind?"

"Nothing aside from what we're facing," she said with a shake of her head. "Did you know that there are underground tunnels in the area?"

"I didn't think that would normally be part of Ceoran planning," I said.

"Yep. There's a whole maze of them. They run for at least six miles and they intersect at these two locations." She pointed to the red crosses she'd marked on the map.

Kieran pulled the coffee-stained paper toward him and mused. "What do you make of this?"

Eric turned the map toward him and studied it silently for a few moments.

"I think this is our best chance at staying off-grid when we move out."

"Nighttime cover too," Emelia added. "Safer than walking out there in the open."

"Alex, what are your thoughts?" Eric asked, kind of stunning me.

This wasn't my forte, nor did I have much training in this sort of thing. But I wasn't going to let this opportunity to prove my worth pass me by.

"I'm thinking that if we could find the tunnel system on an old map, surely others might have found it too. I guess I'm just worried that there could be Scavengers if not Reapers using it to make their way around during the day, or the night for that matter."

I glanced up at Eric and shielded a smile when I saw the beaming expression on his face. I must have said something right because a warm smile coming from Kieran confirmed it.

"You'll be a soldier in no time." Emelia grinned. "Not that you want to be, it's gross and cold all the time."

"Not all the time, don't scare the girl. Only when we have to go out in the snow with no shelter for days," Kieran added. "Even my royal ass can handle it."

"Guys, seriously," Eric snapped playfully. "It's not that bad, in fact those really hot days when we sweat out of our eyeballs really makes up for it."

I burst out laughing, as did the three of them.

"In all seriousness, though, I want to learn all of this. I want to be able to fight for myself," I said. "And for you."

"We'll teach you," Eric said firmly.

"You'll be one of the most badass soldiers out there once we're done, kid. Don't worry about that." Kieran grinned.

"And in the meantime, you've got the three of us watching your six and we have your atomic power watching over us," Emelia added.

I chuckled.

"Alright, let's get out there and start mapping the best way to get to sector seven. The sooner we finish, the more comfortable I'll feel about staying here." Eric folded his arms across his chest.

I beamed with pride and I was sure the dumb grin on my face said so too. Eric gave me a warm smile before he and Emelia started getting their weapons and maps ready, along with rations of food and water should we get stranded—military rules I imagined, not dissimilar to those my dad taught me.

Kieran turned to me when we were alone. "Are you holding up okay with all of this?"

"I am, yeah. Still feels new and a bit daunting, but I think I'm starting to find my feet again."

"What about physically? Are you alright?"

"I am."

He looked at me skeptically.

"I'm fine, really."

"I know how hard healing is for any one of us, even on the smallest scale, and you've done huge amounts in a short space of time. Can't be feeling too hot."

"I'm not one of you though, am I?"

His face hardened.

"It's the truth, isn't it? I'm a freak of nature, some weird hybrid thing that oscillates between good and evil. I don't quite function the same as all of you."

"You're not a freak of nature."

"You're right. I'm a freak born out of desperation."

"Alex—"

"Just calling it how it is." I sighed.

"What about your memories?" he asked, dropping it.

"I remember a lot, but not everything. It's frustrating to be honest, I don't know if I'll ever get it all back. I feel...broken?"

"You're not broken. Just missing a few pieces. When you find them, you'll feel better."

"*If* I find them."

Kieran shrugged. "The fact that you've already got most of them back, tells me you will."

"Maybe. Anyway, what do you need me to do for this mapping thing?"

"Eric's call but I would say for the four of us to split off into two groups; we can scout the area and cover more ground that way."

"Sounds good."

Eric and Emelia came back a few moments later and Eric handed me a small bag and another to Kieran. I peered inside and grinned when I saw a Glock, an earpiece and radio inside.

"Em, you're with Kelly, Alex you're with me."

"Got it." Emelia nodded slinging her own pack over her shoulder.

"Alex and I will scope out the underground since we've got our very own Reaper radar, you two will take the surrounding areas, focus specifically on the path we'll need for plan A, to get out of here."

"Plan B?" Kieran asked.

"Your call, Kelly. Mark it up and we'll reconvene in two hours. Everyone good?"

"Yep." I nodded feeling excited about the mission. I finally felt like I was contributing.

The sun had well and truly set and it was fully dark, aside from the eerie light the moon emitted.

Emelia and Kieran went toward the tall trees which had long since lost their green leaves, and instead loomed like creepy skeletons against the large moon.

"Good luck and stay safe," Eric called to them.

"You know us, Eric, we're the dream team." Emelia winked.

I could practically feel the annoyance rolling off Eric. He was serious and Emelia was the total opposite and I enjoyed seeing the two of them banter.

Once we lost sight of them, Eric and I continued along our path.

"Radar good to go?"

"Always is." I smiled, tightening my hold on the bag.

As we walked silently and close together, we ventured deeper into the woods, with Eric's knowledge of the area and my skill in surviving in the wilderness as our only real guides.

It didn't take long to reach the mouth of the hidden tunnel system Emelia had mapped out for us.

"Stay close and ready, I have no idea what we're going to come up against in there."

"I'm getting creepy clown vibes."

"As long as Pennywise isn't waiting for us, I'm good," he grunted as he worked to clear the overgrown grass covering the hatch.

"Yuck, don't even joke about that." I shuddered and helped him pull it open.

I nearly doubled over to puke when the smell radiated upward.

"Dear God. Something must have died down there." I swallowed back the bile and peered into the darkness with disgust.

Eric flicked on his flashlight and shone it into the pit. The rusty ladder was illuminated first, followed by the vines creeping up along it. All the way down the bottom there was sludge and God knew what else.

"Attach your flashlight to your body, do not lose it under any circumstances."

I did as he said while he secured his around his left hand.

"After you."

"Chivalry at its finest."

He grinned. "You know me."

I rolled my eyes and took a deep breath of fresh, non-stinky air and switched on my flashlight that was hooked to my belt. Then I began to descend.

Once I was halfway down, Eric started his descent.

As soon as I reached the bottom, I held onto the last rung I could reach and carefully tested the ground beneath me. When the squishy soil held my weight, I hopped off and moved out of the way.

I swept my light over the cavern. There wasn't much going on aside from leftover trash belonging to people who appeared to have squatted here months ago, some dead rodents and loads of tree roots which had grown through the soil walls creating a crisscross pattern of veins across the expanse of the exposed earth.

"Clear," I called up to Eric.

When he joined me, he took the lead with Emelia's well-drawn map as his guide.

"It says to continue straight for half a mile."

"And then?" I asked, keeping pace behind him and occasionally checking behind us.

That insidious feeling of being watched wasn't lost on me. I felt every hair on my neck with acute awareness. As we walked deeper the tunnel walls graduated from exposed earth to sandstone. It told me that these parts of the system must have been older and hopefully more secure. The feeling of creepiness didn't lessen, though. It also didn't help that there were creepy markings carved into the sandstone walls. Some looked like alien skulls with giant eye sockets; others were just arrows pointing in all directions.

"God, it's like an episode of *Ancient Aliens* down here," I muttered, taking my flashlight off my belt and instead securing it around my wrist.

Eric stood beside me taking in the creepy images. His eyes cast across the painted cavernous walls before peeling his gaze away.

"What do you make of them?" I asked.

"Nothing, just people being smart asses. Come on."

We walked through the tunnel until it narrowed and reached a sort of fork.

"Which way?" I turned in the tight quarters gesturing to the much wider path to our left and the tighter to our right.

"Right and up."

"Up?" I muttered, checking behind me again, hoping to have seen the last of the alien heads.

"Apparently."

I bit back the nerves and scooted closer to Eric. He didn't miss a thing, as usual, and swept his flashlight behind me.

"Something we should be aware of?" he asked.

"No. It's just creepy down here."

He gave me a quick look and returned his attention to the map and continued down the marked path. I shuddered. The occasional sweep of light from the flashlight illuminated the area enough for me to make out roots from the trees and plants above ground poking through, as well as crumbling walls every few yards or so. The entire tunnel system that we'd walked through so far smelt damp, like a football pitch after the rainy season. I gently pressed my fingers to the wall closest to me where some of the stone had come away confirming it was soaked, which made me wonder how it stayed so wet down here.

A sudden realization found me—if it stayed this wet, it meant that it probably flooded down here too and if we were caught here when that happened, it wouldn't be good for us.

"What is it?" Eric asked when I shone the flashlight at my feet.

"I think these tunnels are prone to flash flooding."

He swept the light across the ground we stood on and ahead. A muscle in his jaw twitched.

"I'd say by the inch of water we're standing in, that you're right."

"What do we do?"

"Keep moving, the water must go somewhere to drain. We find that, we're safe."

I nodded and followed him through the darkness. Once we reached the end of the path, he turned right and then stopped abruptly.

"What is it?" I tried to look over his shoulder as the tiny tunnel tapered to a close at the end.

"There's no up."

"You're kidding."

"Have a look. It's closed off."

I stepped around him, very aware of the proximity in which we found our bodies.

His breath was hot on my cheek as I moved past him.

Just like he said, the *up* we needed was gone. I pressed my fingers along the ceiling and felt around for any sign of a door. When I came up empty, I turned back to him.

"Can I look at the map?"

He held it out and we both shone our lights on it.

For a moment I thought this expedition was over before it even began, but, as I studied the map closer, I recognized something I'd noticed on the way down.

"The creepy alien heads."

"What?" Eric asked, leaning closer.

"Those creepy alien drawings we saw on the walls before."

"What about them?"

"I had this weird feeling like we were being watched in that area."

"Are you sure it wasn't just the weird vibes freaking you out?"

"That's what I thought at first. But no, I think there genuinely was someone, or *something*, watching us. I think the hatch we're looking for is there. I think this part of the tunnel wasn't mapped or, if it was, maybe it was done in reverse, on purpose."

"Good call."

"I didn't like what I felt there though. I've no idea what's waiting for us."

"Did it feel like anything you've felt before?"

"Like Reapers but not, I don't know. It's strange."

"Well, we don't really have much of a choice, do we?"

He was right. I didn't like it though. Slowly we began tracing our way back while I focused on the Reaper radar within. As we neared the alien heads, I slowed and Eric placed himself in front of me, his gun trained ahead.

"How are we looking?" he asked.

"I don't sense Reapers. But there is that *something* else up there."

"Is it safe to proceed?"

"I don't know," I said, feeling the anxiety start to creep up on me. My body was starting to react to the imminent threat. That was the only way I knew that whatever was waiting up there, wasn't good.

"Can we handle this, Alex?" Eric asked, suddenly serious.

"We're going to have to. We need this access point."

"I'm not okay with putting you at risk so blindly. We should regroup, bring the other two with us."

"No time. We have a little less than an hour now to get this mapped and make it back to our safehouse, even though I really think we should wait for your mom to contact us."

Eric sighed, lowering the flashlight. "We can't risk waiting around for a call that may never come."

"I get you don't trust her but—"

"It's not about trusting her, Alex. It's about the reality of our situation. You saw how hopelessly outnumbered we were at the military towers; you saw how quickly the Reapers overran the entire thing. We don't even know if she got out, and if she did how likely is it that they were able to regain control of the towers?"

I closed my mouth and exhaled sharply through my nose. "This is your plan, Eric; I'm just trying to see all possible sides to it. One of those sides is us going into that access point, the other is waiting for your mom to contact us."

"You understand what you're suggesting?"

"I do. But we have no other options here. I'm scared of what's up there. I've never felt anything like it, but I'm more afraid of what tomorrow looks like if we have nowhere left to go, and since you don't think waiting for Morales to get back to us is a good idea, we have to go up."

"Damn it." Eric scrubbed his jaw and looked up at the barely visible lines outlining the door we missed earlier.

My stomach tightened and my mouth went dry.

I did not want to do this. God, I didn't want to do it at all.

"Stay behind me at all times, okay?" Eric said.

"Yeah, got it."

Eric got to work clearing the growth from the hatch door and then carefully and very slowly opened it. After waiting a couple of seconds, he hoisted himself up just enough to peer through the crack.

"Looks clear," he whispered.

I exhaled and focused on the sensation starting to get stronger.

He hoisted himself up into the crawlspace and reached down to help me up.

Together we moved silently through the darkness. There was no sandstone here. The entire thing was crudely dug, barely wide and tall enough for a fully grown man to crawl through. There was no wiggle room, no way to know what else shared this space with us. Using the flashlight was dangerous and being so out of our comfort in the pitch black was terrifying.

As we neared the end of the crawl space, my anxiety started tripling. Every nerve was firing as the dense darkness grew colder and staler and that soul-destroying feeling slammed into me.

"Eric, hurry," I hissed.

He sped up his pace, and just as I saw a sliver of light filtering through up ahead, a sickening stench permeated the small space and a splitting moment of pure fear shot through me. It was too late. I knew it before anything else even happened. A sickly pale, bony hand shot up through the ground under me and wrapped around my wrist pulling me down.

"Alex!" Eric's scream echoed in the chamber above as I was dragged through the dirt, down into the previous dead-end tunnel we'd come from and into another opening we'd missed before.

Chapter Twenty
Lake Creatures

Eric

My heart slammed into my ribs as I threw myself through the cavity Alex had been pulled through. My nails scraped and scratched through the crumbly earth. I did everything possible to ignore the splintering pain as I hit rock and clay at every turn. With a final desperate claw, I broke through the bedrock. I dropped into the tunnel we'd walked through earlier and into the new opening that I saw now ran diagonally to the one in the ceiling. "Alex!"

My knees pounded through the sloshy mess as I clawed my way through the narrow tunnel following her screams.

By the time I pulled myself into another, previously unseen, open cavern, I shot to my feet and looked around. She'd gone quiet and everything was eerily still. "Alex!" I shouted again and then waited.

No response.

"Alex!"

Nothing.

"Damn it!" I yelled into the musty air. "Alex, answer me!"

I flicked on the flashlight and swept it across the space. As the beam of light erratically danced across the cavern, I noticed how much my hands were shaking. There was nothing. No sign of foot-prints. No signs of life. They couldn't have just disappeared. I kneeled and pressed my palm to the wet earth between my feet, hoping to feel something, any flicker of an essence belonging to her, or even vibrations of movement. But there was nothing. It was completely devoid of life. In fact, the entire cave was.

I dragged myself back up and rushed further into the cave, com-ing upon another tunnel, something we hadn't seen on the map Emelia had given us, and continued along. It opened up into an even bigger cavern with a dark, unnaturally still, black lake right in the middle. This must have been where the water drained.

My senses were immediately struck with the stench of death and the heaviness of trapped souls. I shone my flashlight around and my entire body went rigid when the light landed on corpses hap-hazardly discarded around the cave, some right beside the water, others floating face down on its glistening surface.

I pulled my collar up over my nose and let my feet carry me closer. They were all at various stages of decomposition, but they had all been dead for weeks, if not months. My racing pulse settled. None of them were Alex.

Once I managed to think straight, I unhooked my gun which was thankfully attached to my person rather than in my bag which was well and truly lost, and continued sweeping the cavern. It was the worst possible situation. I'd lost the map so I had no idea where I was, and more importantly I'd lost Alex. Kelly and Em wouldn't know where we were or what was down here, and I had no way to warn them. The radios didn't work down here, and the earpieces were useless.

The only thing I could do was keep searching.

But first, I had to work out what the hell was down here with us and what took Alex.

***

Alex

My body was lax and completely numb like the last time I went to the dentist for some fillings. Four injections of anesthetic later, my entire face was numb for hours. Nothing moved and the only thing I could feel was a bone chilling cold blowing on me.

I was wet. My pants were torn, and my shirt was either ripped or missing.

All of that I managed to gather by the way certain parts of me were more chilled than the rest, the parts with exposed skin on mushy ground.

There was a sound of trickling water off in the distance, and weird gargled kind of groans. It didn't sound human but it didn't sound Reaper either which was confusing as the sensation definitely felt like Reaper. I tried to move. Nothing worked. I tried to look around, but my range of sight only went so far. Somehow, by some sheer chance of pure dumb luck, my flashlight had fallen nearby and produced enough light to illuminate a dark body of water and not much else, but what I did see scared me into complete silence.

Panic sent a rush of bile to the surface which made me choke on my own vomit. Reactive tears wet my cheeks and made the creatures off to my right turn in my direction.

I had to get up. I had to move.

My body shook as fear set in and the cold raged through me.

The creatures got closer, and I could now see what I hoped to God I had imagined before. They looked like the alien creatures depicted on the walls when we'd first entered the tunnel system. They were tall, lanky, and their clumsy movements made them appear as though they were moving through a strobe-lit nightclub. Where there should have been eyes, there was only the sickly pallor of their grey-and-white skin; there was no nose, just two, narrow slits and a large mouth that was too round and too large to belong to anything living on this planet. One of them hissed as it approached and bared unnaturally sharp teeth which went all the way around like a lamprey.

The second one shoved the hissing one out of the way and grabbed my ankle and started dragging me toward it, and the further it pulled me, I realized we were getting closer to the water.

There was nothing I could do as my limp body was being pulled through the wet mush.

Think, Alex, think.

I opened my mouth to scream and when nothing came out, my stomach dropped. The creature continued battling the other one for what I assumed was going to be its meal. I couldn't think around the panic coursing through me. They were going to drown me or break me into pieces or eat me. This was not how I envisioned my death.

This wasn't real. This couldn't be happening—

"Alex!"

My eyes snapped up in the direction of Eric's voice. Oh my God. He was going to get eaten too and I couldn't warn him.

"Alex, say something!"

The creature dropped me and turned to the other one. My body landed in unbearably icy water which immediately made my lungs seize up. There was a moment of silence where they just stood staring at each other with their bald, faceless heads tilted.

When the sound of Eric's footsteps got louder, they started toward him. Oh no.

My eyes followed the pair as they kind of crawled on all fours and awkwardly ran on their legs.

When they turned a corner, I lost sight of them from my vantage spot on the ground.

Their clumsy footsteps quietened and all I could hear were Eric's careful ones. I spent all my energy focusing on him and totally missed that where the creature had dropped me, was completely soft and there was no solid structure under me. The water which had simply wet the back of my head, was now covering my ears and with every terrifying minute that went past, I was sinking deeper into the water. This is where all the floodwaters must have gone, which had of course compromised the structural integrity of the entire area.

This could not be happening. I was not going out like this. I tried to move again and this time, thankfully, my right hand shifted, then my left foot. It was a small movement, but it was better than before. I continued struggling against the ticking of my imminent death and through every small movement that freed up my ears from the pool of water, I heard fighting and then a gunshot.

No, Eric.

I had to get out of the water. I had to help, and I would be no helping dying in what I assumed to be a murky, underground lake.

A second gunshot fired and at the same time I managed to free my entire arm from the paralysis. My celebrations were short-lived because the second I pulled my hand free from the vacuum the sludge had created, the semi hard surface on which I'd been floating on, gave way.

Oh, give me a break.

My body went under water, and like I was watching it all in slow motion, my face did too. In seconds that seemed to stretch an eternity, the black water had covered my eyes and all I could see was the darkness with flickers of light from Eric's approaching flashlight. It felt like a cruel, cruel glimmer of hope. I couldn't even splash to tell him where I was, I couldn't alert him at all. I'd disappear beneath the inky blackness and that would be it. I'd simply vanish, cease to exist. No one would ever find my body. I'd sink to the bottom and become one with the lost souls that had succumbed to the lake creatures.

As the seconds ticked away and my lungs involuntarily inhaled the icy water, I sunk deeper and deeper into the lake's depths until I could no longer see anything but my own death reflecting back at me in the obsidian blackness.

***

Eric

"Alex!" I screamed for her.

She had just been here, she had to still be here. I shoved my hand through the string hanging off the back of the flashlight and tightened it enough to know I wouldn't lose it.

My eyes darted from left to right as I ran wildly sweeping the beam of light across the shore of the eerie lake. I stopped abruptly when I saw a hideous, humanoid creature scurrying toward me.

What in Karatoi's name was this and where was Alex?

The second I spotted a depression in the ground where the mud beneath the water seemed to be disturbed, I made a run for it, hoping that I would make it before they reached me.

Before I could make it any further, it cut across the sloshy ground, stunning me with its speed and slammed into my body sending me flying backwards into the air and crashing into the water a few feet away.

"No!" I screamed, realizing how much time this had cost me.

I sucked in a deep breath, coughing up the water I'd inadvertently swallowed and spotted the source of the assault. It was tall, faceless and truly horrific. With awkward, quick movements it ran at me and wrapped its hand around my throat cutting off a breath.

We grappled in the water, all while my mind raced to Alex. She'd been under for too long. I was wasting time here. A rush of panic gave me the last burst of energy I needed to dispose of the creature. I threw it down firing the last bullet in the chamber straight into its faceless head and shoved the corpse out of the way.

I rushed back to where Alex had gone down, fighting against the pressure of the water lapping at my legs and dove in, praying to whoever would listen that I could find her in these inky depths.

My eyes burned in the black pool and my lungs screamed for air as minute after minute passed without finding her.

As the last few seconds of oxygen disappeared, something grabbed onto my hand which made my heart lurch. As soon as I felt delicate fingers tighten around my hand, I gripped her and pulled her up.

Her arms wrapped around me and I hauled her close to my body and pulled.

The moment we broke the surface of the water, I sucked in greedy breaths and turned to Alex, quickly sweeping the flashlight around the shore to make sure we were alone.

"Asteraki mou, say something."

"I cannot tell you how glad I am not to have died in this gross lake." She spluttered, coughing up water.

She looped her arm over my shoulder as we both swam back to the shore.

"Are you okay?"

"I couldn't find my way to the surface, it was all so weird in there, like the water didn't work normally," she said breathlessly.

"What happened?"

"No idea, whatever those things were, had numbed me somehow. Probably to eat me."

"Can you move now?" I asked when we reached the shore.

"Yeah, I'm good. I think it was wearing off in the water. Although, it would be nice to get some new clothes."

When she said that, I immediately noticed that they had scratched her up as they dragged her through the caverns. Her black tank top was shredded, probably from being pulled through the tunnels. Her jacket completely gone, lost somewhere. Upon closer inspection, I felt anger seize my muscles when I saw the cuts and bruises across her body.

"Let me help you."

"No, Eric, don't."

"I can do it."

"I know you can, but I don't want you to. I need your strength, all of it."

I frowned. The notion that she didn't see me as strong enough to fight and protect her hurt.

"Eric, I didn't mean it like that."

"It's fine, I understand."

"Can we please just get out of here." She folded her arms across her chest.

The cold was truly settling in now. The stale air in the cavern seemed to move just enough to cause a chilling breeze on our wet bodies.

"We need to find shelter first," I said sweeping the light in front of us.

With some luck, I managed to find the way back to where we'd come from.

"We lost the map?"

"We did. And I saw more tracks leading into this cave. There are more of them in here somewhere and I'm betting they won't be too happy to see their dead pals."

I handed her bag back, glad that I'd managed to find it on the way here, and started heading back the way I came. Alex stayed silent behind me, but I could sense the heaviness between us and it wasn't just the eeriness of this place.

As we walked past the two corpses who were bleeding into the soggy ground, I noticed that their blood wasn't like ours, it was kind of purple and thick.

"Guess those etchings make sense," Alex said behind me.

"Creepy as hell."

"What are they?" she asked.

"No idea. I've never seen anything like it. But I did see a bunch of dead people back there when I was looking for you."

"You think these things have been here a while?"

"Maybe."

Alex sighed and I kept walking.

"What about Kieran and Em?" she asked.

"We have no way to warn them or find them. Our radios are useless down here. We need to find somewhere quiet and small, with only one way in and out. Lay low, recoup and warm up. Then we'll backtrack our steps and find the map and our way out."

"What can I do?"

"Keep checking for those things, you sensed them before so now we know what that feeling was."

"Okay."

She fell into step behind me and we continued through the musty tunnel system. Once I reached the fork, I stopped and checked the tracks. I'd come from the left, so our best chance of find the map was there.

"This way."

We continued silently until I spotted the crumbled, trodden on mess of the map in the distance. Alex shone her light on it while I checked the damage.

"Can we use it?"

"No," I ground out, holding it up to the light. "It's completely ruined."

"Great."

"Come on." I discarded the map and started back to the fork. "There weren't any safe spots back this way, we need to find somewhere else."

We got to work scouring the small pathways and checking each crevice when Alex stopped and called me over.

There was a small crawlspace, tiny and difficult to get in to but it met all the criteria. It had one way in and one way out. It was big enough for the two of us, though we'd be completely in each other's pockets.

"It'll do. We can seal the entrance."

"I'll find some stones."

Together we set off to find whatever we could use to barricade ourselves inside for at least a few hours, long enough to rest. Once the pile had reached halfway up the entrance, I nodded to her.

"I think that's enough."

Alex crawled inside first and I handed her stone after stone until they were all inside. Then, I squeezed my way in and we set the stones up to form a wall, sealing us in.

Once we were done, I sat back against the makeshift door and wiped off the sweat forming on my neck.

Alex peeled up her soaked tank top and my eyes quickly followed. She winced every time she moved and she kept her eyes down and away from me.

That persistent ache in my gut intensified. Seeing her like that and not being able to do a damned thing to help was torture.

I shuffled my way over to her.

"Before you say anything, I'm not going to heal you. But you are freezing, and we both need to stay warm."

She let out a shallow breath and scooted over. I carefully placed myself behind her and wrapped my arms around her waist when she laid back down.

I buried my chin in her hair and inhaled deeply.

"I'm sorry I'm not strong enough to do this for you."

"You are strong enough, but I don't want to risk both of us being compromised."

"I know, and you're right. It's wise, it's very *me*."

"Very you?" she chuckled, turning in my arms.

"Yeah, you know, logical."

"Oh." She smirked. "I should stop that then, we can't both be logical."

"No, probably not." I cupped her cheek and held her close. Her soft lips explored mine and the cold seemingly vanished. When she pulled back and looked up at me, I couldn't help the grin that formed on my lips.

"I think we're both pretty gross from that nasty lake water, but I think all things considered, this is okay."

"It's totally okay."

She chuckled and settled against my chest. While the proximity was keeping us both warm, I wasn't blind to the fact that she'd nearly drowned and we'd both been exposed to abnormally cold temperatures and water. She trembled consistently until I felt her fall asleep in my arms. My muscles, too, ached with the constant shaking but soon enough, even I felt sleep claim me.

CHAPTER TWENTY
FOUNTAIN OF YOUTH

Alex

A weird sensation caught my attention first, breaking me from my unusually peaceful sleep. I cracked my eyes open and stirred enough to notice nothing seemed out of the ordinary.

Eric's arms were wrapped around me tightly, and his legs tangled with mine. I grinned sheepishly and reached up to brush a strand of hair that had dried on his forehead.

He smirked, startling me.

"Sorry, couldn't help it." He chuckled, pressing a kiss to my forehead. "What woke you?"

"Not sure." I craned my neck again and saw nothing.

Our little cozy cave was the same as we'd left it before we fell asleep and none of the stones had been disturbed.

"Are the creatures back?"

"I don't think so." I sat up and Eric moved beside me readying his gun.

"I'm not about to be surprised again."

"Good idea."

I shuddered thinking about being dragged through a freaking hole and used as a midnight snack for whatever weird alien lurked down here.

"How's your body, are you feeling okay?" he asked.

"Yeah, surprisingly. I feel like that dirty lake might have actually helped." I looked myself over. There had been definite gashes where I imagined any form of water that wasn't crystal clear would have caused an infection.

I wasn't a doctor, so I didn't know how long it took to see anything bad, but I also wasn't an idiot. These wounds looked clean, like they'd begun healing and that was fast, even for me.

"How are you feeling?" I asked.

"I feel great, probably better than when we came in here."

"Interesting."

"Yeah, you can say that." He mused, pressing his ear to the stones.

"Anything?"

"No, nothing."

I covered my hand over the stone near his face and closed my eyes. I could sense something out there. Alive, but not really. I frowned and concentrated harder.

"I hear something," Eric whispered, making me freeze beside him.

We both strained to listen and just like he said, I heard it too. A slow, clumsy shuffling. Not staggered steps like the creatures, but like something heavy, something that was struggling.

"What is that?" I mouthed.

Eric shook his head silently and we both stayed completely still. Whatever was outside was joined by another equally slow, clumsy set of shuffling footsteps. Only this time they sounded like they were dragging something. My stomach instantly dropped. What if the creatures had captured someone else, what if they had Kieran or Emelia?

My thoughts wouldn't stop racing.

The only thing that made me settle down was the fact that the dragging was consistent. They reminded me of zombies in movies dragging their busted limbs around. My skin crawled at the idea.

I sat back on my heels and waited for them, whatever they were, to pass.

"What do we do now?" I asked, keeping my voice low.

"How many bullets have you got left?"

I flicked the barrel of the chamber open. "Three. You?"

"None. I can draw them out and you can cover me. Best bet I think."

"No, I'll draw them out, you cover me," I said and then held up my hand when I saw him about to start another argument. "I'm smaller and quicker, you know I'm right."

"Damn your newly found logic."

I shielded a smile and cocked my brow at him. This was the best way, the only way. I handed him my gun with the last few bullets we had between us.

I slung my bag over my shoulder and we both readied our weapons...though mine was slightly different to the gun Eric was preparing. I could feel the now familiar waves of the power of Esper simmered a little beneath the surface, which was a good sign. We would hopefully work well. Slowly, I was starting to recognize and get used to this feeling. As more time went on, the more it felt like a part of me. I was embracing the feeling instead of fighting it.

We carefully started pulling back stone after stone, and soon the small cavity through which we came was exposed. I peered out and planned my move. As I looked from the right to the left, I spotted two figures roughly fifteen or so feet away. I pulled my head back, heart slamming into my ribs.

I pressed my fingers to my lips and shook my head. Eric got the message. He carefully looked around the corner and observed the figures for a moment before returning to the safety of our cave.

"They're not the same things we saw before," he whispered.

"What the hell are they?"

"This is going to sound totally crazy, but I could swear that I recognize the school sweater that smaller one was wearing."

"What? Where from?"

"That lake where I found you, there were dead bodies all over the place, at least a dozen."

"You don't think they were playing dead or something, do you?" The notion sounded stupid as soon as I said it out loud.

Eric shook his head. "No, I don't think they were playing dead. I think they were actually dead but somehow came back to life."

"Like actual zombies?" I hissed. "Oh, hell to the no."

I was not down for zombies. I could do aliens and Reapers and all sorts of other crazy beings. But not zombies. Hadn't he seen *28 Days Later?*

"At this point, nothing would shock me." He peered again. The shuffling had gotten quieter signaling that they'd rounded the corner. "Maybe that lake does something?"

"Like reanimating the dead?"

"You're healed up; I'm feeling better than ever. Who knows?"

My fingers grazed the previously deep gashes along my arm. He was right. The healing had been quick and now it was almost complete. When I was under the water, the sensation of being enveloped by a comforting blanket seemed to take over my senses as I'd sunk into the darkness. And how did I survive in there that long? I should have drowned, even with my Reaper and Ceoran blood. What if the water had some sort of healing or reanimation powers? That could change everything. It could change how we fought, how we healed. Maybe things could be different with the Ceoran and how we treated our soldiers.

"If you're right, it's a huge deal, Eric."

"I know. We could change everything."

"We need to take a sample."

"We can't, not now, we need to move out and find the others."

"Eric—"

"We are working against ridiculous odds as it is, we have no idea what's waiting for us when we get out of here. This isn't our priority right now. I'm sorry."

I was ready to argue but the stern look on his face told me that it was pointless. He was right, logical, as always. Damn it.

"Alex. We have to go," he encouraged.

Conceding was harder than I expected. My legs felt like they weighed a ton. Leaving here without a chance to bring back whatever that lake did was painful. We were so close. So close to being able to present the Council with something that would leave all Ceoran on an equal standing, if that was indeed what the lake water did. We would no longer lose soldiers because we weren't allowed to heal them. But Eric gently tugged my arm and reminded me of what we had come here to do. I slung my bag over my shoulder and followed him out.

With the lake and its magic properties tucked safely in the back of my mind, I followed him. We quietly made our way out of the small cave and went in the opposite direction to the creatures. Everything inside me was on complete alert. So far, I knew what the weird alien creatures felt like and the weird zombie folk. So, as long as I didn't feel their presence coming through, I was confident we would get out of this alive.

Eric slowed and checked our path. Luckily he was more of a tracker than I was. To me it all looked the same. The same muddy ground, the same crumbly ceilings. Eric, however, seemed to know exactly where he was going. I stayed close and alert.

We made our way through paths I didn't recognize, and finally reached one that did look relatively familiar. I noticed our distinctive footprints in the soft surface. The ladder to the outside world that we came down was up ahead. I did a little happy dance when I saw the opening, making Eric smirk and shake his head.

"How long since we've been gone?" I asked.

He glanced down at this watch. "Almost thirteen hours."

"You're joking."

"Afraid not. I'll go up first and clear it."

"Okay."

Eric started up the ladder and I kept my eyes scanning the small area around me. I didn't feel anything, but it didn't mean there was nothing sinister lurking, waiting for an opportune moment.

"Clear."

I hauled ass up the ladder feeling every hair on my body stand on end as if something was coming for me. It was like that one time back at home when I watched a scary movie and then had to go to the bathroom at three in the morning. I could have sworn something was watching me from every dark, cracked door.

There had been nothing of course, but here, we knew we actually had company.

Eric's hand appeared at the top. I grabbed it and he pulled me out of the hatch. The sky had changed, the light had long since faded but by the time on Eric's watch, there should have been a glimmer of daylight. There was nothing.

"What the actual…" I murmured looking around.

"I know, it's off. Everything is weird."

"Did we walk through some weird time loop or something?"

Everything was eerily still. The sky was devoid of any light or any hint of it even coming. The trees didn't move, there wasn't even a gentle breeze. By our count we were meant to have lost the entire night in the cave and walked out to the rising sun or at least early morning. It was black, infinite in its inkiness.

I glanced around, gripping the straps of my bag tightly. As horrific as it felt it also felt familiar. I shuddered at the thought and shook it away.

"Eric, I don't like this."

"I don't either, asteraki mou."

We walked back toward where we had parted with Em and Kieran but there were no signs of them.

"I'm going to sound really crazy when I say this, but are we sure we're still in the same time?"

Eric swallowed hard and shook his head slowly. "I don't think we've gone through a time loop."

"What then?"

"No idea, but we should make our way back to the safehouse."

"You think they'd have gone back?"

"It's what I would do. Safer to go back to base than wander around, especially when you don't know what happened to the rest of your team."

"See this is why you're in charge and I am not."

He forced a tight smile but he was as on edge as me.

There was nothing to indicate that we had in fact gone through a time loop, everything was the same as we saw it yesterday. The tire tracks were there too. That relaxed me slightly.

As we neared a break in the trees, Eric slowed and then quickly grabbed me and pulled me behind the cover of a large oak.

"What's going on?" I whispered as quietly as I could.

"Scavengers up ahead."

All my senses suddenly perked up. How had I not sensed them before?

"There's a Reaper with them," Eric said softly. "I think it's using a cloaking shield."

"How do you know that if they're being shielded?"

"Might not feel them, but I can hear it. Listen."

I quietened my breathing and stood still, focusing on the sounds coming from the nearing group. The Reaper was barking orders at the humans, the telltale raspy voice that sounded like it was speaking through multiple vocal cords separated it from them. We might not have been able to see it, but the sound was unmistakable.

That would explain it. But not how *I* missed it. Was I really that distracted?

"Stay behind me. We have to go around."

"How many are we looking at?"

"At least a dozen. Too many for us."

"Damn it."

I peered around the trunk and shuddered when I saw a bunch of really disheveled looking males. One of them I recognized.

"This is not good."

"What?" he asked, moving us both back into the cover of the trees.

"The young kid over there." I nodded to the ratty-looking one. "Kieran spared him after wiping out his entire camp when I was on the run and he found me."

Eric's jaw hardened. "That complicates things."

"We can handle some Scavengers."

"True, but there's more than just Scavengers here and that worries me."

There was something oddly terrifying about this particular encounter. He was right, we both knew we could handle Scavengers. We also knew we could handle one Reaper. But the more time that passed, the heavier the feeling became. There was something else off about this. Something that made me incredibly uneasy.

Eric shifted and I felt a very distinct change of energy respond to him, inside me.

As the feeling shot through me like a bolt of electricity, I gripped onto the tree trunk and felt overwhelming anguish creep up on me. I didn't even question it this time. I knew what the feeling meant and what was coming. I closed my eyes for what couldn't have been more than half a second and I saw light, powerful and consuming. I was at its core, watching on in terror as someone bathed in light ran at me, threatening to stop my advance and then there was nothing. Not just the lack of presence or being, but literally nothing. It was over. The end had come and I was right there in the midst of it all.

"Alex?" His face was in front of mine before I could even react. "What's wrong?"

"Something is coming. Something we can't stop."

"The Reaper?"

"No, this isn't about the Reapers," I managed. "Something bigger…"

267

I looked up into his eyes. How did I tell him that in a single moment that lasted less than a breath of a second, I had seen the end? It was sudden, like a fragment of a memory being shoved into my brain. Only it wasn't a memory it was a premonition. Whatever was about to happen would directly set off a chain of events that would lead to the end I had just felt. Eric opened his mouth to say something, but I stopped him by reaching up with both hands and cupping his cheeks.

"Whatever comes next, know that I love you, Eric Raine."

"I don't under—"

Neither of us heard what came next as a deafening explosion rocked the entire vicinity, sending both of us into the air. As I landed heavily into a crumpled mess, I heard Eric yelling for me through the unbearable ringing in my ears. I covered my face, shielding myself from the debris that started to rain down on us. Eric somehow found me through the chaos and grabbed me tight, holding firmly onto me as we both crawled to our knees, still trying to take cover from the unknown attack.

In the distance I heard voices; some belonged to Reapers who spoke with a rushed, gargled kind of tone, the others were familiar. Ceoran, but not the ones we wanted on our side.

Through all the hazy debris around us I could make out an unmistakable shape.

"She's here, and so is the guardian."

"You've got to be kidding me," Eric muttered in response to Ashfield's cold voice as he helped both of us to our feet.

In a matter of seconds, Eric and I were surrounded. The blast that had blown up the entire perimeter of the land we were on was still shuddering when the Reapers descended. *How was he still alive?*

They circled us and stopped, seemingly waiting for Ashfield's orders. What the hell was going on?

"Thought I killed you," Ashfield said flatly.

"Thought you would have tried harder, not a cowardly shot," Eric spat back.

Ashfield looked insulted. One of his thin brows shot up, the other twitched. Eric had struck a note. Now we knew Ashfield had real issues being referred to as a coward.

"Why are you working with them?" I asked.

"Because you, Chancellor, betrayed the one deal you and I made and now, you've left me no choice."

"What are you talking about?" I shouted, finding myself losing my patience with him.

"I don't buy this memory loss story anymore, Alexia. I know you remember what you and I planned. I know you remember me."

"I don't know what you're talking about. You're totally delusional," I tried. I couldn't risk him knowing how many memories had come back and how much of it I had pieced together.

"That's not what you said when we sat up late into the night talking about the changes you and I would make on the high Council."

"You and I couldn't have made any changes even if we wanted to. We're not on the high Council."

"*You* were!" he spat making me snap my mouth shut.

He was eyeing Eric, he was losing his cool and any moment now he could snap, he might hurt Eric and I couldn't handle that.

"You and I, we never would have worked, regardless of what I promised you."

"We could have but you took that from me, from *us*!"

"I didn't do anything. I never wanted this."

Eric stood firmly beside me, the tension in the circle of burning embers grew.

Ashfield took a few steps closer and Eric stepped in front of me. The second he did, he was hit behind the knees, forcing him down to the ground.

"Eric!" I reached for him but I was pulled back by two Scavengers. When I looked back, my stomach dropped. It was the young kid. Dear God.

"Surprised to see me?"

"Don't touch her." Eric broke free from the Scavenger behind him and smashed his fist into the young kid's face. He cried out when blood gushed everywhere. Eric on the other hand received an equally hard punch forcing him back down. I screamed and tried to rush to him but the kid was back.

"Take him," Ashfield commanded.

Two Reapers responded to Ashfield's order and stepped in and pulled Eric back.

Ashfield rolled his eyes. "Does everything need to be so hard?"

"Why are you doing this!" I screamed. "Why are you working with them?"

"Because of you: you and I had business planned and I want to finish it. I want what you promised me." He took two long strides toward me and reached for my face. What started as a gentle, sensual caress turned into a rough squeeze when I turned away in disgust. "As for why I'm working with them, well, they can give me something no one on the Ceoran Council can."

"You're insane!"

"Sanity is overrated. I want me and you to sit on the Council together like we were meant to. Like you owe me."

"I don't owe you anything."

He smirked. "Technicalities. You're right, though, it's not you, rather your family. See, your parents promised me a seat, they promised me that when you and I got together everything would be perfect."

He looked over at the Reapers holding Eric and nodded.

"Take him," he muttered, turning from me. "I want her with me, toss him in the back with the other two."

Eric's eyes darted between Ashfield and the Scavenger and before he was dragged away, I saw panic flash through them.

"Make sure he's gagged. He talks too much," Ashfield ordered.

A gag was shoved into Eric's mouth and the two Ceoran following Ashfield's orders dragged him kicking and screaming.

I looked over to where they'd taken him and gasped when I saw a large truck pull in through the smoke. When the doors were opened, I saw Emelia and Kieran shackled and gagged, strung up to the ceiling, their eyes wide with panic.

"No!"

"You'll get yours soon, princess," the kid whispered into my ear, squeezing my butt before he threw me forward making me stumble into a separate car.

As the door was slammed shut, a gag was shoved into my mouth, a bag thrown over my head and my torn top removed, only to be replaced by a clean smelling blanket.

Then I felt a hand at the base of my skull and a quick, sharp pinch. Warmth followed by a quick burst of nausea hit me before I felt nothing at all.

Chapter Twenty-One
The Ambush

Eric

Rage filled every pore and every cell inside me when I saw them throw Alex into the back of the car. Angry tears raged to the surface as my mind raced through all the horrific stuff I didn't want to entertain.

Beside me, Kelly and Emelia thrashed against their restraints, yelling through gagged mouths just like me.

As the door to the truck was shut, with us trapped inside and Alex being taken away from me, I felt my resolve break. I'd seen what those people had done to others before. I'd seen the aftermath, I'd picked people up from it, tried to put them back together but they were too far broken to be helped.

Alex would have enraged them when she tried to fight them, and Kelly's compassion in leaving this kid alive had now put her in danger. Rage raced through me again and I screamed and screamed until I felt bile heave up and into the gag making me choke on my own vomit.

"Eric, stop."

My eyes snapped up to my sister. She'd managed to chew off her gag.

Her wide, wet eyes were rimmed with red circles as bright as the welts on her body. Her jaw was purple. I looked over at Kelly, he looked the same. They'd both been beaten and tortured. I thrashed again.

"Eric, please. Stop. You'll hurt yourself."

My body refused to stop. If I did, it would all be over. I couldn't stop fighting. I had to get out of here. I had to find her, I had to stop that kid, stop Ashfield…

"Eric…" Emelia sobbed.

My eyes met hers and everything inside me broke.

Compassion was our weakness. It's what had brought us to our knees in the first place. We came to this planet to protect the humans even though in the beginning of our stay, centuries ago, they responded with hate and fear. But we stayed, we chose to forgive and to show compassion because we were meant to be a better, kinder race. Times had changed, we became forgotten to the humans and we lived in the shadows protecting them, though the hate continued to surface within our own kind in the form of Class division and power struggles.

"Eric, I know this is bad. I don't know what will happen to Alex. But whatever it is, she will survive it. You know she's strong. You know she won't give up. We can't either."

What she was insinuating hurt even more than to imagine it. I couldn't do it. I couldn't let my mind go there. I knew their methods of extracting information and very few survived.

"I overheard them earlier, they're taking us all to Compound Three. Ashfield wanted to use the two compounds being so close together as a fort. Eric, this is good. Kieran and I mapped more than half the tunnels. We found a cave that stopped just short of the perimeter to Compound Four. We can get out of this. This is advantageous to us."

My eyes snapped up to hers. The cave. Yes. Good. We could use the cave. We could use the tunnels. We'd mapped the first four miles too. There would only be a few left that were uncharted, and Alex and I knew about the aliens down there and the healing lake.

"What is it? You found something?" Emelia asked quickly.

Both her and Kelly looked at me desperately.

Yes, I wanted to say yes. I nodded.

"What? Something we can use?"

I nodded again.

"A weapon?"

Well yes, but not really. I nodded anyway.

"Oh Eric, that's good news. We found some weird stuff down there and bodies, but I swear they looked...juicy."

Because they're reanimating, and they're savage. They are weapons. We can use them.

She looked around, no doubt searching for something she could use to free herself. I wanted to tell her not to because we could actually use being inside as an advantage. Like she sensed what I was thinking, she stopped struggling to get free and instead looked at me.

"When we get there, they're going to put us in cells, but separately. When that happens, find the nearest exit you walk past. Kieran and I found an old schematic of the building when we were coming back. There's a single meeting point in the south tower, and it's underground. The tunnel entrance is covered, so I don't think anyone knows about it."

I nodded, so did Kelly.

"The only problem is getting out of the cells. But we'll work it out. Just remember. Central point in the south tower in the basement."

We both nodded again.

The truck came to a rough stop. The driver said something to whoever was outside and we were moving again. It must have been the gate.

I made a mental note of the time it took to leave the gate and stop again. Seven minutes.

The truck's engine went off and then more voices.

This was good. This was information I could use.

I kept Alex in the back if my mind, safe and secure and as my driving force to end every one of these assholes.

"Get them into the cells in the north tower," I heard one of them say.

The three of us looked at each other. Not ideal but it wasn't the worst thing.

"Remember what I said," Emelia reminded us.

How could I forget?

The door to the truck was pulled open and my body instantly went on guard. Ashfield wasn't there but a bunch of his friends were, including his brother David. The other was a no show—guess he saw the shitshow about to unfold and decided he didn't want to be part of the opening act. But right behind them all was...Morales. Maybe we stood a chance after all.

She gave me a very small nod before disappearing into the crowd.

Alex

A white light hummed just ahead, pulsating in tune to the rhythm of my own heart. It was unnerving. I breathed in, the light expanded, I breathed out, it settled. There was a familiarity in it, but at the same time I had no idea what I was looking at. I walked ahead and then stopped, there seemed to be something else there, no, someone else. It was definitely the outline of a person silhouetted against the bright orb. The figure turned abruptly and I turned to follow its line of sight. Another figure, a much taller one ran toward it. The smaller figure bolted.

I jolted awake when another bump in the road caused my body to jerk up and then crash back into the leather seat.

Pieces of what took place before I was knocked unconscious fell into place. The dream or whatever it was, remained a permanent fixture in my mind. Why was I seeing this now? Why all of a sudden and what did it mean?

The screeching of brakes up ahead drew my attention. The truck had stopped but the car I was in kept going.

My face was pressed into the seat and the rest of me held down by two strong arms. I couldn't have fought back even if I'd gotten my arms free.

Finally, I felt the car slow before it went down a very steep incline. *Basement parking.* I made a mental note.

When we finally stopped moving, all four doors opened at once and the cool air chilled my exposed torso. Unlike my usual choice of attire which consisted of a cheap Kmart bra, I'd opted for a thick, compound issue crop top. It was my only glimmer of hope through this mess and as much as it grossed me out that anything belonging to Ashfield was touching my skin, I was grateful for the blanket providing some warmth and cover. I didn't want to think about the creep sitting beside me or what he was planning. I didn't want to think about the twisted mind games Ashfield was concocting.

Most of all I didn't want to think about how stupid I had been. I'd almost fallen for his sweet-talking, and worst of all, I thought we were one step ahead when he had been the whole time.

"Bring her to my room," I heard him say.

What? No. Not to his room. Definitely not to anyone's room. My body instinctively went rigid, fighting back the arms holding me.

It seems that their instinctive reaction was to punch me in the stomach. As the fist connected with my gut, I doubled over and coughed into my gag.

"Enough. I want her in once piece."

"Walk," someone ordered.

My legs were dead weight. I couldn't think around the panic let alone walk. That earned me another hit.

"Stop," Ashfield barked, "I don't want her hurt. Do you understand me?"

One of them barked something unintelligible back.

"Move." They shoved me forward.

This time, my legs worked, and my feet started stumbling forward. One foot after the other.

Before long, my feet moved from hard concrete to soft plush carpet and a warm hallway. There were muffled voices, the distant smell of freshly brewed coffee and faint music.

"Inside please."

I was shoved forward, and I stumbled until I found my footing. "Shackle her feet too please, this one has some skills I don't want to be on the receiving end of."

I rushed away and clumsily tripped over my own feet, hitting the ground hard. I grunted into my gag and tried to scramble away.

"Christ, must I do everything myself?" Ashfield snapped.

"Sorry," one of them barked back.

I was roughly pulled into a seated position and my feet were shackled; a tiny chain with about half a foot of give was all I was allowed. A bleak glimmer of hope.

They pulled me to my feet and then they were gone.

The door was closed and the sound of a lock engaging made my stomach lurch.

"Now that we're alone, you and I are going to have a serious conversation, Chancellor."

My entire body trembled as I felt his eyes on me, stalking around me. The sack was thick over my head and I couldn't tell if we were in the dark or in the world's brightest room. All I knew for certain was that I was terrified out of my mind.

For the first time, I was truly alone and truly out of my depth. I was restrained, my arms were useless, I couldn't kick, I couldn't punch and I couldn't call on my power. Out there I could try something, I could run, I could hide, or at the very least I could attempt to use Esper. Here, I had nothing.

Ashfield stepped away from me for a moment and then he was back. I jumped when I felt his cold hand on my stomach and the other on the waistband of my trackpants.

Sweet baby Jesus. No. God no.

"Now you might notice that you can't call on your power here, that's all by design of course. So relax or I'll stab you by mistake."

I froze.

He pulled my sweats down to my ankles. My entire body shook. Then I heard scissors. I had to do a double take to make sure that's what I was hearing.

Definitely scissors.

He was cutting my pants off. What the hell?

"Now, that's better." He left again. This time when he came back, I felt a soft robe around me.

"I'm going to undo your arms so you can put this on properly. Try anything and I will have to restrain you again. Understand?"

I nodded desperately. I would have agreed to anything at this point. Being this exposed in front of him was revolting.

He unshackled me like he promised, and I quickly shoved my arms into the sleeves and tied it tightly around my waist.

"I'm sorry you had to experience all of that," he said as if he was genuinely proud of himself for helping me. "I would let you have a shower and clean up but I'm afraid you'd try to escape. So the best I can do is this robe. Then you can have some fresh clothes. The proper clothes a woman like you should be wearing, not that compound uniform," he said with disgust.

I rolled my eyes under the sack, slightly more at ease now knowing that he wasn't going to do anything to me.

"I had dinner ordered for us, it should be here soon. Don't worry, your friends will be fed as well."

How hospitable.

"Do you want to sit? You must be exhausted."

I refused to entertain this jerk. My back and my neck were so sore I could hardly stand but the last thing I wanted was to be at his mercy and give in.

"Suit yourself."

He padded across what felt like lush carpet beneath my bare toes and dragged over a chair. I heard him let out a long breath, the kind you express when you're trying to be obnoxious.

"I'll take that off your head as long as you promise to behave like a lady."

God. I was going to smack him as soon as my hands were free again.

"Yes, no?"

"Screw you," I said, though it came out seriously jumbled and I wondered whether he'd understood me at all.

The chuckle that came in response told me that he had in fact understood me.

He took the bag off anyway and I immediately threw my hands up to my face to pull the gag off but the invasion of bright lights stunned me momentarily and I slammed my eyes shut, waiting for the throbbing pain in the front part of my head to subside. Then I carefully opened them again, taking in the room.

Familiarity in the design shot through me almost making me double back. He caught the expression and smirked. I quickly looked away.

James Ashfield was wealthy. Obscenely so. The room was most definitely not Ceoran issue. This had under the table dealings written all over it. The large, obnoxious four-poster bed in the middle of the huge room was adorned with golden laced bedding which matched the framed paintings hanging on the wainscoted walls. I took in the décor, and after scanning the room and assessing that the art here was genuine, I was certain that half of the country's saved classic art was in this room. Worse than that, I remembered a lot of this artwork; not from here though, but his room at the old compound, *our* compound.

"Had it moved here when I was informed of a potential risk."

I narrowed my eyes in disgust.

"I know you liked these two." He gestured to the large Monets behind him. "Couldn't in good conscience let them go up in flames when the attacks finally came."

I exhaled sharply through my nose.

Ashfield sat proudly, his legs crossed neatly as he sipped on a tea.

"You can take the gag off."

I ground my molars against the fabric of the gag. I was so mad I probably could have chewed it to pieces. But I was civil, and I removed it like a normal person would. I threw it aside and watched him through narrowed eyes.

He got up and brought back another chair.

"Sit."

"Cram it," I bit back.

"Stop being so stubborn."

God, I wanted to feel the soft cushion under my butt. Ashfield saw me eyeing it. The smug bastard was loving this.

"Can we have a mature conversation?" he asked, gesturing to the seat in front of me.

"*You're* talking about mature. You beat the living crap out of my friends, shot Eric in the back and stripped me after your buddies punched me like a bag."

He actually looked hurt, like I'd offended him.

"I had to."

"Why?"

"Because you kept evading me and you and I have business to tend to."

"So you keep saying."

"So you keep denying."

I rolled my eyes.

"In all seriousness, you really don't know what I'm talking about, do you?"

"For the hundredth time and the love of God, no, I do not know what you're talking about," I said, dropping into the chair. Yep, the cushion was amazing, my butt was very happy and I was going to have to play dumb a little longer.

He studied me for a moment. Then got up and disappeared behind a large, extravagant room divider which looked like it had once belonged to the Shang Dynasty.

When he came back, he handed me a leather-bound book which had his monogram on it. I resisted the urge to roll my eyes again.

"This will answer most, if not all of your questions."

"What is all of this?"

"Official documents from my family." He tapped the monogram. "That's my family crest."

"Right."

"This contains official signatures, arrangements, treaties. You name it. It also contains things I'm sure you've already seen and probably remember."

I looked at the heavy book and then back at him. I didn't know what he was playing at but I was losing patience.

A knock at the door drew his attention.

"Come in."

A pair of servants walked in pushing a cart filled with amazing-looking food. There were fruits, bowls of candy, a massive chicken, all sorts of vegetables and salads, and three kinds of wine. I didn't drink and I wouldn't be starting tonight.

"Dinner is served. You can stay here for the night. I think this room will be sufficient. It has everything you need, a shower included."

"Thought I wasn't allowed to shower?"

He grinned. "I can see you're eager to learn what's in that book and something tells me once you start reading, you won't be going anywhere. So be my guest, shower, relax, eat." He picked a grape and popped it into his mouth.

"You're leaving me here?"

"I'm certainly not leaving you in a cell."

I frowned; I really had no idea what he was up to.

"You didn't think I was really going to throw you in a cell like a common Ceoran, did you?"

"I don't know what to think, Ashfield."

"James," he corrected. "And that hurts. I'm not an animal."

This time I did roll my eyes. "Could have fooled me."

"Now that's the banter I remember. And miss."

I tore my gaze from him.

"Take your time with that book. Enjoy dinner, and I will be back in a few hours after you've had some time to rest and read."

I was certainly not going to enjoy any of this.

Ashfield left, locking the door from the outside. I was alone. I groaned and tossed the book aside then reached for the shackles around my feet. Just as I thought, they were solid, no give at all.

I scanned the room. Everything did look very inviting. This was the worst kind of torture. The food smelled delicious. The shower was beckoning. No. I wouldn't go in there. The creep probably had cameras set up.

I reached for a piece of watermelon and devoured it. I wasn't going to use his shower, but I was certainly going to eat—I needed the energy. I picked up a cracker and there, in the middle of the cart was a small silver key. I snatched it up and examined it. It was a key to the shackles around my feet. I wasted no time releasing myself. Once my legs were free, I stretched them out and picked the book up.

I opened it to the first page and started reading while I grazed on the food in front of me. It started off as expected. Hierarchy of all involved in the Ceoran High Council, including my family and his, all things I remembered. Then there was a list of all the commendable Soldier class families. The Corteza name was there, as was Morales'. I sighed; they were classified as some of the best serving bloodlines, yet they still meant nothing to the *higher* classes.

This sort of treatment and division had to stop.

I turned to the next page and that's where my mood severely dropped.

There was a signed document which was sealed a day after my birth. The document was signed by my parents and James Ashfield's. We were to be raised closely together in hopes that one day we would enter the Council together.

Without me, and my bloodline, the Ashfields would never stand a chance. He wasn't royal enough and his family hadn't done enough. They threw money at everything they could, but it wasn't what the High Council wanted. They wanted talent, skill, *pedigree*. All of the things my family had.

Beneath that paragraph there was a quick mention of his middle brother David and his political advancements—this part was added in much later of course. It also spoke about David potentially sitting on the High Council instead, but then, under that, the charges that were brought against him: rape and battery. Their eldest brother, Jonathan, led that cause. My mouth dried. So I was right and my memory wasn't playing tricks on me. His brother was meant to take this seat with another girl but after that charge, the Council dropped him, which is why James and I were plan B.

The next section, weeks after David's charge, contained documents showing that my parents had once again signed a more official arrangement with the Ashfields. He and I were to be paired in order to enter the Council as noble born Council leaders.

Even though those signatures were most definitely real and what I was seeing was very real, I couldn't believe it, I didn't *remember* this. Unless, I was never told.

The next page was covered with the signatures of all Ceoran Council seats who'd agreed on the class division almost three decades ago. My heart slowed, both my parents and their parent's names were there.

I slammed the book shut and threw it down.

So this was it. I was promised to him like a slave for a Council seat. There was no reason, no explanation. No word from my parents, and there never would be.

Everything I'd suffered through, everything Eric had suffered through, was about a damned seat and had gone to the grave with them.

Chapter Twenty-Two
We'll Dance in Hell

Eric

We were thrown into separate cells and I had little indication of where the other two were. I rubbed the marks around my wrists and hissed when I realized all the skin had been scraped raw thanks to my incessant struggling.

It would have to wait.

I looked around my small cell which was made of three concrete walls and a door of six-inch-thick steel. In the door there was a seven- by nine-inch window with a small ledge, large enough to host a small meal tray and nothing else. The window was locked from the outside and secured with an impenetrable code and padlock combination; I knew because I'd locked up prisoners in cells just like these back in our compound which meant there was no breaking out. I peered through the small space and spotted a clock on the far wall; it was all I could see from my vantage point.

As I reached for the ledge to see if I could pry it off as a makeshift weapon, I heard an urgent tapping coming through the concrete wall to my left. I moved closer and it sounded again. I stopped, concentrating on it.

It came again.

And again, I listened.

There was a definite pattern.

It was Morse code, or more specifically a Ceoran version of it, something only certain members of each compound knew. It was specific to each small group to ensure compartmentalization should something happen and deem that group compromised. We were meant to use it to inform the rest that we were captured without giving away anything.

The code continued. A simple set of instructions kept repeating.

Stay low. Big explosion. Twenty-three hundred.

I sat down on the provided steel cot and looked back at the clock. It was only nine thirty.

Was I meant to just sit here and wait around for something to happen? What if nothing did? What if I wasted all this time when I could have been trying to find a way to get to Alex?

What was happening to her? Would she make it through another hour and a half?

I got up and paced the cell, tried yanking the ledge again and then returned to the cot. I had no choice.

I needed to wait it out. I needed to be smart and trust that she was handling herself. I dropped my head into my palms and dug my elbows into my knees, expelling a long breath. Then I prayed. Something I hadn't done in a long, long time.

The Karatoi were stern, calculating even. And they did only what needed to be done. But today, right here, we, *I*, needed their help. I needed them to come. Alex needed us. And we couldn't do a damned thing being stuck in these cells.

I could only hope that they would listen, that we weren't too late and that something could be done when the time came. Until then, all I could do was hope.

Alex

The book sat heavy in my lap, the secrets it gave up equally as dense. Had my parents really sold me to him? I couldn't make sense of any of it. They had their own standing on the Council. Had they been at risk of losing it? Is that why? I mean I'd speculated before, I'd almost been ready to wager on it, but the confirmation stung.

There must have been a reason, surely. No. It didn't matter why. It was wrong and it was a total betrayal of all my trust and memories. I couldn't understand how someone's family could do that to them and then keep it a secret for seventeen years.

Would they ever have told me? Something inside me said no. That same something wondered whether their hands were tied, whether there was something deeper, more sinister that had forced them rather than money.

We hadn't been as wealthy as the Ashfields, but we were comfortable, I remembered that, we had more than most and we used it wisely both in the human world and on Ceora…unless that was a skewed view of my family as well. At this point, I couldn't be sure of anything.

But the sinking feeling that something had made them do that out of desperation clawed at my insides, setting my heart on edge. I had done desperate things too, hadn't I? To secure a future for me and Eric, maybe they'd done this for reasons equally as important. I had to get out of here, I needed to move, to find Eric and the others and end this madness.

I dropped the book on the table with a thud and popped a few more grapes into my mouth before setting off in search of something I could use to get out of here.

The entire bedroom was filled from corner to corner with useless décor, nothing one could use to smash a door open.

I groaned and stopped, collecting myself to think.

The wardrobe. Surely he'd have something in there. I ducked into the large walk-in and stopped abruptly. This guy was crazy. There was nothing aside from an obnoxious amount of clothing. He had more than anyone I knew. It was absurd.

As for something I could use to break the lock on the door, I was hot out of luck. I carefully padded to the bathroom and then groaned when I saw nothing of use again.

The only thing that caught my eye was a freshly folded pile of clothes, *women's* clothes to be specific, and a shoe box. There was a small, folded note on top.

I hope you find these to your liking, Chancellor. If not, there is a wardrobe to your left with some more. J.

I rolled my eyes and looked to my left, and sure enough there was another door. I toed it open and let out a long sigh. There was an entire row of dresses which happened to be exactly my size. They were pretty, he knew what I liked but they weren't me, not anymore.

I closed the door and returned my attention to the pile on the counter and picked up the first item of clothing. The simple, white and blue T-shirt unfolded in my hands. It was soft, *so* soft and I ached to feel the cotton on my skin. The next item was a pair of perfectly pressed, beige linen pants, the kind you'd wear on your super yacht.

Curiosity got the better of me and I caved. I reached for the shoebox and pulled it open. My mouth gaped. These were absolutely gorgeous. Far too gorgeous to be worn in the middle of a damn apocalypse. They were tan, woven sandals covering most of the foot aside from leaving the toes open. They were complete with a dainty strap around the ankles and a small, conservative heel. I had to give it to Ashfield, the guy had impeccable taste in fashion, if he had indeed picked these himself.

I glanced around the bathroom and cringed thinking back to my earlier suspicion that he had cameras set up in here, but the thought quickly fizzled out. Why would he have rigged his own bathroom with surveillance, that was totally idiotic. I decided that I was going to take advantage of the fresh clothing and I might as well make use of fresh water and towels. I was filthy, covered in grass, that weird lake water, and Ashfield's robe.

A quick scan of the extravagant bathroom confirmed two things: Ashfield loved marble, the entire thing including the toilet was decked out in it, and second, he thought of me as some kind of possession. I was a doll he could dress up and make his own, the dresses confirmed as much which meant he would absolutely give me privacy to ensure I wasn't spooked.

I'd long since ditched that look. I remembered my old self through snippets of memories here and there. There was still a bit of mystery like the relationship Ashfield and I shared and the way I used to be then. I remembered some of it, and why I'd done it but not all.

I couldn't imagine that I would have chosen that way of life. Then again, I thought, as I looked at the pretty dresses, maybe I'd been a different person, one who actually did want this. So why would I have fallen for Eric? I studied the opulence, trying to remember what I was like and whether this sort of thing appealed to me. Deep inside, something stirred, something drew me to it and the way of life. I shuddered and forced the thought down like it might drown me. No, this way of life had no room for Eric, of that I was sure, which equated to me not remembering something correctly.

My family were considered highly at the Council, I remembered that well. It didn't matter now, despite how much Ashfield wanted it so. I was Alex, not Alexia, not the girl he expected to dress up and play politics with.

I shut the door and reached for a clean face washer and some of the bottles Ashfield had mentioned earlier. I grabbed a mandarin and sandalwood shampoo and vanilla bodywash. I scrubbed my body and washed my hair as best as I could, enjoying the water a lot more than I probably should have. This wasn't my home and I shouldn't be making myself comfortable, it only made the reality of my life out there harder to go back to. Once I'd finished and dried off, I dressed in the linen pants and top and slipped my feet into the sandals.

After I was done, I made my way back into the bedroom.

The door behind me opened and Ashfield came back in sporting a fresh suit, clean hair and a beaming smile.

"I really thought you would have preferred one of your dresses."

My dresses?

"I guess you're still used to being out there. It will take time," he mused, walking over to the small buffet and helping himself to some cheese.

"I'm not going to parade around in those for you or anyone else."

"That's fair, but we are going to make an appearance together and it would be nicer if you were dressed for the occasion."

"I'm not going anywhere with you. You're delusional."

"I take it reading about your parents didn't really inspire a change of heart." Ashfield stuffed his hands into his pockets.

"It doesn't change anything, Ashfield."

"That's where you're wrong, it changes everything."

Something in his eyes sparked to life setting me on edge.

"Why am I here?" I demanded.

"To sit on the Council with me."

"No, I'm not going to do that."

He stalked around me, taking in the half-eaten food on the cart and the discarded dirty clothes he'd thrown into the corner.

"Was the food adequate?"

"What?" I snapped.

"The food, was it to your liking?"

"I heard you, I'm just confused as to why you think that's a relevant topic of discussion."

He smirked. "I can ask the chef to make you something different next time."

"There won't be a next time. I'm getting out of here and you better hope you're not around when I do because I won't hesitate to break your nose."

"That kind of language isn't really your style."

For a moment we both looked at each other, like maybe he was finally getting it through his thick head that I wasn't who he thought I was anymore, and I wasn't about to become her either. Certainly not for him.

"I can appreciate that being out there for so long has forced you to make some changes to survive. I'm sorry for that," he said, stepping closer.

"Oh wow. You're really something."

"This whole thing was absolutely appalling. I can't believe the Council actually approved something like that. You never should have been out there."

"Well I was and I survived, without you and your chivalry." I stepped back.

"You don't know how happy I am about that."

"Somehow I don't think you know the meaning of happy, Ashfield."

"James," he corrected and then beamed his obnoxiously white smile at me. "I know happiness. It's with you and you seem to have refused to remember us."

The more he spoke, the more I hated the small flickers of memories and feelings forming in my mind.

There had been something, however small, however ridiculous and unbelievable to the present version of me. He was a means to an end, a relevant player in the game I was playing but had there really been more? Was there a time when I cared about him in some way? It was absurd to imagine but...

Ashfield must have sensed something because he stopped pacing and searched my face. I looked away.

"Ah, you've been holding out on me. You remember something, don't you?"

"No."

"No?"

"No."

"Interesting." He walked around me again and stopped by the large bureau, right under the Monet I adored the most. "Do you want to know what I think?"

"Really don't."

I tore my gaze away from the small bridge with pretty flowers.

"I think that you're afraid to remember what we had because it goes against everything Raine has told you about the old you. And if you accept that it means you're accepting that he lied to you which, of course, the great Major Eric Raine would never do," he mocked.

"The old me cared about something important, something you don't care about."

"I care."

"Oh really?" I challenged. "Is that why you've tried to destroy Eric at every turn?"

"No, that's just jealousy. I'm man enough to admit that. But you and I, we had a good thing, and we cared about the same end goal, Alexia."

Dear God. I rolled my eyes and pinched the bridge of my nose. "Is it too late to request a cell?"

"Haven't lost your sense of humor though." He grinned.

"In all seriousness, *James*, what do you expect from me, now, after everything?"

"Tonight, a show at the Council meeting. Tomorrow maybe a meeting. In the future, I would like you to stand by my side."

My heart slammed against my ribs. I was very clearly out of my depth, there was nowhere to go, no one coming to help. I looked helplessly beyond him to the room with the nice dresses.

"So you're forcing me to be here. As your prisoner."

His jaw squared. "I have never forced you to do anything, Alexia, and nor will I ever."

"Then I'm free to go."

"Door isn't locked."

I rushed over to it and yanked hard, half expecting it to be locked. When it came free, I stumbled backwards, then stopped and slowly turned.

"You're free to leave if you want."

I drew in a breath. "If I want? Why on Earth would I stay?"

"Because if you leave, you'll never get the answers you seek. So, I know you'll stay because you're far too curious not to."

My heart raced, so did my mind. He wasn't wrong. I could walk right now, go looking for Eric and the others, leave all this behind and what? Be none the wiser, leave without any concrete answers. I sighed and shut the door.

"Fine."

"Fine?" His brows shot up into his hairline.

"Fine, I'll go with you tonight. But that's it. No touching, no pretending, nothing. Got it?"

"Thank you."

"I need to dress *appropriately*," I said with as much patience as I could muster, and hoped he got the message to get out and leave me alone.

He left the room, once again leaving me inside with my own sense of despair and helplessness. I kept telling myself that this was a good plan, a solid one. Yet no matter how much I tried to pep myself up, I found that the nerves were building quicker than I could stop them.

I opened the door to the wardrobe once more and found the outfit I'd secretly eyed. It was a two-piece black pant and blazer suit with a silky, burgundy floral shirt. It was pretty and it was me. But it was also a bit big. The pants were a little looser than they should have been on account of me being out there for so long living off nothing but trail bars and pure cardio.

There was no makeup which honestly surprised me; I thought someone as particular as Ashfield would have had everything in here. Instead, I turned my attention to my hair. I pulled back the dark blonde waves into a low bun, left a few strands out around my face and checked myself over.

It was the prettiest I'd felt in years and it kind of irked me that it was playing dress-up for Ashfield and not for a date with Eric. My heart ached, like a little reminder that deep in the back of my mind I was always worrying for him.

After a few more tweaks of the clothing, I knocked on the front door and waited. Ashfield came in a few moments later, his eyes bright with a sickening glimmer.

"Love that on you," he said, standing a few feet away from me.

I didn't humor him with a response.

He didn't seem to mind.

"Shall we?"

"Let's get this over with," I bit.

Thankfully, he didn't expect any sort of hand holding or arm linking. I didn't think I could manage that much. I was about two compliments away from knocking his perfect white teeth out.

I followed him silently through the halls and tried to take note of everything around us. There was a spiral staircase that led up and down but there was no way of knowing how far. There were two brightly lit exits to the left of us, a large command center ahead and then another passage of corridors. All around us the compound was outfitted with security like I'd seen in Compound 1 and very little else. While Ashfield's room was opulent and decorated, the halls out here were a stark contrast: white, clean, minimal.

There weren't very many people around but the few who were around stopped to acknowledge me.

"We're so glad you're safe, Chancellor Wynter," a soldier in her mid-forties said as we walked.

"Thank you."

"Does anyone here know what you did?" I asked, voice dripping with venom he was too stupid to see.

"Of course not."

"You're not going to get away with this."

"As long as I have you by my side, I beg to differ."

"And what if I leave right now, make a commotion and tell everyone that you abducted me and my friends?"

"Then your friends will get a bullet to the head before you even finish your speech."

I stopped walking and looked directly at him. "You're bluffing."

He didn't say anything but he did retrieve a small tablet from his pocket. There were several angles of cells with the occupants clearly visible inside. Eric, Emelia, Kieran, Carter, Clark…everyone I knew. There were dozens of them. All the Ceoran who knew what needed to be done and were willing to give their lives for it.

"Say the word, Chancellor, and they all go to sleep."

"You're a monster."

"I'm simply a person doing business. And so are you."

"Not like this."

"Unfortunately, thanks to your mother recanting when she did, this is the hand we're dealt."

"Yeah, well. Guess she had some sense in the end."

"Needless to say, she messed up a lot of things for us. My family especially."

"And what about your brother?" I hissed.

Ashfield stopped walking and grabbed my arm just tight enough to make me flinch internally but not enough to cause a scene. "Careful with your next words, *Chancellor.*"

"Or what, *James,* are you going to show me what a big man you are?" I said quietly, but with enough venom that there was no mistaking where I was going. "Because I think if you really look back over the history of what messed up your family's standing, you'll find that it sits with that animal you share your bloodline with."

He paled.

"What?" I feigned shock. "Didn't think I knew about your rapist brother? About the things he put your family through, the way the Council booted him out making all of you look like a damn joke. No one on the Council even wants to entertain the idea of you being royalty, let alone giving you a seat."

"My brother did wrong, but we are not the same person."

"Semantics, *James.* You're keeping me here like a prisoner without shackles. You're no different."

His jaw clenched so tightly that I heard his teeth creak.

Never in my life had I felt pure rage ooze out of someone than I did in that moment. I stood perfectly still, silent, waiting. I didn't know what he would do, I expected anything, everything at this point. He was losing his cool, I could see it in the way one of his brows twitched and his clenched fists shook at his side. I refused to move and show him that I was low-key terrified of what he would do next.

"That may be the case, Chancellor, but we have all learned from that very tragic situation and my family have done nothing but offer their support to those two girls. So, I'll say it again, the way tonight goes is your call. Come with me, put on a smile, maybe even dance if we have to, or watch your friends die," he said calmly and then strode on ahead.

I let out a long breath. Well, crap on a stick. My plan was not going well.

***

Eric

The message in the walls kept replaying and I kept checking the time. It was getting closer and I was feeling the tension.

Before I could drive myself crazy, the small window in the door was slid open and a soldier I recognized as Colonel Richard Addams, one of my former classmates at the academy, stood there cementing to me just how much betrayal we faced.

"Food."

"I don't want food," I snapped.

"You're in here for the long haul, Raine. Might as well eat something." He put the food on the small ledge and stepped back. I could only make out his head and the top part of his torso, and nothing but the closed window of the cell directly behind him.

"I'm fine."

"Suit yourself. Your girlfriend will be feasting like a queen tonight."

My eyes narrowed.

"Didn't know?"

I didn't reply.

"Oh, you didn't, well, let me regale you with a story. Chancellor Wynter has agreed to accompany Mr. Ashfield to the Council gala tonight where they will appear together again. And, if he's lucky, which we all know he will be, she will accompany him back to his rooms where discussions will be had to plot the course of our future."

Together again. A jolt of anger raced through me. He must have done something to her or threatened her somehow. She would never have agreed to that, not of her own accord.

"What kind of future do you think Ashfield will possibly provide you?" I spat.

"Out of this hole, away from these menial jobs."

I laughed and he straightened.

"You're a fool to think that he will do anything that would benefit people like us," I said, trying to reason with this idiot.

"We are not the same kind, Raine. You're happy slaving away for them while I want to get out of their shadows."

"Then you're even more stupid than I thought, Addams. You can't honestly believe that Ashfield would help us."

"Oh he's going to do a lot more than help."

"What are you talking about?" I demanded.

"Well you see, when he and Wynter finally sit on the throne like they always should have, all of this"—he gestured around the cells—"will be a thing of the past. The only people in cells will be people like you and your friends going against the Ashfield's rule. Which means, people like me and my *kind* will be free, no longer slaves to serve them."

"And what do you think will happen when they want protection against my *kind*?" I felt the heat of anger rising within me.

"It won't be like now."

"Open your eyes, Addams!" I shouted this time. "You can't possibly be this naive!"

"Only naive person here is you, Raine. You don't honestly think she's going to come back for you, do you?" he said quietly, without any real emotion. "Word on the street is that your little lady up there has regained her memories and I bet you know what that means?"

I balled my fists at my side.

"After she sees where she belongs, remembers how cozy and cushy it is up there with him, with her lavish gowns and royal feasts, do you really think she'll want to come back and slum it in the cold with you?"

When I failed to find any words that wouldn't sound pathetic, Addams laughed and slammed the small window shut, leaving me to my thoughts.

I paced the cell. Checked my watched three more times and then groaned in exasperation. What was happening out there? This was agony. I couldn't wait one more hour. With every minute that passed while I was stuck down here, Alex was forced to endure the bureaucratic garbage they were shoveling up there.

Outside I heard Addams' footsteps slow and stop every few feet or so as he opened each cell's small window, dropped their trays of food off and continued.

"I'm going to rip your throat out, Addams!" I heard my sister shout before another window was shut. Guess she wasn't hungry either.

I relaxed somewhat knowing that Emelia was here on the same floor; the stops Addams had made with his food delivery indicated that the rest of our crew was too.

I wondered whether they had heard the message or whether that had only been for me. Chances were the latter. Had anyone else heard it, Addams would have too. His involvement here made me shake with rage. He was a decorated soldier who'd been recruited by the high Council for his ruthless tactics out in the field. He and I had always been compared, pit against each other. He was all about getting the job done regardless of what the job cost others. That's where he and I differed. I was all for the book, but he went beyond. He didn't care about the cost of innocent lives that might be caught in the crossfire, he only cared about the job. The fact that he was one of the guards down here didn't elude me. He had been placed here for a reason and I couldn't help but think it was because they, whoever tasked him here, knew how tough of an opponent he was for me.

They liked those kinds of people and so, he went far. My biggest concern now was that when he came here, it was swept under the rug as a clandestine mission. He was no longer on the books, and he was no longer spoken about. So, that meant that what happened down here in the basement never filtered up to the royals above. And that meant that no one up there would know that Alex wasn't here of her own free will and the fact that no alarm had been raised in the time we'd been here told me that she had been silenced somehow.

That thought alone made a new rush a fear spike inside me. What if the explosion coming tonight would set off a chain of events that put her in more danger? What if it cost us the one opportunity to keep her safe?

My mind raced, so much so that I'd failed to realize that the message had stopped.

I checked my watch again.

Forty-five minutes.

***

Alex

The hall was decked out in all the glamour and glitz one would expect of an Academy Awards ceremony. It was disgusting to think that out there people were dying and starving in the wilderness, being hunted by savages who knew no humanity, while these people, people I belonged to, partied like it was an afterthought.

My eyes wandered near and far taking in the sights of barely there dresses, gowns made of gemstones and perfectly tailored suits sauntering around the opulent hall. Champagne flowed and food was served, everyone was enjoying the night, completely unaware of the turmoil slithering around inside me like a venomous snake about to launch.

It was all so cliché, the dancing, the food, the service. Of course it was, I thought, looking out over the sea of nicely dressed bodies—surely we didn't do this sort of thing on Ceora, we must have only done it here because we were in human form and that meant emulating what the humans did to fit in as much as possible. I couldn't remember what we all looked like in our true form, but I knew there was a lot of light. No wonder it resembled the Oscars. I was only half surprised that there was no giant golden statue guarding the front entrance. Suffice it to say, they'd learned how to embrace the materialistic things of this place. They didn't care about the cost or the value, it meant nothing to them. As long as it was shiny and new, they would eat it all up.

"You'll get back into the swing of things in no time," Ashfield said beside me.

I never wanted to get back to this. This was hell. Anger made my fists shake but I refused to let him see how upsetting this was.

My family, my friends, people I cared about had sacrificed everything because they wanted to end this horrible class division, because they were sick of seeing the *lesser* class treated like dirt.

Yet here we were.

As we walked through the front doors, heading toward yet more beautifully dressed people, I ground my molars knowing that down below, in the cells, there were regular, working-class Ceoran locked away like animals for wanting to give everyone equality. I spotted a row of soldiers who were our guardians standing just outside. They had nowhere to rest, nothing to eat. They simply swapped shifts and then resumed their duties elsewhere while the pristinely dressed Council members and upper-class Ceoran ate meals I'd never seen being served before, let alone now during the apocalypse. Everything was so wrong.

"We're over here," Ashfield said, guiding us to the front.

Wasn't it bad enough that I had to be here without actually having to sit right up front in everyone's line of sight?

One of the workers who was dressed in a simple, white button-down shirt and black pants pulled my chair out for me. She didn't make eye contact when I thanked her. Ashfield didn't even bother thanking the woman who helped him.

I was seriously going to knock his teeth out as soon as I knew Eric and the others were safe.

The Elders I'd met with a few days ago—who knew what I was—walked up to the podium and made direct eye contact with me. The shivers their looks sent up my spine were close to how I felt when Reapers were nearby. If I wasn't mistaken, I was starting to think that the sensation meant evil. Not of any specific variety or race, just pure, unadulterated evil.

Pulling my gaze away I focused on the rest of the decorated hall. I remembered reading about Monet's paintings and spotting the genuine from the fakes. And just like the ones in Ashfield's room, these were genuine, as were all the vases, pots and sculptures. I shuddered.

The world ended and these people took the artwork to save. It was sickening. There were millions upon millions of people that could have been saved, given refuge in any one of these ridiculous compounds, yet no one, not even those who swore up and down that they cared about the human race, did anything. Why were we even here? Had the Ceoran of old done their job when they first came and neglected to pass on the duty to the new? Had the memo somehow been misplaced?

Somehow, I didn't think that's what it was. Somehow, I thought, no I knew, that it was complacency. They'd been here for so many centuries that they'd forgotten what their purpose was on Earth. They'd forgotten how to care, and considering they weren't even going back to Ceora, they thought what the hell? Why not party it up down here?

"Magnificent, isn't it?" Ashfield gestured ahead.

The long black floor-to-ceiling drapes were adorned with gold threads and crystals that tied into the rest of the color scheme.

The tables below were round and sat ten people; the one we were seated at on the platform slightly above everyone else was long and rectangular, giving everyone the view of the people up front. The Elders had a seat with us. That alone was enough to make me seriously question why on earth I was here. I'd been told about my past and even experienced some of the returning memories about this part of my life but it was still so far out of reach I couldn't quite grasp the lunacy of it.

"No. It's insane."

He scowled. "Remember what I said about behaving."

"Kiss my ass."

A High Council member off to Ashfield's left shot me a sideways look and then quickly returned her attention to her drink when I raised my brows in challenge.

Ashfield shifted beside me, straightening his ridiculous tie. Good, I'd made him uncomfortable and embarrassed.

My attention was drawn to the front when several couples walked in hand in hand and took to mingling like this was some kind of social event. The whole layout looked like an expensive wedding, and it buzzed with the same excitement. It didn't escape me that Ashfield and I were right in the middle, on display for everyone to ogle. I reminded myself to stay collected and avoid rolling my eyes. I had to play this game if it meant making sure the others were going to be spared.

"Thank you all for coming out tonight on this cold evening," the female Elder who'd spoken to me said, eliciting a murmur of laughs from the crowd.

"I want to start by saying how thankful we are that our very own Chancellor Wynter has been spared from the monstrosity of the attacks on our compounds. Let's take a moment to grieve those who were lost and those who have given their lives for their duty."

What a fake cow.

The people in the crowd genuinely looked shaken though. They weren't all bad people. A lot of them knew nothing beyond their walls of safety and I couldn't be mad at their lack of education.

"Now that we have our wonderful, young chancellors back where they belong in the safety of our walls, I would like to officially welcome Mr. James Ashfield of the third generation of Ashfield Ceoran and Chancellor Alexia Wynter of the seventh generation of Wynter-Alexander Ceoran."

The crowd erupted in applause. It was a time for celebration. Their royalty was back, they had a complete High Council again and I felt dirtier than I ever had. I would have taken the gross lake and crawling through mud ditches with Eric over this any day.

Ashfield folded his hand across mine, making me flinch. Up ahead, on the table closest to us, I recognized two Ceoran I hadn't seen in years, but remembered from our compound: his parents. His mother was stoic, sitting quietly in her emerald-colored gown adorned with ruby gems, with a neutral expression pasted on her heavily made-up face that was framed by greying waves of mousy blonde hair. Beside her, his father. A tall, burly man with dark eyes and jet-black hair. His jaw was covered in a speckling of pepper-colored facial hair and round rimmed glasses. He smiled at me, making me kind of double back. It wasn't creepy or sinister, just a genuine, warm smile, like someone greeting an old friend.

I frowned at the weirdness of it all and then looked up at Ashfield when he squeezed my hand.

"We need to stand," he whispered with a forced smile.

I shot to my feet and stood beside him. Were we meant to wave or something? I had no idea.

After about two minutes of grinning like an idiot beside me, he gestured that it was time to sit again. I followed suit completely confused by the bizarre ceremony.

"Thank you both. It warms my heart and I'm sure I speak for the other Elders present when I say that you two are a picture of perfection sitting there."

I forced a tight smile and ignored Ashfield when he, again, folded his hand across mine. I was forever thankful that he was all about *class* and keeping up appearances so he wasn't about PDA. I would have died if he tried to place his arm around me or worse, kiss me.

"While tonight is about celebrating the return of Chancellor Wynter it is also about preserving what we can of our way of life. The world out there has changed and our lives on this planet aren't as safe as they were. We need to start planning the next phase."

Next phase? What the hell is she talking about?

Ashfield stirred beside me. The little weasel knew more than he'd let on. There was a purpose here, a reason he'd brought me and it wasn't just to sit beside him.

"The Council members and Elders will discuss what we need to do moving forward to ensure the safety of all Ceoran. For tonight, though, enjoy the feast, spend time with those you love and enjoy."

I shot up, unable to contain myself. "I'm sorry but aren't we here to protect the people of Earth?"

The entire place, and I mean every single soul, royal and soldier alike, including Ashfield's parents, went deathly still except for James himself. He rose beside me trying to pull me back down but the Elder simply waved her hand at him as if his attempts of controlling his *girlfriend* were tiresome.

"You're right, Chancellor." She forced a tight smile which looked like it bordered on madness. "However, your unique situation having been on the run with the humans and your guardians has allowed you to see firsthand that Earth is overrun, we have nothing further to do here."

"Nothing further?" I couldn't help my voice rising two octaves. "We didn't even try. We sat here like privileged brats while they fought a futile war!"

This time she didn't bother with the fake smile, she shot me a look I could only describe as a pure threat. He eyes narrowed, thin lips pursed into a straight line.

"I understand your frustration, Chancellor, but we have decided that this is the path."

"You have decided. I wasn't here and if I'm right, which I know I am, I am required to be here to sign off on such drastic decisions, am I not?"

Further to her right, another Elder nodded. He had been silent up to this point, completely resigned to his cognac and beer nuts. "She is right, Elder Sim. She hasn't signed off on this."

Elder Sim turned, slowly casting the man a look I couldn't make out behind her waves of silver hair.

"And you mean for us to recount the votes then?" she asked, this time forcing a fake smile.

"If that's what the other Elders and Mr. Ashfield deem necessary."

I held my breath. This was not part of the plan. I didn't want to sit on any voting meeting, I didn't want to be part of that decision-making process when I knew they'd overrule me anyway. I chanced a look at Ashfield. He was three shades whiter and completely livid. He didn't even look at me, instead he glanced over at his mother who looked as emotionless as she had been before. Though this time, though, I did see a slight furrow in her brow. His father, however, just looked uncomfortable. He shifted in his spot, the sound of fabric moving under him obnoxiously loud in the silent room. I'd officially embarrassed Ashfield in front of his parents and everyone else here.

Elder Sim turned back to me, studied my face for a moment and then returned her attention to the crowd who'd since started chattering amongst themselves, no doubt wondering what kind of commotion was about to erupt.

"Very well, we shall host another voting session tomorrow morning where our very loved Chancellor Wynter will also be able to cast her vote."

"And until then, you will wait on making your decision?" I asked.

"We will wait."

"Thank you," I tried to say as politely as I could.

"Now let the festivities—"

The Elder's speech was cut off as the doors at the back of the hall opened up and four stern, inhuman beings walked in. They were tall, dressed in grey kimono-style outfits with very limited facial expressions. They weren't as pale as the Reapers, but they didn't look like us either.

I sat, my mouth agape. My body suddenly heavy, the suit too tight, my skin uncomfortable. A sharp jolt of something shot through me, instantly reminding me of a feeling I'd experienced before. It was the same as in the cave, the same sensation when the creatures had found us.

They weren't quite as messed-up looking but they were definitely the same being. I swallowed hard and looked directly at them. What were these things and why were there others like them living underground in the tunnel systems? Had these creatures killed those humans?

"My dear Officials, I…we weren't expecting you?" The Elder began while the others beside her rose, appearing uncomfortable as their gazes shot from the beings to each other.

Officials? No. This couldn't be happening. Why were they here, we hadn't failed yet! We had time, didn't we? No. No, this couldn't be happening now.

Her voice echoed in the unnaturally silent hall. Some Ceoran sat like me, others stood. I didn't know what them being here meant but it didn't feel good. The air grew heavy and stale, like the oxygen was being sucked out of it, and as the four towering Officials walked toward us, the pain in my chest grew and I doubled over, throwing my hands out in front of me on the table to steady myself. I felt the unease of whatever was coming wash over me.

Ashfield's hand landed on the small of my back and if I wasn't feeling so sick I would have pushed him away, but between the pain in my head and the sickness welling inside me, I could only focus on remaining upright. Without them saying a word I heard a direct message in my head.

Halfling, it is time for you to come with us.

What the actual—there was little more than a second to digest the words before a thundering sound rolled through the room and in a split second, there was a blinding flash then an explosion so loud I thought it'd deafened me.

Everything went white for a moment and then there was nothing. A complete and utter stillness and silence. My eyes shot to the tallest one who'd walked ahead.

In the time it took for me to understand what was happening, the hall lit up in a brilliant flash of deafening noise and more blinding light and then there was a split second of silence where my

311

blood rushed through my head, beating painfully loud in my ears. Then came the sound.

It was an explosion. Low and deep, the rumbling started beneath our feet and then the building swayed like a magnitude six earthquake in a high-rise.

The entire building had been attacked and it was going down. A few feet ahead of me, the ground ripped in two sending dozens of Ceoran into the gaping hole and as my eyes shot up to the Officials, I knew they hadn't done this.

Wide, perplexed expressions etched their unnaturally cold faces and then the ground beneath us disappeared beneath our feet.

We fell.

First there was sound, then there were flickers of light, and then there was pain. I held in a cry as I tried to move my hand which was pinned beneath something heavy and immovable. I tried to shift again, deciding that I wasn't going anywhere until I'd freed my arm.

I craned my neck around and assessed the situation. The white linen cloth that had covered our table was stained in blood and torn to tatters; the chair I'd been sitting on was broken into pieces all around me; and the precariously teetering slab of concrete above me that used to be the floor of the ballroom we'd just been in was holding on by a single, fragile beam which could give at any moment. I had to move and I had to move now.

I felt around with my free hand until I touched the start of the beam beneath my fingers. I focused on the power inside me and called on it. With a gentle, yet forceful nudge I released a burst strong enough to free the pillar and with it my hand.

As the concrete gave way, I rolled, shielding my face with my arms and prayed that I'd gone the right way.

Once the loud bang signaling the crashing of the above floor coming down sounded, I moved, throwing myself out of the way and into a small clearing. The groaning of bent metal and falling debris finally subsided. I sucked in a shaky breath and got to my knees. I'd made it out in one piece. As feeling rushed back into my limbs, sounds quickly filled my ears. There was wailing and screaming, the sound of sirens and the barking of orders.

I looked through a crack in the debris to my left and saw the commotion of feet rushing by. And beyond the feet there were bodies, people strewn across the floor in a tangled mess of limbs and tables. The entire gala, floor and people, tables and decorations had all fallen through the floor. A sickening thought dawned on me. What if everything was gone and this was the only life left? Would the floors beneath us look the same? What if Eric, Em and Kieran and everyone else was dead in the basement? What if this was it?

I had to find them. I searched for an opening, staying quiet in the process. Not only was I evading those damn Officials coming to take me out but I was also hiding from Ashfield, if he had indeed survived. There was a gap in the rubble a few feet in front of me. I could squeeze through it if I managed to move some of the stuff blocking my way.

I started shifting whatever I could and then stopped when I heard my name.

"Alex!"

I kept going, quieter this time.

"Alex!" he called again.

If he thought I was dead, maybe he'd get out of here and leave me alone.

"We have to go now, sir!" one of the soldiers yelled.

"Not without her!"

"We'll find her. We need to get you all to safety first. The structure is failing."

"I'm not leaving her!"

"Sir, we will find her. You are of no use to us here. You need to get to safety first."

I ground my teeth and stayed silent. The fact that he was acting like I meant something more to him than a ticket to the top made me fizzle with a new kind of anger. If I didn't know the guy, I would have thought he was sincere in his worry for me.

Once the soldiers finally dragged him out, I waited for a few minutes to make sure no one was about to start digging around for me, Officials included. When I heard the Ceoran start searching for survivors a few feet from me, I started shifting the mangled chair legs from my way and made the gap large enough for me to crawl out of.

There was nothing identifiable left. What the initial explosion didn't incinerate had broken when the floor we'd been on crashed through the level below, the concrete and steel beams that fell had crushed everything else. Flickers of small fires still burning were scattered amongst the debris all around me. My eyes burned as the smoke billowed.

Getting to my knees proved more difficult. I stumbled and crashed to the ground several times before I got my bearings and quickly crawled over to a downed pillar and hid.

The lady who'd pulled my chair out was huddled in a corner. Her eyes widened when she saw me and I pressed my fingers to my lips.

"I'm getting out of here. You with me?"

For a moment I thought she was catatonic. But when I repeated myself she finally nodded.

"Good. We need to move now. Stay low and follow me."

Together we silently navigated our way through whatever floor this was and found our way to an opening. I peered outside and worked out that it was a corridor filled with survivors rushing toward another opening. Like the rest of what I'd seen, this was severely damaged too, and thanks to my super disheveled appearance, no one paid me any attention as the woman and I made our way along with the crowd and down the stairs.

I stopped when I heard voices I didn't recognize ahead. "The Chancellor is our priority. Understand?"

The voices belonged to Ceoran, not the Officials, but that sense of dread that alerted me to their presence in my vicinity grew inside. I had to get out of here. My eyes darted around us, I had to hide.

The woman I was with quickly took off her torn white shirt and gave it to me. I pulled it on, yanked my hair out of my bun and hung my head shielding my face. She stepped around in front of me and wrapped her arm around my shoulder practically shielding me. Once the soldiers moved past our location, she stepped away and nodded to the next staircase. We sprinted for it, heading down to the basement.

There was no one down here.

The building had exploded somewhere in the middle which had somehow preserved the lower levels making them appear as if nothing had touched them. It made me think that the explosion had been carefully orchestrated.

"Eric!" I called and then waited for a few moments. "Em?" I tried.

There was no response.

The woman tugged on my arm and pointed to a small cabinet by the end of the hall. I rushed to it and opened the cover. There was a switch labeled "All Cells."

Before I could flick it, a loud booming voice sounded behind me.

"Get your hand off that switch, Chancellor!"

I spun on the spot coming face-to-face with a stocky guard. My eyes immediately widened when I realized that he was training a gun at me and I was unarmed. The woman beside me sulked back.

"Alex!" Eric's muffled voice came from within one of the cells.

"So, she has come for you," the guard said, a small grin appearing on his lips.

"Don't do anything stupid, Addams!" Eric's voice came in response.

"I won't have to if the pretty lady just does as I ask."

"And if she doesn't?" I challenged.

"Then I will have to do what I've been tasked to do."

"You do realize Ashfield won't hesitate to shoot you himself if you lay a finger on me."

Addams seemed to think about that for a moment while I thought back to why his name was familiar. As he cocked the gun releasing the safety, it clicked—he was the other soldier who always challenged Eric for first position on their ranking board.

"So the way I see it, Colonel, is it?" I flicked off the cover of the switch board. "You don't have much of a choice. Wait around here for whoever comes out of those cells to finish you off, or use that gun and shoot me and wait for James to decide what he's going to do with you."

His jaw twitched, so did his eyes.

"If I remember correctly, in that cell behind me, is the only other Ceoran who was good enough to beat you. Reckon you're still good enough to take him?" I tested.

When his knuckles blanched around the gun, I lifted my brows at him.

"What's it going to be? Up for a challenge?"

He didn't wait around. He hightailed it out as soon as I flicked the switch.

Within seconds, Eric's and Emelia's heads popped out of their cells, followed by Kieran and Carter and all our other friends.

"Oh my God!" I rushed forward and threw my arms around Eric, nearly bowling him over.

"Jesus, Alex. I heard the explosion." He pulled back and searched my face and then my body. "Are you okay?"

"I'm fine, but we have a serious problem and we have to move, like right now."

Before I could explain, the door at the other end of the cell block was blown open and a swarm of Ceoran soldiers rushed in, and right behind them, the Officials.

"Run. Now!" I said, grabbing the woman's arm beside me and starting back up the stairs.

There was no time to think. All I knew was that we had to get out. The Officials knew who I was and whatever they needed me for was going to spell the end of life as we knew it on Earth. That didn't just mean the end of the Ceoran here, it meant the end of protecting the humans that made up this planet, *my* planet. I knew this as home, we all did. Most of us were brought here for our missions before we were even old enough to know what our lives were destined for. Others were born to Ceoran who'd lived here for generations before them.

Everything I was working toward for a world of peace and equality had meant nothing, everyone fighting for me was expendable, and now it was up to me to change that.

I found the hallway that led to our escape.

I threw myself at it and flinched at the momentary pain but when the lock gave way, I shoved it open, wide enough for us to get out.

As we broke free, the building caved in on itself and I could only hope that everyone got out.

"We need to get to the tunnels!" Emelia shouted.

"Head to the south tower!" Kieran yelled.

We all changed course and started for the looming building peeking through the ash and flames on the horizon. It was now or never.

Chapter Twenty-Three
The Rising of a Ceoran

Alex

Kieran kept pace while I ran ahead. There was no telling who would try and stop us and I couldn't afford to lose any more time waiting to find out.

The Officials were here for me and I had no idea why, but it didn't take a wealth of Ceoran knowledge to understand that it wasn't just for a casual chat about the state of affairs.

"Go right!" Kieran shouted behind me, firing off a few rounds at the fast-approaching Ceoran behind us.

I hooked a right and kept going. Morales was ahead, waiting at the base of the tower, her arms flailing wildly, guiding us all into the building and to the stairs. Beside her were more Ceoran I didn't know, but they ran in with Katya. Friendlies, our friends.

We threw ourselves in and she and two other soldiers slammed the doors shut behind us, barricading them with a beam of wood.

"Go!" she ordered. "There's a team waiting for you!"

Eric broke off and ran back to help her keep the door closed.

"Stay with the others!" he shouted to me.

"Got it!"

The rest of us continued running down the stairs and found the entrance to the underground tunnel network.

Once we were all inside, I heard Morales scream and then more gunfire broke out.

I was confident that the Officials hadn't gotten in but rather Ceoran who had already been inside the tower had found her.

"Stay to the left of the tunnels and keep your eyes open," I instructed, watching my group make their way into the darkness.

There was more commotion behind me and where the system of tunnels broke into a three-way fork, I heard another crack. It wasn't an explosion.

No sooner had I turned around than I saw what was causing the influx of sound in the otherwise quiet underground.

There were dozens and dozens of Ceoran and Reapers who had made it down into the tunnels fighting the small army Morales had sent.

I didn't think twice when I broke off from my group and ran toward them.

I didn't have eyes on Eric but I heard another crack which I now assumed belonged to him.

As yet another loud crack shattered the otherwise silent tunnels, I caught a glimpse of a fiery figure blurring through the passages at outrageous speed.

For a moment I stood transfixed as pure awe consumed me. Why was this familiar? Why did I not fear it?

As I ran back toward the sound, I noticed that the tunnel was widening, taking us to a large clearing beneath the terrain the compounds had been on.

As the fiery figure sped past at dizzying speeds, I felt an overwhelming sensation of understanding course through me. Every time I had been in the woods alone, running from the Scavengers and Reapers long before I *met* Eric and Emelia, I had heard this sound. The cracking. I had always assumed that it was just gunfire, or lightning off in the distance, or commotion out in the wilderness carried on the wind, I'd never associated it with what I now realized it really was.

It was Eric.

Did all Ceoran do this? Could I do this?

As his form flickered between human and Ceoran, the loud crack signaling the transformation every time, my eyes finally focused on the blurry image. It had always been him out there with me, like he said but so much closer than I ever knew or that he'd even told me.

Tears pricked my eyes. It was magnificent, awe-inspiring and completely breathtaking to witness.

As more time went past and the fighting intensified more sounds of what resembled thunder carried through the night, and I noticed that it wasn't just him. Other Ceoran were doing the same, backing him, fighting on his side, on *our* side.

Eric's fiery figure slowed and faltered.

He was hurt. A large and violent gash spanned across his left bicep all the way down to his forearm. Anger gripped me in a vice. Too many people had been hurt because of what I was. Protecting this secret. Protecting something which we knew was fleeting.

As he was tackled to the ground by another Reaper, understanding coursed through me, just like it did out in the forest when Ashfield's convoy found us. There would be a definitive end, sooner than we imagined. It would be in the form of fire and destruction, like a supernova. It would burn from the inside out. How I knew that I didn't understand. I'd felt it in the depths of my soul.

One hundred years from now, Ceoran and other alien species out there wouldn't even know Earth had existed. Maybe they'd talk about the gentle people here like a myth, something the younglings spoke about in hushed whispers while their elders conversed.

I couldn't let that happen. I wouldn't.

There was goodness here, people that deserved to be saved, however few were left now. Most had withdrawn from the cities, laid low and took to hiding wherever they could to avoid us and the Reapers.

I could stop this happening now. I could give them a world to come back to, to get out of hiding, to live again.

All around our people were falling, gunshots and fiery blasts cracked through the darkness, shuddering through the earth beneath my feet. We were falling by the second, Ceoran hellbent on killing us in the name of going home tore through the space. We wouldn't survive this.

A cold, sickening feeling made me recoil.

We would be annihilated before we'd even started.

Like he sensed me, Eric's fiery face turned in my direction. A small yet monumental shift within me made a trail of nerves light up inside.

His eyes burned through mine in absolute clarity, despite the fiery form he was in right now. I didn't know if I could do that too. Maybe I was too much of a hybrid to have enough juice to pull that off. But the small instances of fire that raged to the surface and made my skin glow red said otherwise.

I focused on the way the fire in my veins felt and lit up beneath my skin like it did those few times out in the woods when I scared the hell out of Clark and Carter. I'd been afraid of it but I now knew what it meant. I focused on the feeling again and let it pour through me. Just like Eric, but way less cool, I saw the glow of Ceoran power come over my skin. I wasn't completely engulfed, my human form was prevalent, and the glow only seemed to illuminate me giving me an almost angelic glow—ironic considering what freakish DNA was running through my veins.

Up ahead, another five or six blurry Ceoran rushed between the fighting figures and took out the Reapers who'd come down in the forest earlier and somehow found us down in the tunnels, probably in all the openings Eric and I had found when we were scoping out the area. Emelia's map had shown a serious tunnel system down here so it wouldn't have been hard for them to find a way in. I recognized Emelia's elegant maneuvers long before I even saw her face. She grinned the second our eyes locked.

Eric rushed forward and body slammed two Reapers and threw another down before he even made contact. Kieran and Clark appeared behind me and turned into their Ceoran forms. Bodies of light crashed into bodies of blackness and loud booms reverberated through the cavernous space.

I'd never seen them do this before. I was in absolute awe as their fiery bodies fought the oncoming army who seemed to be growing in numbers despite how many we took out.

Another group of at least ten Reapers appeared on the path leading down toward us. When they launched into the offensive, a niggling feeling inside me roared to life. I was moving before I even worked out where I was going. I had to help. This was my chance. My duty. My body kicked me into gear like my brain was just along for the ride. I ran off to the side, away from the Ceoran and toward an opening that would lead to an uncharted part of the tunnel system. The same heavy feeling that coursed through me as the creatures carried me toward the lake started to fire through me, we must have been nearing it now.

Kieran shouted after me and then Eric broke away from the group. I couldn't afford to slow down to tell him to stay back. Something told me that even if I did, he wouldn't listen. I ran, feeling the heat off my own face burning through my skin. Was that normal? Or was it something to do with the fact that the Reaper blood inside me was fighting the intrusion of the Ceoran? It didn't matter. I'd have plenty of time to contemplate my messed-up genetics if I survived this.

Eric quickly gained pace and had practically caught up to me as I tore through the uncharted tunnels and came upon the shoreline of the creepy lake. Reapers came at us, at least a dozen now but so too did the creepy lake creatures.

They launched forward taking Ceoran and Reaper alike as their lunch while the rest of us battled around them.

"Stay on your toes and face the Reapers head on," Eric said, his voice airy, like it was disembodied and surprisingly calm.

I'd almost expected him to tell me what a stupid idea this was, or how I was underprepared, which to be fair wouldn't have been an unexpected call. The last time I went off on my own, I damn near got us both killed. Not to mention the entire compound being unable to return home now.

A nauseating pit of guilt crept up out of my belly and crawled all over me. I uprooted them all. But they had a chance to fight; the humans who'd died because of them didn't.

Then just like that, the guilt was gone. There was purpose now.

"Got it." I nodded, dodging a snacking creature.

Together we advanced. The Reapers, now well aware of who Eric and I were, kept a steady pace. They weren't attacking us with the usual savagery I'd witnessed. These guys were coming at us with tactile precision, as Dad would have said.

As each Reaper took their given orders seriously, I waited and watched. Calculating which one would go where and what Eric and I could do as a team to kill them. I remembered this: he and I worked well together. We had a strong connection that bordered on lunacy if you asked me. In my own head, I was still that eighteen-year-old girl who was butt hurt about losing access to the internet, and not a leader who could singlehandedly change the course of fate.

But with each Reaper I took down the leader inside me started to flourish. She was born of the embers and the ashes of her past life, she had been a warrior, a savior and she was fierce and indomitable.

Up ahead more Reapers converged, and I stepped forward turning my face slightly to Eric. With a single look, I knew he was on the same page as me. We could do this. We had to.

"Take them from the left," I said.

Eric nodded.

I returned my eyes to the front and felt the power of the Ceoran blood race through me and surge alongside the darkness of the Reaper's. Game on.

I ground my teeth and rushed forward.

In that moment my body moved of its own accord and the power backed me up. Eric ran past me, his body glowing bright and dangerous. As he connected with the first Reaper, I ran dead ahead and threw my hands out at the pair who'd decided to take me on.

Eric's form flickered as he fought hand to hand with the Reaper as though each pull of energy was making him lose his grip on his true form. Each hit made him falter but he fought hard, as did I. Together we took them on and eliminated our respective threats.

As Eric shifted back into Ceoran form and his body glowed bright, a desperate, determined rage fueled me and in one powerful crack of power I felt my soul separate from my body as if I was watching on from the outside. My entire body glowed blue and violet, oscillating between the bright and vibrant colors. The Reaper blood and Ceoran energy collided and created an absolutely perfect balance I'd never felt before.

The fragments of those memories I yearned to reach that lay hidden just behind the sheath of the Clean Slate started to chip through the wall holding them back. As each pull of power poured out of me, the fragments came just as fast and freely.

I ran forward.

Memories of holding hands with Eric as we lay side by side falling asleep beneath the stars.

With each powerful foot that I rushed forward, parts of me that remained dormant, exploded to life.

Images of my life with him flashed through my mind, showing me how deeply we loved, how selflessly and truly. There was no doubt in my mind now that I loved him beyond measure and that he loved me the same.

I ground my jaw and called on everything inside me. This was true, raw power that I now felt and *remembered* was only used sparingly because each time we brought this much power forward we risked burning out.

I remembered James. I remembered smiling, with him, in his home, with his parents.

Tears burned my eyes at the memory. It had been real. Not make-believe, not just duty.

I ran, fighting every Reaper that crossed my path. Anger and confusion burning through me as more memories slotted back into my mind.

I remembered leaving James, telling my parents I was in love with Eric…telling them I was so sorry for the mess I'd made.

Tears poured out of me freely as Eric ran beside me taking out every Reaper that came upon us.

By the time I reached the larger group of Reapers, our friends had joined us. Clark threw himself into the fight, his Ceoran form flashing to life; right beside him Emelia and Zayne did the same.

Like muscle memory that had been ingrained into my very being, my body took over and I let all the energy out following them into the fight.

The entire cave was lit up in a brilliant blue hue and it exploded outward like a breaking star. Everyone around me took cover but they didn't need to. Like the energy knew who it needed to target, it flowed through Eric and the others without hurting them, while every Reaper, lake creature and Ceoran who was not on our side was obliterated in a burning blaze that stole their last breaths in a matter of seconds.

I screamed as the energy was ripped from me on and on, the seconds lasting an eternity, the pain forever etching into my bones and my blood reminding me of who I had been and who I was now.

Before the final blast of energy was taken from me, I saw Eric running toward me.

With a final breathless scream, I let go and fell into the beckoning darkness.

Light.

Dark.

Pain.

Nothing.

I sat up and looked around. I was alone. The cave system was empty and the darkness was lifting, in its place a soft hue of light was breaking through like the dawn after a raging storm.

Where was the light even coming from?

My eyes ached like they'd been sandblasted, and my fingers tingled where the power had erupted.

"Hello?" I called out to a silent cave.

I stood and slowly walked around. Where was everyone? Had I killed them? No, I couldn't possibly…I saw my power spare my friends, it didn't hurt them and I would have felt something, wouldn't I?

The light pulsed gently all around, bathing the cave in a soft glow. What was going on? I checked over myself, it wasn't coming from me…it wasn't coming from any Ceoran either considering I was alone. I looked up, it wasn't the sky, I was still deep in the cave, yet there was a gentle source of light that seemed to just be…

"Hello?" I tried again.

This time, I heard a soft pair of footsteps behind me.

I turned on the spot ready to fight.

When my eyes landed on two people I couldn't possibly be seeing, I closed my eyes, counted to three and then opened them.

"Mom?" I whispered. "Dad?"

"Oh, baby." My mother ran to me and hugged me.

For a moment I stood frozen, so afraid to move because if I did, I'd wake up and realize that this was just a dream.

But it was just a dream, wasn't it? I had passed out or died…and this was my mind trying to make the transition easier.

They were exactly as I remembered them from before Eric wiped my memories. They were my real parents, the parents I never had the chance to mourn properly because I'd asked him to initiate the Clean Slate.

"You're not dead, sweetheart," my dad said as though reading my mind.

"Daddy, I…I don't understand."

He cupped my cheek and my mother tucked a loose strand of hair behind my ears.

"When we died at the Hampton Compound, our bodies were left behind. But we went home. We're still out there, darling, we're watching over you and all you do," Mom said.

"You're still out there?" I whispered.

Dad nodded with a big smile. "We're always out there, when we die on our host planet it's simply the vessel which ceases to exist, our essence lives on, we're back home now, on Ceora. You know this. You remember it now, don't you?"

I nodded wordlessly.

"I want to come with you." I felt tears burn my eyes. *I'd missed them so much.*

"You need to go back now, you still have so much to do, with your friends, with the Ceoran and with Eric." Dad hugged me.

"What is this?" I asked, taking both their faces in.

"This is the In Between—you're neither here with us nor back on Earth with them."

"And I have to choose where to go now?" My breath quickened.

"No, sweetheart. You must go back, you need to end this," Mom said.

329

"I'm not sure what I can do." The tears spilled over.

"The Officials won't stop until they've wiped everyone out, they want their Ceoran back on Ceora; they don't want them wasted on Earth. To them this planet is dying, it's too late, you heard what the Elders said. The Reapers have overrun it and if they don't destroy it, the Reapers will find us. They'll find Ceora."

"How do I stop them?"

"You must find the Bridge and seal it. The Reapers won't be able to get off the planet and the Ceoran who are left will be able to end them."

"But if I seal the Bridge the rest of us will never be able to leave. We'd be trapped here on Earth."

Dad nodded.

"I, I can't make that decision for them, it's not my place…"

"You are their leader, Alex, you must."

Before I could say any more, they both kissed the top of my head in turn.

"Be brave, be fierce. You can do this," Mom said.

"What about the Officials, why are they coming for me?"

Mom looked at me and then frowned. "Because I made you into what you are. You cannot exist, not like this. It's against our rules. It makes you dangerous."

"You're talking about me being half Reaper."

She nodded.

"So that's why they're after me. I'm an abomination."

"That's why Silus wants you too. You're a very powerful weapon."

"But he didn't know who I was before…"

"No, he knew one such being existed, and he had worked out that the being he was after was at our compound and—"

"And I exposed myself to him when I asked him to heal Eric. This is too much." I shook my head, anger replacing my weariness. "I never asked for any of this."

"I know, and it was wrong of me. But can you understand a mother's desperation to save her child?" Mom pleaded with me.

"You asked a mythical being to infect me with Reaper blood," I said sternly.

"It was the only way you would survive."

"Maybe I wasn't meant to survive!"

She turned her face from me.

"You were always meant to exist, Alex, one way or another," Dad added.

"And what about your desperation for a Council seat, did you arrange that too?"

My father was the one to frown this time. "We had no choice, Alex."

"Why?"

"There's no time to explain this now."

"Then make time!" I shouted, aware of the tremble in my voice and the pull inside me—I was being dragged back to my body.

"When you were born it was to secure our future; later it was to secure yours. The Ashfields knew about what I did. You were at risk if I didn't..."

"They blackmailed you."

They both nodded.

"And the Reapers came for you anyway," Mom ground out.

"The attack on the Hampton Compound was designed to take you alive, but Eric got to you first and got you out. And you knew that the Clean Slate was the only way to stay hidden after that," Dad explained.

"And James, his brother…"

"His brother was never going to make it to the top, the Council knew he was a loose cannon long before he did what he did. His parents knew it too. That's why the documents were signed early on. I changed my mind, I wanted you out of that life but, but it was too late."

"And the Ashfields wanted control." I bowed my head.

"Yes, Alex. They wanted to control the very thing you and Eric are fighting for."

"I agreed to it myself because of Eric. To protect him, for equality." My memories were back now.

Dad nodded. "You loved him more than life itself, Alex, you wanted the world to know it and this was the only way to make sure that could happen. With you and Ashfield on the Council, your vote could change the way Ceoran exist for centuries to come. You would have set the new laws into effect and once that was done—"

"I would have left Ashfield."

"He knew there was no romantic future, but he wanted in for his own reasons," Dad said.

"His parents' reasons you mean."

"Yes," Mom said.

"What were their reasons, what is the end game here? I don't understand." I thrust my fingers through my hair.

"I'm afraid that is something we don't know." Mom frowned.

"So all of this was for nothing. I'm exposed now anyway; they're coming for me, and to top it off the Officials are here too."

Mom's eyes widened.

"You're certain?" Dad asked.

"Pretty certain. I was standing before them when the building I was in went down and now I have nowhere to go. Eric is in danger and James is determined that this can all be salvaged."

"I'm so sorry," Mom whispered, her eyes welling with tears.

"Don't be sorry. Be helpful, what do I do now?" I asked.

Mom didn't answer but Dad did.

"Go back to your friends. You know how to end this, Alex, no one can do it but you."

"If I do this, I die right?" I whispered.

Mom hung her head and Dad squeezed my hand. My breath caught somewhere between a sob and laugh.

"So, that's it. I close the Bridge, seal everyone's fate and die."

"It is your destiny, baby," Mom said gently.

I shook my head. I couldn't speak. I couldn't say anything else.

I let them both embrace me because deep down, no matter how much anger and helplessness coursed through me, they were my parents and I loved them. No matter what mistakes they made, no matter what I was facing now I had to go back, finish this thing and do what I'd set out to all those years ago.

Eric, Emelia, all our friends, the Ceoran who died for us and the ones who would sacrifice in the years to come were my responsibility. I couldn't let James Ashfield and his family win, I wouldn't let the Officials take me out before I was finished, and I sure as hell wouldn't sit idly by as more of our people were destroyed for a system that no longer worked.

As I glanced back up at my mom's stricken face, the pull around my body intensified. I opened my mouth to scream for them and lifted my hand to her outstretched one but before I could take my next breath, I was yanked backwards and then there was darkness.

My eyes snapped open, and the roaring of simmering power inside my veins disoriented me. Where was I? Was this real, what just happened?

My vision came in and out of focus. My name was called. The faces around me flickered until Eric's form solidified in front of me.

"Easy," he said when I tried to get up.

When my body reacted by giving me a ridiculous splitting headache, I sat back down and tipped my face up instead.

Eric's hand moved to my jaw. His eyes coasted over my face and then my body. Scrapes and scuffs dotted the parts of skin that weren't shielded by the suit I'd destroyed, and the rest, away from his hot gaze, was covered in goosebumps from the intense stare.

"Are you with me?"

"I'm here…" I whispered. "Eric…I, I saw my family."

A knot formed in his brows. "How?"

"I fell and when I woke, they were there."

"What did they tell you?"

"The Officials know who I am. They want to destroy me because I'm not meant to exist, Eric. We have to seal the Bridge and we have stop anyone from coming or leaving."

He bowed his head knowing what that meant. The sacrifice was ours to make, one I would have to decide for everyone around us.

He looked at his sister and at our friends who watched us in awe. My eyes travelled back to Eric.

"Why are they kneeling?" I whispered so only he could hear.

His hand found mine. "They see your true form now, Asteraki Mou."

A small breath escaped my lips as I looked back to all the Ceoran who'd made it into the cave after I had wiped all the baddies out.

"You saved us," Kieran said, dropping to his knees. "I've only ever heard about this, I've never…I never thought I'd see it in my lifetime."

Emelia was kneeling, Morales too. Before I knew it, the entire group who'd fought for me and for us, was on their knees.

"I'm not following…" I whispered looking up at Eric and then the others kneeling before me.

Katya, Lisa and Leah, I remembered them all. My eyes watered, they had been my friends. Zayne and Kristian smiled, pure awe filled their eyes.

Eric squeezed my hand in his, drawing my eyes back to him. "That power you just used, that wasn't like what we can do. You have the blood of the Karatoi in you, Alex. It means that you aren't just one of us, you're one of them. One the most powerful beings to have ever lived in this universe and along with the Reaper blood, well you can imagine how dangerous that makes you to them."

"Holy…wow…" I looked around again.

"It is why you and only you can seal the Bridge," Kieran said gently.

Tears welled in my eyes as I stood.

"The Ceoran in you has risen," Eric explained.

"The time has come, whatever you must do next, we will follow," Kieran said.

"It's too soon. I'm not ready," I whispered.

I looked from one face to the next. I knew what he was telling me and I knew he was right, just like my parents.

My mouth gaped. No, no I couldn't do this yet. I had so much left to do here, so much more I wanted to experience…

"I'm afraid, Eric."

"I know, Asteraki Mou, but you won't be alone. I'm always going to be with you."

My eyes flicked down to the space between our hands.

Was I strong enough to do this? I didn't know. It was terrifying. I knew how the Bridge had to be sealed, I knew and it scared me. Fear coiled around my heart, but so did understanding—my essence would close it, and I would be gone. I'd be like Mom and Dad, existing somewhere out there, maybe on Ceora maybe not, but I wouldn't exist here anymore, I wouldn't exist with Eric. He didn't know that part and I would never tell him.

Tears poured out of me.

Eric kept talking but the rush of all I'd forgotten and all that was coming back to me was too much.

All my rambling thoughts were pushed aside when Eric brought his hand to my cheek again and gently guided my face up to his. In the eternally slow second it took for his lips to meet mine, a million tiny sparks of energy raced through me and urged me to react. I did. I kissed Eric back, ignoring the fact that there were a bunch of people watching us.

A breath was stolen as his fingers twisted through my hair, reminding me of how gentle and destructive our world could be.

Eric was the same. A dangerous pit of power, a silent reserve of unbridled energy ready to protect and serve whatever cause he deemed worthy.

I pulled him closer, letting a comfortable warmth roll through me. In that moment I wasn't afraid of the fate of the world resting on me, or the fact that I was only eighteen years old and expected to give my life up for the cause.

Eric kissed me again. And in that moment, every time I'd ever felt alone, alienated, out of my own body and different to everyone else, made sense. I wasn't everyone else. I was something more and that something more was going to shift the paradigm.

Eric's lips curved into a beautiful smile; Emelia nodded reassuringly beside him. Kieran stood tall and proud like a big brother, and in that moment, I wanted to squeeze them all into the biggest hug known to man and maybe weep. I was bordering a frenzy of irrational nerves, but I reined it in and stayed cool. If I was going to do this, it would have to be real and I couldn't afford to let myself look like I was melting with fear inside.

With a simple nod at all the Ceoran who kneeled before me, their hearts and beliefs on the line, I stood tall, proud, ready to be their leader, ready to end this.

And it all started now.

Chapter Twenty-Four
Make Time For What Matters

Alex
Two Weeks Later

Eric pulled the covers back and lay down beside me. I found myself giggling before I could stop the reaction. He responded by pulling the covers over our heads and nuzzling his mouth against the crook of my neck.

"Do we really have time to be doing this?" I chuckled as his hand slipped down to my throat and his lips quickly followed.

"Well, we're not doing anything else right now, we've got free time."

"Shouldn't we be resting?" I twisted my fingers through his hair and arched my back to get closer to him.

"Is that what you want?" He pulled back and met my gaze, eyes hooded and full of fire.

"Ah, absolutely not?"

He chuckled. "So, I'm allowed to continue?"

"Yes," I whispered, pulling him closer. "You're always allowed to continue."

"Those are the sweetest words, Asteraki Mou."

"You know you totally melt me when you say that?"

"Asteraki Mou?" He smiled against my mouth while his free hand dipped down to my hip and coasted across my stomach.

I nodded. "Where did you learn it?"

"My mom, my adoptive mom, she was Greek. She always called me that. When I met you, I knew you were my star too."

"That's beautiful, Eric."

He smiled and then kissed me before pulling back again. "I love you, Asteraki Mou, always."

Heat spread through my body as the words were forgotten and all we focused on were the touches and the careful caresses.

"Do you remember this?" he asked.

Once I woke after the *Rising*—it's what they called my freaky power move back in the cave—my memories had come back, the Clean Slate completely reversed. Like Eric said, it was unheard of. Morales reminded me of it every time we spoke, she was flabber-gasted...so was I.

He knew that I'd remembered everything but he did it anyway whenever we were close. I think he just liked hearing my response.

"I'm sorry I ever forgot."

He continued tracing gentle lines across my bare stomach.

It dawned on me that there was a very real chance neither of us would walk away from the coming fight. That thought sent a rush of fear over me and I tightened my hold on Eric. The gentle kiss we were lost in suddenly became desperate, laced with an edge of sheer panic I couldn't control.

He pulled back, his forehead touching mine as both our bodies remained tangled, close, but not close enough.

"What is it, Alex?"

"Nothing. Kiss me."

"Hey," he tipped my chin up and searched my face, "you're scaring me."

"It's nothing. Stop talking." I nudged him down until he was flat on his back and I lowered myself over him.

His fist tangled through my hair and pulled my face down to his, kissing me deeply.

A small sound lost between a moan and sigh left his lips when I brought our bodies together and got lost in the sensation I knew I'd been missing for so long.

Eric sat up bringing me with him. His lips brushed over my jaw and then my thundering pulse and still lower. I sucked in a sharp breath and pressed my cheek against his.

If this was it, if this was going to be one of our last moments together, I wanted to remember it forever, I wanted him to know how I felt, how much he meant to me and how deeply he made me feel.

He must have sensed the shift in me because the careful, slow and patient movements were replaced with hurried and desperate ones.

Both of us were on edge, filled with anguish and urgency.

If this was the beginning of the very near end, then tonight would mean everything.

There was a bright light ahead, beckoning me toward it. It wasn't scary or calming, it was just there, yet I knew I had to go to it.

As I neared, I looked up at the inky sky. Pinpricks of light glittered all around me. I wasn't seeing the sky from the same place I was in now, I knew the constellations and this one couldn't be seen from this particular location. Dad had ingrained that knowledge into my head from the day I could talk. "Memorize the stars, Alex, memorize them and they will help you some day," he would say.

I frowned and focused on them. There were three bright orbs, lining up. That was a specific event, one I knew but couldn't recall right now.

My eyes coasted across the blackness and landed on the bright light forming ahead. It was the Bridge…it was open and there was a figure, no, no there were three. Two very tall ones, they didn't look human, and one much smaller. It was me, I knew it all the way to my bones.

As I neared the Bridge, I saw another, running faster, getting closer to me.

Urgency replaced my curiosity. I had to get closer to the me in my dream. I had to see.

With a simple thought, I was right there. My eyes widened when I saw myself jump and then the light was gone.

I woke with a jolt and fanned my face. That was just strange, too weird to even begin to understand. It was the same dream I'd had over and over. I was starting to think it wasn't just a dream, but it clearly wasn't a memory either since I'd never experienced anything like it. Could it have been a *premonition?* Was that even possible for me? Emelia had some Seer ability, so it wasn't totally out of the realm of possibility.

I sat up and composed myself. When I realized that the bed beside me was empty, I frowned. Eric was gone, so was his tactical vest and gun. I craned my neck and tried to listen out to where the others were in the house.

As I made a move to get out of the bed, a sharp, rolling pain speared through my core and shot out to my limbs. I held in a surprised gasp and swung my legs over the bed and looked down at my arms. My entire body was trembling, covered in glowing veins. The same, weird, scary as hell thing I'd seen before I almost went postal on Clark in the woods when we were on the run with Kieran and Cater. I balled my fists in my lap and closed my eyes, taking a deep breath.

I had to calm down and get this under control. This wasn't good. I wasn't naïve. Maybe the end was actually nearer than I initially thought. Mom and Dad didn't say when it would happen, and maybe they'd just failed to mention that it was around the corner. It was all going to start with me nearing the source, getting closer to Esper. I could feel it beckoning me. The power of Esper and Reaper battled inside me, each one wanted dominance over the other and every time that happened I slowly pieced together that I was nearing the end of my road.

Once everything had settled enough to take some proper breaths, I listened out for where everyone was.

Emelia's voice beamed through the paper-thin walls which immediately made me flush. If I could hear her so easily then last night...

"Alex, get your butt up!" she yelled. "I made food."

I groaned and peeled myself out of the bed, padded over to the wardrobe and pulled out some comfortable compound clothing. I shuddered thinking back to the clothes Ashfield had stashed in his wardrobe for me. Plus, he had seen me in my underwear. To say that I'd felt violated was an understatement. A shiver of anger rolled through me.

I took a deep breath and got dressed in a pair of sweats which had the dainty Ceoran Council logo on them.

Once I managed to make myself look presentable and most definitely not blushing like an over-ripened tomato, I braved the outside world.

In the kitchen, Emelia and Kieran were busy plating up food for our small army. We had a new addition though, Eric and Emelia's mom – Commander Morales. I stopped by the door, unsure of what was going on.

Emelia met my gaze and gave me a tiny shake of the head. I could read a sign when it was flashed before me. I sat down and took the plate Kieran handed me.

"Thanks."

"Eat up, troops, we have a big day ahead of us," Kristian said, chowing down on a sausage.

"Where did you guys get all this?" I asked.

"I took supplies from the kitchen before it all went to hell last night," Morales said.

"How did the mission go?" I asked.

Morales had been going off on small missions with several of our soldiers each night since we'd broken free from sector seven. Last night was a smaller military installation she and Emelia had broken into in order to find out more about where Ashfield had gone and whether the Officials were getting close to finding out my location. We'd only been safe here for as long as we have because Commander Morales and her contacts had it secured. It's why she was the commander and the rest of the soldiers obeyed her, the woman knew her stuff.

"Ashfield is still in the wind but the Officials are getting impatient," Emelia explained delicately sipping on her coffee. "There was chatter among the Ceoran on the ground that they were rallying some more heavy-handed soldiers, some not from around here."

"From where?" I asked.

343

"They call them the Collective, they're somewhere out beyond the Milky Way," she said.

A chill settled over me. "It won't get to that."

"If it does...if they come into the equation, we're all done. They rule over everything, their say is final, what we say or do won't matter."

"I know that," I bit. "So, how do we avoid them being called in?"

"Manage the situation here," Morales said simply.

"Sounds easier said than done." I sighed. "Are we safe here?"

"For now, yes. It doesn't mean we let our guard down, Chancellor," Morales explained.

"She is one of us, you don't have to call her that," Kristian said.

"I appreciate the charade you've got going here; however, Chancellor Wynter is here for her protection and that is all."

"Alex is here because she is our friend," Eric's voice sounded behind me, making every hair stand on end. "And she is here because she is fighting *with* us."

He stood behind me, his hand resting protectively on my shoulder. I didn't know whether I should have been cautious to show affection here but then when he got closer, I shut that thought down. If Eric wasn't backing away, I wouldn't either.

"When order is restored, things will go back to normal, Eric," Morales said.

"No." He shook his head, his voice full of venom. "Not everyone here lived by the book."

"Now that is rich coming from you," she said back to her son.

Eric's lips formed a straight line.

"Weren't you the one who shut her out because of *the book?*" she challenged.

"He did what he thought was right," I spoke up. *And there won't be a back to normal,* I wanted to say. I didn't have the heart to tell them about what I'd learned, not yet. That was between me and Eric for now.

Morales's brows shot into her hairline.

"And since I am a Chancellor, and I do have standing here which you seem to respect, I'm going to say this once, the Ceoran who are here, including me, are all fighting on the same side against the same enemy. I don't want class division mentioned here again. Not in my presence, not ever. Is that clear?" I looked directly at her before I cast my eyes over everyone else.

Eric stood proudly beside me; the others all beamed and nodded.

"Thank you for the food, and for the shelter, Commander Morales." I nodded and then excused myself.

Eric followed me to our room.

"I'm sorry," I said.

"For what?" He closed the door behind him.

"That was out of line, I was rude. I shouldn't have..."

"Thank you."

I turned to face him. "You're thanking me?"

He walked over and sat on the edge of the bed, his brows furrowed and face serious.

I sat beside him and dropped my head.

"I feel like an idiot, I shouldn't have spoken to her like that, or anyone."

"You stood up for me."

"I sounded like a dictator. Like one of *them.*"

"No. You were just, and you were right." He turned his face toward me slightly. "Back when I found out she was alive, and Em arranged for us all to meet, I was in shock. I didn't know what to expect."

"She's always been about the job. I remember that now."

He nodded and forced a tight smile.

"I've never been able to stand up to her, it just feels wrong and I can't, I can't make myself do it. After the fact, I feel like an idiot, I have all these things I wanted to say, and none of them come out."

I took his hand and held it tightly. The admission hurt to hear, and the way his face and shoulders dropped made anger rise to the surface.

"She was never cruel, it's not like she treated us poorly, but she was never kind. Em and I were just a means to an end, you know?"

"I remember Em telling me your mom died of toxins when we first met, during the Clean Slate Alex in the woods."

"Not surprised, she would have made anything up to save explaining to you that we were the children of a mother who didn't really want a bar of us and that our stepmother tragically died in a house fire."

"A house fire?" I didn't think I knew that part, I didn't remember him ever telling me.

"Yep, so mundane. She was a soldier who'd run countless missions and that's how she went out."

"Em blames herself."

"Em was home with her, said a candle tipped over and that was that."

"Jesus," I whispered.

"She wants her mom; it's why she's so determined to keep Morales around," Eric said flatly.

"And what about you?"

"I want my mom as well, but not at the cost of losing you and everything else I've worked for."

There was a pause, Eric seemed to disappear into his head for a moment before he let out a long breath and took my hand.

"Do you think she loved your dad?"

"I think in the beginning she must have. But then the job called and she answered."

"I'm so sorry, Eric."

"Don't be." He wrapped his arm around my shoulder and pressed a kiss to my forehead. "But I do want to ask something of you."

"Of course, anything." I cupped his cheek.

"If I become like that. Stop me. Please."

"Eric, you won't."

"I've already crossed that line before, with you. I can't, I won't do that again. Promise me."

"I promise," I said. I would do anything he asked me.

He expelled a long breath and stood, pulling me to my feet. He wrapped his arms around me and rested his chin on top of my head.

"We have a long road ahead of us," he said.

"I know. I just hope we all get out of this."

"We will. We have to."

He turned toward me and took my face in both his hands. His eyes searched mine and then every inch of my face.

"Did they hurt you?" he asked.

"What, when?"

"When Ashfield took you away."

"No, Eric. He didn't do anything." I sighed. This is not a conversation I wanted to waste time on.

He closed his eyes and nodded. "I lost my mind when I saw them take you. I couldn't think around the rage."

"I know what you mean." I let out a quiet breath and then gingerly brushed my fingers across the bruises on his face. They'd hurt him, I could see the pain in his movements, though he'd never tell me that. It'd been two weeks since that fight and he still wasn't healed. That didn't sit right with me. Something was wrong. "I can help you."

"No, not with this, Alex. It's not worth it. You need to conserve your energy."

"You're hurt."

"I'm okay, see." He pressed my palm flat to his cheek.

His eyes flared.

"You don't have to lie to me," I whispered.

"Just like you don't have to lie to me."

"What do you mean?"

He looked away for a moment, like he saw the deliberation in my face about Ashfield. He must have seen it for the last two weeks and didn't bring it up because every time he tried, I shut him out. There was so much going on inside me, with the dreams and the *rising* that I didn't allow Ashfield to cross my mind, nor did I want to waste time talking about it. He didn't *do* anything to physically hurt me, but how he made me feel was inexcusable.

But I could see that Eric needed the closure, he needed to talk about it and so I relented.

"Something happened. Didn't it? I can see the way you were on edge, especially last night."

I got up and paced the room, wondering how to frame it. I didn't want to lie or make light of it. The whole thing left me on edge and feeling disgusting. But I also knew Eric. I knew what kind of fire burned in his core; it was much too similar to mine to be naïve about the way he would react.

"He wanted me to dress the part, to look like his promised partner on the Council high table and I guess wearing gross lake drenched clothes didn't meet his requirements."

"How do you mean?"

"He pulled my clothes off, well, more precisely, he cut them off me."

"He cut your clothes off your body?"

He hadn't raised his voice or made any indication of anger flaring, but his body did go rigid, his jaw squared, and his face turned a shade of pale that didn't look healthy.

"That was all, he gave me his robe and just, it was gross. I felt disgusting, he touched me like I was a long-lost girlfriend or something, and all I wanted to do was rip his throat out."

"He touched you," Eric said calmly. Like the statement was solidifying Ashfield's future in his mind.

"I know you're raging right now. Believe me, I was too. But right now, this thing we're facing is much bigger than Ashfield's perviness."

"Ashfield is a predator. That whole family is like that."

"I know. I do. But I don't want you risking your life or this job because of that. Okay?"

"I can't promise that."

"Eric—"

"What he did was beyond unacceptable, Alex. It was criminal and wrong. And if I do see him again, I cannot promise you that I won't..." He trailed off, looking away for a moment.

I could understand his rage. I felt the same. But a part of me shut it all out and processed the event as something that I needed to move past. He was right, though. It was criminal and it was wrong, I shouldn't have made light of it or ignored it.

"His family comes from a long line of twisted freaks who live above the line of law. You already know that his brother David was accused of raping two girls in his direct line of report. They were soldiers, girls none of the Council members bothered to even vindicate."

"I know, I just didn't know it was never looked into."

"No one could prove any of it of course, because he is who he is, and they were just *nobodies* who happened to attend a party he was throwing. They booted him off the running for Council, that's all they could do."

"I know. It's disgusting."

Eric scrubbed the back of his neck and let out a long breath.

"His family had covered up criminal acts both of the older brothers had committed long before any of that came to light."

"Because of the Class Division."

"Exactly. And they did a hell of a job keeping it from almost everyone, including you."

"Jesus, Eric." I covered my mouth with my hand and shook my head. "Did you know them? The girls?"

"I did."

"How are they now?"

"One of them is doing okay, she found comfort in counselling, but the other, she didn't."

"Where is she?"

"She killed herself not long after."

"Damn it."

"The Ashfield name is a cancer here, you know this. But they bring in the votes and the money so everyone looks the other way."

"Which is precisely why you can't go after them. But I can." I gave him a pointed look.

"You have to stay away from them, at all costs, Asteraki Mou. This isn't something that we can afford to get cocky about," he said sternly. "This game they're playing doesn't allow for anyone of my class to win, do you understand?"

"No, I don't, Eric."

He sighed, running his hand through his hair. "If they get to you, I won't be able to do anything to protect you in their domain."

"You're stronger than they are."

"Yes, but my position isn't. I fight them, I get thrown in jail, my sister, all our friends, everyone who is on your side, loses, and they get you exactly where they want you."

"Surely there's more we can do, the Council will see what they are, we have to expose them."

"Council knows who and what they are. Nothing has changed since the Clean Slate and the memories you had. You were there at the tower with him, did they seem to care, did they bother at all to find out who was being locked up in the cells beneath their party?"

I dropped my gaze. No, they didn't care. He had people on his side that I never in my wildest dreams would have thought were capable of switching sides like that.

"I've wracked my brain for more than four years trying to work out how to do that. They're impenetrable, there's nothing, at least nothing I could find."

"Then we have to make them slip up," I said.

"I don't think people like that slip up."

"Not intentionally."

"Where are you going with this, Alex?"

"The same rules don't apply to me."

"Now I really don't like where you're going."

"Hear me out."

"No." He shook his head, shooting to his feet.

"Eric, please."

He turned abruptly on the spot, his eyes flaring. I'd seen that look only once before and it was in the forest, when I first saw him facing down those Reapers and it had scared the hell out of me.

"This is so dangerous I can't even begin to comprehend how you think this could possibly be a good idea."

"I didn't say it was a good idea, but it can work," I said.

"And what if it doesn't?"

"Then I'm screwed."

"I can't believe we're having this conversation."

"Well, we are. And the sooner we sort something out, the better chance we have of making this work."

"No, no, Alex. I will not get behind this. You're talking about using yourself as bait, walking right up to them so you can make him slip up *somehow*. Do you realize how insane that sounds? Especially when we have bigger problems like the Officials coming to wipe you out, Silus hunting for his weapon of choice and who even knows what the Council are concocting."

The Collective, I wanted to say, but it didn't seem like a good idea to throw gasoline of the raging fire.

"Even if it's my choice. Even if I know I can do this?"

"It's dangerous and stupid and as your Guardian, which by the way, I still am, I'm here to override anything that might put you in danger. So yes."

"This is ridiculous."

"You can be mad at me all you want, that's fine, but at least you'll be safe and alive."

"For how long?" I snapped.

He looked at me, nostrils flaring.

"I'm meant to seal the Bridge, seal countless Ceoran's fate, probably die in the process and for what? Nothing will change. I will die, you will all live on in the same, barbaric existence the Council have imposed on you since the beginning of time!"

His shoulders shuddered and I quickly shut my mouth.

"What did you just say?"

"Forget it." I turned to leave but he grabbed my hand and tugged me back to him.

"Alex, please tell me I didn't hear what I thought I did."

My courage vanished.

"That's what my parents said. I seal the Bridge; seal your fate and I die."

He dropped my hand and took a step back. His hands went to his head and for a moment he stood silently, transfixed before he shook his head, muttered something under his breath and then shook his head again.

"I cannot live out the remainder of my life, however short it may be, knowing that nothing will change for you." I was crying now, helpless, angry, raging.

Eric tried to come to me, but I shoved him back.

"I will not let things end like that," I whispered, evening out my voice before giving him a quick look. "It's my choice and I choose to die for something!"

Chapter Twenty-Five
Those Who Stay and Those Who Leave

Carter and Zayne were clearing out the kitchen and setting out the maps and schematics we'd be using for the next phase of our mission. As it stood now, we had to rethink everything we'd been planning; the Officials would be on the lookout for me and if they hadn't already gathered a decent Ceoran army they would soon. It meant we couldn't rely on finding allies like we had before because we simply couldn't trust that the Ceoran we reached out to weren't compromised.

And despite Eric's reluctance to consider my plan of infiltration, I still thought it was a good idea. Maybe my confidence was starting to kill my braincells and take over whatever logic I usually led with. In my obsession to make Ashfield and his family pay for what they'd arranged years ago and what they'd pulled more recently, I'd lost sight of the objective. It didn't even matter in the grand scheme of things. But it did matter to me, to those girls who never got justice, and our people, people like Eric's line who would forever live under the same archaic rule.

My new power and the very real and obvious show of what I could do kind of set everyone here on edge. It was surreal and a bit daunting. I didn't know whether they secretly feared me or just thought I was a freak. At least Eric didn't treat me any different. I, on the other hand, felt relieved. I had answers for why I'd always felt so alien growing up compared to my Ceoran brothers and sisters, and even after the Clean Slate, at school, I didn't fit in. Not just because I wasn't human like the rest of them, but because I wasn't anything normal.

I wasn't cut from Ceoran or human, or even Reaper cloth. I was a mixture, a concoction of things that shouldn't have been and I existed somewhere in between. I was just a vessel for some freaky essence to be housed so when the time came I could seal the Bridge. Unfortunately for me, what my mother did out of desperation to save me made my destiny a skewed mess. Instead of the Karatoi offering me eternal protection until the time came to seal the Bridge on Earth, they now sought me out to destroy me because I was a threat—I alone possessed the knowledge of both Reaper and Ceoran power; I could see how that made me dangerous.

I sighed and looked up at Eric. His back was to me as he and Katya worked quietly making coffee for us all. I couldn't hear what they were talking about but he seemed a lot calmer and his mood a little lighter. They each handed us a cup and when Eric came over to me, he gave me a quick look, the kind that said he wasn't ready to talk about my plan or the bombshell I'd dropped, before tearing his gaze away. Great.

When we were all seated, Morales got up and gave me a fleeting glance before addressing the rest of the group.

"I've gone over all the options we have and the ones we no longer can entertain. The chatter I've heard on the inside is that the Ashfield family was, and remains, responsible for the internal attacks on our compounds, along with someone trusted that we haven't yet identified."

My eyes shot to Eric.

"Someone?" I asked.

Morales all but shrugged. "He's working with someone who knows all your moves, all your plans, Chancellor. We don't know who yet but whoever it is has a deep involvement with James."

"To what end?" I asked, although I felt like I knew the answer.

Morales took a deep breath and looked around at all the faces giving her their undivided attention.

"It would appear that Silus wants something we can give, and in turn he can give us something we want."

"Alex for the Ashfields," Carter supplied.

"Exactly," she cleared her throat, "It is my understanding from the last seven years of working undercover among them, that the Ashfields plan on using Alex to gain full control over Ceoran lives. Right now, they have the protection of Silus so we can't attack. And like the Reapers, they care not for equality or any kind of democracy. So, if they do this, the first thing they will do is take out her guardians, it will leave Alex open and vulnerable, giving the Reapers access to get exactly what they want from her. So the way I see it, we're in a tough, unwinnable situation however we play it right now."

"What do they want from her?" Lisa asked.

"Her essence," Morales said flatly.

"Why?" Clark asked looking at me.

"Alex?" Morales asked.

Ah crap.

"You don't have to say anything you don't want to," Eric said sternly, giving his mother a pointed look.

"It's fine. They should know."

He shook his head like he was disappointed I was going against him and sat back.

"I'm part Reaper," I said. "There's no roundabout way to say that, I guess."

"What the hell?" Clark snapped, getting up. "You're one of them?"

"Clearly I'm not," I shot back.

"This is madness."

"Then get the hell out and stop wasting everyone's oxygen here," Eric snapped.

My mouth closed. I was totally speechless. Evidently, Clark was too.

Eric gave him another pointed look. "The door is there, Clark. Get the hell out if this is a problem for you or shut up and let her talk."

He sat back down.

I dared to look up at the rest of them. Granted, everyone looked a little shocked, probably a bit paler than usual but they were all still here.

"How did that happen?" Lisa asked gently.

"I was sick when I was born and a mage was able to combine my blood with theirs to heal me," I said.

"And you're, well you're still you, you're one of us."

"I am." I looked down at my hands. "I have some of their powers, some of their strengths and some of their weaknesses."

"So why do they need your essence?" Zayne asked.

"Her essence will allow the Reapers to utilize that perfect molecular composition, allowing them to cross the Bridge which will give them free access to any planet they desire," Morales said.

"And they hit the jackpot considering she harbors that power, being a part of the Karatoi," Eric added.

"Right. So I'm able to close and open the Bridge, but my role is to seal it so nothing can get in and well, we won't be able to get out..."

"Damn. This is huge," Carter muttered.

"Meaning we'll be stuck here, forever?" Lisa asked seriously.

"It's the only way," I said quietly.

"So we're screwed, either way then. We can't give Alex up obviously, and we can't do this without working with Silus considering we can't get to the Ashfields," Clark said.

"Can't we just find them and attack? Kieran asked.

"There is no proof, therefore we cannot rely on a coup. We have to do this off the books," Morales continued, almost cringing at the idea.

I could imagine how hard that was for someone like her.

"So, what's the play then?" Kieran asked, leaning back in his chair.

"In my opinion, based on everything I have seen and heard"—she looked at me and then at Eric—"Alex and Eric will stand the best chance of getting out of this if they split up from the rest of the group."

Well, I was not expecting that.

Neither was anyone else judging by the explosive reactions that raced through the kitchen.

"That is crazy, I'm sorry but they cannot take on everyone out there alone," Kieran snapped.

"They won't have to," Emelia said.

"I don't understand," Lisa said looking between me and Eric and Morales.

Emelia looked at me and a small smile formed. "Eric and Alex can cover each other, there's a certain frequency that her power vibes on, partially thanks to the Reaper blood. I picked up archival evidence on it when I was digging around Council files."

"But you just said how important it was to keep her safe. We're safer in numbers," Lisa said.

"Numbers don't always equate to safety," Katya said.

"In this case I think it does," Lisa challenged.

"No. We will only be in their way. You saw what Alex can do. That level of power is beyond anything we have to offer. Eric on the other hand, because of his position being directly linked to her, can assist."

Eric's jaw hardened at the conversation unfolding between the two friends,

"I'm sorry, I get where your priorities lie, Raine, but I can't sit around and do this when she is clearly unhinged and one of them." Clark got up. He'd never gotten over his fear of me and what he saw in woods that day.

"Choose your next words carefully," Eric muttered.

"You can count me out of this. What I saw in the woods was enough for me. I'm done. You and your missus are on your own. I want out." He collected his things and left.

"I'm sorry," Lisa said, quietly following suit.

"Lis," Katya shot, "you can't be serious!"

"I can't, this is too much." She didn't look at me before she followed Clark out.

Carter didn't look at me either before he took his leave after the other two.

I didn't expect everyone to be on my side, but I didn't expect to feel so hurt by it when it stared me in the face.

I swallowed hard and got up.

"Don't worry about them, you have us," Katya said gently.

I knew she meant well but I couldn't right now. Zayne, Kristian and Kieran all looked at us.

Morales remined silent, so too did Eric beside me.

Leah got up. "*We're* with you, Chancellor," she said firmly.

"We need to close the Bridge, otherwise none of this matters. If we don't, then whatever we do, whatever we've done, will be for nothing," I muttered and turned to leave.

"Alex…" Kieran said but I didn't stay to hear anything else as I left the kitchen and made my way into the bedroom, closing myself off from them and that conversation.

I heard rushed footsteps come after me and reach the door.

I felt my composure slip and annoying tears overwhelm me. Before I could stop myself, I felt a sob building. I slid down the door and crumpled into myself. It was shameless and totally overpowering. I couldn't stop crying and I couldn't catch my breath. It felt so pointless and *childish*.

Two gentle hands cupped my elbows and I looked up. Through the haze of tears I saw Eric's pained expression.

"That was completely out of line, I'm sorry you had to experience that."

"They're right though," I said.

"No, they're not."

I pulled myself together and got up, pushing past him. I stopped at the window and pressed my hands to the frame above my head.

Eric stopped behind me, his presence was strong. I could feel him more than I could before, I could feel the anguish inside him, the turmoil, his rushing thoughts. I lowered my head to the glass and willed the intrusion out of my mind. I couldn't do this; it was too much.

"Alex, talk to me."

"I'm not well. I can feel my control slipping."

"You're still here."

"No," I said without turning, "I can feel things, things I couldn't before. I can feel you, I can feel everything inside you like they're my own feelings."

He shifted.

"I can't stop it, everything flows into me and it's messy and it hurts. I can feel it all, the light, the darkness…and it's insatiable, it's calling to me all the time, pulling me in and drowning me. I can't swim above it because as soon as I do I get pulled under. The darkness feels better than the light now and I, God, I *want* to be there. I want the dark."

"Alex, I…I didn't know."

"It just started happening, after the cave, I don't know why but I think it's the Reaper blood. I think it's taking over now that I've *awakened*."

He stepped closer and I felt his hands land on my hips. I leaned back into him, resting my head on his chest.

"I feel my control slipping, I feel this anger and rage I've never felt before starting to consume me."

"I haven't noticed anything. You're still the same, kind woman you always were."

I turned in his arms and leaned back against the window, searching his face.

"I know I won't walk away from this," I said.

"No one can know that."

I forced a tight smile when he brushed my cheek. "I know you know how this works."

"No, not always."

"Everything I've dreamt so far has come to light. In my dream you and I, we fight, and there's this moment where we have to choose what happens next. I didn't know what the dreams meant before but I do now. You try to stop me, we can see the Bridge, it's just on the horizon cresting the darkness of the woods and that's where it...I can't see beyond that because that's where my story ends."

"You and I will never fight, Alex. There's no way that could happen. Ever."

"Maybe. I hope not."

He frowned and pulled me tighter against him. He didn't want to believe what I was telling him, but deep down I felt the fear begin to consume him. The thoughts around what was coming and what we might be faced with tore him down.

Eric Raine, ever the brave, ever the strong, was falling faster than he could hold himself together.

I wondered whether there was a place for him beside me in my pit of despair that tasted so good it hurt. No, I decided then and there. I wouldn't bring him down with me. He was too good, too pure.

I swept my hands across his biceps and up to his face, easing his worry with a simple thought. I gently pulled him down and kissed him, knowing that no matter what I said or did, he wouldn't let this conversation go and it would eventually destroy him.

So, I dug a little deeper, finding the threads of fear inside his mind and I pulled, forcing a wave of calm and love into him. He wouldn't be afraid, he wouldn't feel the pain I did because that was something I could still control even if everything else eluded me.

"When the time comes, Eric, know that we did everything we possibly could to beat this thing. Know how much we loved, how much I care. Know who we were before I became what you'll see at the end."

"The time won't come, Asteraki Mou, I won't let it."

"I hope you're right."

ACKNOWLEDGEMENTS

Taking on an entire series while pregnant and completing a master's degree was another level of challenging circumstances I'd never experienced, but, taking on this second book with a toddler, a new job and family life was another. But here we are, only thanks to an incredible team that saw this through from draft to the gorgeous little book you hold in your hand.

Firstly, to my incredible team at Vulpine Press who have always had my back and showed me endless support.

To my family who were patient with cancelled plans and rescheduled lunches.

And to myself for telling me when I needed to slow down, breathe and recoup. We did it!

Based in Melbourne, Violeta M. Bagia is a multi-genre author with a passion for delving into challenging and thought-provoking topics. With a Master of Arts degree under her belt, Bagia brings a depth of understanding to her writing that enriches every narrative. Whether crafting tales of futuristic worlds or weaving intricate narratives of love and human connection, Bagia is a storyteller with a passion for exploring human emotion. When she's not crafting exciting new worlds, she's out there exploring the wilderness, trying out wild new moves in her martial arts classes or, eating chocolate on the couch with her dogs.

w: writepointcoaching.com
t: @vmb_author
i: violeta.m.bagia_writer
f: Violeta M. Bagia